A CARRA KiNG
AN INSPECTOR MATT MINOGUE MYSTERY

JOHN BRADY

STEERFORTH PRESS
SOUTH ROYALTON, VERMONT

For Hanna
And for Chris and Mary Brady, and Matt Crowe

For information about permission to reproduce
selections from this book, write to:
Steerforth Press L.C., P.O. Box 70,
South Royalton, Vermont 05068

Library of Congress Cataloging-in-Publication Data
Brady, John, 1955–
A Carra King : an Inspector Matt Minogue
murder mystery / John Brady. — 1st ed.
p. cm.
ISBN 1-58642-018-6
1. Minogue, Matt (Fictitious character) — Fiction.
2. Police — Ireland — Dublin — Fiction. 3. Dublin (Ireland) — Fiction.
I. Title.
PR6052.R2626 C37 2001
823'.914—dc21
00-012962

FIRST EDITION

Everyone is born a king . . . and most die in exile.
—OSCAR WILDE

Excerpt from a report delivered by the Hon. James Black and Mr. Trevor Dewdney to the Committee on Quaker Relief to Rural Districts in the Western Counties of Ireland delivered in London, 1849.

The crowning of the Carra King, culminating in a pilgrimage and celebrations on a nearby hillside, is an event of great significance in the locality, as it marks the beginning of the growing season. Though not an event of note in the locality in at least a lifetime, it has been revived this past year, doubtless due a need among the people to celebrate their delivery from the Famine.

An unmarried man, or an eligible bachelor as the expression is used here, is chosen to carry a stone bearing what local folklore holds to be the image of Crom Dubh, an ancient king converted by St. Columkille to Christianity. The Carra King stone, weighing in excess of a hundredweight, is held on the back by leather straps and carried to the hilltop where it is blessed and revered. This task is made even more onerous by a regimen of fasting and sleeping outdoors on the heather, practices reminiscent of the ascetic traditions of monastic life long ago, and indicative of a link with the voluntary privations in tests of manhood we read of in folklore, all preparatory to undertaking a *geis,* or a mighty test to establish honor in ancient Irish society.

For a night and a day, people gather on the bare hillside and in the vicinity to pray for a harvest and the prospect of a short winter with families well provisioned. As with the other festivals held in the country, this is also the occasion for other transactions and socializing, with news being exchanged, marriages discussed and, as can be expected among a people known for their love of music and storytelling, dancing and fair atmosphere.

Dr. Power, a physician, who has practiced in the locality for twenty years, related to us pieces of local lore which suggested that the Carra King may have some of its origins in barbaric practices which had persisted after the arrival of Christianity in the time of Patrick and Columkille. The original king, Dr. Power surmised, may have been party to tyranny and disputes of succession that eventuated in a situation Dr. Power suggest was not unlike the well-known tragic figure in the Bard's "Danish" play. . . .

CHAPTER I

THE DRIVER BRAKED LATE for the lights and the Fiat began to slide. Larry Smith cursed and eased off the pedal. What the hell was he doing with this law-abiding routine, stopping for an amber traffic light on a Sunday morning? He shifted into first before the car came to a stop halfway across the white line and groped under the seat for the pistol. It hadn't shifted.

A Toyota van turned on to Strand Road ahead. Some fella delivering the Sunday papers? He looked across the bay. The tide north of Dublin was out. Lambay Island like a slab sitting on the gray, flat water of the Irish Sea. Frigid looking, the color of water out of the washer, or an old, battered saucepan. There was piles more rain on the way too. What a poxy start to the day.

Even the golf clubhouse looked like a dump. It'd been twenty years since Zipper Brophy and his brothers had destroyed that clubhouse. There'd been two days of questioning, he remembered, and a hammering from head cases in the Special Branch. All because a lot of Guards were members. Zipper was dead three years now. It was pure heroin, one of the first loads to hit town. Zipper'd always been careless. It was April first too, of all days, and they found him in the toilet out at the Jolly Rover, that dump that had burned down in Finglas last year. Plainclothes Guards all over at the funeral too, trying to mix in. They'd almost caused a scrap with Zipper's brother outside the church.

He looked in the rearview mirror again. The early mass in Sutton was started already. He shifted in his seat to get a better look at the sea. He thought of the last holiday he'd had with Yvonne. It'd been like a honeymoon all over again in Portugal.

He yawned until the tear almost broke away from his eye. He'd been shaky enough getting up. He drew the pistol out from under the seat and laid it in his lap. Nice weight to it, balancing there, and the little knob under the trigger guard. He'd been on the move for a month now, after he'd heard the rumors. Moving around every night had left him restless, washed-out. You couldn't really get a night's sleep like this. He couldn't even use the cell phone to talk to Yvonne. Someone had heard the law could get in on the new ones even. Well how was that anyway, wasn't it an infringement on a person's basic rights and all that?

He leaned over the wheel and stared at the red light. He should give up on the Fiat really. The blind spots were making him jittery. Cheaper to fix the smashed wing mirrors, sure, but it was burning a bit of oil now. He swore at —

A screech and a flicker in the side mirror made him drop his hand on the pistol. He looked out the passenger window. A seagull drifted down onto the footpath. That's all it was? He looked at the twisted edges on the mirror frame. Both of them smashed in the one night a fortnight ago. Christ, if he got his hands on the little bastards. His back was tightening up on him already. He leaned over the wheel again but it didn't help. He let out the clutch a little, let the Fiat roll into the junction.

That van ahead was taking its time. Well what if he were to just drop it all and get into Australia or someplace? On his own, and then send for Yvonne after he was set up right — and on the QT of course. Shouldn't be that hard. A car, a Renault, was cruising up to the lights now. There was only the driver. He looked up at the red light again. Christ, were they broken or what? The road ahead looked suddenly huge and empty. He couldn't be sitting here in the middle of nowhere on a lousy, rainy Sunday morning. He let out the clutch.

The banging came steadily from the back. He jammed the accelerator to the floor. The Renault had come through the junction. The back doors of the van were opening. Spots appeared on the panel of the passenger door, and a burning smell stung in his nose. He banged the pistol on the ashtray as he went to find second gear. Glass showered across the seat at him. He kept the wheel turning. The growl and burr of the impacts didn't seem to be so loud now. The glove compartment shattered a split second before the windscreen went white. He banged at the glass with the end of the pistol but it wouldn't give.

The first shot hit him in the shoulder, knocked him hard against the door. The steering wheel went nuts and then locked as the Fiat mounted the footpath, slid along the seawall, and stalled. He heard himself shouting. The spots on the steering wheel were blood, he knew. He wondered when he'd begin to feel his arm, why he wasn't panicking.

He rolled out onto the footpath. The glass grinding into his elbows didn't register with him. He thought of the rocks under the seawall, if he could get over there.

"Who are yous?"

The Fiat twitched with more impacts.

"We'll work this out . . . !"

Seaweed, he smelled; rubber, oil, sewage.

"Give me a chance to talk . . . !"

He waited. Still nothing.

"Just tell me what you're *after* . . . !" It wasn't a shout now, a screech that ripped at his throat. "Just let me fucking *talk!*"

The buzzer from the open door was driving him around the twist.

"Whatever it is . . . ! Come on . . . ! Who *are* you?"

There were more shots from the front. It was a steady pattern now, like those drum rolls he used to do in that band the social workers organized for them back when they were in fifth class, that stupid community band. Something stung as it flew into his cheek. He pressed his face to the panel by the wheel. The bullets slamming into bodywork resonated through his cheekbone.

"Jesus," Larry Smith whispered. "Yvonne."

Running feet were zigzagging his way. They weren't stopping, slowing down even. The panic broke over him then. He shoved the pistol around the side of the bumper, fired twice, ducked back.

Larry Smith was turning to see if others had come up behind him when a bullet shattered the base of his skull. It was a firearm of similar caliber if not the identical weapon, the Garda press release stated two days later, that was also used to blow parts of Larry Smith's head across Strand Road. The postmortem report contained three further sentences which were to be much remarked upon in the Murder Squad. They concerned what appeared to be the marks of a kick to the face delivered, it seemed, prior to the coup de grâce.

{ 5 }

. . . . .

"Lads," said APF Colm Brennan. He waited until they looked over at him. At least they'd see the uniform and cop on that he was Airport Police. "Lads? Come on now, for the love of God. This is Dublin Airport now, not a bloody rave-up. Yous can't be blocking the way here."

There were five of them now. Brennan looked around at the faces of these die-hard fans of Public Works. Nobody had actually complained. The trouble was that the big fella, the dopey-looking one with the four hundred studs in his ears, had started drinking out of something from inside his jacket. He could be fifteen or he could be twenty, couldn't be sure. But he was the one to watch. He might lose the head handy enough, that one.

"Well, turn it down at least. Do you hear me?"

The big fella threw his hair back, began nodding to the beat.

. . . *teenage babies die at night* . . .

Brennan thought, God, if he heard that stupid song one more time. Where were those fellas living with their depressing frigging "tunes"? Hadn't they heard there were jobs out there, the Celtic Tiger going around roaring money now? He waited for the big fella to look over. Not a chance, no. And the others were ignoring him too. The young one with the tights for pants and the yellow hair and the thing in her nose was swaying and dancing and grinning. A taxi pulled away from the drop-off area by the terminal doors. The driver beeped as he passed. The big fella waved and raised his fist.

"Yeaaaahhhhh!"

Brennan clutched the walkie-talkie tighter behind his back and glanced over at the video camera set high in the wall. The big fella turned away. He was taking another swig out of the bottle.

Enough was enough. Brennan stepped over.

"Look," he said. "That's the limit."

The big fella dropped the bottle inside his jacket. He stared at some point on Brennan's chest.

"What's A, P, F? I mean, you're not a *real* cop, are you?"

"Airport Police, and yeah, I am a real policeman. Now turn that thing down, get your gear and move on."

"— The F, though. There — APF. F stands for something. Right?"

Brennan stared at him.

"Airport Police and Fire Service. Take your mates too."

"So it's like fires too, you have to put out fires, right? Like, *big* fires?"

Brennan stared into the bloodshot eyes. He couldn't tell if it was just the slagging or something else on the way.

"Okay," he said. "That's it. Out of here. It's over, let's go."

"Well wait a minute here." The big fella wiped his mouth with the back of his hand. "I've got me rights haven't I? No one's hassled here, are they? All we're doing is seeing the band off."

He lit a cigarette. His eyes stayed steady on Brennan's. A guitar riff howled behind him. The big fella started to snigger and turned away, shaking with laughter. Brennan looked from face to face, down at the ghetto blaster, the bags, the rucksacks. Badges everywhere, paint, beads, studs. And they thought Public Works was still the local lads, their pals. Gobshites. They didn't even cop on that Public Works had their own frigging jet at the far end of the airport. That they were going off to do a video somewhere. That worldwide success didn't begin with the bloody band climbing out of taxis and buses like ordinary Joe Soaps and pushing trolleys up to the bloody check-in. He wished he could tell them.

"All right then," Brennan muttered. "Don't say I didn't tell you."

A minibus with tinted windows had stopped near the doors.

"Look," the big lug called out. "It's the lads!"

Brennan knew that he'd left it too late. He made it in front of the girl. The others moved around him. He thumbed to transmit, hoped to God Fogarty or someone had been keeping an eye on things. Not a bloody Guard in sight. The girl got by him. There were hands pawing the minibus. The big fella had his face plastered up to a side window on the van. Fogarty, the supervisor, answered on the radio.

"They're mobbing a van here," Brennan said. "We need to get people out."

He began shoving the teenagers away.

"Leave the van alone!" he shouted. "That couldn't be them!"

The girl with the face full of hardware shrieked the name of the lead guitarist. Brennan squinted in the window himself. Could it be someone from the band? The tint was so bloody dark.

"Get back!" he grunted and he shoved the girl.

He caught a glimpse of a sticker by the bottom corner of the windscreen. Squiggly writing, dots, a piece of a moon. Oh Jases, he muttered. Where did they put their CD signs now, those diplomatic plates? Well it was their own bloody fault. He turned and grasped the big fella's collar.

The doors to the terminal slid open. Fogarty and Jimmy Doyle and the new fella what's his name were coming out full tilt now. About bloody time —

The big fella turned. The loose look on his face had turned to something narrow and Brennan knew he'd have to get a hold of him rapid, pull him off balance. Behind the lug, though, a window on the van slid down to reveal two startled brown eyes staring at Brennan. Masks, he wondered, but no, some of those things the women wore because. . . .

APF Brennan opened his mouth to say something and then fell backward as something connected with his cheekbone.

•   •   •   •   •

Chief Inspector James Kilmartin was on a roll now, and he knew it. He slid off his stool and hitched up his trousers. Minogue knew the routine: the cute countryman, nobody's fool — so look out. He looked at the faces in the huddle around "The Killer" Kilmartin here in the bar of the Garda Club. One of the Guards, a red-faced sergeant, kept shaking his head and rubbing his eyes. Every now and then he'd repeat things Kilmartin had said and he'd chortle softly. Kilmartin leveled a finger and swept it around slowly by each of the Guards.

"So it's getting dark now," he said. "This poor Yankee tourist, he's getting kind of worried, isn't he?"

Over at the far end of the bar Sergeant Seamus Hoey was rolling depleted ice cubes around the bottom of his glass. Minogue counted back: it was seven months since Hoey had transferred out of the squad. He now worked in Crime Prevention. Kilmartin still thought this was hilarious, annoying, stupid. A Guard didn't just *opt to leave* the squad, especially to join a joke shop like Crime Prevention. On top of that he'd become a teetotaler of nearly one year's standing. Kilmartin had stopped slagging him about that after Minogue had asked him whether he'd still be making the jokes if Shea had succeeded in his suicide attempt. Detective Garda Tommy Malone, who had taken up Hoey's position in the Murder Squad, was staring at the goings-on in Hoey's glass. He seemed to be mesmerized. Malone was simply knackered, Minogue decided, same as himself. The few pints had slammed the door on the adrenalin that had kept them going these past few days.

Kilmartin's voice grew louder.

"I mean here he is, out in the back of beyond, down amongst the *buffs* of County Clare . . ."

Kilmartin looked across at his friend and colleague, Minogue, and his wink gave way to a leer. Minogue raised an eyebrow to register the slur against his native county. This seemed to enliven Kilmartin.

"So anyway," he went on voice, "here's this fecking tourist, this poor iijit of a Yank, beginning to wonder if he'd been given proper directions at all. Researching his ancestors, walking in ditches, and staring at oul cow sheds — you know the routine! What happens but doesn't he fall over this courting couple in behind a ditch . . ."

The red-faced sergeant began to chortle. Kilmartin paused and leaned back, let his tongue trace his bottom lip.

"Now you know what *they're* up to," he said.

The sergeant laughed outright. Malone drifted over to Minogue and laid his glass on the counter.

"Another pint, boss? My twist."

Minogue shrugged. Hoey had followed Malone over now.

"Is this the Family Member one?" Hoey asked. "Or the Old Log Inn?"

"Family Member," said Malone. "But we won't know for a while yet."

Minogue looked at his watch. Half-six. Kilmartin had insisted on taking them all to the Garda Club. Sure didn't they have plenty to celebrate, God damn it, was the chief inspector's tack: a) Tynan fighting off the decentralizing shite from the Department of Justice for another year. Who'd have thought he'd be coming to our rescue at all? Then b), finally getting the chief supers with their whinging about dispersing the squad buried for another year too? Tynan again, strangely enough, and this time telling those yobs just how bad crime had gotten here in Dublin with the frigging jackals and hyenas and wolves doing their own take on the Celtic Tiger rigamarole? Not to speak of c) Hoey's promotion, the speed of it and all . . . ? And not to mention d) that bastard Harte finally coughing up for the Dunshaughlin shooting?

Laughter erupted from around Kilmartin. Minogue had missed the punch line again. Now Kilmartin was heading their way. Minogue tracked the chief inspector's approach, the slow rolling gait, the faked punch to the stomach of the laughing sergeant, the clumsy headlock and guffaws. High spirits entirely, and why not: Kilmartin was away on three weeks leave as of this evening. He could nurse his sore head on the plane to Boston tomorrow. As of one hour ago, in fact, Minogue had become acting head of the Murder Squad.

Kilmartin drew up opposite Malone.

"Well now, Molly," he said. "Anudder one, den? My twist and all, now."

"No," said Malone. "Thanks." Kilmartin turned to Hoey.

"Coke, Sergeant?" Shea Hoey seemed to consider it. Kilmartin eyed him. "I don't want you drinking your way into Bolivia now, but," he added.

The barman pointed the remote at the TV across the room. An ad for a hamburger chain came on. Minogue wished he'd eaten before the three pints. He thought about sausages in Bewleys. What day was it today anyway? Thursday he was to meet his daughter Iseult for lunch. The baby was due in three months. *Trimester,* that was the word: her last trimester.

The spinning globe and floating letters slowed and jumped off the screen. Small pictures then turned into movies as they sprang to the front. A military vehicle unloaded food next to a dusty track. Sudan? Or was that last year? Next was a dusty plain. The camera moved from a close-up of bleached bones to a shimmering horizon. Next came a scene of a riverbank protest. Had to be Ireland. Yes, slurry had killed thousands of fish in Cork.

"Oh I know when my money's no good," said Kilmartin and moved off to the Guards at the far end of the bar.

Too lazy to get up, Minogue watched Hoey begin to flip a beer mat. As well as studying for his sergeant's exam, Hoey had taken to conjuring tricks. To cod his new missus, was Kilmartin's theory. Not so. Áine Finnucane, not Áine Hoey, had brought Hoey to the inner-city school where she taught remedial. A lot of hard cases, Hoey had reported: broken homes, some already into drugs, families in and out of jail. So Hoey had prepped himself with sleight-of-hand tricks to get the kids' interest. He'd ended up more or less hypnotizing them, Hoey reported, but wasn't sure if he'd gotten through to them about anything else. That didn't seem to matter to Hoey. He kept returning on a regular basis to "put on shows" at other inner-city schools. Áine, a woman Minogue liked a great deal indeed because of how she laughed as much as what she had done teaching and building in Africa, had told Minogue that a lot of the kids in her school now called Hoey the Magic Cop.

Malone dropped some coins on the counter.

"All right," he said to Hoey. "Show us the married man trick. You know, where you make the money disappear?"

· · · · ·

Airport Police and Fire Officer Derek Mitchell, twenty, and six weeks into his new job, checked his walkie-talkie and headed out toward Dublin Airport's long-term car park. The breezes which had played around him by the doors to the freight depot were gusts out here.

He waved at the Guards sitting in the squad car by the ramp. One of them managed a nod. "Don't strain yourself," Mitchell murmured. The news that the Guards were going to make a new Garda station at the airport was only a rumor anyway. This squad car sitting by the ramp up to the terminal was for show now. That mob of fans had been turfed out and four of them had been arrested. Even Fogarty hadn't seen anything like it. It was the van with the tinted windows showing up that'd torn the arse out of the situation. No wonder those Saudi Arabians would be thinking we were all bloody barbarians. Well, they should talk: the women in masks, veils, or whatever, hiding their faces. And for what? Like furniture covered up. *Chattels,* that was the word.

It had taken three Guards to get the big lug into the squad car. The one who had clocked Brennan. He was sixteen, it turned out. Derek Mitchell sort of felt sorry for Brennan. Brennan, who should have known better, was going home with a thick lip. He might even be concussed someone said — but that was maybe Brennan already taking a dive with compo in mind. Using his head better now after getting clattered than before Brennan, yeah, aiming for an easy way out. It was Brennan had told him the Guards were going to set up a station at the airport, that the APFs would be in the ha'penny place then.

The wind was rising. He zipped his jacket up higher. It took major work to push the button through the frigging buttonhole on his collar. His thumb hurt like hell from pushing the edge of the button. Bollocks: it was too tight now.

He rubbed his thumb hard against his forefinger and watched a plane make its approach over the Irish Sea. It just hung there. Stats: at any given moment a million people were flying up there. That was day and night too. Where'd he read that? He rolled the volume dial of his walkie-talkie over and back. Now, think about it: was he the only person in the world, the civilized world like, to think about how mad air travel was?

All they were basically were metal tubes, for God's sake, tons of weight, full of people getting fired through the air at five hundred miles an hour. Madness really. People reading the papers, having their dinners, watching films, sitting on toilets, sleeping — all five *miles* up there.

He turned and looked around the sky. There were dirty gray, rolling rain clouds to the west. It was getting colder. He eyed the canopy over by the fire depot. It'd be a quarter after seven before he'd log into the last checkpoint next to the decks for the drop-offs. They should give him a car or something, like for the dog patrols on the perimeter rounds had. A bike even! Ah it was exercise, wasn't it.

The windscreens were covered with clouds. It made Mitchell dreamy. The long-term car park always looked full. That was because people parked as close as they could to the walkway. A lot of the cars had the flashing lights that told you the alarm was set. What a bloody pain the alarms were out here! If people decided to ignore the notices about the alarms, then they actually deserved to get their cars robbed. Well not *ignored* exactly, but the Guards didn't care much to be told about alarms going off. A good gust of wind could do some of them. A lot them didn't have automatic resets either. There was a surge of engines from the far side of the hangars. A car started up a few rows over. He walked on. He knew he'd given up checking every car. He walked slower, tried to get a system going where he'd be covering all the cars in both directions, row by row. There might be video in here now, no matter what Fogarty had told them about it taking another few months at least. There could be cameras just for keeping an eye on patrols. But he didn't have to be the FBI for God's sake, did he. Just cover himself, that's —

He was quick but still late. He let his hand settle on his hair instead and watched the damned hat tossed rolling down the roadway between the rows. It bounced as the brim rolled under. Then it lodged against a wheel and fell over like a really bad actor in a really bad cowboy film from a million years ago. He stared at the hat. There were specks of rain on the windscreen of the Golf next to him now. He picked up the hat, jammed it on his head, held it there.

He walked faster now. There was a blue Escort with an English number plate. He stopped, turned away from the wind, and jammed his stupid hat between his knees. He peeled back the pages in his logbook until he got to to the notes he had scribbled down from the patrol board. It was a blue Escort, *Dublin* registration, they were looking for. Someone had scribbled VIP and TV on the sheet too. He wondered if the other patrol APFs bothered with the board at all. Robbed cars was the Guards' job anyway. As in, those two layabouts sitting in their squad car back at the ramp. Someone had told him the Guards didn't try anymore because there were so many being stolen, in Dublin at least. Brennan had wised him up to the fact that it was only for insurance that the Guards had to post the bulletins to them. Well he'd better keep a note of it, just in case. Show he was on the ball at least. The pages flapped and clung to the pencil. He wrote blind anyway.

His eyes watered from the gusts now. He looked back down the rows he'd done. A right iijit he must look, his hat jammed between his knees, the pages still flapping and cracking in his other hand. No wonder the probationer APFs got the long-term patrols for months. He managed to close his notebook with one hand and slip it into his pocket. It was going to lash rain any minute: de-fin-itely. He looked across the rows of car roofs. They were all one color from this angle. A blue Escort? There were probably dozens of them here. He bit his lip. A raindrop smacked his hat brim. Part of him had decided not to go back down those rows again anyway.

CHAPTER 2

MINOGUE RUBBED HIS EYES. The bar at the Garda Club was filling up. He'd seen Liam Nugent wave from the door, swing his imaginary hurley stick. Minogue had to wave his fist at him, of course. Nugent, a Wexford man recently promoted to CI and doing well in Fraud, shrank in mock terror. County Clare's chances of getting to the quarter finals in this year's All-Ireland had come to depend on Wexford getting beaten by Kilkenny — again. Minogue's eyes drifted back to the television.

The weatherwoman clicked a wand thing she kept in her hand. He rubbed his eyes again. When he opened them he could see Ireland's weather in relation to weather systems across Europe. They were having a tough time of it with rain and sleet in northern Italy. Apparently the Austrians were getting some lightning bolts. Weatherwoman clicked again and satellite pictures slid by. A cold front was on the way from Central Europe.

Minogue thought again about staying. Kilmartin had made his mind up, settling in with a mountain of sandwiches in front of him. He'd turned serious now too, laying into the System. Minogue didn't want to hear it again but he caught the odd phrase: What exactly were Guards supposed to do in these situations, Kilmartin wanted to know — duck?! Wear suits of armor? Put their hands in their pockets, and look the other way? Or whistle a shagging jig, maybe? What chance did we have when push came to shove? Et cetera.

The policemen huddled around Kilmartin examined their drinks, cast longer glances at the television. Kilmartin wasn't going to give up. Where was the incentive to follow through if the system was stacked, he demanded. Had to hold our ground, didn't we? Oh, by Christ wasn't the public was being codded! Face facts: crime in Dublin was out of hand. Larry Smith had been only one in a whole mob of gangsters. And the young offenders — oh don't get him started on that one! A mess entirely. As if one of 'em stabbed you and robbed you it wouldn't hurt as much or something! You could buy a gun in a pub in Clondalkin for seven hundred quid. Ah, what was the point of talking . . . !

Hoey was heading off now. Malahide was a long enough commute. Minogue asked him how the new house was working out.

"I'm trying to get a lawn going," Hoey said.

"What's a lawn?" Malone asked.

"They have them down the country," said Hoey. "Green things."

Kilmartin had started into the joke about the taxi driver and the prostitute. Minogue swiveled the stool about and looked around the room. He spotted a woman in conversation with a superintendent in civvies. Lawlor, that's who he was. Lahlah. It was "Bridges" Lawlor a few years ago. Minogue had seen him on television a lot this past while. People's feelings toward the Guards was his thing, he half-remembered. The community policing thing, building bridges. That was it, building bridges in the poorer areas of Dublin so that the gangsters would be rooted out by their own communities.

The woman looked familiar. The big glasses on her put Minogue in mind of a frog. He tried to place her, believed he was coming close, but soon gave up trying. Lawlor seemed to be explaining something complicated. She didn't often return his smiles. She nodded every now and then, but her eyes went often to the ruck around Kilmartin.

The weatherwoman and her maps disappeared in a flurry of stars. She was replaced by sliding words and the twirling logo of Radio Telifís Éireann. The shine on that, Minogue thought, we're international now, we have everything. And why not. Taxpayers, a lot of them probably German taxpayers still, would be paying for Kilmartin's junket to the States. He'd be visiting Quantico of all places, to get the lowdown on how the FBI profiled their serial bad guys. He wondered what they'd have made of the likes of Dublinman and all-around thug, drug dealer, vandal, robber, and scut Larry Smith.

Kilmartin was well into his joke now. The taxi driver had been informed by his passenger that she had no money for the fare. A face appeared on the screen, a telephone number below it. Kilmartin's voice was louder but Minogue still caught most of the words from the announcer. Touring the west of Ireland in a rented blue Ford Escort.

"No sign of your man yet," Malone said.

The snapshot looked like the regulation crop of a group scene. A wedding maybe. The large, even teeth, the tan, they could only mean American. Minogue wondered what exactly it was that made the face so easily typed. The beefy neck? Some stock expression of ease and entitlement. Well after all, he'd grown up and belonged to people who owned the planet more or less. Cheap petrol, big cars. Hamburgers; planes that went to space and back. Big smiles, genuine a lot of them; guns in every house. Prosperity. And Daithi Minogue, whose letters came less frequently now, and who hadn't been back for a visit lived there. The pang sliced hard across Minogue's chest and he felt suddenly almost desperate.

"That Yank, the tourist," Malone repeated. "What's his name again?"

"Shaw-nessy," Minogue said.

"What do you mean Shawnessy? Shock-nessy." Minogue eyed Malone.

"That's how they say it over there."

"How do you know?"

"There was a fella on *Miami Vice* once. A crook, a lawyer. Shawnessy, they pronounced it."

Malone looked up from his work balancing beer mats and frowned.

"Now do you believe me?" Minogue asked.

Malone's house of beer mats collapsed. He shrugged and swore and grabbed his glass. Stress, Minogue thought as he yawned with a sudden aching weariness, another meaningless word. The screen filled with burning buses. A lanky teenager throwing a rock froze and shrank, and was yanked back in miniature to a corner of the screen. Was that Derry, Minogue wondered.

"Jesus Christ," said Malone. "Is that going on tonight? It fucking well better not be."

"It's archival footage."

"What?"

A British army Land Rover sped over a roadway littered with stones. A petrol bomb burst against its roof.

"History, Tommy. It's old stuff."

Someone with a scarf wrapped around his lower face was caught and frozen in place as he hoisted a petrol bomb. He too was dispatched as a fading, still shot to the bottom of the screen. The making of a great athlete, Minogue believed, that kid. Probably in his thirties or even forties by now, with kids, a few pints in the local, a half-decent house paid for by Her Majesty, the trousers getting too tight on him. The pictures slid back to reveal a dimly lit studio, where four people sat around a table.

"Maybe the locals ate him," Malone said. Minogue turned to him.

"The American, like." Malone nodded toward Kilmartin.

"They did say the west of Ireland, didn't they?"

"Our American cousins are here to enjoy history, Tommy. Not to live it."

He looked back at the television. Spotlights revealed the panelists one by one. Minogue sighed. God, not that windbag from the university again. Worse, that hairy, know-it-all journalist what was his name, the one wrote about Ireland disappearing. As if.

Then Kilmartin's fist crashed into his palm. One of tonight's designated gobshites to edify, a detective with a long nose that he constantly rubbed with the same paper hankie, made a solemn nod. Kilmartin's eyes were hooded now. He pulled back his thumb, pointed his finger at his head, dropped the thumb. He eyed the red-faced sergeant who began to nod slowly himself.

"Smih' goh' hih'," said the sergeant.

The phrase was a take on another Dublin criminal family member's reaction to the news of Larry Smith's murder. Together with a mostly mangled Dublin accent, it had done the rounds of Garda stations for months now.

"Play hard, die hard," said Kilmartin.

"Damned right, Jim," said the sergeant. "That's the way she goes. A-okay."

"One hundred percent effective," Kilmartin said, his voice gone soft now. "Yes sirree . . . *The Larry Smith Solution.*"

Minogue looked around the room. He'd missed the transition from hilarity to gravity. The woman with the glasses, frog-woman, hadn't. She was watching Kilmartin intently. Lahlah's smile had faded. His eyes shifted from the group to the barman leaning on the bar listening to Kilmartin.

Sure that his message had reached and clutched and held the minds of his colleagues, and surer still that they'd hold it forever, Chief Inspector James Kilmartin arched his back over the counter. He looked with a lazy defiance from face to face. Murmurs of approval ran through the group of policemen. Glasses went to mouths, a flick of the head from several. The red-faced sergeant put his fist on the counter and pulled an imaginary trigger. The brotherhood, thought Minogue, the clan.

"Job well done there, Jim," said the red-faced sergeant. "No complaints here, let me tell you."

Superintendent Lawlor tweaked his nose and turned to talk to frog-woman. I know her, Minogue thought, I do. Who the hell was she anyhow? He watched her feign an interest in what Lawlor was saying with some newfound fervor. Her eyes went toward Kilmartin again. Lawlor kept talking. She looked down at the empty glass Lawlor was pushing around on the countertop. Lawlor's face eased when she reached for her bag. He nodded to Minogue as he passed on the way to the door.

●   ●   ●   ●   ●

Derek Mitchell turned away from the gusts. He looked at the sky again.

"Make up your bloody mind," he groaned.

The raindrops were beginning to bead and run together on the car roofs now. He'd come back around by the long-term car park again, on the trot this time. Ahead of him were the rows of cars he had passed earlier. It'd be no use saying that it was raining. Five minutes and he'd be finished, anyway. Or drowned, shag it.

He slowed to look in the window of a newish Volvo. The stick thing must be a control for the stereo. The CD changer was probably in the boot and — His hat flew off and sailed over the roof. He watched it bounce off the roof of an Opel. He was beyond being annoyed. There was a certain elegance to it, he had to admit. It rolled down onto the bonnet and fell on the tarmacadam. He stepped around the front of the Opel in time to see the hat on the move again. It rolled on the edge of its crown, wobbled, and changed direction. Drops of rain hit his forehead. The hat began to roll in a circle, it rebounded off a wheel, and fell over. Gusts still stirred it.

He took his time strolling over. He picked up the hat and rubbed it with his sleeve. To hell with that stupid folder of regulations: this bloody hat was staying under his arm until he got back indoors. He looked down at the mossy growth already working its way into the tarmacadam here. Then he slowly returned to his hunkers. He stayed there for a half a minute, moving from foot to foot, staring at it from different angles. He had already decided to call in. He just didn't want to make an iijit of himself.

No, it wasn't the color that had caught his eye, he thought while he waited for the shift super to show up. It wasn't even red, for God's sake. But somehow he'd known right away what it was. That was before he'd checked the car, even. It was only after he'd stood up again that he'd realized it went right back under the bumper of the car anyway. He'd walked around the back of the car, seen the sticker: Emerald Rent-A-Car. The Emerald Isle, he murmured: if this was what he thought it was, this was trouble. His fingers kept the hat rotating in his hands. He hardly noticed the rain soaking into his hair.

He looked over at the Escort again. It looked different now, as though everything had moved away from it and it stood alone, changed. It wasn't what might be in the car that was getting to him. It was how normal everything seemed, how weirdly ordinary and dull and boring. More than creepy: the hairs were still standing on the back of his neck.

No sirens, no squad cars. Where the hell were they? He tugged on the antenna, rolled the volume dial until it hissed. No one was talking, why not? He didn't want to call in again. It'd sound like he was losing it or something. The drone of lorries slowing on the dual carriageway carried over the hiss of traffic. He watched a jet rise above the terminal and followed the quivering trail from the exhaust. The rain was getting heavier.

When he looked back he saw Fogarty and two Guards heading his way. Fogarty, the fat bastard, was huffing and puffing. Derek Mitchell stepped back to the bumper of the Escort and thumbed his notebook open.

"All right there, er," he heard Fogarty call out. "Derek?"

Mitchell watched squad car lights flicker from across the car park. More of them, well *finally*, like. He held onto his hat. What if it wasn't blood though? The two Guards looked him up and down. A handset came alive with a staticky country accent. Fogarty gave up on the hair.

"Over there," he said to Fogarty. He had to clear his throat again. "In there, under the exhaust pipe. You have to get down here to really see it."

• • • • •

Malone hit eighty in spots on the airport road. Minogue didn't ask him why he was driving like a bloody lunatic. Maybe he was trying to keep pace with two unmarked Opels that had passed them near Whitehall. The Nissan leaned hard into the bend as they closed on the roundabout at the entrance to the airport. Minogue felt the tires bite. He looked at the shredded supermarket bags fluttering in the hedgerows.

"They're after shutting the whole airport down?" Malone asked again. Another unmarked, a Granada, came up behind, flickering light askew on the roof.

"That's what they told me," Minogue said.

Maybe he could get a sandwich. But the grub in the terminal restaurant always had a peculiar taste. It had taken a few years to dawn on him that the taste of everything he'd eaten or drunk there over the years had something to do with him sitting across the table from his son with the minutes winding down for the boarding call. The lump in his throat, Daithi Minogue's pale, slack face. Hangovers, the dull and persistent pain that came up his chest to his throat. Daithi's "it's only six hours away, Ma" didn't wash with Minogue either. Well it wasn't six anymore, it was more like twelve to the West Coast.

The Minogues' only son liked the States. Kathleen Minogue still sent him the Positions Available every Wednesday. He was in no hurry to get married. Semiconductors seemed to be most of his work. Why not head back to Silicon Valley here in Dublin, the new economy? Well . . . Daithi Minogue was sure he was being earmarked for an operation in Silicon Valley. Silicon Valley was where it all came together, Daithi had explained.

"So it's a full-scale thing," said Malone. "Since that incident with your man. In Monaghan?"

"I suppose," said Minogue.

The tires began to growl. Malone let the steering wheel drift a little. The Nissan tilted suddenly to the right as Malone turned off the roundabout.

"Brian Whelan," Malone said. "Right?

Minogue nodded. Garda Brian Whelan, two years on the force, had been making what he and his partner believed was a routine check of a vehicle parked on a street in Castleblayney, County Monaghan, two weeks after Christmas. The car had disintegrated when Whelan opened the passenger-side door. The remains of Joseph Brogan, known as a tout of checkered reliability to the RUC and the Guards, were found among the wreckage of the car. The talk was still that it was settling scores and staking out territory for a gang made up of IRA men. This was during a cease-fire.

The first roadblock was next to a landscaped knoll that hid the cargo terminals from the traffic. The shrubs hadn't flourished in the four years Minogue had begun noting them on his trips here. He wound down his window and slipped out his photocard. A Guard with watery eyes and blond hairs growing high on his cheeks laid his hand on the roof of the Nissan. Had the bomb squad arrived yet, Minogue wanted to know.

"Ten minutes or so," the Guard replied. "No smoke yet, but."

Shrmooaak, Minogue registered. County Cork, and not inclined to hide it.

"There'll be a site van along by and by," he said. "Steer them right, like a good man, will you."

"I will."

No "sir." Minogue looked up at him.

"Ye'd better meander over that way," the Guard said. "Everything that side of the hill is locked up tight, so it is."

"Tighter than that Munster cup you have below in Cork, I hope," Minogue said. The Guard's smile revealed pointy teeth. A fox, Minogue thought. A Cork fox.

"Clare, are ye?"

"Not on your shagging life," said Malone.

Malone coasted down the empty road. Minogue's belly growled again. He strained to catch a glimpse of the car parks on the far side of the shrubs. A Guard in full motorbike regalia waved them down a roadway away from the car park. A line of flagpoles followed the curb. Most of the flags were tangled in their ropes. Snapping and straining, the American one still floated free.

Caty, his son's fiancée, with no *h* because it was the Polish version, had fallen in love with Ireland. Minogue wasn't sure what or whose Ireland she was in love with. She wanted to live here, learn Irish; walk the back roads, talk to everyone, learn everything. Caty was a sociologist, raised in a devout Polish-American family in an outer suburb of New York City. Her grave accounts of immigrants in American cities impressed Minogue. He didn't understand how she could see Poles and Irish as similar though, the centuries of oppression thing.

He remembered her sitting on an outcrop over the Burren not two months ago, writing notes. A strange sight entirely, with the stone fields all about her. It was one of those pet days, with roaring sunshine and the clouds low and fast, when even the hills seemed to be on the move. Interrogating him afterward: what had happened to all the families in these ruined villages now hidden under hazel and ivy? Was it true like Daithi had told her, that he'd wanted to move to the States himself years ago? Were Clare people really musical, second-sighted? Was the Celtic Tiger destroying the real Ireland? And why did everyone seem to talk ironically here anyway?

"Jases," said Malone. "It's a right bloody maze here."

He turned the Nissan down toward a collection of dumpsters and airport vans clustered around the back doors of what looked like a warehouse. Several uniforms moved around between the vehicles.

"Yellow," said Malone. "The lorry. There we are."

He parked by an airport van. Minogue checked the battery before he pocketed the cell phone.

"Does anyone really think it's booby-trapped," Malone said. "Your man's car?"

Minogue shrugged. A Guard stepped down from the rear door of the communications lorry. Minogue stepped out onto the grass and turned his back to the wind. He looked around the sky. At least it had only been a shower. But instead of the wind slicing at his face, he imagined for several seconds the air full of glass, pieces of torn metal scything through the shrubs, the blast hitting them before they'd even hear it. He stopped buttoning his coat. Couldn't happen, he almost said. There was a peace deal in the works. The sharp ache in his chest ebbed slowly.

He rapped on the door, stepped in. Two technicians were seated side by side in front of a console. One tugged on his handset and raised the pencil he'd been tapping on the counter.

"How's things, lads?" Minogue asked.

Someone was smoking. Minogue glanced at the monitors. He stopped at the one that held steady on the hatchback of the Escort. The picture shuddered, shrank to allow other cars in and then closed on the Escort again. The technician closest to the cab of the lorry turned and lifted his cigarette from the ashtray. O'Reilly, Minogue thought.

"Pretty close now," he said.

Minogue watched him suck hard on the cigarette. Some skin problem, a face like a well-cooked pudding, a wispy mustache. O'Reilly tapped at the partition door into the cab.

"So what," came the voice from the door as it opened. "Ask them if I give a shit. Go ahead. This isn't one a their bloody concerts, their *gigs* here. This is a security shutdown."

Minogue's eyes returned to the monitor. The camera was steady on an armored lorry parked sideways across the entrance to a car park.

"Fine and well," the voice went on. "Make whatever calls you want. That's your business."

Minogue recognized the soft voice, how the speaker managed to squeeze in a light cough in the middle of a sentence. *"Make whatever ah-uh calls you want."* A mannerism, Minogue wondered, or a conscious put-down.

The speaker backed in through the partition door. The cell phone clenched in his hand was identical to Minogue's. Superintendent Damian Little stared at the phone as though it had bitten him. He addressed nobody in particular.

"Fucking yobs," he murmured. "Did you ever hear the like?"

O'Reilly smiled and unplugged his headset. The police radio traffic was constant now. Little straightened up and looked at the two arrivals.

"Will you lookit," Little said..

"How's Damian?" Minogue asked. Chiseled, they'd call that jaw; action hero model, maybe. Did women really like that class of a fella? The Adam's apple standing out on his neck, the veins running beside them. Weights, Minogue understood vaguely, something strenuous and even close to a torturous rapture that photos of athletes showed so clearly.

Little grasped Minogue's hand. The grin spread to a tight smile. Right, Minogue remembered: that little-boy gap between his teeth, what he remembered along with Little's intensity that came through so strangely in his drawl. The almost slow-mo, gentle tone Minogue associated with teachers on automatic, priests in confession maybe. As though you were on the slow side, and the speaker was taking account of it.

"The undertakers themselves. How's Matt?"

"Fair to middling, Damian. That wasn't us you were referring to now was it."

Little's leather jacket creaked as he brandished the cell phone. Minogue plucked out his own and waved it. Little smiled.

"For fuck's sake you wouldn't believe it," he said. "Show business."

Malone stepped around Minogue.

"Well, stop the lights," Little said. "Tommy Malone. Moving up too, huh?"

"Dead on," said Malone. "How's it going."

"Don't mind me, I heard you left the Killer whistling over a case there."

"Only rumors."

"Ah you should have come over to us when you had the chance, man!" said Little.

For all Malone's physical abilities and the hard-chaw self he brought to work, Minogue still couldn't imagine Malone as one of the Emergency Repsonse Unit cowboys.

O'Reilly tapped on the monitor. Little's smile dropped off his face. He leaned in over the screen. The camera covering the army bomb disposal lorry drew back to reveal a huddle of figures gathered around what looked to Minogue to be a small tank. The gofer, they called it now, this drone that had been bought with much fanfare from an outfit who'd perfected the design in Belfast.

It began to move, stop, move again. A voice on the radio said "Switching over." Little touched a button by the monitor and the policemen were staring at pavement and the bottom of a tire. The picture jerked and turned to frame a row of parked cars.

"Aw Christ," said Little, and he turned away. "They'll be ten minutes before they send in the damn thing. And for what? This isn't bomb territory, this thing."

Little clapped his hands and began rubbing them hard together.

"Here," he said. "Give you a laugh. Do you know who that was on the phone there? Trying to give me grief? Go on, guess."

"Your daughter's new boyfriend," said Malone.

"No. He's still in a coma. Try again."

"We don't know, Damian," said Minogue.

"Public Works. That's who."

"Who are they?"

"Very funny," said Little. "Don't you like them? *Streets of Shame?*"

"'Nobody's home,' Yeah, yeah, yeah."

"I bet you have all their CDs, you bollocks."

"Not gone on them," said Malone. "I'd be more a GOD man these days."

Little gave a breathless laugh. It took Minogue a moment: Girls Over Dublin, the latest rage group. Little looked over at Minogue.

"Well, Matt," he said. "'Do you believe in GOD?'"

Minogue kept his eyes on the screen. He remembered the pictures on the ads for their smash hit CD. They were like those Chagall pictures, couples flying over a city. Nice. Only one of them, a Fiona, had claimed she was lesbian, he'd heard, and the bishops and archbishops had been smart enough to keep their mouths shut, let GOD's publicity genius spin in the wind over the free controversy they wanted.

"Girls Over Dublin," Minogue said. "Or the Man Himself, Damian?"

"Ah, what's the use," Little said. "You're in the Dark Ages, the pair of you. Get with it. It was their big-shot manager on the phone, not the *celebrities* themselves. Should have heard him, I'm telling you. You know him — Daly? Baldy, tries to wear a ponytail. Jumped-up gobshite."

Minogue looked up from the screen.

"So Public Works are held up here are they," said Minogue. "Along with us ordinary mortals."

"How'd you get this number, says I to him," Little went on. "This line is a vital link in our communications. 'Senior officer at Garda HQ,' says he. Like I'm supposed to fall down and adore or something. 'We have a very tight schedule,' says he. Rules don't apply to him of course."

The drone was on the move again. It spun slowly. Minogue caught a glimpse of several cars.

"So he starts to push," said Little. "'Couldn't we just go around the side and slip away,' says he. 'We have a private aircraft.' Well Dublin Airport is closed down, says I. In its entirety. No exceptions. On my orders. Now get off my fucking phone or I'll run you in for obstructing the Guards. You fucking weasel."

Minogue almost smiled. What would the celebrity manager have made of Little's gentle tone, the delivery.

"Is that what you said," he said to Little.

The lights reflected off wet tarmacadam were throwing glare at the camera now.

"Nearly told him to set his hair on fire and put it out himself with a lump hammer," said Little. "Christ, you'd think he'd be *thanking* us. If the car's wired, goes up . . . Well, I mean, I know it's not going to happen, but . . ."

Minogue looked up.

"So: not a word of a warning here, Damian?"

Little shook his head.

"Ask 'em how long more," he said to O'Reilly.

O'Reilly adjusted the earpiece and bent the stalk for the microphone while he waited. Little tugged at his ear and swore under his breath. The drone wasn't moving. Minogue glanced over and traced the lines cut into Little's forehead.

Raw meat heroes, Kilmartin called Little and his former cohorts. Still the fitness maniac, Minogue supposed, Little coached Garda teams, and his contorted face had appeared on the front pages of newspapers a few years ago: GARDA OFFICER, 42, PLACES 4TH IN DUBLIN CITY MARATHON.

Kilmartin disdained and envied the reputation the Emergency Response Units had built. He'd put out rumors that Little's training regimen involved booting trainees in T-shirts out of helicopters up in the Glen of Imaal and making them survive their two-day stay in the open by eating snails and bits of weeds. Some of Kilmartin's inventions had turned out to be true.

Damian Little had had to do the sideways waltz into Communications after a disastrous ERU raid in a border village. Shot eight times, the suspect lived. He turned out to be a Special Branch officer. Trigger Little suffered no public rebuke, however. Minogue heard that he had become separated from his wife.

The cell phone chirping was his own. He opened it and listened to Larry Griffin, a site specialist, describe the progress of the site van in the thickening traffic outside the airport. He held his hand over the mouthpiece.

"Damian. Can I point the site van up here while we're waiting?"

The drone was moving again. This time it emerged from behind the armored lorry. A screen filled with its jarring progress as it swung about and advanced by a line of cars. The radio came to life. Minogue asked again.

Little picked up a headset.

"Bring 'em up alongside, sure," he said.

Minogue's stomach rumbled again. He dropped the phone in his jacket pocket.

"Ah bollocks," said Little. "Bollocks, bollocks, *bollocks* . . ."

Minogue looked over at the still picture on the monitor. The voice on the radio sounded bashful. Problems with a key were enumerated. Little swore. The picture shook again. The drone was reversing. Little put down the headset.

"Bollocks," he said. "Here we are with a ton of the best detection and control stuff in the world. The sniffer reads fine. The controls are dead on. But we can't put a frigging key in a frigging lock."

"Like you're Einstein," said Malone, "but you arrive home pissed."

A bag of crisps even, thought Minogue. He scribbled the cell phone number on a pad and waved it at Little.

"Cut the shagging panel and be done with it," Little muttered. "Jases. We'll be here all night."

"Derek Mur . . ." said Minogue. "The airport security lad?"

"Mitchell," said Little. "APF, they're called. Airport Police and Fire. Joeys, we call them. But they don't much like that. Especially being as they're going ahead with putting in a station proper here soon enough."

"Where'll I find this Mitchell fella?"

"Staff canteen at the near end of the terminal."

CHAPTER 3

It took Minogue and Malone twenty minutes to corral cups of tea, a bag each of cheese and onion crisps, and a quick account by Derek Mitchell of how he had turned up the missing car. Fogarty, the supervisor, had been too talkative for Minogue not to notice. Fogarty was worried about being caught on the hop. So he should. Mitchell might be new on the job but maybe he'd turn out to be the only fella patrolling with his eyes open too.

Minogue sipped his tea, took in Mitchell's modest qualifiers. Mitchell had heard nothing of car thefts or break-in gangs working the airport. Five times — and Minogue had put a small tick in his notebook each time, so he knew: "I'm only new here like." Minogue stared at his notes and tried more combinations for APF: Airport Police and Fire; Always Planned Fiascos.

Malone prodded Mitchell a few times about his APF colleagues. Mitchell kept to the modest route. He didn't seem to notice he was repeating himself: a) there were lots of cars there; b) it was just lucky he had a knack for cars and numbers; c) "I'm only new here like" number six; d) they all check the lists on shift. Like hell, Minogue wanted to say. Áine's Police Fella; Awful Patrol Folk . . .

Fogarty had brought them a smudgy photocopy of the patrol and duty schedule. Missing persons and stolen vehicle lists were displayed prominently on the wall of the office by the schedules and the radio plug-ins. Too prominent, too neatly aligned.

The plastic taste of the tea grew sharper. PVC tea. Malone asked Mitchell to go over the route again. Mitchell drew his finger east from the horseshoe area by the terminals toward the long-term car park.

Could he remember the exact times for the checkpoints? Mitchell thought that he could.

Minogue stood. The aftertaste from his last gulp was pure plastic. He dropped the cup into the can.

"Take your time there," he said to Mitchell. "And don't be worrying. There are no wrong answers, now."

Malone joined him by the door.

"There has to be video here, Tommy. Get a layout of where they have them. And see what they cover, like a good man. Then we'll start rounding up the tapes."

Malone eyed Mitchell straining to get his times right.

"Fogarty is fussing around a lot. He'd be the one for the —"

The first man in the door was wearing sunglasses. Minogue didn't recognize him at first. More people piled in. Soft leather jackets, a woman with very short hair, a brace of cameras around her neck. Fogarty came next. He looked very pleased with himself. Perfume — men's or women's, Minogue couldn't tell — began to take over the room. Someone was smoking Gauloises or Gitanes too.

"Won't be long, lads," Fogarty said. "We'll have you en route ASAP."

Minogue recognized the manager. Daly: bald on top, that ponytail, just like Damian Little had said. The band members looked shagged. Daly took off his sunglasses and rubbed at his eyes. Minogue began to smell whiskey off someone's breath. Fogarty began rounding up chairs. The group shuffled and glanced around the canteen. Mr. 21 Byrne, the nickname off the bus he'd been born on. Crowley, the Crow. Mooney, that was the drummer's name. A nephew of neighbors of Kathleen growing up in Harolds Cross, Minogue recalled. Kevin Mooney, Batman, the fans called him. Daly threw up an arm and looked at his watch.

"Soon as we can," Fogarty said. "First up. You can slip out there and go around the side of the terminals. Be off in a flash."

Batman Mooney sank into a chair and lit a cigarette. He nodded at Malone.

"How's it going there?"

Malone chewed his gum hard, burst a bubble behind his teeth.

"Not so bad," he said. "Yourself?"

Mooney shrugged and blew out smoke. He ran his fingers through his stubbly, streaked hair and looked at them. Minogue watched the photographer twist on a lens and focus on Mooney. He mugged for her.

"Trapped in Dublin," he groaned. "Sober . . . ! Aarrghh! Help!"

She moved around him. The camera shutter went off in bursts. A heavyset man with an earring and a brush cut came through the door. He nodded at Daly and shook his head once.

"Fuck," muttered Daly. "*Fuck!* When, then, for Christ's sake?"

Daly yanked a cell phone out of his pocket. Did they make them that small now, Minogue wondered. His own phone began to ring. Damian Little: the site van was here. The bomb squad finally had a key in. They were ready to open the Escort.

"Jesus Christ," said Daly. "Is every Garda phone engaged these days?"

Minogue closed his phone.

"Not anymore."

"What's that?"

"The phone," said Minogue. "Don't be phoning us anymore now, like a good man. We need the lines kept open."

Daly looked to Fogarty.

"Guards," Fogarty said. Daly took in Minogue's expression

"Garda, ah . . . ?"

"Minogue. We're waiting too."

Daly raised his hands and let them drop. The camera was clicking again. Minogue walked to the doorway. Malone paused by Batman Mooney.

"Thanks," he said. "The picture? She'll keep it under her pillow, you know."

"Great. Catherine, yeah?"

"That's right." Malone said. "Me ma."

Mooney gave him a blank stare.

"Are you really a cop?"

"Me?"

"Yeah, you." Mooney nodded at Minogue. "Him, he looks like a farmer. So he must be a cop, right? You, though, I'd be wondering."

"Yeah, I'm a Guard."

"And your ma's into the scene? With the music like?"

"'Course she is. We all are, man. I've a niece runs her own fan club on yous."

Batman Mooney sighed. He drew hard on his cigarette.

"Tell the niece I'll be looking for her at the Point concert next month," he said.

"I'll tell her," Malone said. "Thanks very much. Oh, and by the way."
Mooney stopped in midstretch.

"She asked me to remind you," Malone went on. "She wants her blouse back."

. . . . .

The rain was coming in sheets across the lights now. The plastic cracked, hissed. Christy Griffin was cursing. Not real cursing, Minogue reflected. There was no real relish, no comfort to it.

The rain had soaked in under Minogue's arms. He reached up to help Griffin pull down the plastic again. They'd need a couple of lights in closer after they had sealed the back of the car. He balanced on one leg to look down at the side of Shaughnessy's face again. An anorak, a mountaineering type of coat. It looked like it was made of that dear stuff, the Gore-tex, it was called. A black T-shirt.

Malone had been helping tie the plastic by the front bumper. Pasty-faced, the eyes darting around on him. Well, Shaughnessy's face wasn't as bad as Minogue had expected. Except for the color, that is. Griffin was talking.

"Where do you want the opening left?" he asked again. Minogue stood back.

"Too blowy, Christy. Let it die down a bit, take the pressure off us here."

He held the plastic tighter and studied the hand. He couldn't see any scratches or bloodstains even. The lividity in the face didn't help. This man wasn't dead the six days he was missing. He handed the flap to Griffin and hunkered down by the taillight of the Escort. A runnel dropped onto his neck.

"Hold it over me, Larry, for the love of God, man!"

Malone had moved in beside him.

"Jases," he whispered.

"Head first," Minogue murmured.

He studied the drawn-up legs. A twenty degree tilt, he guessed. The blood would have come out steady enough.

"The blood drained from the head for the few hours before the air did its bit."

Malone wiped rainwater from the hair above his ears.

"Drained into someplace under the boot," he said. "Then leaked out?"

"Three or four hours is as much as you'd get blood draining out, Tommy."

"Kept pouring — draining out, like — when the car was left here?"

Minogue went down on his knees. He squinted at the stain.

"See the dent in the panel there?" said Griffin. "You'll find a hole there."

Minogue stood. His head pushed at the plastic.

"Thanks, Christy."

Griffin rearranged the roof. Minogue waited for a lull in the gusts before stepping out. The rain hit his face like needles. Malone backed out after him. Griffin's face sticking out of his hood reminded Minogue of a big, truculent toddler.

"Have to keep it tight, Christy. No choice now. Give it a half an hour."

Griffin began to secure the tent around the Escort. "Bloody awful," Minogue heard him mutter. Two more scene technicians showed up from the site van. Minogue reminded them about rain coming in under the car on the blood. He handed Malone the phone.

"Keep tabs on Mitchell, Tommy, will you? And poke around with any other staff. Press him on the times again. It'll count for a lot if we can fix the time. I'll do me calls from the site van. We'll see what we have to do if the rain keeps up."

• • • • •

"Sixteen million," Damian Little repeated.

The heater in the site van hadn't made much difference. Minogue's coat was saturated. His shoulders felt like they were encased in half-set cement.

"That's quid too," Little added. "The last album."

Minogue checked his watch. Little rubbed the window and peered out.

"No tax either," said Little. "Not a bloody penny. They're artists, you see."

He turned to Minogue again and cocked an ear.

"That frigging tent of yours might be flying up out of there yet."

Griffin and his crew were still securing the scene. Minogue had watched him driving masonry nails into the tarmac to hold ropes over the tent.

"I've a young fella mad about them," Little said. "Wanted the price of a ticket there a few weeks ago. Guess how much?"

Minogue shivered. He looked over the diagram he had sketched of the boot of the Escort. There'd be blood collected under the spare wheel.

"Tenner," he said.

"A tenner?" Little scoffed. "Where have you been? Go on out of that."

"Twenty, then."

Little tapped the side of a video camera case.

"Twenty-two fifty! And that was a deal, I was told. A *deal*."

Minogue studied the copy of the passport photograph again. The nose, maybe that was the Irish part of Shaughnessy's face.

"Not a penny tax," Little was saying. "The States, Japan. Oz. Everywhere. They spend half the year in the air."

"Art," said Minogue. "We've plenty to spare. Why not spread it around?"

Little laughed. It was clear to Minogue that Damian Little had had this conversation before and that he would have it, in varying forms, again.

"Art? Ever notice when they sing, all of them now, not just them — they all sing in American accents?"

"What age are you now, Damian?"

Little waved a finger at him.

"Don't try that one on me. Nothing to do with it."

Minogue tested the sleeves of his coat with his elbows. Wet through, a strange musty smell. Had the rain died down a bit?

"Sixteen million," said Little. "That's a hell of a lot of jack for stuff that doesn't even rhyme half the time."

"'*Let the storms come, take them all | Shake the pillars, make them fall,*'" said Minogue. "If it's rhymes you want."

"Jesus, I can't even hear words half the time."

"What about 'Graveyard Baby'?"

Little rubbed at the window.

"Here's someone over now."

Malone, bareheaded, water dripping down his face, appeared in the doorway.

"Christy Griffin says come on out," he said. "The rain's dying down for the while anyway. He wants his orders."

Minogue got up slowly. Christy Griffin says. Was that the way professionals worked? The backs of his trousers clung to his legs. He could almost hear his joints creak. Mr. Shaughnessy awaited. Six days missing, he had been, now missing no longer.

.　　.　　.　　.　　.

Kathleen Minogue was standing in the doorway. It had been the phone all right. Morning, then.

"Sorry, love," she said. "It's work."

He rolled onto his back.

"It's five to nine," Kathleen said. "I have to be off."

He listened again to the distant traffic on the Kilmacud Road.

"Raining still, is it?"

"No. He said he'd wait."

"Who said."

"John Tynan."

Minogue yanked back the duvet and sat on the edge of the bed. It was gone three when he'd hit the sack, he remembered. He pulled his dressing gown off the hook and headed for the stairs.

Kathleen followed him.

"I'm away now," she said. "Anne's outside."

She opened the door, she took a step back, she kissed him. The air across his ankles made him shiver. The hedge by the window was clustered with raindrops. From the kitchen he heard the fanfare for the news. He rubbed his eyes again. The exhaust from Anne O'Toole's Volkswagen floating up over the hedge had a blue tint.

"Hello. John, is it?"

"And yourself. All in order, are you, save for the late night?"

"Touch and go for now. I'd be hoping for a fit of clear thinking shortly."

"Good. A cup of something now would speed the process, would it not?"

Minogue watched the ancient and badly driven Volkswagen Polo take the bend around by the shops. The shocks were gone now, it was burning oil. My wife, he thought, my wife in that damned jalopy.

"You'd be doing me a favor," said Tynan. "That cup of something on Mary Street. Upstairs by the window?"

Bewleys, Minogue gathered.

"Three-quarters of an hour then?" Tynan tried.

Minogue scratched a loose fiber on the knee of his pajamas.

"Fair enough. Should I be bringing anything with me?"

"Yes you should. Your ablest recollections of last night at the Garda Club."

Minogue stopped scratching. He watched his fingernail turn pink again.

"Do you know a journalist by the name of Gemma O'Loughlin?"

"So that's who she was," Minogue murmured. "Or what she was."

．　　　．　　　．　　　．　　　．

Minogue couldn't take his eyes off the couple signing to one another at a table by the fireplace. They seemed to be getting such joy from their silent conversation. Tynan's driver, Sergeant Tony O'Leary, was eyeing them too. He watched O'Leary resume his pretend study of the massive stained-glass window over Mary Street below. Maybe O'Leary was replaying or plotting the perfect stroke on Ballybunion. A golf nut, O'Leary. He had done a stint with the UN in Africa and there had been a picture in the newspapers of him playing golf on some dusty plateau there.

Tony O'Leary had returned to duty in Dublin just in time to put his foot in it and thereby come to Tynan's attention, ultimately to be posted to the commissioner's staff. O'Leary had remained stubborn in his re-fusal to recant a statement about an arrest he'd witnessed. His state-ment had been used to defend and then acquit a thug with a long criminal record, who'd alleged mistreatment by nine arresting Guards during a free-for-all in a pub on Talbot Street. O'Leary had crossed a line within the force.

Tynan pushed his cup and saucer to the center of the table.

"Should have recognized her, I suppose," said Minogue. "But there's so many of them these days."

"She was on a PR tour with Conor Lawlor. She's just finished re-searching a series on the Guards for the papers. We'd been hoping it'd be a positive item."

"Is this the same Gemma O'Loughlin who let FIDO out?"

Tynan looked away. Last year's competition for schoolchildren to de-sign and name a new Garda mascot had produced unintended results. Gemma O'Loughlin had ferreted out one of the more cynical Garda rank-and-file takes on what that mascot should be. New legislation and a cascade of regulations and guidelines for arrests, for ensuring the rights of an accused, had caused many Guards to throw their hands up. *Fuck it, drive off* had actually been put in print in the daily newspapers.

"She's adamant," Tynan said then. "The tone, the general agreement among the Guards there. Vehemence, she described it as. Ferocity."

"Drink, John. Spoofing. Come on, now."

"And the bit with the gun?"

"Fingers — no guns."

"She's sticking to it. 'Any citizen would reasonably conclude . . . et cetera.' That Kilmartin meant the Guards had done it. At the very least condoned or approved it."

"Larry Smith?"

"Larry Smith," Tynan said.

"Selling papers. You know how they are."

"Jim doesn't dispute saying it. I had a chat with him this morning."

"Off-duty," Minogue tried again. He knew he didn't sound convincing. "The Garda Club? Let off steam in? Have a few jars, bit of bad language. Remember?"

Tynan studied the crowd by the cash register.

"Well now," he said. "What *should* 'The Larry Smith Solution' mean to a citizen when she hears it from the senior Garda officer who was in theory responsible for the murder investigation of Larry Smith?"

Minogue thought of the clips in the news a few weeks ago. Larry Smith's brother Charlie, "The Knock," jabbing his finger into the camera. The Guards wouldn't get away with executing his brother in cold blood: they hadn't heard the last of the Smiths by a long shot.

"Listen, Matt. Let me be clear here. There's no talk of chopping Jim. Much less asking him to fall on his sword."

"But there's some class of hairshirt bit called for, I take it."

Tynan clasped and then released his fingers.

"There'll be a court injunction landing on her editor's desk if he decides to leave her insinuation that we're covering up anything in the Smith case."

"When do these articles come out?"

"Well they're not sure now. That's their line anyway. She was doing a series: 'The Changing of the Guard,' or so we thought. Now they propose to open with this Larry Smith case. Want some previews? 'Seriously disaffected.' 'Malaise.'"

Minogue sipped more coffee. He felt O'Leary's eyes on him. "Listen to me now," Tynan said. "Do I care a damn what Jim Kilmartin thinks, or doesn't think, about the criminal justice system, juvenile offenders, the murder of a Dublin gangster, the prison system, or the price of eggs in a modern Europe?"

He tapped his knuckles twice on the marble tabletop.

"A little tact, that's all. There's enough talk about things being out of hand. Racketeers, drug barons."

Minogue sat back.

"I didn't hear what Jim said. So how could she? She was further away."

"You're used to tuning him out when you want to. She heard enough."

Minogue watched Tynan shove crumbs from a scone to the edge of the table. He wondered if Tynan would drop any hint that he had engineered Kilmartin's absence for three weeks. A right operator, was Kilmartin's take on Tynan.

"So," Tynan went on. "You're acting CO now. You may receive inquires from the media. That's why we're having a chat here. There are people who might let things slip by accident on purpose, if you take my meaning."

Kilmartin had left bruises in his wake on investigations, Minogue knew.

"There could be inadvertent remarks," said Tynan, "internal or external to the squad. Remarks that could be construed as lending credence to any innuendo leaking out of this article, this series."

Tynan's eyebrows crept up.

"Translation: watch your back. And watch who you say what to."

"Why did Lawlor guest Gemma O'Laughlin into the Garda Club?"

Tynan's eyes stayed on his for a moment. His jaw moved from side to side.

"Ask me a hard question, why don't you. The idea was to allow her a glimpse of hardworking men and women relaxing off duty. The chat, the jokes. Good-natured, decent Garda officers. Sure, it was PR. But now we have her telling the public that the Murder Squad doesn't know the difference between over*seeing* and over*looking* things in the investigation of the murder of a criminal."

"Come on, John. The place is lousy with gossip. Always. She knows that."

"Do you hear me arguing? The Larry Smith case is still open, isn't it?"

"The Smiths would love to stick it to the Guards."

"Sure," said Tynan. "But do you think that there are people who believe or want to believe that a death squad murdered Larry Smith because the law couldn't get enough of him?"

"No, I don't."

"Wrong answer. You're not a tabloid man. So you're not up on this."

"You'll get someone to plea bargain," Minogue said. "Wait and see. Sooner or later we'll have some gouger sitting waiting on his lift to court and he'll decide to sell us whoever killed Smith."

"But there's been no movement in the case, is there," said Tynan. "Flat, right?"

"Well Intelligence summaries float in every week. But there haven't been any fresh leads for months now."

"Jim's still trying to ram the file back in the letter box of Serious Crimes?"

"Sorry. We've tried. Can't touch them. Get the RUC on it."

"Paramilitaries down from Belfast still?"

"We'd still be going for that, yes. A contract, maybe. Drugs in it somewhere."

Tynan licked his fingertip, picked up a crumb from his plate and examined it. A cell phone chirped at the far side of the restaurant. Minogue watched O'Leary slip a phone out of his jacket, pluck out the antenna, and turn away.

"So," said Tynan. "We can expect more of those damned posters going up all over town." He glanced up and saw that Minogue didn't get it.

"No," he added, "not the Citizen Against Drug Dealers ones. The phony ones that Smiths got up."

Right, Minogue remembered. No one had discovered for sure who had paid for the ones that had appeared weeks after the Smith killing: WANTED FOR MURDER OF LAWRENCE SMITH, HUSBAND AND FATHER: THE STATE AND THE GARDA SÍOCHÁNA. He, like others, had put it down to some kind of bitter retort by Smith's family or cronies. Smith himself, Smith the pusher and ringleader, had appeared on CADD posters as wanted for murder by causing overdoses and even several suicides.

"Enough of that," said Tynan. "Last night, the airport. The American." Minogue thought back to the wind whipping at the nylon tarp over the car.

"He was beaten to death, John," he said. "Left in the boot of a car he rented."

"How long is he dead?"

"A couple of days anyway. He might have been still alive when he was dumped in the boot."

Tynan was watching O'Leary now. The sergeant pushed down the antenna and nodded at the commissioner. Tynan looked at his watch.

"Was that our ten o'clock?"

O'Leary nodded. Tynan looked back at Minogue.

"Tell me again, Matt. Sorry."

"He was badly done about the head. I didn't spot signs of a scrap yet."

"Two or three days you're thinking?"

"Probably," Minogue said. "It was there the whole time, I'd imagine," he went on. "There was a dent, and a break in the seal under the spare tire. I'd bet the car was driven hard somewhere. Hit a rock sticking up in a boreen or a rock flying up under it maybe."

"Why only yesterday evening then?"

"Derek Mitchell had his eyes open, if you're asking. Security. He's new."

Tynan stared at the sugar bowl.

"Is this because he was an American, John?"

Tynan glanced up and then resumed his study of the sugar lumps.

"Well he was booked into Jury's for Saturday night," said Minogue. "His ticket out was for Monday. Missing Persons told me the nearest they had was a stay in a bed-and-breakfast in Sligo on the Wednesday. The C65 went out a week yesterday."

Tynan settled his cup on his saucer and turned the spoon to face Minogue.

"I'd be expecting better after we do a press release."

"All right," said Tynan. "You'll need to know this. I had three calls from the States about Shaughnessy. One of these calls was from the State Department. Shaughnessy's family was distressed to learn that he had not returned on schedule to the U.S. One call from our Minister of Justice."

"We're going as fast as we can. We phoned him in as probable just after we secured the car last night —"

"— Let me finish now. The second call was from the American ambassador."

Tynan gazed at Minogue.

"And he expressed his thanks in anticipation of our keen efforts in the matter."

This was what unsettled Kilmartin the most, Minogue thought: Tynan's faculty of transparent irony. Kilmartin took it to be sarcasm.

"Thanks in advance," said Minogue. "That's always nice. A sort of a bonus."

Tynan's eyes wandered the table top now.

"So Shaughnessy's family were alarmed then," Minogue tried.

"His father had an associate here in Ireland phone us. That associate told me Shaughnessy's people were concerned — well before the missed plane."

Minogue sat back.

"That associate is Billy O'Riordan. Hotelier, horseman, and bon vivant."

Minogue recalled newspaper photos of a broadly smiling, chubby man holding the bridles of winning horses; cutting ribbons for new buildings. Shaking hands with public figures; Cancer Society; visiting sheiks; stud farms; helicopter rides to remote islands: the whole bit.

"He'd had calls from Shaughnessy's mother too. She divorced the father twenty years ago. She had custody afterward. She'd been trying to get in touch with the son but couldn't. O'Riordan wanted to help in any way he could."

More offers of help, thought Minogue. Wasn't that great.

"I hear you. What I mean is 'we here in the squad hear you.'"

Tynan folded his arms.

"You know who Shaughnessy's father is?"

"A Mr. Shaughnessy. Shaw-nessy."

Tynan shook his head.

"The mother went back to her maiden name. Something to do with the fact she got an annulment."

"That's the pope saying you were never really married, as I recall."

"That's it. The son came with her and he had his name changed to hers."

"At her wish, or the son's?"

"I don't know," said Tynan. "But she used to be Leyne. Yes, your case, well, his father is John Leyne."

Minogue's wandering thoughts, his cresting irritation disappeared.

"Well now I know," he managed.

"Leyne's Foods," Tynan said. "As in probably billionaire by now. Irish emigrant makes good. Boston."

Minogue stared at the patterns in the stained-glass window.

"Okay," he said finally. "We'll be in the spotlight."

Tynan nodded.

"Amicable," Minogue muttered. "Is that the word they use for a good divorce?"

Tynan paused before answering.

"'Happy families are all the same . . .'"

"'Are all alike,' you mean," Minogue said.

Tynan almost smiled

"You mucker," he said. "And you from God-knows-where, the back of beyond in West Clare. Go after a bit of promotion, can't you."

Minogue was surprised at how fast his irritation returned.

"Leave me alone to do my job."

"Is that about Leyne?"

"That too. He'll take a number, like anyone else."

"Did I suggest differently?"

"Well don't poke me about promotion either. I don't want to end up like Lawlor."

Minogue tried to remember if he'd seen a photo of Leyne recently in the papers. Some acquisition or other, a takeover. As tough as any of the homegrown billionaires over there. He looked back at Tynan. The commissioner's eyes had glazed a little.

"Here you are quoting Chekhov —"

"— Tolstoy. And I didn't quote him. It was you started it."

"But you know it don't you," said Tynan. "The follow-up too probably."

"'Every unhappy family is unhappy in its own way.'"

"Well thanks," said Tynan. "Chances are, I wouldn't be hearing secondhand about your damn views from the bar of the Garda Club spouting off about who had a hand in the fate of a washed-up criminal warlord, or capital punishment, would I, now?"

Minogue looked down into his cup. No divinations from milky coffee froth.

"James uses the term to refer to his long service as a hardworking Garda officer in the city of Dublin."

Tynan pursed his lips.

"I'll remember that," he said. "Another thing about our friend Shaughnessy, or Leyne. O'Riordan left broad enough hints. 'Some acrimony,' he says. The mother kept young Shaughnessy away from the dad for a few years earlier on."

Sudden sunlight flooded through the windows, caught glass, and dazzled Minogue. His sneeze erupted with barely a moment's warning. He opened his eyes to see O'Leary watching him fumbling for a hanky.

"No effort spared," said Tynan. "All resources necessary."

Minogue wiped his nose slowly. No effort spared. A tycoon's son. Sounded like a messed-up son. He crumpled the hanky into a ball and placed it on the saucer. No: a waitress shouldn't have to deal with that. He dropped it into his pocket.

"When's the PM?" Tynan asked.

"Early afternoon, I believe. Pierce Donavan freed himself up."

"You'll attend?"

"I'd better, I suppose."

Tynan arranged his cup and saucer on his plate and stood.

"Phone me direct if you have any hitch in seconding staff."

Tynan handed him a card.

"A new cell phone number for Tony O'Leary," Tynan said. "You still have mine?"

Minogue took it. O'Leary was on the move already. He returned the limp wave.

"I'm going to check if it was Tolstoy, you chancer."

Tynan's eyebrows inched up, stayed. As close as he'd get to a smile, Minogue knew.

CHAPTER 4

Éilis put down her cup. She placed her cigarettes and lighter in the drawer under her keyboard and she looked around the squad room. Like she'd just landed from Jupiter, Minogue thought. Eleven years they'd worked together. The "clerical" didn't mean anything: she ran the place, not Kilmartin. Her gaze settled on Minogue. Kilmartin had phoned, she told him.

"That's nice," Minogue said. "Do you want a cup of tea?"

She resumed her survey of the squad room. Minogue squinted at the power level on the cell phone. Was it faulty, or did it just drop to zero all of a sudden?

"On the head of that rírá at the airport, says he."

He looked up from the keypad. There was something extra in her voice now.

"And wants you to phone back."

He nodded. She didn't look away this time.

"Couldn't reach you, he says. With that cell phone you have in your hand."

Minogue cocked an eye at her.

"Says to remind you to think about the on/off switch on the phone. That it'll make a big difference."

"Thank you, Éilis."

She turned away and picked up the phone. Was that a sigh he had heard out of her? A lot of herbal teas lately, shorter hair, fewer smokes. Kilmartin had heard that Éilis was going out with a civil servant, high up in Finance, a Euro-boy.

"Fergal Sheehy's on holidays," she said.

"You checked already, did you."

"But Farrell's in."

Minogue knew that the officers he wanted drafted in from the pool had been on the move recently. Fergal Sheehy had been transferred to Stolen Vehicles. They were swamped and there had been a dander in the papers about it. Farrell had been in Serious Crimes for six years. He now floated between Drugs and Fraud task forces. Tynan had set up task forces to hit drug dealers when they tried to move their money. Sheehy had gotten in with the Farrell — Jesus Farrell — in part ownership of a racehorse called Stick-Up. The name had been Farrell's idea. Sheehy maintained it gave the horse a psychological edge.

"Farrell," said Éilis into the phone. "Tell him Kilmartin."

Sergeant Eoin Farrell had come by his nickname three years ago after a meticulously planned setup engineered by himself and the then co of Serious Crimes aimed at nailing a gang of bank robbers some years ago. The leader of the gang survived being shot several times in an exchange of fire on Móibhi Road only to awaken in a hospital bed with Farrell, his estranged boyhood friend from Rooskey, County Roscommon, watching him. The first two words he uttered then were to instantly cling as the definitive nickname for Farrell.

That wasn't all, however.

A cousin of Farrell's had gone character witness for the wounded gang leader but the sentence was fifteen years all the same. Kilmartin heard a rumor that Farrell had later met that cousin at a point-to-point horse race some weeks later and gotten into a barney over some words exchanged — set-up and shot-seven-times. The cousin did not press charges after Farrell gave him a hiding, Kilmartin reported, because the cousin claimed not to have known that the gunman had actually opened up with a submachine pistol on a Garda pursuit vehicle.

"Curse of God on it," Éilis hissed. She had definitely dyed the hair, Minogue decided. *Titian,* was that the term?

"Voice mail. It's a damned disgrace, that's what it is. I *hate* it."

"I'll be attending on the PM, Éilis."

"Well who's the ringmaster here for this, so?"

"John Murtagh. I don't know who'll work the airport yet. Fergal, I'd like. Tommy Malone and myself will be pairing up for today at least."

Éilis nodded at the door to Kilmartin's office.

"Will you be wanting in there?" she asked. "The extra line, the leather chair?"

Minogue put down the photocopies of the overnight faxes from the States, the Missing Persons press releases. He peered through the blinds at Kilmartin's office.

James Kilmartin had been as quick to scorn as he'd been to get on the right side of the Euro-junket-consulting-conference carnival that had become mainstays of upper-level positions in the public service. And he'd played the fittings and furniture game shrewdly. New office furniture, made-to-measure suits, and requisitions for conference facilities had followed in short order. Kilmartin had made Minogue try out his new leather chair, rabbitting on about ergonomics and invisible stress. The time was long gone, Kilmartin had declared, when the head of the most respected unit in the Gardai had to hang his head when he had VIPs domestic and foreign coming through his offices.

Minogue felt a sneeze coming on. Conducting site work in the pissings of rain for a few hours last night was hardly conducive to health. He stood very still, his eyes on the blank Trinitron at the far end of the conference table in Kilmartin's office. The sneeze didn't come.

"Are you storming the palace, is it," from Éilis. "For the duration, like?"

"No," he said. "I won't bother me head. It's only a holiday, not a coup."

He trudged back to his own partitioned cubicle. Malone called it the Art Gallery, Kilmartin called it Bedlam, Éilis checked regularly to see if Minogue had put up new Magritte postcards. He dropped the Shaughnessy file on his desk. He didn't believe Kilmartin's excuse for not catching the Boston flight this morning. The diversions to Shannon or Manchester would've all been swallowed up by now.

There was a section of a newspaper folded on top of the phone. He opened it and turned it around. He barely saw Iseult's name at the beginning of the first paragraph before a sneeze made him buckle. It hurt. He leaned on the table and waited, his teeth clenched. Damn, was that prostate? Prostrate from the prostate.

He sat up again. It was one of these free papers they gave out, three-quarters advertising. Garden furniture, vaccuum cleaners, new kitchens. He didn't recognize the thing in the picture. It looked kind of like a sausage. Maybe it had been arranged with the harsh lighting to show up the shadows of the barbed wire so sharply. Vicious, really. He wiped his nose. Éilis was standing in the doorway when he turned to sneeze again. John Murtagh had shown up from somewhere too.

"Nice one there," Murtagh said. "A bit of celebrity there boss."

"Nice what?"

"This gets delivered around our place," said Éilis. "Does she know about it?"

Minogue wiped his nose again. He picked up the pages. The *Holy Family*? He knew Iseult had been working with modeling clay recently. He knew because he'd caught her trying to lift what felt like a hundredweight of the damned stuff up the stairs to her studio. Six months pregnant, up till all hours working on things. Hormones were no excuse.

The *Holy Family* . . . ? The dinner plate looked real. The eggs and rashers and brown bread were close but they looked a bit dead. But that was probably the idea. Plaster, it must be. Or could it be plasticene — then his eyes locked onto the words: ". . . father a senior officer in the Garda Murder Squad . . ."

He sat back, held the paper away more. There was mention of County Clare in the interview. Holy wells at Barnacarraig; childhood visits to the zoo. Her first Holy Communion; altars and holy picture. Blood and flowers: what the hell was that supposed to mean? He skipped through the paragraph. "Bold . . . startling . . . searing . . ." A quote from a gallery owner that Iseult Minogue was prodigously talented. Family violence, Ireland in turmoil: a paean. A paean?

The last paragraph had pregnancy, love, rage. Then there was an admission that people would easily interpret this as a reflection on her own personal history as a woman in Ireland. An artist on fire. Minogue let the paper fall on his desk and he sat back. *Christ on the cross.*

"That's the first thing I thought of," Éilis said.

He had said it aloud? She nodded at the paper.

"There's that iconography there," she added. "It's obvious."

"What's obvious?" Murtagh asked.

"Motifs," said Éilis. "Plain as the nose on your face. See the cross there in the background? Behind the table there?"

"Motives," Minogue said. "What motives?"

"*Motifs*, I said."

"Looks good on you, boss," said Murtagh. "And the missus, of course."

The missus, Minogue wondered; the *missus* will freak.

"It's the rearing," Murtagh added.

"Iseult's going to be famous," said Éilis.

Minogue looked from Éilis to Murtagh and back. He studied the picture again. A greasy Irish breakfast. The barbed wire, the crucifix. Motifs?

"She makes a point of saying it's not her," said Éilis. "Personally, like."

Minogue let it drop back onto his desk. Murtagh picked it up and whistled.

"Don't you get it?" Éilis asked again.

"Tell me what to get, Éilis."

"It's like that poem, Larkin. 'Your mum and dad, they' — well, have you heard that one? Philip Larkin?"

"He'd dead, but, isn't he?"

"'Your mum and dad, they . . . mess you up.' Do you get it now?"

The call from Kilmartin saved Minogue.

"What," was Kilmartin's greeting, "are you bloody paralyzed and you couldn't use a phone? Too heavy to carry, was it?"

"Forgot, Jim. The battery was low. I must have forgotten to switch it back."

"Get off the stage," said Kilmartin. "Pack of lies there! Try again."

"All right. I turned it off because I don't like the damned thing."

"You're a bollocks, Matt. What use is a cell phone if you won't use it!"

"I'll try again. To adapt better."

"I'll line you up for a course on it or something. How to *relate* to it."

"You're on holidays, Jim. What do you want?"

"The fella at the airport. He's ours now, I take it. Who is he? The Yank?"

"Don't you like holidays, Jim? Give 'em to me if you —"

"Shag off, will you. You'd only waste them canoodling around dives in the arse end of Paris or something. Who's the new case, I said."

Minogue tried to condense it into three sentences.

"Leyne," said Kilmartin. "He went big with frozen foods first didn't he? Potatoes, was it? Chips."

"I think it was."

"And the whole frozen food thing took off. Yes. What's the son doing here?"

"A tourist, it looks like."

"Looking for his roots, was he?"

Minogue waited for Kilmartin to work his way around to asking about Tynan.

{ 47 }

"Robbed at the airport? Then murdered?"

"We're not up on placing him yet."

"Jesus. 'Céad Míle Fáilte,' et cetera. How long's he missing?"

"Six days. We can place him in a B & B in Sligo. He was booked into Jury's Hotel here, but never showed. Then he didn't appear for the flight either."

"He traveled bed-and-breakfast down the country but then he went back to tycoon class when he hit Dublin?"

Minogue's eyes prickled. He held the phone away. The sneeze didn't come immediately. He tried squinting at the fluorescent lights with his eyelids half open. Kilmartin was still talking.

"That's right, Jim," he tried.

"What time?"

"It was getting on for half-three when I jacked it in at the site."

"What? He phoned you at half-three this morning?"

"What did you ask me again, Jim?"

"Tynan! I asked you if you'd heard from him lately!"

The sneezes rocked Minogue. Four in a row: he scrambled for paper hankies he hoped he'd kept in the bottom drawer. A final sneeze left him head down, dripping onto a file folder. He let the phone down and swiveled around. He wiped the phone last.

"Mother of God," said Kilmartin. "That's dog rough, what you have. But I'll tell you one thing, we're all victims of foul play here. You getting pissed on at a site last night, me getting the treatment from the Iceman. Eight o'clock this morning for the love of God. The frigging Inquisition. When did he pounce on you?"

"Nine or so."

"What's he want to talk to you for? It's me he'd want to slice and dice."

Minogue let his eyes wander along the frosted glass wall of his cubicle. He lingered on the black-and-whites of the footprints from the Dunlaoghaire Park murder. Ninety quid Nike runners, half-burned. His eyes finally settled on the road map of Ireland. Sligo. Had Shaughnessy been heading up to Donegal or down to Mayo? Where had the "touring the west of Ireland" bit come from anyway?

"Well, there's a series being done on the Guards," he said to Kilmartin. "He said to watch what I say."

"Talk about the understatement of the frigging century. Are we running a police force or a PR outfit, I hope you asked him. Where did he put in the knife anyway?"

{ 48 }

"He got word of some items overheard at the Garda Club."

Minogue thought he heard the intake of breath in the pause.

"Is that a fact now," Kilmartin said. "Let me tell you about *that*. That's what has dropped us all in it. Hey, did you recognize her there? That bitch, what's her name . . . ?"

The Holy Family, Minogue thought. Iseult on a rant about patriarchy.

"Well she sort of looked familiar but . . ."

"I only got word on this newspaper thing, this *profile* thing, at one of Tynan's come-all-yes there a month ago. I mean to say, does anyone actually go for this ra-ra stuff, open-house, *relationship* shite? Anyone who's been in the job more than six weeks, like? Anyone with time on the beat? Anyone with a brain bigger than a shagging *pea*? Anyone smarter than Lawlor trying to feather his nest for promotion?"

The counties had yellow borders. County Sligo was the collar on the teddy bear that was the map of Ireland. Donegal Bay there, then the ocean. He'd never liked Sligo. He didn't know why really. Maybe it was because it was in the way of getting to Donegal, his real destination on holidays years ago.

"Well?" Kilmartin said again. "Am I tarred with the Smith thing?"

"I don't know, Jim. Things get around though."

"Ch-a-rrist! A man can't voice an opinion without some gobshite hiding in a corner and making a big deal about it! Had she nothing better to do?"

Minogue detached the phone from his ear. Hard to blame Kilmartin really.

"Well how in the name of Jases did that bitch get into the bloody club in the first place anyway? Answer me that one, if you can! Lawlor brought her, that's how. It was Tynan started this whole thing, getting the press to play ball — and now look!"

Minogue's extension buzzer stopped Kilmartin. It was Murtagh.

"A few things coming in," Murtagh said. "They had Shaughnessy on the news this morning. Woke a few people up. Four phone calls came in to Missing Persons. Donegal, two of them, one from some place called Falcarragh. A local station. A call from a couple who run a bed-and-breakfast near town."

"Falcarragh," Minogue said. "Which days?"

"Early last week, before the Sligo B & B. The other one's a guest house in Glencolumbkille."

Glencolumbkille, almost as far west as you could get in Donegal.

"Here's a wobbler for you," Murtagh went on. "A call came from the museum."

"The museum, here in Dublin? To do with Shaughnessy?"

"Yep, above on Kildare Street. There's a Seán Garland phoned. Says he thinks this Shaughnessy came in for a chat awhile ago. Yep, a week or ten days back. He thinks Shaughnessy was asking about something or other. But here's the thing: he didn't come in as any Shaughnessy, says Garland. Garland saw the picture in the morning paper. He thinks that your man used the name Leyne. So there."

Minogue dabbed at his nose and pulled out his photocopy of the Fógra Tóradh notice. Missing person: Patrick L. Shaughnessy. *L* for Leyne? Why didn't he know the dead man's middle name?

"All right, John. Give me a minute here."

He underlined Glencolumbkille, took his hand off the cell phone's mouthpiece.

"You're on the move it sounds like," Kilmartin said.

"The news this morning seems to've stirred the bushes a bit."

"I won't keep you — just keep me posted if Tynan goes haywire on this rubbish at the club, do you hear me? While I'm away?"

"To be sure."

"Write this down; I forgot to give it to you."

Minogue copied Kilmartin's son's address. The Palisades? White flight?

"If anything comes up, in the papers or otherwise," Kilmartin said. Glencolumbkille, Minogue thought, the strand beyond the folk village there.

"And here's Brian's fax number."

Minogue scribbled it down.

"And his e-mail —"

"It's all right; I'll phone if there's trouble."

"Here: is it Jamesons with you? Or do you expect Bushmills?"

"Don't trouble yourself."

"Oh, and what does Kathleen dab behind the ears, Maura wants to know."

"Bushmills too, I think."

"I bet you don't even know. You bostún."

"Chanel number something. A black lid. It's pricey."

"What isn't these days. All right oul son, mind the trams now."

"Jim?"

"I know, I know — you're in a hurry. I'll be off if you'll let me. What is it?"

Minogue pinched hard at the bridge of his nose. What had possessed him to come up with this question now?

"Larry Smith, Jim."

Minogue stared at his notebook while he waited.

"What about him? What's your question exactly?"

"Just wondering, that's all. You were the conductor on it."

"Well I had to be, didn't I. It was hot from day one. It had to be done right. I took it because there'd need to be high-level consult . . . Wait a minute. What are you saying? What do you want?"

"Is there even a remote chance . . . ?"

"Well Jesus. That's how the damage gets done, isn't it. Not by direct inquiry, oh no, never that way. It's the slow way, the innuendo, the bloody gossip eating away like an acid at the thing until finally — you're actually asking me? You who worked on it with me, you who sat in on all those briefings with Serious Crimes and those gunslingers, those bloody *headers* from C2? You can't be serious. No way."

"Just asking."

"You already said that! 'Just asking' my arse. See? She's gotten to you even!"

Minogue wondered if it was Leyne's Foods was the first of the frozen foods which had shown up in the supermarkets years ago. American Style Frozen Foods.

"Look," Kilmartin said. "It was one or other of a pack from Belfast, I'm telling you. Devlin or Harte — they're known hit men who take contracts. You know we can't get them on this. Come on now — you spent two days at the site with me, didn't you? There was nothing. Are you forgetting? The dum-dums were down to bloody bottle caps by the time they went through him. Don't you remember? Is it her, the widow, what's her name? Or is it the brother, what's his name, Charlie, rabblerousing for an inquiry? He's an iijit, but he's sly. The fucker. But they're all like that."

"Neither, Jim. No. Look, mind yourself over there now."

The rueful tone in Kilmartin's voice then didn't surprise Minogue.

"Hah," Kilmartin said. "The FBI. We could show them a thing or two, couldn't we? I'm telling you, we could. The cases where the crime lab is between your ears, hah? The Yanks . . . don't talk to me."

Minogue thought of the cocked thumb last night, Kilmartin's squint as he aimed: Smih' goh' hih'.

"You're telling me," he managed.

He ended the call, eyed the duration. The state could pay the airtime on that one. He had kept the newspaper clipping from last week's newspaper, the preview for the forthcoming series on the Guards. He took it out of the drawer. "The Changing of the Guard": a bit glib really. But that was good journalism, wasn't it. "The Old Guard" later on: well, there was something noble and steadfast about that. Holding fast against a tide of criminality. Plain and simple stuff, no guff and cant. He slipped the pages back into the drawer and stared at the phone. No he wouldn't phone Kathleen right now. He sat back, tried to plan his next hour. Couldn't.

Larry Smith and Company, limited. The simple fact of the matter was that Larry Smith had played cowboys and he wound up in the middle of a road in Baldoyle with bits of him all over the tarmacadam. Hollow-point bullets, brutal. James Kilmartin, a senior Garda officer no less and no more frustrated than 99 percent of the Gardai, had been caught off-guard voicing his satisfaction out loud. So. In the heel of the reel, who cared about how the streets of Dublin had been cleaned of at least one serious, lifelong gouger. A vicious little bastard in his own right, incurable.

He eyed the page on Iseult again before folding it and slipping it into his pocket. He headed out into the squad room proper. Murtagh had already entered the times on the board. The credit card trail, he thought. Receipts from the States cleared in about a week now. Éilis was copying the file.

The green light from the photocopier flared and died by the corners of the cover, but some escaped to run across Éilis's neck. He returned her blank gaze for several moments. What was bothering her?

"Emerald Rent-A-Car?" he tried.

"Not yet," she said.

Minogue tried to map the days and places but he was soon stuck.

"This museum thing, John, if he says he's Leyne. What's going on there?"

"Maybe to get the royal treatment researching the forebears and all that," Murtagh said. "The lig in, the 'influence.' Researching the forebears and all that? Instead of lining up like Joe Soap at the genealogy office."

"Garland," Minogue said. "I've heard of him."

"Wait a minute. He's got a fancy job title as I remember."

Murtagh fingered his notebook. He looked up with a faint smile.

"'Keeper of Irish Antiquities.'"

"I thought that was Maura Kilmartin," from Éilis. Minogue gave her the eye.

"Garland does lectures too, so he does," said Murtagh. "Public lectures on history. The Golden Age. Monks and what have you. How we civilized Europe."

Minogue searched Murtagh's face for irony.

"Anyway," Murtagh went on. "Shaughnessy's in Jury's Hotel until the Monday. He picks up the car at Emerald, down off O'Connell Street. He makes sure he's booked back into Jury's for the weekend, starting Friday. Plane's out on Monday. He's planned five days of touring then."

Murtagh rapped the board with his knuckles.

"If Donegal is good, then Shaughnessy's there on Tuesday. Say he's on the road most of Monday. Donegal town's six hours driving anyway."

"What if he went through the North, but?"

Minogue rubbed at his eyes. He heard cracking sounds from somewhere near his sinuses. If this cold went to his chest he'd be shagged for a fortnight.

"Her Majesty's would give us time and place on this, John. Without much sloothering around the issue, I mean. It's not political."

Murtagh scrutinized the map.

"Might have gone through Strabane." He tugged at his lip. "Up to . . ."

"Letterkenny," said Minogue, "and points north. Derry maybe."

He squinted at the timetable again.

"Who exactly filed the C65 to Missing Persons anyway?"

Murtagh capped his marker. Éilis answered the phone.

"I don't know yet. But there were the calls from the States. And Billy O'Riordan."

"All right so," said Minogue. "Find out exactly, will you?"

Éilis was holding the phone up when he opened his eyes again. Three sneezes this time. His nose felt like a burst football.

"Fergal Sheehy," she said. "He's on. Needs the money, says he. Will you brief him now or do you want him to stop by on the way to the airport?"

CHAPTER 5

MALONE TURNED THE NISSAN into Beaumont Hospital. The autopsy was set for eleven.

"How many's this for you?" he asked Minogue.

"This'll be thirty-seven."

Malone cleared his throat again. He yanked the ticket from the parking robot thing and drove through as the boom lifted.

Minogue hated this hospital. Unreasonable, he knew, but he couldn't shake the feeling that all this space here made it too quiet. Easy for him to say, was Kathleen's take on this. He hadn't been jammed into Mercer's Hospital or Jervis Street in the middle of a Dublin summer for a bloody delivery, had he?

"The ma got her knees done here," Malone said. "Lovely place, says she. But glad to get out early all the same."

Minogue stole a glance at his partner.

"Says it's haunted," Malone went on. "Too long on the drip, says I, losing the head. No, says she. Saw them."

"Saw who?"

Malone parked next to a plumber's van. He let his seat belt roll back slowly into its chamber, looked sideways at Minogue.

"Kids, she says. From the Starlight."

Minogue tried to fix the year of the fire at the Starlight dance hall. He'd helped to direct the ambulances delivering the teenagers' charred bodies. How often he'd thought of the dozens of ambulances grouped around the front of the then new hospital, their sirens off, their lights sweeping uselessly still. He remembered it being so terribly quiet. Then, when some of the parents and families began to show up —

He checked the phone again, stepped out after Malone. Wind and unreliable sun had dried much of the tarmacadam now. There were pools still in the shadows by the walls.

"Still no sign of a wallet," Malone said. "Passport or the like, huh."

"I'll phone the lab again, I suppose."

Malone scratched at his lip.

"Picked up a header, hitchhiking," he said. "Bang. Took everything. What do you think?"

"Keep it in mind," said Minogue. "But why's the car at the airport awhile?"

Malone held the door open for the inspector. Minogue paused, eyed Malone rolling his free shoulder. A boxer's reflex as the bell went, he wondered. Was Malone so twitchy before every PM?

"Okay," Malone said. "He meets another Yank on the road somewhere. He gives him — or her — a lift to the airport. This hitchhiker sees Shaughnessy's loaded. Right? Shaughnessy's a yapper, say, likes to spoof a bit. So he let's things slip, about his da, et cetera. Moneybags, all that. Name dropping, see? He digs his own grave with his mouth. This hitchiker's back in Reno or wherever the hell he came from. And we're fu — we're banjaxed."

The hallway was busy. Minogue watched a man with papery skin pushing his own wheelchair ahead of himself. Two kids being walked quickly by their mother, flustered, annoyed; one of the kids with tear stains on his cheeks, the other one looking blankly around.

He slowed to take in the monument to the Starlight kids: THEY SHALL NEVER GROW OLD.

"Come on," he said to Malone. "It's gone eleven."

An orderly stood by the window next to the lab offices eating a KitKat. Through a window Minogue spotted Pierce Donavan's battered Land Rover. The state pathologist had brought it to every site since Minogue had started with the squad. Gerry Hanlon, Garda photographer, was reading the paper at a table. There were voices from the change room.

"Are we all aboard, Gerry?"

Hanlon closed the paper. A pathology assistant whom Minogue had once mistaken for a cleaner two years ago came in from the door behind them. The door to the change room opened.

"Ah, well now. The Clare connection, by God!"

Donavan's greeting put Minogue in mind of a genial uncle, the sort of man who'd fart for the entertainment of children; a man who'd show kids how to make the best bows and arrows. A man who would always wave at trains.

The reserve that Donavan's ebullience concealed was not widely known. A heavily armored introvert, he had married late to one of his students. She practiced as an obstetrician now. Minogue wondered what their dinner-table chat was like. A sometime insomniac who wrote poetry at night, Donavan had given Minogue one of his self-published volumes several years ago. It was after Minogue had become distraught during the autopsy of a child beaten to death by his mother's fella. The mother had been out trying to borrow money to buy heroin.

Donavan had stopped the PM, sealed the room, bought a packet of fags. He had stood smoking with Minogue at the delivery door to the lab for a half an hour. Later he and Minogue had gone for a walk near his home in Howth. The inspector often recalled that cliff walk. The sun blinding them from the bay, the wind freshening as they rounded the outer edge of Howth Head. Minogue's fury and despair and hatred had ebbed as if by magic then.

"Garda Malone," said Donavan, "is it?"

"How's it going."

"You're traveling in high society there, Garda Malone. Mind that boss of yours."

"How's the care at home, Pierce?" Minogue asked.

"Orla's fifteen. She has a boyfriend with a ring in his eyebrow. You decide."

"You want him to move it to his nose, is it?"

"She'll do that handy enough, I'm thinking. Well: the both of ye in attendance for the American, is it?"

"I'm principal, Pierce. Tommy'll be in and out."

Donavan glanced at Malone before he headed back to the change room. Minogue heard him break into song.

"Are you right there Michael are you right?"

"Do you think that we'll get home before the night?"

Minogue shook his head and turned to Malone.

"Check on anything coming in on the squad lines, if you please, Tommy."

"You don't need me in on the, the thing here?"

"Later maybe. See if we can start a paper trail on his credit cards. He's hardly traveling without any, now. Find out what the interviews are looking like at the airport. I'm a bit worried that we'll need to be getting a lot of staff in a hurry."

"I'll tell Sheehy."

Minogue stared at the pattern of the floor tiles again, the marks from wheels. Fergal Sheehy would hardly be at the airport yet. The site van and four forensic technicians were working the car park. Swords and Finglas stations had coughed up eight staff between them to keep up with interviews.

He looked up at Malone.

"We'll be there by dinnertime, tell him. One or so. Tell him to push Fogarty. The security log books, thefts and break-ins at the airport. Any gang related especially. Allegations even. Bang heads if he has to, tell him. All the way up to Tynan."

"Okay," said Malone. "But let me ask you something. This Fogarty fella, the security chief there. He was shaping up kind of cagey last night. What do you think?"

"He was edgy all right."

"He knew the patrols were bollocky," Malone said. Minogue nodded.

"That's on the menu to be sure," he said. "But what's the story on video at the airport?"

"It's a bit dodgy yet," replied Malone. "There's surveillance indoors but . . ."

"While you're at it," Minogue said. "Phone Eimear at the lab and see what they've turned up from the car that we'd need to move on right away."

Malone had his notebook out but he hadn't written anything. He nodded as Hanlon and the assistant moved around him and entered the change room.

"I'll see you inside then," said Minogue. "Later on. No hurry."

A second pathology assistant was putting on a plastic smock next to Donavan. Minogue slipped off his jacket, introduced himself, eyed the headline on the sports page left on a chair. His nose began to tickle, but the sneeze didn't arrive.

"Tipperary always pull one out of the bag," Donavan said. "The whores."

Minogue felt his nose block, blotting out the stale, sweet smell he'd had with him since he entered the lab. A mercy, the timing.

"Well the Clare crowd let us down badly this year, I'd have to allow, Pierce. Maybe we should stick to the football for a few years."

Donavan rearranged X rays in a folder.

"How are yours," he murmured. "Is it different when they're grown?"

Minogue shrugged.

"Did I tell you I'm going to be a grandfather?"

"You did indeed mention it. Ye're all fired up and ready?"

"We'll have to get the clautheens out of the attic, I told Kathleen."

Donavan clipped the X rays on the panel.

"How well you kept them," he said. "Up beside your Communion money?"

Donavan had eyebrows like a damned haystack, Minogue decided. *Hirsute,* that was the word. Donavan waved at the X rays and tugged at his beard for several moments. Then he tapped one with his knuckles.

"There," he said. "There's sure to be brain damage. The skull is fractured here. And here. You can see actual bone fragments there. Look."

A male, Minogue thought. Rage, strength. He tugged the cuffs further down on his wrists. Was the elastic tighter on these new ones? The assistants wheeled in the body from the cooler room. Hanlon placed spools of film on the bottom shelf of a cabinet over the sink and closed the door. One of the wheels on the trolley squeaked. It caught and spun and squeaked again.

"I'll be wanting to see how many separate impressions we can see in that area," said Donavan. "How many times he was hit."

Minogue's nose felt ticklish again. He heard the assistant grunt as he lifted the top end of the bag. He retrieved the clipboard and tested his Biro again.

The trolley was being pushed to the wall now. The white plastic bag lay like a pupa on the table. The decay had been slowed by confinement in the car, but the heat had bloated the body. The seal on the zip still reminded Minogue of a tag at a sale. He looked around at the shelves and the cabinets, the clock. The second hand crawling, stopping almost if you looked at it directly. Christ. Half-eleven. The sharp click of instruments being laid on the table seemed very loud. The squeak of Donavan's crepe soles on the terrazzo slowed.

"Good," Donavan said.

Minogue moved back to let Hanlon prepare for a set of photos. Donavan wheeled over a cabinet with four drawers. On top lay a clipboard with a schematic diagram of the body. Donavan had written "Patrick Shaughnessy." Another clipboard had a sheet of graph paper topmost. Donavan eyed at the clock and scribbled the time on the graph paper. He nodded at the assistant.

"Cut the seal, Kevin. And thank you."

Minogue listened to the high-pitched wirps of the flash recharging. Hanlon took seven, eight photos of the back of Shaughnessy's head. He took the ruler from beside the head and replaced it with the others on the table. Donavan stood to the far side of the table. His eyes remained fixed on Shaughnessy's neck.

"Good," said Hanlon.

The assistants rolled the body over. Minogue glanced over at the tagged bags of Shaughnessy's clothes in the corner. The long-sleeved polo shirt might even be a wool blend. The green khaki-style trousers and the jacket were outdoorsy, were they not. He squeezed his eyes shut for a moment. Was it himself, he wondered, or had the light gone dim a little. Radio Na Gaeltachta continued to play faintly from an aged transistor radio jammed between specimen jars over the sinks. A subdued conversation with odd episodes of forced humor between the interviewer and his guest, a poet now deceased, gave way to a spirited tune on a concertina. Minogue concentrated on the meandering notes. Why did a concertina always sound like it was about to fly out of control.

"'The Pigeon on the Gate,'" Donavan said. "Noel Hill?"

"None other," said Minogue. "You'll get honorary citizenship to Clare yet."

He looked back at Shaughnessy's swollen face. The lividity always reminded him of a bruised apple. He watched Donavan's hands. The pathologist's commentary continued in a monotone. A habit, Minogue knew, because Donavan rarely used a tape. The deceased bled profusely from open wounds . . . A lividity pattern indicates he had lain in a position head below horizontal after the injures were sustained. . . .

Donavan turned to the clipboard and wrote 5+ beside the head on the schematic. Blood had clotted and glued Shaughnessy's hair to a plastic shopping bag. Three hours at most to stop that blood flow in the open air, but probably longer in the tight, airless boot of the Escort. Minogue's eyes slid out of focus. Hitchhiker, Malone had been speculating. The new

Galway Road had you across the River Shannon in little more than an hour. You could be in Galway in less than three. With Shaughnessy dead, the blood draining into the wheel well —

The sneeze surprised even Minogue.

"God between us and all harm," said Donavan. He lifted the arms one by one, turned them and then began a detailed examination of the hands.

Hanlon stood waiting. His thumb tapped softly, slowly on the back of his camera. Donavan let down each hand in turn and he walked to the X ray panel. He stared at the X ray of Shaughnessy's hands.

"Nothing there yet to indicate resistance," he said.

He returned to the table and examined the left hand again.

"Nothing," he said again. He glanced over at Minogue.

"He wasn't expecting it, Matt."

Minogue realized that he had been holding his breath. He had been imagining a conversation: a lonely stretch of road, raining maybe. Shaughnessy feeling sorry for some unfortunate hiker with his thumb out. A girl, maybe? The boot lid open to pack in a rucksack or to take one out: *From Boston? Really? How about that! Sure, let me put that in the boot — the trunk —* . . . Or getting out, most likely: the hitchhiker could even have picked that spot. *You can let me off here, I've got a better chance on an empty bit of road.* Shaughnessy's opening the lid of the boot, he's reaching in. What was he hit with?

The squeak from the opening door was Malone. Donavan didn't look up from the clipboard. Minogue moved to the sink. Malone eyed the body.

"We have a move," he said. "Fella phoned in from the press. A photographer, says he took pictures at a do. He's checking now but he's almost sure Shaughnessy's picture's in the paper from ten days ago. A reception of some kind out in Goff's, the horsey crowd out on the Naas Road."

Goffs, thought Minogue. High glam: millionaires, film stars, sheiks and princes, pop tarts — any celebrity might show up at these world-renowned bloodstock auctions.

"Name of Noel O'Hagan," Malone said. "The photographer. He's a freelancer. He says there were other newspaper fellas there too. It was a kind of a celebrity gig. There should be other pics somewhere handy."

Malone looked over Minogue's shoulder at Kevin, Donavan's assistant, who was letting a stream of water play on the bloodstains by Shaughnessy's ear.

"And the rented car," Malone said. "Shaughnessy was number eleven to rent it. It's a year old, the Escort."

"What's the story so far on the contents?" Minogue tried.

"I checked with Eimear again. They've inventoried the boot already. Very messed up. The bit of board over the spare wheel and that, well it's broken. Like, something heavy had been dumped on it."

"The weight of the body?"

Malone shrugged.

"Eimear says she doesn't think so. There was something more compact, says she, but right heavy. And there's a good-sized ding on the bottom of the car. Major, like. A bad road? That's what left the hole under the boot, it looks like."

"What's the situation with prints, might I ask?"

"There's a crew working through from the boot," Malone replied. "They're still at the inside of the car like. There's no wallet yet. Passport, camera — nothing. There was a fair-sized bag of laundry. All man's clothes. Guidebooks, maps, bits of stuff like biscuits, empty Coke cans. He smoked, or someone in the car smoked. Eimear says they see hairs coming from the carpet now too."

"Are there good prints coming out?"

"Well yeah, as a matter of fact. A lot, even from the outside. They'll start the comparison search on Shaughnessy's this afternoon."

Donavan was humming. Minogue tried again to pin the name of the tune.

"Ten renters before Shaughnessy," he murmured.

"That's the story so far," said Malone. "Yeah. And then there'd be cleaners, staff borrowing the cars out there."

Minogue watched Donavan's assistant wiping pieces of sponge on the body in a circular motion, dropping the pieces into a specimen bag hanging at the sides of the table — "The Moon Behind the Hill," that was the tune. Donavan stopped humming. Minogue turned back toward the pathologist.

Water still trickled from the hose at rest by Shaughnessy's elbow. Donavan was finished the external? Patrick Leyne Shaughnessy would shortly be sawn and eviscerated.

The music gave way to a too-chatty presenter with a strong Ulster accent extolling the virtues of Clare music in general. An impertinence, Minogue decided.

Malone murmured by his shoulder now.

"Spots of blood from around the lid of the hatchback," he said. "They're in being typed.".

The click of more instruments being laid on the stainless steel brought Malone's glance to the table. He bit his lip, looked back at Minogue.

"Clobbered in the open doorway, the boot, what do you think?"

"Well it looks like he didn't react," he said. "But there's a spray pattern to sort out still, to be sure."

"He knew the guy, then," Malone went on. "Or the fella ran up, got his first one in?"

The whirr always reminded Minogue of the dentist. Malone's blink lasted too long. Minogue eyed at the saw that the assistant was readying. Donavan leaned over his clipboard, staring at the schematic of the back of the body.

"Say he'd been drinking," said Malone. "Closing time, you know? After hours even. A session maybe, buying rounds of drink and all. All hail-fella-well-met until they're outside. Say he's been blathering away with the few jars on him. Money talk. Fellas go out with him. 'Give us a lift there, will you . . . '"

"Easy done, all right," Minogue said.

Malone eyed the body for several moments.

"Well-to-do, you know," he said. "Lots of *stuff*, like. The watch, the clothes. You know the Yanks, the way they are, the way they look. Maybe Shaughnessy's pulling tenners out of his wallet all night. So it's a local. I say we're going to find two fellas, two drinking partners. They wait their chance, wallop him, follow through — maybe in a panic, or pissed — finish the job. Then they decide to hide the body back up in Dublin. Where it belongs, to their way of thinking?"

Minogue thought of the American tourists he'd first seen as a kid. He'd been mesmerized by the diver's watches, those expanding metal watchbands, the tanned, hairy forearms. Perfume, the jaws always going on them. And now? He'd seen video cameras the size of paperbacks, outdoor gear and packsacks with pockets and straps for everything. Still the big, capped teeth, the ready smiles, the ponderous way a lot of them walked. All overweight? Swaggering? How they seemed to occupy that part of the path or the space where they stopped to look around.

Maybe Mr. Patrick Leyne Shaughnessy had seriously pissed off some unemployed, restless, and angry young fellas, men very goddamned fed up of hearing about a booming economy, fed up of watching tourists pulling endless amounts of cash out of their wallets.

Donavan was looking over. He pointed to Shaughnessy's head.

"This abrasion up here by the right side of the temple," he said. "That starts at the cheekbone in actual fact."

Minogue stepped back to the table. Malone, his face tight, followed.

"Falling, you could guess," Donavan added.

Minogue couldn't see any difference in colors where the skin was scuffed. Hanlon maneuvred around him. Lots of blows says rage, drunken; panic: the basics here.

"How many times was he hit?" he asked Donavan.

"Well now. You have the base of the skull fractured, with bits of it up here. See those little bits on the X ray there on the right?"

Donavan picked up a scalpel and examined the blade.

"We have corresponding scrapes here on the right side of the head as he went down. I would hazard a guess that the first blow sent him to the ground. Defenseless, maybe even mortal. An iron bar?"

Hanlon leaned over the side of the table and snapped three pictures. What hitchhiker would be walking around with an iron bar handy?

"So other blows landed after he went down. Here's a pattern on the side of the face that backs that up."

Minogue followed Donavan's finger. Kevin helped to turn the head.

"But, thing is, there'd be more to it — a collateral fracture even — if he was hit on cement now," Donavan went on. "Or a roadway. I don't see, I don't recognize, gravel or tar here yet."

Minogue's mind slipped away again. Shaughnessy opening the boot lid: he'd have heard someone step up behind him? A word, a shout? He hadn't raised his arm to fend of the blow. Drunk? He looked at the board. Shaughnessy was a hundred eighty-three centimeters. That was just over six feet. Hit hard the first time, Shaughnessy would have gone forward and down at the same time. The spots of blood on the underside of the hatchback looked like the outer edge of a spray pattern, fair enough. It could also be from clumsy, strained efforts to shove Shaughnessy into the boot. Eighty-nine point something kilos, about two hundred pounds: over fourteen stone? Well that'd take lifting. For an instant Minogue saw a pack of teenagers flailing at Shaughnessy.

He looked down at his notebook.

"Can I take photocopies with me today, Pierce?"

"'Course you can."

Donavan looked under his eyebrow from Minogue to Malone and back. Minogue glanced over at his colleague. Malone's jaw was slack, his tongue was working slowly against the inside of the cheek.

"We'll go in now," said Donavan. "Kevin?"

Minogue nodded toward the door. Malone followed him over.

"Follow up on the newspaper thing now instead of waiting," Minogue said. "Get this fella, the photographer again. O'Hagan, is it?"

Malone nodded.

"If Shaughnessy was on the society pages there'll be other pictures somewhere. Pinch these photographers if you get waltzed around. Call in uniforms, even. Get Éilis to have the warrants express if we need them. I'd be thinking there'd be other pictures of the same crowd or the same do somewhere in their files."

"Contact proofs," said Malone. "That's what they do first, right?"

"That's it. And then do a check with the lab again."

Malone looked up at the clock.

"No great hurry back now," said Minogue. "But you're buying dinner today."

Kevin drew up jars from a cart he had wheeled over and placed six of them beside Shaughnessy's left arm. Donavan switched on the saw for a test. Minogue became aware of a new ache at the base of his neck. He kept his gaze on the jars. Kevin placed the roll of labels by Donavan's clipboard and began writing in Shaughnessy's name and the date. Minogue forced himself to look over Shaughnessy again.

Donavan's gloves looked very tight. Maybe they were some new type of plastic or rubber. He should really put on glasses himself. The saw might throw up bits of . . . He watched Donavan draw the scalpel up from Shaughnessy's pubic hair. The radio began to play a reel. Donavan finished the Y with a sharp flourish. There was a flute and a harp, airy sounds that reminded him of a windy May morning. Kathleen was off tomorrow. Phone Iseult and . . .

The tissue parted by the rib cage as though it had been unzipped. Minogue held his breath again. It took an effort to keep his feet planted now. He let his eyes out of focus. He was already there, just in time: that turn in the lane by Tully, that sliver of sea off Bray.

Donavan turned the diagram around. Minogue recalled the deft slicing of the liver, the pathologist's unwavering hand as he held the sample for the jars.

"I can't tell," said Donavan. "But it wasn't more than a couple of hours before the systems shut down. A sizable meal, call it. Do Americans have big appetites?"

Irony? Minogue didn't know. He squeezed the back of his neck. He looked around the conference room and tried another mouthful of tea. Pretty poor. He eyed his notebook next to the stain from the cup. His writing had definitely changed after Donavan had opened the skull. He remembered fighting against the noise of the saw, wandering through the woods by Carrigologan, stepping around the stones and the long grass in Tully. "Drink?" he had written under INTERNAL.

Malone had found out that both of Shaughnessy's parents would be coming over. Geraldine Shaughnessy, the mother and Leyne's ex, hadn't remarried. Leyne himself was already on the plane, someone said. It was O'Riordan, Leyne's old pal in Ireland, who had identified the body at four in the morning. It had been at the joint request of the mother and father. A representative of Leyne had faxed through the confirmation to Tynan's office this morning.

"The blood alcohol will be done by three or so, I imagine," said Donavan. "If you have the queue jumped. As per your routine fashion."

"Thanks, Pierce," said Minogue. He looked down at his notes again.

"Do you be over Glencree much still?"

"Most Sundays," said Minogue. "More, now the autumn is here."

"Do you suffer company?"

Minogue managed a smile.

"Stop off at the house, can't you. We'll take the one car up."

"Do you hear me arguing? Remember me to Kathleen."

CHAPTER 6

MALONE JAMMED SECOND GEAR as he sped away from the lights. He accelerated hard on the motorway.

"You know what gets to me?" he said to Minogue. "Like, *really* gets to me?"

"Tell me, why don't you."

"It's when they're finished. I swear to God, man. I can take the face being pulled back down; I can. The *brain* flopping around on the table even."

Malone glanced over at the inspector.

"It's when they tie up the bag."

"The bag," Minogue said.

"With the stuff inside it. The organs, like? They shove things back in, inside the rib cage. Now that's what *really* gets me. Know what I'm saying?"

Nowharamsane. Minogue yawned. He'd been counting: seventeen APF officers on the roster. A couple of hundred staff. Cleaners, baggage handlers, drivers. Maintenance, delivery people, bottle washers. Shop assistants, pilots, stewardesses. Passengers, passengers' families saying good-bye to passengers. Passengers' families saying hello to passengers. Sheehy'd need twenty officers to make a dent in this.

"Reminds me of well, you know. The Christmas? A turkey or something. Sick, isn't it?"

Minogue followed a plane's approach out over the sea. The plane seemed to hover there over Howth. A holding pattern.

"But you have to hand it to him," said Malone. "An art. That's what it is."

The flaps down, Minogue thought, and the wheels were claws searching for a place to perch. Fifty, sixty tons, were they? Jesus. All in the space of a lifetime, this stuff too. Neither his father nor his mother had been inside a plane.

"And the size of the needle, but," Malone said and began pulling at an eyebrow.

Minogue shifted to get his notebook out. He had the phone open when it rang. It was Tony O'Leary. The family was flying in from the States very shortly.

"It's Leyne's jet they're coming in on," said O'Leary. "Boss wants to know how you stand on it."

Minogue looked out at the broken lines of the motorway rushing by them. As if O'Leary didn't know.

"Strangely enough, Tony, we were on the way to the airport."

"He's tied up until after four. He wants you to represent him."

"Haven't you phoned Lawlor? He could do that handy enough."

"Says will you phone him if you can't."

Minogue let a few moments go by.

"The mother and Leyne, is it?"

"That's it. Probably a few people with them. Justice is sending Declan King."

Assistant minister for Justice, King was an ex-Guard turned barrister. King had been dubbed King Declan by Kilmartin in disdainful, edgy regard for King's talents as the minister's principal arm-twister for Gardai. An intense pain in the face, Kilmartin avowed.

"And wants you to brief Leyne," O'Leary added. "Within reason."

The Nissan leaned in hard on the bend. Minogue realized that he was squeezing the phone hard against his ear.

"Give me a minute there, Tony," he managed, and muffled the receiver. He turned to Malone.

"Take it handy for the love of God, man. And pull in after the roundabout. We might be changing the menu here."

He took his hand off the phone.

"Let me see if I have this right, Tony. The commissioner of the Gardai wants me to brief Leyne on a murder investigation that's hardly gotten started?"

"That's what he wanted."

O'Leary must have been holding his breath too.

"Leyne is an American, zillionaire frozen food tycoon and I am a Garda inspector."

"He says he'll let you in on the thing soon's he can."

"Where do we take him? In town I mean."

"There's a press conference set for the Shelbourne Hotel."

A press conference, Minogue thought. *I* can't be running around like an iijit, chaperoning some fella," he said. "I have to break this case right away. It's speed now, at this stage. He knows that.

"I can't be running around the city like an iijit. Tell him that, will you."

O'Leary said nothing. Minogue stared at a flattened Coke can in the grass.

"All right, Tony. Where's himself at the moment anyway?"

"He's caught up with a task force on criminal assets."

Minogue rather liked the indignation warming his throat and chest.

"But he'll definitely be out for the press conference though," O'Leary said. "It can double for your public appeal, if you're having one."

"I'll see him there then. And I have a shopping list."

"Say the word."

"Fergal Sheehy's going to need a dozen officers to get started in earnest. He has five there with him now. Forensics's still working the site so the van's staying put. I'll call you in about fifteen minutes and give you a list."

"Absolutely."

Minogue thumbed the end button twice. Absolutely? He watched the airport buildings rise slowly above the hedges as Malone braked for the roundabout.

"Go on in, Tommy. I need to look around. The security office first."

Malone waited until they had stepped out of the car to ask him.

"What's O'Leary want?"

"*Céad míle fáilte* for our American friends, Tommy. Lucky I have the spare tin whistle in the boot."

"Are you serious?"

"I am. Can you sing 'Danny Boy'?"

"Bollocks! I get sergeant out of this. Just for agreeing to be here."

Minogue stepped in front of his colleague. He gave him a hard look.

"All right so. No more playing to the gallery, Tommy. I'm a lot more annoyed than you are. You'll be staying with Fergal at the airport. I'll go back into town with the VIPs and head a press conference afterward."

Malone's grimace was almost too much for Minogue.

"Just drive. And don't be making faces at me."

· · · · ·

Fergal Sheehy was perched on the edge of a table littered with printouts and maps of the airport. He nodded at Minogue, returned to squinting at the map. Minogue took off his jacket. The coffee stain was still there. That bucket-arsed shopper with the five hundred shopping bags after the Christmas sales had ambushed him in Bewleys.

"I've been looking," Sheehy said. "There's holes all over the place."

"The schedules?"

"The whole thing. Sure, they have video at the terminals but — here, have you been in to the monitoring room yet?"

"No."

"There's three areas basically: indoors, approaches to the terminal — that's the one they pay the most attention to for drive-ups and vehicle bombs. Then there's a camera over the main entry for traffic flow. That's it. There's plans and all the rest of it to get full coverage by the end of next year."

Sheehy pushed himself up off the table. He nodded down at the maps.

"That car park's blind. So there."

Minogue slipped his jacket back on.

"Fergal. I have to sit in on some class of a briefing with the mother and father when they land. Then I'm off to town again. Press conference and appeal."

"Well that's very nice for you. Who have I got here?"

"Tommy. I'll put in the call for staff in a minute."

"When do you want the powwow?"

"Aim for seven."

Minogue headed down the hallway that led to the public areas of the terminal. There were five security officers waiting in chairs in the hallway. He took the stairs down to a door which opened onto the arrivals. He looked up at the screens but then remembered Leyne had his own plane. He counted: seven hours flying, more maybe. Plus five, for the time change. Leyne and the ex-wife had left Boston four in the morning their time.

He spotted Declan King talking to a ruddy-faced man in a navy suit. King made his way over.

"Matt?"

"Good day to you now, Declan."

"Kieran Hayes. He works out of CDU."

Minogue didn't fight back much against the clamp Hayes issued as a handshake. He took in the ruddy complexion, the well-tended hair, the heavy jaw. "Works out of" meant nothing: Hayes was a cowboy. Minogue wondered if members of the new mob had been given protective duties too.

The latest incarnation of Emergency Response was called The Cobra Squad. Minogue had heard "take down" and "Cobra" in the same sentence at a session in Ryan's pub a few months back. At first he'd thought they were talking about a film. Someone had told him that this Cobra Squad was to be the latest hammer for paramilitary gangs in the South.

Hayes raised his eyebrows, excused himself. Minogue watched him thread his way through the lineups. He began to pick out the other detectives stationed around the building.

King kept looking around the arrivals hall.

"You're up and running on this?"

Minogue looked at him.

"I'm only only asking because you can expect Leyne to," King said. "Do you know him, or of him?"

"He's some class of a tycoon. That much I know."

"Very direct. Down to earth. He'll — oh, here we go now."

Hayes was pointing to a door marked NO ENTRY. Minogue followed King. At the end of a short corridor the inspector found himself in a carpeted room a little smaller than the squad room. In lieu of real windows were two stained-glass panels full of detailed Celtic ornaments. An exit sign hung over the door to the left. An olive carpet, puffy-looking leather sofas, indirect lighting, and low tables.

One of the detectives, a skinny, graying fella with the look of a fox about his profile gave Minogue the nod. Minogue couldn't remember the name, but he was almost certain that it was the same one who had been front and center in an infamous *Irish Times* photo of a demonstrator being given a hiding at a Euro summit in Dublin several years ago. Minogue eyed the stained glass and the paneling.

A door opened behind him. The man who came through was a lift from of a movie or a magazine, an American magazine. The eyes flicked around the room, he turned, said hi to King, and left again. Minogue perched on the back of a sofa. King tugged at his jacket, checked his watch.

"He has a tendency to take over," King said with what might have been a smile. "He may get in your face."

The door opened again and drew in the stink of cooking and engine oil and rubber. Customs officer, looking very pleased with himself. Minogue couldn't remember seeing one spruced up to such splendor before. There followed a short, broad-shouldered man, plodding more than walking into the VIP reception area. It's the pope, was Minogue's first thought. He almost said as much. Startled, he stared at the lined forehead, the stoop, the jutting jaw. The remains of curly white hair fell halfway down over his ears. Even from across the room Minogue could see the membrane of dried spittle in the corners of Leyne's mouth.

Behind Leyne, and nearly a head taller, came a woman with rust-colored hair, a pale complexion, and red-rimmed, blue eyes. The cut of the maroon trouser suit Minogue had glimpsed in fashion magazines, but the face was from a winter's day walk on a country road in the west of Ireland. Forty-eight, he remembered from the paper, and she didn't take the sunglasses route, it seemed.

A bulky, well-groomed man in his forties followed. He hesitated, his briefcase held tight by his leg, and then stood to Leyne's right. Principal handler/flunky, Minogue decided. He wondered how many more Leyne had brought with him.

He looked over again. The multimillionaire hadn't grown an inch since he'd last looked. The head like a boulder or the like, so out of proportion to the frame. Now she wasn't much short of six feet, he decided. These were Patrick Leyne Shaughnessy's parents, he thought as he stepped forward, and half-wondered where his annoyance had disappeared to: Mrs. Geraldine Shaughnessy and her former husband, Mr. John Leyne. The long and the short of it.

·   ·   ·   ·   ·

The Mercedes soaked up the motorway with a faint whistle. Minogue glanced back at the cars following. Mrs. Shaughnessy had insisted on being shown the site where her son's rented car had been found. Minogue remembered her jaw quivering, the handkerchief held to her nose. Leyne had stood beside her, pushing back long strands of hair teased up by the breeze. He'd studied the car park with a bleak gaze for a long time. Minogue wondered if the bored disbelief on Leyne's face was just the shock, or was it from something else that had occurred to him quicker. The look of a tradesman, maybe, surveying an impossible job.

Leyne turned to him. Minogue didn't want to look at the man's mouth, the yellow film stretching around his mouth like a fish or something. There was a sour smell in the car too that Minogue didn't want to be aware of anymore.

"So," Leyne said. "Tell me, what's really going on here?"

Minogue focused on the driver's eyes in the mirror of the unmarked Opel ahead. Mrs. Shaughnessy was talking to Declan King there, with Kieran Hayes looking around the front passenger headrest, glancing at the Mercedes every now and then.

Freeman, Leyne's assistant, was sitting in the passenger seat, chewing slowly on something. Minogue's gaze went to the driver. The car was Billy O'Riordan's, the driver an ex-Guard, apparently.

"Well," said Leyne.

The Irish accent seemed to have soaked through the twang Minogue had heard at the airport. Freeman sat forward a little and turned.

"If this was back home, you'd think robbery," he said. "A mugging, maybe."

"That's definitely a line of inquiry," Minogue managed.

"Look," said Leyne. "Let us know where we stand."

Minogue gave him a blank look.

"You're the expert, right," he said. "Tri . . . Tan . . ."

"Commissioner Tynan," said Freeman.

"That's him. He says you're the goods. But what else would he say? Now look, we need to get to the point here. You can speak your mind, you understand?"

"I've told you what we know so far," Minogue said. "There's nothing to embellish. We're going after leads the best we can. That's about it so far."

Freeman adjusted his glasses again. He started to say something but Leyne waved him off.

"Look, there, Inspector, is it?"

"Matt's grand."

"Matt. You can appreciate where we're coming from. How we talk, the way things work. You know. The States? Have you been?"

"No. Not yet. But I have a rough idea."

"Well I've been both sides. I watched the Yanks getting off the tourist buses, Christ, I don't know when — Eisenhower, that's how long ago. Looking for fairies and leprechauns, the half of them. All I'm saying is, level with me. I'm not going to give you shit. Hell, I'm in no position to. You're not Dublin are you?"

"No."

"Where?"

"Clare. West Clare."

"Family?"

"Two."

"Grown up, are they?"

"Most of the time."

"How long are you married?"

Minogue looked out the window.

"Sixty-seven years," he said.

The driver's eyes locked on to his in his mirror. Freeman stopped his chewing and looked at the dashboard.

"So it's your first marriage then, I take it."

Minogue nodded. Freeman resumed his chewing.

"They told you how much of a pain in the ass I am?"

"In a manner of speaking, yes."

"How'm I doing?"

Minogue looked across at him. Leyne's eyes were more watery than he'd noticed earlier. The jaw was set even harder. There were blood vessels right up to the iris.

"You're doing all right so far."

"Only all right?"

"The shock hits people differently, Mr. Leyne."

"Ever had someone close to you murdered? Die suddenly?"

Minogue looked around the face. The skin was papery near the eyes too. "I don't mind you poking," he said. "But when I do, I'll tell you. I've a job to do, that's all."

Leyne turned back to the window. A sagging van belched clouds of diesel smoke.

"You're a gentleman to spare Geraldine," he said. "But I'd like to know. What's your gut instinct?"

Minogue looked through the back window. The security squad would be jumpy if the traffic slowed any more.

"I can't say. Your son was out of sight for quite a number of days. We're trying to place him."

Leyne closed his eyes, let his head back against the headrest. He rubbed at his eyes and sighed. The driver pulled around the slowing traffic by Collins Avenue. He was directed through the junction by two Guards on motorcycles. Three kids waved at the cars. The Mercedes picked up speed again.

{ 73 }

"Jeff," Leyne said then and opened his eyes. "Are we connected?"

Freeman took a cell phone from his briefcase.

"It's Billy O'Riordan I want."

Freeman consulted an address book, he dialed, and he listened for a moment. He handed it to Leyne.

The potato millionaire eased himself into the corner. His eyes lost focus.

"Billy? It's John," he said. "Yes. Thanks. Christ, I don't know. About twenty minutes ago."

Minogue eyed Freeman taking in Summerhill. Not that appetizing an entry to Dublin's fair city even with the boom times. Freeman leaned in to him.

"Definitely in shock," he whispered.

Minogue returned Freeman's gaze. Concerned, sure, but hired concern?

"We left Boston at four," Freeman added. "Didn't sleep much . . ."

Minogue glanced at Leyne. He was pinching the bridge of his nose while he listened. His eyelids fluttered but they stayed closed.

"It's not personal," Freeman whispered. "You can appreciate that, right? He's used to running the show his way."

"Damn it, Billy," Leyne said then. "The hell would I know?"

An old man, Minogue realized. The suit and the tan and the darting eyes twitching and floating in the pouches of skin didn't make him any less than sixty-eight years old.

The Mercedes was waved through red lights by the bridge. Freeman spoke behind his hand now.

"Mr. Leyne's never forgotten his home country."

Leyne said all right and handed the phone back to Freeman. He looked out at the new offices by the quays.

"Did Jeff give you more of the hard ass and soft heart routine there?"

Freeman sat back with a rueful smile.

"He better have," Leyne went on. "That's what he's paid to do. Here, see that pub?"

Minogue took in the newly tarted up pub as they passed.

"I worked there for six months on the buildings," Leyne said. "Years and years ago. Carrying concrete blocks up to a black-haired bastard, a brickie. Jimmy Morrissey, from Leitrim. I had a row with him one night. The size of me, huh. He beat the shit out of me. A great education, he gave me that day."

He nodded at Freeman.

"But Jeff here came up the veal route. Didn't you, Jeff?"

Freeman smiled.

"Summer house on the Cape. Aspen, Jeff?"

"Aspen," said Freeman. "Yes, sir. Worked two seasons in a pizza joint there."

Leyne tapped on the window.

"That bastard Morrissey did me a big favor. I went home to those ten acres and got started on learning everything I could about chips. Potato chips. People thought I was mad. I got a job in Mitchelstown. Two jobs."

"Crisps we call them here," said Minogue. "Chips you get out of a chipper."

Leyne strained to look back at a passing building.

"I hate Dublin," he said. "Still. And I shouldn't, should I. Things have come on a lot here, haven't they?"

"I suppose."

"Film industry, the music? Gone mad on the digital economy and all that?"

The car turned sharply around Merrion Row. The trees seemed to be drooping very low over the railings in the square.

"You have a garden, I hope."

"I do."

"Do you grow spuds?"

Minogue thought ahead to Kathleen's disbelief when he'd tell her tonight.

"I do."

"You don't care that you can get them dirt cheap from Cyprus?"

"No."

It wasn't scorn Minogue heard in Leyne's voice, but he couldn't be sure.

"It's in the genes, is it? Since the Famine?"

"There's no way to know."

Leyne cleared his throat. Freeman looked at him and then at Minogue.

"What would anyone know about that anymore," Leyne murmured. "There's only microchips or television or something. Video games. Stores — shops. Who cares. There's no past anymore. History's over, isn't that it?"

"My great-grandmother was the only one left," said Minogue. "Out of nine. A Quaker family in Galway took her in."

Leyne made to say something but he stopped. Minogue watched the back gates of the Dáil swing open to admit a car. Too many damned Mercedes in Boomtown Dublin now this last while. He returned Leyne's gaze.

"The man she married had buried seven brothers and sisters," he said.

"Enough left to take on the landlords though? And then the Black and Tans."

"I suppose. I've a brother keeps score, over the centuries."

Leyne sighed.

"British Queens, my da used to grow," he said. "Duke of Yorks. The Kerr's Pinks. Idaho Reds . . . Sir Walter Raleigh and the glorious spud. Rotting in the fields. People dying in ditches. But I'm no scholar. No. I'm too busy working for a living. I *pay* people to study something, and then I pay them again to explain it to me. I must be mad."

Two Garda motorcycles blocked the traffic at the lights by Baggot Street. The Mercedes surged ahead. One circuit of Stephen's Green and they'd pull up at the Shelbourne. Minogue looked at the Opel ahead. What was there in Geraldine Shaughnessy's manner, her appearance, that he'd recognized but couldn't detail as he'd watched her standing in the airport car park by the tape? A teacher maybe, a nun?

"Microchips or not I hear Dublin's falling apart," said Leyne. "How bad is it?"

Minogue recognized a newspaper seller at the foot of Harcourt Street. The man, a boy when Minogue first knew him, with a loose eye and sloping drag-foot gait, squinted at the cars. Behind him on a bus shelter was an ad for GOD. It was the original one, the close-up black and white of a shaved head with a tattoo on her neck and a ring in her eyebrow. The mocking, hollow eyes staring at him from any point he looked. Would Leyne be satisfied to know that the suicide rate was now ahead of England's?

"Cup of good coffee's nearly a pound," he said. "Bistros. New television channels."

"That's all you can tell me?" asked Leyne. "Not the part about Dublin being full of drug addicts? Or that there are Irish farmers paid *not* to grow things?"

The trees in their full spread and the glimpses of the pond between the shrubs lifted Minogue.

"Not what DeValera and the 1916 crowd had in mind, I tell you."

I tell ya, Minogue repeated within. The American and the Irish had him off balance yet. But more than the accent, he had heard something familiar in Leyne's talk. Steeling himself for a news conference, no doubt: the inevitable intrusion of police and gawkers and cranks. Revisiting old scars too, maybe. A past marriage, a return bout in a private struggle against the old country he had turned into a villain so he could escape it. Better not tell him the Irish weren't emigrant laboring men anymore.

Minogue stole a glance at Leyne. This short multimillionaire had gone far. He'd parlayed a crop that had kept his ancestors alive — and then decimated them — into convenience food, and he'd made a big pile of money at it. And no, it wasn't bitterness he'd been hearing in Leyne's asides. It was something else, and he had heard it before. It was that zest and disenchantment which came out too often as scorn, and maybe that lasting ache was a watermark in Minogue's fellow citizens no matter where they ended up. Always returning, always leaving, he wondered. Everything counts, and nothing matters?

The car pulled over to the entrance of the Shelbourne. Minogue counted three squad cars, a half-dozen uniforms, and as many in plain clothes stepping out onto the roadway. He spotted the hard chaws further back, eyes everywhere, one talking into his lapel, another with his jacket unbuttoned, the pistol jammed up under his arm. He looked at the faces of people held back on the footpath.

"Christ," Leyne said.

"It's going to be okay," Freeman soothed. "You've taken your six o'-clock —"

"Yeah, yeah," Leyne snapped. He turned to Minogue.

"We're going to have to hang tough, right? You know what I'm saying?"

Minogue took in the wet eyes, the raspy breathing. He saw veins under the skin along Leyne's neck now.

"You have your own people to answer to, I know," Leyne said. "All I ask is, don't make it harder for Geraldine or me."

He nodded at the small crowd on the pavement.

"I don't know what these journalists are like here but I wouldn't cross the street to piss on one of them if he was on fire."

Leyne's piercing eyes darted around the scene for several moments more.

"It'll come out sooner or later," he whispered. "Every family has its things."

Hayes opened Leyne's door. The food tycoon grabbed Minogue's arm.

"My son was murdered," he said. "The money's no good. I can't get him back. I can't go back to fix things. Do you know what I'm saying?"

Minogue nodded. Leyne stared into his eyes again.

"You're thinking, 'Some goddamned Yank,' right?"

Minogue watched Freeman adjusting his collar.

"I'm an Irishman. I wandered off, I suppose. But I'm an Irishman. Okay?"

Minogue nodded.

"I'm a pain in the arse all my life. And I look like hell, don't I?"

"You'll be okay. Just go easy on yourself. Don't react to stupid questions."

"I don't mean appearing on TV here," said Leyne. "Hell, that's nothing. What I mean is the father bit. The parent thing. You're the old school there, are you? No divorce or that, Mass on Sunday, all that . . . ?"

"No."

Leyne grabbed his arm again, squeezed.

"Listen," Leyne said. " Do I look like a man who's interested in bullshit? In my condition? Let's talk man-to-man here. I never stopped being Irish. An Irishman, do you get it? The main thing here is, whatever you do, remember I'm behind you. All the way. You hear me?"

CHAPTER 7

Leyne leaned in, pushed a nest of the microphones back. Minogue wondered what it was about Leyne's face that now reminded him of a fish. Another journalist placed a recorder on the table. Minogue stopped counting: there must be a dozen Guards around the room. Tynan sat in next to him.

"Thanks," he said. "They want to start right away?"

"I suppose. What do I tell the parents that I don't give to a press conference?"

Tynan raised an eyebrow.

"Don't be dragging your feet," he said.

Minogue eyed Gemma O'Loughlin chewing on a pen at the back of the room.

"I'm giving the bare minimum, John."

Tynan put on his Easter Island face, looked out at the small crowd. Mrs. Shaughnessy was now sitting next to Leyne. He leaned toward her and said something. He put his hand on her arm. She seemed not to notice the hand.

King read the release. He didn't use the word *appeal*. That was left for him, Minogue realized. The lights dazzled him. He almost missed his cue but a television camera swiveled and settled on him. He heard himself begin, and he flinched at, but was grateful for, the clichés that flowed easily. Minogue looked over to Leyne and Mrs. Shaughnessy several times. The light had done something to her face. She sat upright, with that out-of-reach look Minogue hadn't learned to type conclusively over the years. Anger, sure, he supposed. Grief; tiredness; helplessness; disbelief. All of it.

Leyne sat forward and studied some point in the far corner of the room. Minogue took in the dogged, strained face. The pope was right, but something neanderthal about the jutting jaw too.

Minogue's armpits began to prickle. He moved the sheaf of papers he'd used as a prop and glanced at King. King cued Mrs. Shaughnessy. She blinked and a tear slid down. She held up a finger to stop it. She sounded close to breathlessness. Leyne's hand went to her arm again. There was a sudden flurry of camera shutters. Minogue saw the journalists writing more.

It occurred to the inspector that Mrs. Shaughnessy did not like asking for help. That she had practiced what she was going to say. That she was not going to lose her poise. She called her son her only son. She said she had a deep affection for Ireland and his Irish roots. That his visits to Ireland had been high points in his life. She paused and bit her lip. Her son had even thought of moving to Ireland to live. Her voice wavered, she closed her eyes. Thirty-something years in the States and her accent almost wholly Irish still, Minogue realized. Her mother and father, two brothers and two sisters still lived in County Cork. They were strong farmers; well up.

Justice, she said then. Her son would rest but his parents could not until — Tynan was sliding a note across. It had been folded once. "Release cause?" Minogue shook his head. Mrs. Shaughnessy finished. To Minogue's surprise, Leyne said nothing but rose. He and Mrs. Shaughnessy were ushered away from the table. Minogue tried to count the flashes but gave up after ten. Two Guards in uniform blocked reporters from following the couple. Then King threw the conference open for questions.

The first one was from Seán Barrett, a hack who had thought himself an impregnable insider with the Guards until Tynan had come to the commissioner's job. No more midnight jaunts on drug busts for Barrett, no more helicopter tours of uncovered arms dumps. Barrett, Kilmartin had heard, was more than pissed off at his fall from favor.

Minogue told Barrett he couldn't release cause of death until he was sure of it. Had the postmortem been performed? It had. There was some doubt remaining? There were details that required careful examination. King picked out a face Minogue didn't recognize. An English accent, by God. He took in the leather jacket, the hair, the earring.

Was Mr. Shaughnessy the victim of organized criminal groups? Try disorganized, Minogue wanted to say, as criminals tended to be. No, he replied instead. There was nothing to suggest this yet. It was very early in the investigation. It would naturally fall under our consideration. Were there criminal gangs operating at the airport?

Minogue sidestepped it, threw in a decoy: unprecedented. The tabloid had to have its chance then. Minogue saw King almost grimace. The reporter hung on, poked the air with his pencil: Was the Dublin area now acknowledged to be suffering from an epidemic of violent crime? Was there not documented lack of security, an alarming lack of security, at the airport? Was Shaughnessy targeted as a tourist?

Tynan weighed in. Minogue watched Gemma O'Loughlin scribbling fast. Tynan's tone was almost kindly, the tone that Kilmartin most suspected: this wasn't the occasion to discuss trends and statistics or crimes. This was investigation, not extrapolation. There was no confirmation or even assertion that the murder had been committed at the airport — hence our appeal for info on Mr. Shaughnessy's whereabouts over the last several days and weeks.

A radio journalist next.

Had Mr. Shaughnessy been reported as missing? Yes, for eight days. A search made? Fógra Tóradh issued to all stations Tuesday morning. Had there been any measures beyond the ordinary taken to locate Mr. Shaughnessy? Minogue had expected it earlier. He noticed that Tynan was sitting forward with his elbows on the table now. The Make My Day move, Kilmartin had called it, like I want the meeting over. Full resources of the Gardai brought to bear, came Tynan's reply. Particularly tragic when the crime victim was a visitor to our country.

King took Gemma O'Loughlin next. She glanced at Minogue several times as she spoke. Had Mr. Shaughnessy's family been the subject of any security concerns in the past? Prominent positions, well known, et cetera . . . ? King steered it to Tynan. Public figures was Tynan's tack; the world we live in; extra measures. Minogue looked from face to face in the front row while Tynan did his slow rehash of the Garda appeal for sightings of Shaughnessy. He let his thoughts go to the maps in the squad room. Donegal, with roads over the bogs like the twists and leavings of thread or wool on the floor after Iseult had been doing a tapestry.

·   ·   ·   ·   ·

A handful of reporters remained seated. The camera crew had nearly finished disassembling. Tony O'Leary sat on the edge of the deserted table. Minogue watched hotel staff carrying away chairs.

"All right," said Tynan. "You're headed back out to the airport?"

"Probably."

The day was running away on him. He'd need to be back into town again by half-six to get his head straight for the briefing. Traffic . . . ?

"But after I check with Éilis."

"Tony'll take you out so," said Tynan.

O'Leary had parked the commissioner's Opel at the taxi rank by the top of Dawson Street. Minogue rolled down the window. He was glad of the noise along the green.

"I'll set up a meeting," said Tynan. "Tomorrow early, say. Give them a bit of time to get themselves together. They have nothing recent on him, on the son, you know that? But Mrs. knows you want to talk to her."

Minogue took out his phone.

"Did Leyne tell you anything on the way in?" Tynan asked.

Minogue switched the phone back to standby.

"He told me he was still an Irishman."

"Did he run us all down as backward iijits, Guards included?"

"More or less."

Tynan nodded.

"But I fell to thinking," Minogue resumed, "well, that Leyne has the look of a man not in the whole of his health."

Tynan stared at Minogue's forehead for a moment.

"You wouldn't be the first to notice," he said. "There's keen interest in that very subject. He's sitting on about two hundred million dollars."

"He didn't mention that to me on the trip in from the airport."

Tynan didn't bite.

"Well did he tell you anything?"

"He did but I don't know what it means. 'It'll all come out eventually,' he said."

"What 'all'?"

"Family, I think," Minogue said. "The son was a bit wild."

Tynan stared at the open door of the Opel then across the roof at O'Leary. "I'll walk it, Tony," he said. "Meet me up at the office."

O'Leary glanced at Minogue.

"No he wouldn't be loaded, Tony. We'll be okay."

Minogue followed Tynan across to the broad footpath that surrounded Stephen's Green. The commissioner was a brisk walker.

"All the free advice I get," Tynan said. "Now Tony is supposed to carry a gun and take bodyguard training."

"Have you . . . ?"

"Threats? 'Course I have. Tell me, what'd you make of Mrs.?"

"I don't know. Genteel, if the word means anything anymore. Are she and Leyne, what's the word —"

"Amicable? They are now. The marriage lasted only a few years. He didn't fight the settlement."

"Well-heeled, is she."

Tynan slowed his pace for a moment.

"Get the notion of preferential treatment out of your head. Face the facts: Leyne's high profile, and we'll be in the spotlight along with him. There's a lot of other baggage as well: the Leyne Foundation, the half-dozen companies he has a stake in. Biotech, food processing, mining."

"I know a little bit more too. He was a lousy parent. A lousy husband."

Minogue thought of Leyne's grip on his arm as they stepped out of the limo for the press conference.

"A philanderer I was told," Tynan went on. "Not a boozer, but."

Tynan turned sharply in through the gate into the green.

"So how'd he strike you?"

Minogue watched two kids feeding lumps of bread the size of tennis balls to the ducks. The pond was gray today. Downy feathers lay on the scum by the walk.

"He wants what he wants," he said. "Whatever that is. Guilt too, maybe, about the son. And he said he'd, er, back me up."

"Well that's nice to hear," said Tynan. Minogue eyed him.

"Back me up against a wall maybe, John. If I don't come through the way he wants."

They turned by the fountain for the German airmen and headed down the walk toward the Harcourt Street gate. Minogue tried to hold on to the sound of the flowing water as long as he could.

·　　·　　·　　·　　·

Éilis answered. Murtagh was on the phone but he'd said he wanted to talk to him. Minogue waited. Sitting in the passenger seat of the commissioner's car being sort of chauffeured around didn't feel glam so much as stupid. O'Leary adjusted the volume on the radio. Dispatch was trying to reroute a payroll van and its escort around an accident scene on the North Circular Road.

"Okay," said Murtagh then. "Good. Are you in town, boss?"

"I am. I hardly got a look in at the airport before this jaunt back."

"There's stuff coming in, pictures. Pictures of Shaughnessy at some dos. The races, some get together with the music crowd. He was socializing hot and heavy before he went west."

Minogue wondered if Murtagh had intended the wit.

"There's a photographer at the *Evening Press* doing some legwork for us. He's been phoning around fellas he knows in all the papers. So far we have Shaughnessy at four different dos. Four, no less. Quite the lad."

"Who's with him, or near him, even?"

"Yes. I'm looking at one just in over the fax. It's spotty and all, but he's got a girl under his oxter in one."

One night stand? Minogue wondered.

"Find her, can we?"

"The snapshots are being couriered over."

"Nothing new on placing him after he left Dublin?"

"No. But I was just talking to Serious Crimes about the airport. Kevin Cronin's got names from stuff late last year. Cars robbed. There was a mugging in one of the car parks. Never nailed down, but Cronin says he could point us to a few gougers who should be in the know. Here's the catch: one's in the Joy. The other one's out of the picture in England somewhere."

Minogue yawned. He might as well go out to the airport and shoulder his share of the interviews.

"Listen, I forgot," he said to Murtagh. "Get Éilis to update the appeal in the press release as soon as she can, will you? Along with anyone who used that car park at the airport — I forgot to put in about any snapshots or videos people might have taken there. Coming and going, like."

"Okay. Remember the call in from some fella in the museum? Shaughnessy was talking to someone in there . . . ?"

"Go ahead, yes."

"When he signed himself in as Leyne? I have a name on the woman he talked with there: Aoife Hartnett."

"Is she handy?"

"No," said Murtagh. "She's on her holidays, wouldn't you know it. Away off in Portugal is the best I can give you right now."

"Since?"

"Em. A week back."

Minogue looked down at the book that had slid out from under the seat when O'Leary had braked hard at the lights in Whitehall. Where was Asmara again? He thought back to the name of the woman who'd called in from the B & B in Donegal.

"John," Minogue said. "The call-in that said something about Shaughnessy may be traveling with a woman. That was Donegal, wasn't it?"

.   .   .   .   .

He took another drink from his cup. He grimaced and searched around the room for something to get rid of the taste.

"I don't know what that is," he sighed. "But coffee, it ain't."

Malone and Sheehy seemed to be surviving the tea. Malone tapped on the list again.

"This fella's on the level. Coughlan. The APF. He's going to drop Fogarty in the shite."

That wasn't the plan, Minogue wanted to say.

Minogue watched a feeble, fussy granny enter the airport restaurant on the arm of a hungover-looking man in an ill-fitting suit. Not the emigrant Paddys of old, he thought, with the string around the suitcase at the dock for the night sailing.

"Want to bet Coughlan or other fellas have a chip on the shoulder," Malone said. "And they want to drop their boss for something?"

Minogue shrugged.

"There are no direct pointers yet," said Sheehy. "The patrols all log in the checkpoints but sure they might as well be sleepwalking, some of 'em."

"How are we for response from people who parked there over the week?" Minogue asked. He looked down at his scribbles. "Five people so far, is it?"

Sheehy nodded. Malone looked at his watch.

"Half-four," he said. "There's only six or seven security staff left to do."

Minogue looked down at the personnel lists and the companies under contract.

"Is this it, Fergal? The whole shebang?"

"There's a few missing," Sheehy said. "But they'll come through."

"All right. What's the story on the vicinity search?"

Malone said that the dumpsters were still being checked. They'd located the tip where the terminal rubbish was disposed of.

Minogue thought of a rubbish tip, flocks of seagulls circling and squabbling. He'd better go down to the site, close it up. The technicians had come up dry. They'd worked it all morning. He checked his watch.

"Let's head down to the security office," he said. "We'll deal out what we have."

He turned to Sheehy.

"We'll aim for half-seven. At the squad, if you please, Fergal. Run up summaries, like a good man, and smarten us up on where we're headed with leads from here anyway."

Eoin Gormley, one of the newest forensic technicians, and Paddy Tuttle, probably the longest serving, were in the site van.

"Well, men," Minogue said. "We'll give it the once-over again."

Tuttle talked to Gormley about cigarette butts on their way across the access road to the car park. Minogue's bad shoulder ached worse. He thought about his brother's gnarled hands, how he could hardly walk down the lane on the farm now.

The tarmac in the car park looked soft. There were clumps of moss like sponge by the cement bollards. The Guard on shift was leaning against an unmarked car. Minogue studied the space within the tape, the holes where the tarmac had been taken up.

"A right lot of rain we've had," said the Guard. Soil samples, the contents of the boot, Minogue was thinking: that comb under the seat. The odometer said Shaughnessy had gone nearly 1,400 km. He stared at the stripped section of tar by the back of the Escort.

"Anything definite to tell us he was attacked here?"

Tuttle tugged at his ear.

"Do you want the considered version or the man-in-a-hurry version?"

"Whichever you like, now Paddy. No miracles expected."

"That's where the back bumper was, see? The 'B'?"

Minogue looked along the chalk line.

"We 'scoped and scrubbed for blood all up and down there before we took that patch up. The rain would've carried it off fair enough, but there are plenty of crevices in the tar that'd hold it. Minute though, very minute. It'd be degraded there fast too. Acidy. The compounds in there, well . . ."

"Tires, shoes?"

"There's residue all over the place," said Tuttle. "But you'll never distinguish them. That's going nowhere. We measured under where the wheels were. There's a difference all right but that's good for nothing, time-wise."

"Cars parked there before, you're going to tell me," Minogue murmured. "And will do so again?"

"I measured just a half an hour after to compare," Tuttle went on. "Sure the damn stuff comes back up again. Spongy. The time of day. A bit of sun . . ."

"Paddy. The site: I know you're not a betting man now."

Tuttle looked away toward the terminal. The sky had brown tints.

"Sorry, Matt. I couldn't really."

"'Forensic science wouldn't support it'?"

Tuttle nodded.

"Eoin?"

"Ditto. You'd be reading tea leaves."

"It's in the car you'll get anything here," said Tuttle.

Minogue tugged at the tape. Emerald Rent-A-Car had an option to leave their car at the airport but Shaughnessy hadn't taken it. Had he changed his mind, or had whoever driven the car thought they could lose it for a while? Some bloody scut, he thought again, a hitchhiker, traveling on Shaughnessy's credit cards. Match the entry to the exit from the Aer Lingus passenger lists: point of entry passport controls from the ferries. But if they'd come through the North he'd have the UK control data to reckon with.

Tuttle was still waiting.

"Sorry, Paddy. Yes. Thanks. The car, yes, we have that, to be sure."

The Guard helped them take down the tape and fold the uprights.

·   ·   ·   ·   ·

Inspector Minogue was getting to know the Swords Road a bit too well. He thought of the trips back from the airport each time they'd brought his son and de facto daughter-in-law out for their flight back. Kathleen silent, her crying done. Daithi pale, himself bewildered. The trips were getting spread out now. There had been three trips in four years — a trend — and Daithi wasn't sure about this Christmas either. Wasn't sure, quote unquote. The job was intense. It was the price you paid for the fast track. If he's not coming home at least once a year well . . . Kathleen had started the sentence often but had never finished it.

A low-slung sports car with a laughing driver and a woman pushing back her long hair rocketed by only to brake sharply as a taxi passed a van at a leisurely fifty miles an hour. Malone kept trying to see the driver.

"Jases," said Malone. "That's what's his name. Isn't it?"

Minogue blooked over. A Porsche, by God, and a turbo at that.

"It looks like him all right."

"Yeah, I knew it was. The film fella. *A Rebel Hand*. What's his name?"

Malone gave the inspector a sly look.

"Fannon. Gary Fannon."

"Will I flash the badge? Have a go at him for the driving?"

Minogue studied the gestures of Ireland's enfant terrible director while he waited for the taxi to move out of the fast lane. Who was the girl?

"He was doing ninety," Malone said. "Seen him bombing along in the mirror. Eighty in anyhow."

"Ah, leave him alone."

"Why? Are you hoping to stay the good side of him? Get hired?"

"He's a cultural icon, Tommy."

"Icon? Is that the same as a fucking chancer?"

He stood on the brakes in time to leave six inches or so between their Nissan and the van ahead.

"Shit — sorry. What's he like, Leyne?"

Minogue waved him back to watching the road.

"The son and him weren't that close, right?"

"He wants to help," Minogue said. She was a singer, the girl, wasn't she? What was her name? "He told me he'll back me up. Anything I want."

"Me too?"

"No. Only me. You're from Dublin. But I'm a countryman."

"Fu —. That's not very nice, is it."

"Dublin's a kip, Tommy. Mr. Leyne so pronounced it. Sorry, but."

Malone squirmed in his seat and tapped the steering wheel.

"Anything you want, is that the story?"

"Correct," replied Minogue. "So that's two anythings now. One from Tynan, one from Leyne."

Malone shifted again.

"You mind me asking you something there? The Killer's always gotten under Tynan's skin, right? And vice versa, like. Right?

Ryeh, Minogue heard. Loike.

"'Cause yours truly runs the shop with a shagging hammer in one hand," said Malone. "We're the elite and all that. His style, right?"

"He has his ways."

"Yeah, yeah. What I'm trying to say is, well . . . Tynan and you are on, ah, good terms. So Tynan'd be happy if, well, you know what I'm saying."

The Porsche had attracted a lot of attention ahead. Malone raced the Nissan in first.

"I know this Shaughnessy's high profile," he went on, "so we're in the spotlight? But, like, Tynan's got to be happy the way you-know-who is off in the States. 'Specially the timing, right . . . ? And with the Larry Smith thing hanging . . . ?"

The Porsche headed up Griffith Avenue. Going to the Gravediggers by Glasnevin, Minogue decided. He'd heard from Iseult that was where visiting movie stars and glitterati checked in. Ambience, sawdust on the floor, pints of Guinness.

Minogue didn't rise to the bait. The traffic was slowing again. Malone U-turned back to Home Farm Road.

"When do we get a session with the Mr. and Mrs.?"

"Tomorrow," Minogue replied. "Mrs. had the most contact with him, the last contact over there."

Malone turned up the radio at the mention of pursuit. Three suspected shoplifters were legging it down Parnell Street. One of them had flashed a knife. Another had used a baseball bat on a cashier. Two squad cars were heading over. Malone turned it back down.

"That's who it was," he said. "Now I have it. Only I can't think of her name."

"Who?"

"Leyne's missus. That's who she looks like, that film star. I can see the face exactly but. Way back, I'm talking about now. The oldies."

"How oldie, exactly?"

"Ah, ages ago. Your time probably. Tall, cool type. Ended up marrying some king or the like . . ."

"Grace Kelly?"

Malone slapped the wheel and turned to Minogue.

"That's her! How'd you know?"

CHAPTER 8

THE LAB HAD SENT EIMEAR KELLY OVER. She sat by Murtagh's desk reading her notes with an intent frown. Minogue sat on the edge of the desk. How did the windows get so grimy so fast here, he wondered. Éilis clapped bundles of photocopies on the top of the photocopier.

Murtagh had photos up on the boards.

"He says he's waiting on ones from two other fellas," he called over to Minogue. "They're freelancers."

Minogue scrutinized the faces. Everyone was having a good time apparently. Shaughnessy had a big sunny smile. No guile in it; a bit of a gom really. He held a glass of wine in one. O'Riordan had the hat right, just like Vincent O'Brien, as he held the bridle on the racehorse. Leopardstown, a big race in the calendar: the Prime Foods Cup for four-year-olds. Shaughnessy was in profile there. Two women, one of them O'Riordan's age. A trainer, by the look of him, up front with O'Riordan too.

The inspector sipped his tea and looked down the timetable on the board. Murtagh had updated the map with pins for Shaughnessy's Dublin dates too.

Murtagh pointed at a group standing in front of a doorway.

"That one there," he said. "That's at an auction in Goff's. The fella on the left is a Saudi Arabian prince. Can you tell? Ha ha."

O'Riordan was beaming at the Saudi prince. Minogue studied the camera slung over Shaughnessy's shoulder. A sleek-looking model; couldn't tell the make.

"An art exhibition," said Murtagh. He tapped the photo four times with his finger. "Kind of hoi-polloi there. It was Donohoe took those two. They're in the papers last Sunday week. That's Shaughnessy talking to some art dude. Film people showed up. Julia Whatshername was supposed to show but she didn't."

"Tough," said Malone. "Pops up a lot, doesn't he. How'd he get his intros?"

Murtagh shrugged.

"Connected through O'Riordan? He's keen on the socialite bit."

Fergal Sheehy arrived. Murtagh held up his mug. Sheehy sidled over to Éilis and said something out of the side of his mouth. She scowled and tapped the photocopy bundle one more time, hard. She began dropping the copies on the table.

"Eimear," said Minogue. "I know you'd like to get home. Start us off will you?"

Minogue checked his list in his notebook. Blood from the bootlid typed the same as Shaughnessy's. No receipts on the floor of the car. Fine particles from the seat covers in the front not yet matched to belongings found in the car. Nine fags in the ashtray: lipstick traces plain on at least four. Tests? A week at least.

"Eimear," said Minogue. "The inventory from the boot again. Have ye tried all the clothes for fiber matches?"

"All the jackets. Yes."

There were signs of someone's efforts to wipe prints. Lab staff had lasered the seats for latent prints and had found plenty. The comparisons were started already.

"The hairs you're talking about," said Murtagh. "Emerald gave me a list of customers they'd rented the Escort to. The car's only six months old. There's a total of eleven separate contracts on it, all of them tourists. Holland, the States. Germany. Some of the staff at Emerald are allowed to take the cars home too. And there's delivery drivers and cleaners too."

Minogue read down the inventory again. Michelin was misspelled.

"So far the wallet and the passport," he said. "Camera, video camera — did he declare stuff on arrival?"

Murtagh shook his head.

"Nothing, but it'll take a final search tomorrow at Customs to make sure."

"Any start on a Bórd Fáilte office, John? Visitor's books?"

Murtagh bit his lip and scribbled on his notepad.

"I'll start right after. Slipped my mind."

"He wasn't packing much for a jet-setter," said Malone. "Four shirts, including what he had on when he was killed. Jeans, two other pairs of pants. Shoes, well three pairs."

There was no booze in the car. Shaughnessy smoked. There were wrappers from bars of chocolate, two empty Pepsi cans, fragments of crisps, apple cores. They found paper hankies, the inside of an *Irish Times*. He studied the list of books and maps again. Two all-Ireland road maps but no marks on them. An ordinance survey for Donegal with a stamp on it from a shop in Donegal town. *Life in Early Ireland* by Professor Seán O'Tuama. Hardly meant drunken nightclub louts wavering in the middle of the street at 3 A.M.

A Bórd Fáilte accommodations book had been folded open at Donegal. There were two national monuments and sites books. Minogue had spotted one of the titles browsing in the Official Publications office on Molesworth Street himself and wondered if anybody ever bought them. *Land and People in Early Christian Ireland*. A dictionary of Irish placenames. Had Shaughnessy written postcards? Minogue blew his nose as quietly as he could.

"Eimear," he said then. "Are ye finished with the books? Prints, I mean."

She told him they'd need another day at least to fluoroscope all the books. He'd loved Ireland, the mother had said; had thought of moving here.

"Ah ye're great, Eimear," he said. "Now I know it's early, but maybe ye had something on placing the car at all? Those plastic shopping bags in the boot?"

They were generic to the shopping chain all over the country.

"Shit," said Malone.

She'd already sent one receipt found in a bag to a man in the head office of Powers supermarkets to locate the shop. It was dated for two weeks ago.

Minogue leafed through the shots of the boot again.

"The damage to the car — John, did you phone Emerald on that?"

"I did. It's news to them. They have no record from previous rentals."

"What broke the panel over the spare wheel? Because he traveled light . . . ?"

Sheehy cleared his throat.

"I'd be thinking I put the two things on the same line. The bang on the bottom of the car and the broken panel there over the spare wheel."

"What," said Malone. "You mean a big load in the back, and that broke it?"

"Going over a good-sized bump, and you with a load in the back, sure you'd give it a right good belt, so you would."

"A boreen, are you saying, Fergal?"

"I am. And if you didn't know the road. And if it was nighttime . . ."

"And if you were pissed," said Malone.

Murtagh tapped on his watch. It was three minutes to six. Minogue nodded.

Murtagh rose and wheeled in Kilmartin's Trinitron. Minogue asked Eimear about the hair from the comb. He received approximately the answer he expected. It was pretty well useless until more hair from the same person was had. Minogue thanked her. Did she want to hang around and see whatever they'd put in from the press conference? She declined and asked for squad autographs instead. Malone told her about the Works stuck at the airport, the autograph for his ma. Sheehy offered her an overused Northsider joke about a marriage proposal. Eimear Kelly, a champion middle-distance runner for Dublin, starting with her primary school days in Finglas, asked Sheehy if Kerry people had learned to cook their food yet. Malone opined that he'd heard Kerry people hadn't even finessed it to killing their food before they started chewing it.

Sheehy affected to be stoical and even gently sage about Dubliners. He stroked his lip, sighed, and started on the airport details. There were twenty-something — wait, twenty-three — vehicles still in the car park checked in the same time or before Shaughnessy's. There was no way to pin Shaughnessy's car to a time until all the others had been claimed.

"People actually leave their cars in a car park in the airport for days on end?" Malone asked.

"Gas, isn't it," said Sheehy. "The most of them are only a few days, but it's getting popular."

"If he was done outside and then the car was parked at the airport," said Malone, "then someone had enough of a cool head to dust the shagging trail by taking the ticket from the car."

"Or a clean-up man after the event," said Minogue.

Murtagh turned up the volume. The first shot of the news item was of the whole table. A voice-over introduced Mrs. Shaughnessy and played the last of her words. A tear glittered but didn't run.

"Here, look," said Malone when Minogue came on. "You're baldier than I thought you were, er, boss."

The next shot was of Tynan. It was prefaced by a remark that the Gardai needed the help of the public. The Garda commissioner stared out at the viewers as he spoke. The Iceman indeed, thought Minogue. The help-line number appeared on the screen. Then the newscast veered off to a civil war in Africa.

A phone was ringing already. Murtagh lifted it and waved it at Minogue.

"You're on the telly," said Iseult.

"You're in the paper," he said. "A paper, anyway."

"Looked quite extinguished I'd have to say," she said. "Tie done up, the hair combed."

Minogue's head had began to feel very heavy.

"Thanks for the slagging now," he said. "I don't get half enough on the job."

"Ah grow up," said his daughter. "Has Ma seen the Neighbors thing yet?"

He watched Sheehy pointing to the entry to the car park on the map of the airport. Eastlands, they called it. They christened car parks now?

"I don't think so, love. Why don't you phone her, find out?"

"Ah, I couldn't. That'd be showing off!"

"Better you explain it before she sees it cold herself."

"What do you mean, 'cold'? And this 'explain' bit?"

"Well phone her up and do whatever gostering and the like you want."

"I thought you were beyond that kind of thing. Since when does art need to be — ah, now I get it. She's going to think it has to do with . . ."

"That's right. Think it over, now. I have to go. We expect to be busy. People phoning like."

"Oh the brush-off now, is it? Well I've me own things to do, you know."

Minogue pushed his fingertips hard into his temples. Touchy, he'd forgotten.

"We'll talk later, can we, love? You're taking everything handy now, I hope?"

"It's not a *disease*, Da. You're like Pat: 'Sit down, dear. I'll do that, dear.'"

The inspector squashed the urge to ask about Pat, how his lectures were going. Iseult's husband lectured three days a week in Limerick. Kathleen had been sharply rebuffed again the other day with her inquiries. She had been petrified to learn from Iseult herself that she, seven months pregnant, had been waist high in the sea by Killiney one evening recently. What in the name of God did she do that for? Wasn't it cold, wasn't the water dirty, couldn't she have lost her footing even with Orla there? Didn't she know how dangerous the tides were there? Iseult had cut her off. Didn't Kathleen know about intrauterine intelligence? That babies learn so much in the womb? Imprinting? That they respond to music and talk?

Minogue remembered Kathleen trying to understand what Iseult was saying. He had turned up to a lunch date with Iseult to find her sound asleep on a seat in a great hall in the National Gallery. She was sprawled under an enormous picture, with a guide tiptoeing up and down next to her. Imprinting, she told him while she ate a meal bigger than his: her baby would feel the beauty she felt. A piano recital at the opening of a Cubist exhibition was proof, she told him. She'd never felt him — or her — move around so much.

"It'd please me to know you're not going to be bungee jumping or the like."

"Ah don't be fussing! I'm only going out into the bay proper, for a real dip."

"You're serious? I can't tell. I want to sleep —"

"It's all arranged. Orla's da. He has a boat."

"Any chance you'd swap that for a walk in the woods by Katty Gallagher?"

"What are you going to do, roll me up to the top?"

"I might. Tully, then — no climbing? A little pick-me-up in Jerry Byrnes on the way home —"

"— Oh you're cruel, so you are! I haven't had a pint since I found out."

"Sorry. I forgot. Watch me drinking one then, can't you. Imprint that?"

"Ah you're a bad pill, Da!"

$$\bullet \qquad \bullet \qquad \bullet \qquad \bullet \qquad \bullet$$

The smell of fresh tea brewing had made Minogue even dopier. He nibbled slowly on the biscuits. Nearly eight million a year passing through Dublin airport. He listened to the two detectives Murtagh had detailed to handle the call-ins. No, he assured one of them, they didn't have to okay a follow-up by him. Murtagh was the ringmaster for communications within the squad, or what was now technically a task force. What procedures need they follow to secure resources from other Garda departments, a Serious Crime specialist, for example, one of the detectives wanted to know. Demand instant compliance, Minogue had murmured. Only half joking, he told the most visibly surprised, a Liam Brophy new to the pool from the Kevin Street station. Run it first by John Murtagh if he, the inspector, was not there.

He reminded them that all lines in were monitored and recorded. He warned them again that while most of their calls would be coming in through the switchboard, there could be directs. These were often the most valuable. They needed to be handled with extreme care. The request for a trace was automated now: the orange button to the side of the redial. Signal immediately to a squad member if a direct came on: don't worry about being overcautious. A corpulent, fuzzy-redhead detective named Boyle asked if they'd be detailed interviews on follow-ups.

It was only when Minogue was listening to Sheehy explaining why it would take so long to go through the flight lists for stand-by passengers that he remembered he had meant to phone Kathleen. He thought of the barbed wire, how Iseult had wound it around the piece. What have we done, I done, Kathleen must wonder, that my daughter could think like this. Nothing personal Ma, it's art?

Sheehy moved on to a summary from Serious Crimes. A Danny Donegan from Fairview had tried a small ring of car specialists at the airport several years ago. One of his cronies, Peter "Bongo" Murphy, had been done for breaking into cars there. Murphy was currently in jail for later offenses: house breaking, several shops, a lorry load of beer he'd robbed at a new stop on the N 11, and tried to fence solo in Galway. Serious Crimes were stuck for staff as usual. They'd try to get time for follow-up on them. Drug Squad and Intelligence were a compiling a list of operations they'd handled that had any airport connection.

Charlie Blake was the current liaison officer between the Gardai and the Airport Police and Fire Service. Minogue studied Blake's profile while he spoke. What kind of a bird would have a beak like that nose of Blake's, he wondered. The divinity that shapes our ends indeed. The way he tugged at his nose: was that body language for I don't want to be here or I don't really know what I'm talking about? Minogue picked up another biscuit, eyed it. Shouldn't, he thought, and bit into it.

There was no organized ring working cars at the airport recently, Blake believed. The passenger baggage flows had all been done since the new terminal went up. Hoax runs had turned up excellent results. Money spent on state-of-the-art electronics, the imaging and the sensors, was paying off. The last paramilitary run on the place had been two years ago: a header from a breakaway bunch of the UDA tried to place incendiaries. The APFs had done a joint snatch with some of Trigger Little's squads. Minogue remembered a would-be bomber claiming that one of Trigger Little's squad had shoved a gun in his mouth and pulled the trigger.

"Fergal," said Minogue. "We keep on hearing video and electronics and the whole rigarmarole. So how come we find nothing on the car park?"

"'Upgrading,'" said Sheehy. "'Updating.' 'Long-term area's not a priority zone.'"

"It would be if there was a shagging car bomb parked there," said Malone.

Sheehy put up his hands. Minogue studied the map on the board again. He followed in his mind's eye the access road in from the motorway.

"So I think we'll have to ask . . ." Sheehy was saying. Minogue scrambled to retrace the comments he'd been half-listening to.

"To be sure, Fergal. I'll phone myself and turn the wheel."

Promised the world, he thought: seconding two detectives from Serious Crimes, short of staff or not, to go full-time on airport leads was little enough for Tynan to take. He looked at the blank TV screen. No phones ringing. The nine o'clock news would deliver?

"'Touring the west,'" said Minogue. "Where'd that one start?"

"The girl at Emerald," Murtagh said. "She's certain. He asked how long to Donegal. She advised going through Sligo and staying out of the North."

And he might well have taken her advice, Minogue thought. He'd push that over to Tynan too. The commissioner could decide for himself who'd put in the request for assistance from the Brits on border traffic. The phone rang.

"Yes it is," the detective said. He waved at the group by the boards. "Good. What's her number?"

"John," said Minogue. "The one who thinks he was traveling with a woman. Did you get anything there?"

"It's the one in Sligo, Mrs. Rushe. I had a chat with her about four o'clock. She said that Shaughnessy showed up looking for a place. 'Nice enough, American.' Half an hour later, a woman shows up and signs in. 'Irish, well dressed.' She had her own car, but Mrs. doesn't know what kind. Signed in as Sheila Murphy. 'Nice girl,' mid- to late-thirties. Well spoken. It was only the next day Mrs. got the idea that the woman and Shaughnessy might be connected. Chatting at the breakfast, they were, says she."

"A color even?" Minogue tried. "The car, I mean?"

"Nothing on that. I'll have to try again."

"They left around the same time anyway," said Murtagh.

"Does Mrs. know who was sleeping where that night?" Minogue asked.

"She doesn't be inquiring, she says. As long as there's no messing going on."

B & Bs in rural Ireland not checking for wedding rings or the like? Now there was progress, Minogue reflected. He'd tell Leyne that too, if he was asked.

Murtagh nodded at the computer screen.

"There's no Sheila Murphy in the crime box," he said. "Social Welfare has thirty-seven Sheila Murphys. Twenty-something of them could match the age."

"Any description of this woman to go on, John?"

"'Refined.' 'Casual, but well turned out.' She thought Dublin first, but says she heard a country accent under it. Very fair hair, stylish do. A pageboy kind of cut, Mrs. said, the way you see it in the magazines. Jeans though. An over-the-shoulder class of bag was all Mrs. saw. Paid cash."

"She went out later on in the evening?"

"She did. So did Shaughnessy. Mrs. heard one of them coming in about twelve. Only one, she thought, but then she heard some whispering. She didn't check who went where."

"A one-night stand?" asked Malone. "Did you ask her about the sheets?"

Minogue leafed through the photos again. He lifted out the one taken at the opening of the art exhibition. The woman's back was to the camera. You could only see from her shoulders up. Her hair was blond.

"A hairdo like that, maybe?"

Murtagh sat back.

"I suppose. I'll be looking out for it."

One of the detectives handed an information slip to Murtagh.

"Call in from Donegal, a garage in Gweedore. A fella thinks he sold petrol to Shaughnessy awhile back. He doesn't remember any red car. He's going to go back into the books and see."

"Follow it," said Minogue. "Get a statement out of him. The day's the first thing we need — and if there was a woman in the car too."

The phone rang again while Murtagh was plotting a route on the map with the end of his Biro and guessing the times it took to drive without stops. Minogue watched Brophy writing up the information form. The other line rang.

"A bit of life now," said Sheehy. "Maybe we'll get the jump yet."

Minogue wrenched his gaze away from Brophy's Biro. The biscuits has done in his appetite. He wondered about soup. He should phone Kathleen and let her know he'd be late. As is she didn't know. He was getting a headache. The phones had gone silent again. He didn't want to go checking in with Tynan.

Éilis was signing for an envelope from a courier when he stepped out into the squad room. Murtagh had taken the package already and had opened the flap. Photos slid out. Contact sheet, seven or eight 8 x 10s with yellow stickies on them.

Murtagh laid them out on his desk.

"These are the indies your man contacted for us."

It was Sheehy who spotted her first. Minogue looked at the tag.

"That's the same gig," said Murtagh. "The art exhibit. Look: Shaughnessy there next to her. Give us the other one there — see: the hair, the collar. That's her."

"Here she is again," said Sheehy. He pointed to a group standing in front of a blown-up shot with fields and stones stretching to the horizon.

"Not the one with the belly and the dickey bow," said Malone. "The Humpty Dumpty looking fella."

Murtagh had pulled off the tag.

"That's some European Commission somebody. And that's her, according to this guy, O'Toole. Aoife Hartnett. The Humpty Dumpty fella there is Seán Garland. Dr. Garland, a big one in the museum. The opening of some exhibition at the National Museum. The . . . C-a-r-r-a? Carra Fields, it looks like."

"O'Toole," said Minogue. "The photographer? Have we a phone number for him there?"

Murtagh scribbled on a notepad and slid it whole across to Minogue.

"Casual enough there," Malone murmured. "Shaughnessy I mean."

Minogue studied the group again. Murtagh read out the list of names Turloch O'Toole had written on the tag. Museum staff, a member of the

European Commission with a French name. Some smiler from Mayo County Council, another one from Bórd Fáilte. The daughter of the schoolmaster who'd stumbled across the site. Minogue let his eyes rest on the photo for several moments. He turned to Malone.

"Portugal, huh," said Malone.

Murtagh slid a file folder out from under the photos, took out two pages stapled together, and laid it on the table.

"There's a copy of that statement from Garland there. It's an approximate about Shaughnessy's visit, when he showed up — as Patrick Leyne, mind you. There's staff phone numbers and extensions there. Her address is Terenure somewhere. It's on the search we sent to Aer Lingus to see what flight she took."

Minogue couldn't make out much of the other pictures in the backdrop behind the group. There was a piece of a diagram with back spots and some pattern, half of the title visible: The Carra Fields, a Stone Age enclosure of 3,000 acres that was causing people to rewrite all the history books. Was it Kathleen who'd mentioned them awhile ago? Kilmartin?

"John," he called out. "Can we get ahold of Garland this time of the day?"

Murtagh was halfway through a bag of cheese and onion crisps. He looked around for something to wipe the grease off his fingers before he plucked at the file.

CHAPTER 9

THE VOICE WAS SHRILL, querulous. Seventies at least, Minogue guessed. Rambling probably, was Mrs. Garland.

"Who is it again?" she demanded. "A Guard?"

The piping, haughty tone was sweetened with what he believed must be a Cork, a *dignified* Cork, accent.

"Minogue, ma'am. I'm an inspector in the Guards."

"Minogue? Clare, sure where else. You're a Corofin Minogue now, are you?"

"Further west, ma'am. Where might your son be?"

"You must be some class of a fish then. Or a seal maybe."

"Above Ballyvaughan, I —"

"— There's nothing above Ballyvaughan. Except for stones. Clouds maybe."

"And well I know it, ma'am, from trying to coax —"

"You're not trying to cod me, now, are you?"

"Not a bit of it. Is your son expected home soon?"

"There was a Dan Minogue in Foreign Affairs. Are you one of his maybe?"

A headache had dulled his thinking, gutted most of his patience.

"We're better known as the Murder Squad. But for now I'm merely —"

"Murder? What murder? Is Seán all right?"

"Sorry, ma'am. Of course he is. It's a different matter entirely."

"Well God in heaven, man, you put the heart crossways in me!"

"I didn't have the chance —"

"All you had to do was open your mouth, sure."

"I really need to talk to Seán, ma'am. Could I trouble you to direct me to him, as promptly now as I can ask, without giving offense."

"He must be a cousin then," she said. "Dan. Very direct but always civil. The nicest man you could meet. Oh, charm the birds off the trees. A real favorite with the lassies, so he was. This was during the Emergency of course."

Minogue let out the deep breath he had been holding. He slouched in the chair and surveyed the squad room. His eyes settled on the newspaper article about Iseult.

". . . DeValera, God be too good to him," she went on, "he put a lot on Dan's shoulders. Churchill summoned him to Downing Street in '41. Our neutrality was an act of war to the likes of Churchill. Of course he hated anything Irish — *hated* it. Dev knew he'd picked the right man in Dan, of course: with the charm came the iron. Oh I can tell you it was not business as usual for Mr. Churchill that morning!"

"When would he be expected home?"

"'Mr. Churchill,' says Dan, with that lovely soft Clare accent, 'Mr. Churchill. We feel for the plight of your people and the free peoples of Europe. We know what it is to lose our freedom, so we need ask no lessons in tyranny or freedom from you' —"

"Mrs. Garland, I have to ask you again if you would put me in touch with your son as soon as —"

"'Understand that we too have beaches, Mr. Prime Minister.' And as if that wasn't enough, he looks the old bulldog in the eye, without batting an eyelid: 'Speaking for my own family, Mr. Prime Minister, I am from the west of Ireland. My uncle was shot dead in 1920 by Black and Tans. He was a farmer with fifteen acres. Now, with all the might and force you could muster to invade my country, you would still have to cross the Shannon to the west of Ireland. And there' —"

"Indeed, ma'am. I —"

"Whist, will you! 'And there,' says Dan, 'there you'd meet me and my family.' Never entered the minutes, needless to say. Churchill almost threw a decanter at him, so he did. Oul toper, God forgive him. Hated Ireland, always. You'd be proud to claim relation with the likes of Dan Minogue! A huge funeral . . ."

"I must commend you on your memory."

"Hah," she scoffed. "Patronizing a woman of fourscore years. I worked for Dev for thirty years. Now, that was long before the corner boys and counter jumpers insinuated themselves, you'll understand. Long before the sloothering and shuttling off to Brussels and Strasbourg and the like, olagóning for grants and favors and handouts. Begging to be let sit with the fat boys over there, with their shiny suits and their sleek —"

"Mrs Garland, please: I don't want to waste the resources of the Gardai sending out Guards to find him."

Mrs. Garland said nothing. Minogue listened harder to the rustling sounds.

"Hello?"

"Don't be interrupting me! I'm checking his appointments here."

Minogue looked across at Murtagh. He was on hold on another call. He grinned wearily and shook his head. He heard Mrs. Garland whisper, pages turning.

"Now . . . Here we are. Yesterday was . . . Wait . . . What kind of people are we?"

"Pardon?"

"Set-aside: do you know about that?"

"I do, ma'am."

"Do you now. We have farmers paid by the paper boys in Brussels *not* to grow anything. And a lot of them spray the fields to prove they can't put in a crop there so's they'll get the grants. Poison, man — rank *poison!* Can you credit that? With everything we have, someone in Brussels tells Irish farmers to set aside land, a thing we fought and died for — even to *poison* it — and we *do* it? Sure land means nothing anymore. What have we turned into, answer me that. With the year of our lord two thousand bearing down on us . . . We might as well call ourselves a new name. Euroworms or something. Is that the way to start the next thousand years, is it?"

"Hardly."

"Here we are now. Seán is at one of his regular things. They go to a restaurant below the back of Merrion Street there. Do you like Gilbert and Sullivan?"

"Which place, ma'am?"

"L'Avenue."

"He's at a function there is it?"

"He's eating his dinner there. They go off to a pub afterward. Tuohy's. Do you know Tuohy's? Do you know what they did to it?"

An ex-football player had lavished a million and something pounds to disassemble a country pub and reassemble it, board by board, in the middle of Dublin. Minogue gave her no chance to start in on it.

"Thank you, Mrs. Garland. I do. Here's a number for me if I should miss him. If he phones, would you be kind and tell him that I'm leaving this minute to find him, ma'am?"

·   ·   ·   ·   ·

Minogue threw more water on his face. Still his eyeballs ached. He studied the droplets falling from his nose into the sink. The sneezing hadn't yet proved a cold was here. Maybe it was working its way express and stealthily to his chest though.

Malone was waiting for him by the door. He had phoned L'Avenue, gotten to speak to Garland. Garland had told him he'd wait for them there. He nodded at Murtagh hunched over his desk.

"John's gotten ahold of the sister. The Hartnett woman's, like."

Minogue took an extension and listened. Fiona Nolan was close to hysterical. Murtagh asked if she could give the key to a Guard and they'd let themselves in. Caught between panic and suspicion, Fiona Nolan said she'd have to discuss it with her hubbie.

Murtagh kicked off against the desk. He rolled no more than a foot.

"She's freaking out, boss," he whispered.

"Get her husband to bring the key then."

"See what she — Yes. Mr. Nolan? Yes. Garda John Murtagh, attached to the Technical Bureau."

Nolan asked if there was an investigation in which his sister-in-law figured. Murtagh rolled his eyes, gave Minogue a look and pointed at the phone. "Can't," Minogue mouthed. He put down the extension. He heard Murtagh begin to explain to Nolan as he headed for the door.

Malone took Thomas Street. He drove directly through the Coombe to Kevin Street where they met with the last of rush hour. He said *L'Avenue* several times, trying out different inflections each time.

"It's *oo,* Tommy. Not *yew.*"

"Lava-noo."

"You're close."

"Doesn't sound right. Sounds like Lava Noo. Who learned you your French anyhow?"

"Nobody. I picked it up."

"Garland's gay, I betcha."

"Why?"

"He lives with his ma."

"You were living at home until not too long ago."

"That's different. That was on account of the brother."

Minogue answered Murtagh's call as Malone drew up in front of the laneway. He eyed the painted sign for L'Avenue high up on the wall.

Nolan, the brother-in-law, was willing to let them into Aoife Hartnett's place, but only in an hour.

"What," said Minogue. "After he's been through it?"

"I suppose," said Murtagh.

"Tell him to smarten up, John. We're not across from one another in court."

"I leveled with him. He's worried. He'll come around quick enough."

Malone turned into the laneway. There was an interior design place, a cake shop with a Russian-sounding name, an architect's office that looked like some of Daithi's Legos from twenty years gone by.

"There's nowhere to park," said Malone. "I'll park back out by the bank." L'Avenue was half full. There were skylights, vines that looked real, wrought iron dividers. Garland was sitting with two men and a woman. One of the men looked familiar. He had the guarded expression of someone who's well known. Minogue couldn't place him.

"I'll come quietly," Garland said.

Minogue managed a brief smile in return. The size of the head on this fella, he thought. And why did he remind him of a pigeon? The giant's head, the ruddy face over swelling wattles, and a spotted bow tie stole Minogue's attention for several moments. On the end of his short arms were fingers like sausages. Minogue made an effort to keep his eyes on Garland's face.

The others at the table returned the inspector's nod. The woman smiled. Garland grasped his jacket. He eyed the inspector.

"God, your timing is perfect. Inspector?"

"Matt."

"A close call entirely — Colm here was about to extort more wine from us."

Garland must have told them there'd be a Guard coming to call. Glamorous, no doubt, a whiff of danger, something to tell their cronies about.

"Oh yes," Garland went on. "He was getting ready to explain the subtexts in *A Rebel Hand*."

That's who the Colm was: Colm Tierney, newspaper columnist, prognosticator. Minogue's nose began to tickle. He searched his coat pocket for hankies but he couldn't find any.

He knew the surge of irritation wasn't just from having a cold coming on. There was something about these people here that annoyed him. Crank he was, and prejudiced. He knew it, and he felt badly about it, but he knew that wouldn't alter much of his impressions later.

"Colm's the man, I don't know if you're aware of it now . . ."

Garland waited for Minogue to blow his nose.

"Well Colm broke the news that Ireland had disappeared several years ago. 'The man who lost Ireland,' we call him."

Tierney's lips pursed. The smile, or whatever it was supposed to become, never made it. He looked down instead at the glass he was turning on the cloth.

"I keep on finding it," said Garland. "But he doesn't believe me! He's our resident postmodernist — here, did anyone hear the one where some scientist crossed a Mafia boss with a postmodernist?"

Malone had entered the restaurant. He spotted Minogue and made his way over. Minogue finished blowing his nose and glanced at Garland. He'd caught a bit of the punch line, something about an offer you couldn't understand.

"Can we chat here at one of the empty tables?"

A waitress followed the three. Minogue asked if the coffee was fresh. He gave Garland the once-over again.

"It's like I was saying to you on the phone, Dr. Garland," he began.

"Seán. Please."

"Seán. We're trying to locate Ms. Hartnett. We need her help in our inquires."

Garland looked from Minogue to Malone and back.

"She's gone to Portugal. That's what I know at the moment."

"Did she tell you anything about the hows and wheres of her trip?"

"Well, in a word, no. She has oodles of overtime built up, so — well, she did mention to me that she'd found a seat-sale thing . . ."

"Did she give a name, a destination?"

Garland's frown changed his face completely.

"No," he said after several moments' thought. "She'd be just notifying me as a courtesy now, not asking me. We're civil servants and all, but it's more like a, well, a crowd of academics really. Aoife'd decide on leave and such, like."

"Traveling on her own?" Minogue tried.

"Well now. I really don't know."

"'I'm going to Portugal' or 'We're going to Portugal'?"

Garland scratched under his chin.

"No, no," he said slowly. "I'm afraid not. No . . . Now, is this connected with this American that you were looking for, the man who was found the other day?"

Minogue nodded. The coffee arrived in a small cup. He glanced up at the waitress. Was there something else, she asked. A bigger cup, a lot less jazz on the speakers, windows. A pint; at home with a book. He smiled and shook his head.

"Now I'm worried," said Garland. "What can I do here, what can we do?"

"Sorry, Mr. Garland. Seán. We've been in touch with others about Ms. Hartnett's whereabouts. She has or had a sometimes boyfriend, and a sister here in Dublin. The sister thought she was going with a gang from work, a girls' week type of thing. That's what she told her. So here we are. Do you and she work together on a daily basis, now?"

Garland's frown deepened.

"No, not every day at all," he said. "But we'd be bumping into one another pretty well every day. Aoife headed up project teams with the OPW. We have regular meetings and consultations. Now, it's very informal too, of course."

"The Office of Public Works, is it?"

"Yes, sorry. We work very closely with their Historic Properties section there. That's their National Monuments Department."

"The last time being . . . ?"

"Thursday, I think — yes, Thursday. I thought back after you phoned. I left the office at lunchtime. She was going off to lunch as well. Aoife had been meeting with people to do with an interpretive center."

He glanced down at Minogue's notebook.

"After one," he added. "I remember. 'How'd it go,' I asked her. 'Great,' she said."

"She left alone?"

"So far as I know yes. I was talking to someone. Des McNally, yes. Out in the hall by the stairs, and she went by."

Minogue wrote two *l*s for McNally.

"We do be flexible in this environment," said Garland. "Everyone works hard. There'd be stress at certain times, of course, like any other . . ."

He returned Minogue's skeptical gaze. Then he gave a short laugh.

"Stress you're thinking — in a museum? Not like your work now, but . . ."

The missed sleep, the late-night calls, Minogue thought. The hunkering over a corpse, for hours sometimes; the ever new bafflement and disgust, the moment of truth for families and lovers.

"Ms. Hartnett's in a high-pressure job, do you mean?"

"Well no, not exactly. She's an assistant curator. She has responsibilities for several key parts of heritage. There's an awful lot going on these days."

Minogue leaned in over his cup. A couple was steered to the adjacent table.

"Tell me what that means in her case, will you?"

Garland put on a puzzled expression.

"I'm not sure now that this is where we should be going, now, er, Matt."

Minogue let the pause linger. He knew Malone would be giving Garland the look. That quiet barrage of indirect scrutiny, the restrained irritation, the aggressive indifference of a seasoned Garda to the fate of anyone who tried to bollock him usually had the desired effect. He lifted his cup and looked around the restaurant. Not bad at all, at all, the coffee. He watched Colm Tierney finish a glass of wine. Ireland's disappeared, he thought. Had it now.

"What I mean," Garland said then, "is that of course I'll be very glad to help out in any way I can."

"I'm much obliged, Seán," he managed. Garland sighed.

"I'm not comfortable discussing a colleague's professional life," he said.

Minogue watched Malone poke gently at the edge of his eyelid.

"Maybe I've given you the wrong impression here now, meeting here with a bit of socializing going on. I forget sometimes, you know. We tend to, well you can tell, try and stay informal. To someone outside looking in, it might look different."

Minogue nodded. He looked into his cup.

"Sorry now," Garland went on. He gathered himself in his seat. Fifteen stone, Minogue was thinking. Was that a hundred kilos?

"But I have to step back into my job and be duly cautious."

"Don't be sorry at all," said Minogue. "Enough said now. At this moment there's a Guard on his way to Ms. Hartnett's place to see if we can locate her, now."

Garland sat back.

"My God," he whispered. "You mean we have reason to be worried, do we?"

"Well now. This much I can tell you, Seán. We can't find Ms. Hartnett on any flight out of Dublin. I'd be most obliged if you were to keep this to yourself, Seán. We need to contact others, her family. It may all turn out to be a misunderstanding. A series of misunderstandings."

"But Aoife is not under investigation by the Guards, is she?"

"Not a bit of it," Minogue replied. "Now, you were good enough to phone us about a visit from this man who is the current focus of our investigation. Did you know anything about what he and Ms. Hartnett discussed with this American?"

Garland adjusted his dickey bow again.

"Well I don't really," he said. "It was only after me seeing the picture in the papers that I remembered him. I wonder if Aoife herself knows who he is, sorry, who he was. You see, we get a lot of people and groups and requests coming through the department. An awful lot."

Garland leaned in over the table.

"Culture and history and heritage, they're all very hot issues now. We're answerable for a lot more than digging up an oul pot and putting it in a glass case for a busload of schoolchildren to gawk at now. The way histories are handled and researched and presented is all very contentious."

"There's more than one history now?"

Garland gave Minogue the eye in return.

"Oh there's a right can of worms there. There are any number of people and interest groups and the like — stakeholders, they call them — in heritage now. That's a side of the job that takes a lot of time and training. It takes delicate enough management by times, I can tell you. I have three staff with MBAs, even."

"So you're busy, then," said Minogue. "Inquires, visitors, conferences?"

"All that and more, to be sure."

"Would Ms. Hartnett have discussed the visit with anyone else at the office? The American, I mean. Mr. Shaughnessy. She kept notes maybe?"

Garland looked up at a recessed light for several moments.

"To tell you the God's honest truth, I've no idea. Aoife's very organized. She'd probably have a note if there was something to it. She'd certainly have come to me if there were prospects from this thing, this meeting. But she's a fierce busy person. She's project leader on a big site plan that's moving ahead fast."

"Which, now?"

"The Carra Fields, out in Mayo."

Minogue knew that Malone had heard too.

"There was an opening of an exhibition about that recently?"

"There was indeed," said Garland. "With all the plans and models for the interpretive center laid out. Marvelous. It rewrites a lot of history, so it does."

Minogue met Malone's eyes for a moment.

"I've a colleague who'd like to persuade me that Mayo people are civilized."

"Well now he's got you," said Garland. "Stone Age people — late enough on in the Stone Age, to be sure. There were thousands of them — a huge cleared enclosure, with grazing and crops. And a big surprise was that there were no fortifications or the like. All of them living a grand existence without the rowing and beating one another we have later. Can you imagine?"

"Very civilized," said Minogue. "For Mayo. A Garden of Eden."

"Oh, I could go on and on," said Garland. "It's excited a lot of interest in Europe. It's the most important site since, well, we know what happened at Mullaghmore."

"To be sure," said Minogue.

An interpretive center in the Burren area of his home county had been left half-completed after protests about it had overruled the local peoples' support for it.

"Aoife can give you the ins and outs of all the things that need to be juggled and managed for this one. God knows! It's not just money at all, at all. She worked on Mullaghmore too. I remember she saw it coming too, the showdown over that. Anyway, the Fields will be a showpiece entirely. There'll be no slip-ups with this one. It was heritage funds from Europe that made the big difference."

"She's putting the finishing touches to this whole project, you say?"

"Oh yes," said Garland. "We have the funds, the plans approved. We're into tenders already and the nitty-gritty. There's great support all over. Sure the planning and approval process was nearly a love-in. A lot of that was due to Aoife. She has that combination: a real expert in her field, and she knows how to manage outside of the fieldwork. Ideal."

Minogue searched Garland's face for any irony.

"We're ahead of the pack here in Ireland," he went on. "People are coming to Ireland for a lot more than the forty shades of green now. They want to see nature yes, but they want to see a place and a people full of history too, people on the periphery of the continent. I'm not sure that we know what we're sitting on here."

Minogue watched a customer looking down the wine menu. These Carra Fields was nearly as far into the west as you could get without falling off into the sea.

"Yes indeed," Garland added. "Like the economists say, we have good fundamentals, in the line of history. Tremendous historical resources."

"Our time has come, has it," Minogue said.

"It has indeed," said Garland. "And not a moment too soon."

"How do you mean?"

Garland rubbed at his nose. He looked at Minogue's writing in his notebook.

"Well, it's an open secret the way things had been going," he murmured. "So much had been lost."

"Lost," Minogue said.

"Yes. Chalices from monastic sites were dug up and melted down hundreds of years ago. Finds that were never reported. Standing stones used to hold up fences. The Béara Chalice, do you remember that?"

"From the field down near Ballyferriter there a few years ago?"

"That's the one," Garland said. "We had to give thirty thousand pounds to the finder for goodwill. Honest man he was, that turned it in, and him after turning the field one October and there was the chalice lying there with a big dent in it from the harrow . . . But sure what matter. A bog will push stuff up and you can never tell when or where. The thirty thousand was to tell people they'd be well paid to turn in things rather than be conniving or just breaking things up and selling them. And nowadays any fella in off the street can buy any number of electronic gadgets."

"Like what?" from Malone.

"Metal detectors — curse of God on them. Well I remember the meetings we used to have back in the early '70s, when we got the first of the satellite images and we had a bit of money to do the aerial surveys. Oh, you'd laugh — or cry, maybe."

Garland looked over his shoulder at the group he had left.

"It was Hobson's choice there," he said. "We had to decide back then if we should even be making public the digs and the finds until after we had the sites set up and secured."

Minogue had a second after the tickle before the sneeze erupted. When he finished blowing his nose he looked up to find Garland staring at him.

"Tell you what I can do," Garland said. The fingers, so short that the inspector couldn't stop staring at them, were tugging, poking under Garland's chin. "Come around to the office with me. I'll see if there's anything lying around there that'd give us any help."

CHAPTER 10

GARLAND WHEEZED AS HE WALKED down the lane to the car. His gait reminded Minogue of a hen walking ahead of a vehicle trying to get into the farmyard. The inspector slowed.

"It'll be me looking through her appointment diary," Garland said. "More than that, I'd have to get advice on."

Minogue took in the flushed face, the chest rising and falling.

"You can see the situation, now, can't you?"

"Fair enough."

Malone drove around the green and down Dawson Street. He asked Garland about the mummies. Everyone wanted to know about the mummies and when they'd be back. Not a day went by without someone asking after them. What about the bog man, Malone asked then, the one that looked like a shoe. And the bloodstained tunics from the 1916 Rising, were they out being cleaned or something? Minogue almost smiled. Malone, like thousands of people probably, wanted these grisly, tatty, extravagant relics, the meat and potatoes of childhood visits to the museum, back on show. Garland sidestepped Malone's inquiries. He began talking about regional museums, sites, interpretive centers, restoration. Minogue eyed the group of young men drinking cans of something by the Kilkenny Design shop.

Garland told them that Viking Dublin was unexpectedly popular now. There was an interactive exhibit on Swift's Dublin being set up too.

"What, we'd get to talk to him," said Malone. "Have a pint with him?"

Two Guards on duty by the gates to Leinster House eyed them as they passed.

"Virtually," Garland said. "Go around by the car park here. The staff door."

Minogue eased his way out of the Nissan. A Guard who had been sitting in a squad car closer to the Shelbourne stepped out. Minogue met him halfway. The Guard looked over the photocard and then nodded at Malone. Minogue had forgotten who the statue was that they passed in the middle of the car park. A quartz streetlamp began to buzz and glow dimly by the corner of Molesworth Street.

Garland was having trouble finding his key. Minogue looked up to the camera over the door. Garland huffed and puffed, said damn, keyed in. A security guard met them inside the glass cubicle. Garland helloed him and signed in.

"Anybody above, Kevin?"

The security guard had long hair.

"Studio lad I think."

Garland led the two detectives down a hall to a staircase. Minogue pinched the bridge of his nose but he couldn't clear it. He glanced at the names on the doors, the titles: resource outreach coordinator, curators, field facilities.

"Where do you keep the mummies now?" Malone wanted to know. Minogue heard Garland's wheezes.

"Ah that'd be telling. Let's say they're under wraps for now."

A door opened on to a newly decorated foyer. It was gray with bottle-green signs, its lights hidden under a plinth by the ceiling. Garland opened a door that led into a large windowless room lit only by three security lights set into the ceiling. Moveable partitions ran the length of the room.

Minogue took in the computers in each cubicle. Postcards from Thailand and Donegal and New York, Israel, those rock-cleft palaces in Jordan. He slowed to eye a poster for the Carra Fields. Why the hell leave it black and white with masses of clouds looming overhead? Lugubrious, mystical Celt guff. Of course, that was it: the writing on the bottom was German. Calculated, marketed: smart.

Garland and Malone were waiting for him by one of three doors. Garland tugged at his ear. Dr. Aoife Hartnett (Litt M, MBA). Minogue tried to figure out the number of years that had taken.

"Tell you what," said Garland. "Let me just go into the studio and ask them if Aoife's checked in since. Come in and have a look if you want."

The third door: multimedia. That was something to do with computers. The hum from it was music. There were cartoons on the door about engineers, computers with faces, a Murphy's law, a caveman with a laptop under his arm.

The man facing the computer screen turned in his chair and pushed it back on its rollers. He didn't stand.

"Dermot," said Garland. "You're the night owl entirely."

Minogue nodded at him.

"Dermot Higgins," said Garland. He had to ask Malone's name before introducing him.

Minogue registered the stubble, the cropped hair, the T-shirt of a fake Egyptian fresco with microchips among the figures. If he'd tidy up the face, his dark looks would fit handily on a paperback cover: a hero, the shirt in flitters and lathered in sweat, carrying your basic swooning, busty heroine away from a burning castle.

Minogue's eyes strayed to the monitor. The screen filled with fog and slowly cleared to reveal a map of Ireland. Small pictures the size of postage stamps surfaced from the map and began to glow and pulsate.

"Any word from Aoife there, Dermot?" Garland asked.

Higgins shook his head.

"No," he said. "Haven't heard since she went, er . . . ?"

"It's okay," Garland said. "They know she's on a holiday." He turned to the two detectives.

"Bet you don't know what this is, on the screen."

Malone leaned in to study the screen.

"The Carra Fields," said Minogue.

"Well, full marks to you, Insp — Matt."

Higgins clicked a mouse on one of the small pictures glowing in Mayo.

"You click on the site," said Higgins. "And — wait a minute. I'll get the sound up properly."

He tugged a set of headphones from a socket by a set of speakers and flicked buttons on what looked to Minogue to be a small stereo. The crack and rumble from the sound system startled him.

A bódhrán drummed vigorously, like a tattoo for battle before an orchestral background flooded in. Synthesizer, Minogue wondered. The screen dissolved and re-formed as a picture of an ancient village. Sounds of hammering and sharpening, birdsong, and distant voices began to take over. Work and daily life — that must be the idea. The picture faded and was replaced by another, this one of what looked like a family in an old house, gathered around a fire.

The voice-over, a woman, spoke in the present tense. "Greece is a collection of warring tribes yet," she began. "In Mesopotamia, the Sumerians are beginning to use uniform language. The pharaohs' tombs will not be built for two millennia yet. There are clan fights and bloodletting across Europe. In these Carra Fields live four thousand people, farmers and herders. They have a peaceful culture. They worship gods of crop and sun and water and air. They are highly organized, cooperative people. They are on average four inches taller than adults in Europe."

The pictures fading into one another mesmerized Minogue. He managed to glance at the others. Even Higgins looked lost in his gaze at the screen. The changed tone in the narration brought him back to the screen now.

"They will continue to live here for another fifteen centuries," the voice announced, "living in peace and then becoming a forgotten people at around the same time as Babylon falls. The Valley of the Kings will be abandoned to the desert and the Romans will dominate half the known world. Greek civilization will flourish and then fade, as will Rome's. The Middle Ages will dawn and then fade. The first planes will pass over the west coast of Ireland before the world will know the Carra Fields again."

Images began to fade and arrive faster now. Long, walled fields, loose-stone dwellings, kilted and breeched ancients laboring happily among crops, sounds of cattle lowing. Who are these forgotten people? the narrator asks. An intricate pattern of stones made into a wall formed the rest of a burial chamber. A fire burning in an open field at night. The narration gave way to music again.

Higgins hit some keys and the screen returned to a map of Ireland. He rolled away again and folded his arms. Minogue looked around the room. A half dozen computers, several high-tech mystery boxes, lots of wires, cluttered desks, shelves overflowing.

"Deadlines," said Garland. "History doesn't wait for anyone now."

"Is this part of Ms. Hartnett's project?"

"She's the coordinator," said Higgins. "She set up the project and sorts out who and when and that."

Garland turned to Minogue. He nodded at the screen.

"Dermot is bringing us into the modern age. We're set to launch a CD-ROM in, when is it?"

"Five weeks," said Higgins. "That is the plan."

"This'll be a first," said Garland. "You can put any language to it."

"Great," said Minogue. Garland shifted his weight.

"Sure there's no word from Aoife, Dermot?" he asked. "A card, maybe?"

"Well I haven't seen one yet. Sure she's only gone awhile. Ask the others, but I'm pretty sure."

"Does Aoife know the ins and outs of this stuff here?"

Higgins looked up at Minogue and scratched at the stubble on his cheeks.

"Well not the technical end really. The putting together of it. She knows how to run it, the software, I mean. She's in on the testing and all. It's a team thing, you see, it's not just computers. We have a graphic artist and a programmer too."

"Do you get a lot of visitors here?" Minogue asked.

"With Aoife, like?"

"With or without."

Higgins looked over at Garland before he spoke.

"There'd be people coming by fairly regularly though, I suppose. Sponsors, computing people. I don't be here in the mornings, so I don't know."

"Dermot's in Trinity College," said Garland. "The multimedia center there. The greenhouse-looking place by the train station. The Oh Really, they call it."

Minogue said, "You mentioned sponsors."

"Oh yes indeed," said Garland. "One of the banks, Bórd Fáilte, Apple. There's the European heritage money too of course."

Minogue gazed at the screen with the map of Ireland and glowing buttons.

"It's really something," said Garland. "Isn't it? No matter where you are in the world you can travel through Irish history — without leaving your chair."

Minogue looked at his watch.

"Tommy, will you follow along with Mr. Garland there? I'll be along in a few moments. Let me just look at this stuff a minute."

Higgins opened a can of Pepsi and rolled back to the computer. There was a stack of empty lemonade cans built on a ledge by the door. Minogue watched the mouse cursor flick about the screen, pages and pictures and boxes, folders opening and closing.

"A lot of pressure on deadlines, is there?"

Higgins didn't answer for a moment.

"As much as you'd want," he said.

"Part of the job, is it?"

"Yeah. No big deal though."

Higgins sipped Pepsi and looked back at the screen.

"It's an appliance," he said. He began clicking again. "That's all. Think of a telly. A car. A cooker. A stereo. You know?"

Minogue watched the erupting pages of words and colors, the dancing icons.

"What's the end result going to be again?"

"A CD-ROM."

A small window with an image of a sunset picture over a Celtic cross sprang up on the screen. The blurriness was intentional, Minogue realized. Higgins clicked a button under the cross. Minogue shifted his lean to his other foot. A film, by God.

A box of words appeared beside the film window. Lines rolled by themselves.

"Memory's cheap now," Higgins murmured.

"Memory?"

Higgins glanced up.

"To run the thing, sorry."

"RAM, is it?"

"Are you into computing?"

"No."

"Use them at work?"

"My colleagues do. I know how to run a search, a database."

"Ever see your photofit crowd in action?" Higgins asked. "The composites?"

"A few times."

"Impressed?"

"I certainly was," said Minogue.

The window disappeared, the mouse tugged at another, widening it.

"You can never have too much memory. To run the software, like."

"A lot of this can go on the Web site," Higgins went on. "Ovation."

A type of chocolate, Minogue thought. There was that subdued, almost dismissive tone to Higgins's voice now, a mixture of ardor and indifference that was familiar to Minogue. He had heard it off

Murtagh, the voice trailing off as he lost himself in some tricky bit of computing.

"Ovation?" he tried.

"Online Visitor Information. Doesn't really fit, but."

"Did you make it?"

"No. I put things together behind the scenes. Are you a superintendent?"

"Inspector."

A window opened on the screen. Something called Director flashed on.

"What's Aoife done?"

"Nothing that I know of. Do you know different?"

"I work with her. Aoife's the real thing. We'd be nowhere without her."

"Nowhere?"

"With this. That's her voice I used in the commentary, you know."

The screen went dark. The bódhráns began, and the screen began to fade into a map of Europe. A plaintive tinwhistle. God, not another one, Minogue thought: when could we drop the sorrow and moaning, the suffering history stuff?

He watched the slide show move from Vikings to Medieval Dublin, sounds of battle gave way to the marketplace. There'd be plenty more of the battle sound track, he reflected.

Higgins clicked the mouse and the screen froze. He took the can of Pepsi and squeezed it with his fingers in and out.

"It's a new paradigm," he said. "Do you have paradigms in the Guards?"

"We have a specially trained squad alright, but it's very hush-hush. How did you get to hear about it?"

Higgins continued to flick the mouse around in short, precise moves.

"With digital technology and telecommunications, we broadcast. We send out, like. People can download the information. Words, pictures, sounds, short movies even. We don't wait for people to come to us anymore. No need to wait for planeloads from Cleveland to hit Shannon for this."

"Tourism you mean. Or entertainment?"

Higgins spread his hands. Why that gesture — indifference, resignation, indecision — reminded him of a priest's gestures at mass, Minogue didn't know.

"Heritage, isn't it?"

Minogue stared at Higgins but he had turned back to the computer.

"All working out is it?"

"Everything's on target, yes. We're looking good."

Malone was walking through the doorway, Garland fussing behind him.

"Do you have a number I can reach you at, Dermot?"

"The museum number. There's voice mail now."

"I mean outside of the place."

Higgins turned back to Minogue. Garland was saying something to Malone about a meeting date next Monday that Aoife would be chairing.

"Why?" Higgins asked. "What for?"

"Just a chat maybe. Talk about virtual reality or the like?"

Higgins eyebrows arched.

"It's neither," he said. "I'm just a programmer."

Minogue laid his card on the table next to the mouse. Higgins picked it up. He scrutinized it and looked up at the inspector.

"Minogue? Is that you? I thought I heard Muldoon or something. Wait a minute. I know you. You were in the paper the other day."

"I don't think so."

"Not you, wait. It said you were with the Murder Squad. A sister of yours? Some family connection? Something to do with the arts."

"Iseult; I've a daughter," said Minogue.

Higgins rapped at the table with a knuckle.

"That's what it was. She's the one with the *Holy Family*?"

⬩   ⬩   ⬩   ⬩   ⬩

"Quite the yapper," said Malone, "is what he is. Cagey too, but wouldn't let on."

"Drawers weren't locked?"

"No. I just walked in and started on her desk. While you were playing video games out there with Super Mario."

Malone edged the Nissan up on the footpath by a cordoned-off hole in the street near Dawson Street.

"Heard of Ovation, Tommy?"

"Like a standing ovation?"

"Same word, yes."

"A new brand of johnnies. Condoms, like?"

"Try again."

"Chocolates."

"Jimmy's right about you. A right barbarian. All right, try 'online'?"

"Methadone clinic?"

"'Interactive'?"

"This one's easy: all the way on your first date."

"Try telecommunication, then."

"Another easy one. Phoning the 'mot to see if she'll take me out for a few jars. Come on, will you. Give me a tough one."

"'Download.'"

"Same thing. You drink a feed of beer, like, you *download* them."

"Haven't you picked up anything from John Murtagh?"

He'd try Murtagh then. The same Murtagh remained a computing enthusiast. He complained about bugs and crashes but he enjoyed fixing them. Minogue couldn't understand it. He recalled Éilis taunting Murtagh about something called Flight Simulator.

"You want a Big Mac?"

Minogue sighed. It was Murtagh who had gotten him onto McDonald's. His embarrassment hadn't abated over the years.

"I could get you a sambo but they're lying around all day."

"Nothing with cheese anyway, Tommy. Thanks."

He dialed the site van at the airport.

Fergal Sheehy answered. He asked Minogue to wait a minute while he double-checked. Two detectives were interviewing one of the security staff about a row earlier in the day. It was about the Public Works fans getting overexcited the other day. There had been four arrests and charges of assault on three of them.

"How many tickets are still outstanding from the car park?"

"Thirty-something," Sheehy said. "I sent three lads out looking up and down the cars to see if we could spot any on dashboards."

A group of teenagers walked by the Nissan. One of them stopped and held his coat up to shield his lighter. Minogue tried to count the rings in the eyebrow.

"What's the story on the video cameras put there, Fergal?"

Sheehy moved something around near the phone. There was a slap as something hit the floor nearby. Sheehy muttered something. The teenager caught up with his friends, elbowed one, and turned as he walked to eye the Nissan. "Yes, it's a Garda car, son," Minogue murmured, "and don't walk into the parking meter."

"Don't be talking to me about video," said Sheehy. "Joe Kerr is in charge of that stuff it looks like."

"Is it a cod entirely, Fergal?"

"The nearest points to the car park are duds. Black and white, dim. Useless."

Minogue didn't want to press Sheehy. He checked the clock on the dashboard again. He couldn't put off phoning Tynan much longer. He thanked Sheehy, asked to be remembered to his horse.

Malone returned carrying two bags. The scar tissue over his left eye shone as he sat heavily into the driver's seat. Minogue knew that his colleague liked eating fast food in the car.

"We head back then?"

"Let me phone Tynan's office, Tommy."

"What for? Have we anything to give him?"

Minogue pushed the antenna in and drew it out again several times.

"Well, no. There are no go-aheads from the site yet. The timetable's full of holes still. The freephone call-ins, or lack thereof . . . tell me that Shaughnessy had a magic car that doesn't need petrol —"

Minogue let go of the antenna and stared across at his colleague.

"What?" asked Malone. "There's no cheese in it. I heard you — What? What're you looking at?"

"Does Aoife Hartnett have a car?"

Malone looked down at his Big Mac. He shook his head once.

"Oops," he said. He turned the burger, eyed it, and bit into it.

CHAPTER 11

THE VOICE ANSWERING, a man's, had an edgy, suspicious tone. Minogue wondered if the detectives going through her apartment were listening in too. Aoife Hartnett's brother-in-law was put out at being called by his name immediately. He asked Minogue to repeat the introduction.

"A technical bureau, did you say?"

"Right, Mr. Nolan. I'm the officer in charge of the investigation. We're hoping to contact Aoife. We need her help in relation to a case."

Minogue checked his notebook. Yes, the Escort had put up fourteen hundred kilometres. Murtagh had pulled up a Micra for Aoife Hartnett on the computer.

"I know," said Nolan. "The American. Look, now that I've got a chance to speak to you — I'm getting very worried about all this. I don't like it at all."

"It's goodwill, Mr. Nolan, and we appreciate your help. I can tell you that there was no thought of seeking a warrant. We're concerned too."

"Oh it's not the property I'm talking about here. There's nothing to hide on Aoife's part. I mean that the whole family is this close to complete panic here at this stage. It's as much now as I can do — wait, hold on a minute."

Minogue heard the phone being placed on something hard, Nolan calling to one of the detectives: *not while I'm on the phone.* Minogue eyed the traffic slowing by the wall of Trinity. Malone continued to suck hard on a large Coke.

"What are you getting at?"

"Is her car there, Mr. Nolan? A Nissan Micra. Where would it be parked?"

"Let me go and look."

"May I talk to the senior detective there?"

Minogue asked Detective Garda Liam O'Connell what he'd found.

"Lives alone, it looks like," said O'Connell. "No signs of disturbance."

"Passport yet?"

"No. There's bills and bank things and that but damn all else."

O'Connell's voice dropped to a murmur.

"Your man, the brother-in-law, is getting twitchy about us looking around in the wardrobe and the like."

"Okay," said Minogue. "He's a solicitor. If he says enough, don't be cute about it — just walk away from it. Any sign of travel plans?"

"Can't tell if she took a suitcase or that . . . clothes, I don't know."

"What's in the place then?"

"Built five years ago. It's a two bedroom. She has a computer in one of them. Tidy enough. Kitchen's well looked after. Tins of beer, some wine around. Locks are good. Place left tidy. She has a deadbolt and a serious chain on the door. Neighbors, well one is a couple, no kids. Meagher. Works in the bank, wife's in insurance. Other ones not home. He thinks it's a teacher or the like. Lecturer. They're renting."

"No stash?"

"Jewels, prize bonds, the old heirlooms? Not yet."

"Where's the car parked? Her spot, like?"

"I think there's rows of places out the front of the whole place with numbers. Wait a minute, here's your man back —"

The phone changed hands.

"— I can't see her car!"

Minogue heard panic clearly in Nolan's voice now.

"Do you think she left it at the airport?"

"God, no — why would she . . . ?"

Minogue knew by the tone that Nolan didn't think so either. If you lived in Dublin, you wouldn't park overnight at the airport.

"She could have driven to Belfast for a flight," said Nolan. "Or Shannon . . . wait, who'd fly from Shannon to . . . Jesus. Listen, look . . ."

"Mr. Nolan. Give me some time here now. Have you a pen and paper?"

"You think something's happened to her but you won't say it straight out."

"I don't think anything. Help us on this. Can you —"

"Wait a minute. This is upside down here. You're telling me you want me to help you, or should I say help these Guards here going through Aoife's belongings? What's going on here? You haven't told me half of it."

"Give me a minute," Minogue said. "And I'll tell you what we know —"

He held the phone away from his ear when Nolan interrupted. Malone glanced at him and rolled his eyes. He had wolfed down the Big Mac. Now he took the straw out of his drink and began stroking his nose with it.

"No," he said when Nolan paused. "I'm not suggesting that. Your sister-in-law met him several times."

"I never heard of him, well, until this thing."

"She was seen at at least two functions he attended. I want to ask her a few questions about him."

"But she's not actually 'missing' is she?" said Nolan. "I thought you had to be gone for weeks before they — before you — used that term. Right?"

Minogue listened to Nolan breathing through his nostrils, the phone moving about. Malone began to crush his straw.

"Listen, Mr. Nolan. I don't want to alarm you or cause distress now. Miss. Hartnett can't be found. We have to step through this door. You can help us, help all of us, and speed things up."

"What, then? I mean, of course, but this is such a shock."

"We have the number of her car, the Micra. I'm going to issue an appeal on it. Tonight, even, on the news, but certainly tomorrow. It's green?"

"Light green," said Nolan. "A mint kind of green. It's about four years old. Aoife bought her apartment two years ago. I remember helping with the move."

"No fella?"

Minogue didn't care how it sounded. He eyed Malone.

"Current, like," he added.

"No. There was Gerry Whelan until last year. We got to know him fairly well. He's off in Brussels. I think it was the long distance thing wore them out."

Minogue's Biro had hit a greasy patch on his notebook. He scribbled hard to write it. The damned hamburger had made his fingertips slimy.

"W-H-E-L-A-N?"

"Yes, I think. He's an economist. Something to do with the OECD?"

Minogue skipped down the page and found a part that would take the pen. He tried to recall what OECD stood for.

"Brussels, I think," said Nolan.

Magritte, thought Minogue, and saw the floating loaves, the clouds, and the levitating hats. We'd all be Belgians soon anyway.

"Would you or your wife know her travel agent now? Had Aoife done other trips like the one she mentioned, the Portugal idea?"

"Oh sure. She used to do them more, the weekend in London kind of thing, but she was more careful with the money after she bought the apartment."

Minogue tried Nolan for places he'd heard Aoife Hartnett traveled to by choice. Liked Paris, he knew: went with Fiona, and he'd had the kids for five days — that was a few years ago. Munich for some conferences; a university thing on archaeology somewhere in Austria. A Celtic thing, he thought. She hadn't done a huge amount of traveling in the job this past while that he'd heard anyway. Still liked going down the country the odd weekend. Such as?

"Oh, B & Bs. Hotel packages. Galway, I think. She really likes Clare, a lot."

"Little wonder."

"Pardon?"

"The west, you say."

"Yes. She's been up to her eyes at work, you know. It's not that she doesn't like it. She was out to Mayo and Galway there over the summer. That was work, I think, but she'd stay on until Sunday or even Monday morning."

"The Carra Fields?"

"You know about that? Yes, that's starting up. That's right — look, I'm going to have to tell the mother-in-law. Right?"

"That would be a good idea, Mr. Nolan."

"I don't know what, or how I'm going to do it. Mrs. H is just out of the hospital, you know. Maybe Fiona will — Christ . . . ! Excuse me. She'll flip. It's all so, you know, so sudden. What am I going to say anyway?"

Minogue looked at a passing bus painted over to look like a soccer match.

"Make a list," he said. "Look it over a few times and then phone every third or fourth. Tell them to phone the others. It takes the pressure off you."

"She loves her job, you know. She's not the type to, you know?"

Minogue tried to figure out who the goalie making the impossible save was up by the back of the bus. Bonner? He wondered if Nolan would say it.

" . . . To do something to herself, I mean."

Minogue let the pause stretch.

"I hear you," he said. "It makes it all the more important to get details from people who know her."

"The kids just love her. She brought our Emma on a dig there last summer."

Emma. He'd overheard Iseult trying out that one on Kathleen one evening. She'd been slagging? Emma; Rebecca. What was wrong with Pat and Mary?

"Aoife never forgets a birthday. As busy as she is, and all . . ."

"Will you ask at home, Mr. Nolan, and get back to me, soon as you can?"

"The mother has high blood pressure you know. She nursed the husband after the heart attacks."

"I'm sorry now, Mr. Nolan. Far better that a member of the family relays it first. Here are two phone numbers for you —"

"Maybe she just *had* it, you know? Got sick of work? Everyone gets that . . ."

"True for you."

"Just needed a break, a bit of space? Well she'd *like* to have kids, I know that. The whole career thing, the biological clock, I mean. It's so tough."

A hiss from the phone caused Minogue to check the battery strength.

"There's no way I can say 'foul play' to Mrs., you know. No way."

"Say we'd like to get in touch with her, Mr. Nolan. That we're concerned."

"Christ, wouldn't it be a gas if she just phoned tonight from somewhere. London, maybe? 'Changed my mind, stayed in London! Surprise!'"

"To be sure it would."

"When will this go to the media again?"

"I'll be asking the press office to issue it as soon as I can. We'd like to be okay with the next of — her family, I mean, before it comes up on the news."

"That gives me a few hours, I suppose."

"We can't be waiting. The nine o'clock news tonight will be definite."

"You'll phone as soon as you have news?"

That's my question, Minogue wanted to snap at him.

"Depend on it."

"Okay then, I have to work on this. Okay. I'm going to start on it. Okay . . . ?"

Minogue pushed the end button several times. He stared at the charge level. Malone had rolled the wrapping into a ball. He was chewing on ice cubes now.

"What's the story with the brother-in-law? Freaking, is he?"

Minogue nodded.

"Her car's gone, right?"

"It's not parked there anyway. It might be in a garage getting serviced while she's away. Have to chase that now. I don't see her driving to the airport, but."

Malone lifted a bag of chips from his lap.

"No thanks," said Minogue. "How much do I owe you?"

Malone shifted in his seat and stretched his neck.

"You're all right. I'll eat them. Buy me ten or twelve pints sometime."

An ambulance with flashing lights sped by. Minogue thought of the evening ahead of them. He'd just have to take the time to map it all out tonight.

"Shit," said Malone. He threw the empty chip bag on the floor. "Rain's back."

Minogue studied the fine drops forming on the windscreen. He hoped Malone wouldn't turn on the wipers yet.

"Will we head?"

"Wait and let me call into Tynan. Before I forget."

Malone tugged at the collar of his coat, grabbed the steering wheel, and then flicked at the wiper stalk.

·   ·   ·   ·   ·

O'Leary had kept him on hold for two minutes.

"It's all right, Tony. I don't need to bother him if that's the case."

"Are you in town?"

Minogue slapped Malone's arm. He'd kept jerking the stalk to get more windscreen fluid on the glass. The wipers squeaked. Minogue flicked them off.

"Nassau Street, Tony. I'm on a cell phone."

"He'd like you to come by then. Soon as you can."

"I've nothing, Tony. We're still clearing a path here."

"He's in a meeting. He wants you in on it. So: will I tell him you're on the way, Matt?"

Brusque for O'Leary. Minogue studied the raindrops on the bonnet.

O'Leary said, "Concerns your case, says to tell you."

"What can I tell him that I didn't tell him two hours ago, Tony?"

"It's different. There's people pushing info here. The father, Leyne, is here. There's a meeting, in the commissioner's office."

· · · · ·

Malone drove along Andrew Street. He barely stopped at the junction of Wicklow Street.

"Is this a regular gig or what," he said to Minogue.

The inspector had been thinking of a hot whiskey.

"What gig," he said.

Malone accelerated hard up South William Street.

"Well I don't recall any get-togethers between Tynan and the Killer, do I."

"Really."

"Well, fella might think, you know."

"A fella might think what?"

Malone raced through a red light by York Street flats.

"That you have the inside track here with the Iceman. Mr. *Excitement*."

Minogue looked at the parked cars. An Irish coffee would do it. For the taste, not for the bite from the whiskey.

"A fella might get a puck in the snot," he murmured. "For insinuating."

Malone waited for a lorry to move out of the junction by Kevin Street.

"Why are you so touchy about it, then?"

"I'm not."

"See? I told you you were."

"There's no inside track. It's social with him."

"How could it be social only?"

"Because I say so. Because it can't be any other way."

Malone looked over. The hooded eyes, the tightening to one side of his mouth, could only be Dublin, Minogue knew.

"That a fact, boss? Twice today we've been bounced around."

"It's part of the investigation. There's pressure. Don't you be adding more."

Malone's eyebrow stayed up. He dropped a gear and raced the engine.

"Get used to it," Minogue said. "There'll be others looking over our shoulder on this one. Ask Jimmy about his digestive system when he gets back."

"Is that the one about the surgeons being able to make a map of his guts based on the big cases he'd run?"

"That's it. So don't be picking on me. I'm only an innocent country-man up here in the Big Smoke trying to get by."

"Me arse and Katty Barry to that," said Malone.

Minogue couldn't but laugh. It turned to a cough. He tried to volley back with his own concocted Dublin accent but he lost it halfway. Malone kept correcting him on how to pronounce *bollocks,* á la East Wall. Minogue started laughing again. "Owney a culchie," Malone said. He kept jabbing the inspector all the way up Camden Street. Sodbusters. Sheep shaggers.

Minogue hadn't realized just how good a mimic this gurrier colleague was. Cork met Kerry, Kerry met Mayo and even Clare. Malone got bet-ter the more he said. Minogue heard Kilmartin, his own throwaway ex-pressions, even Sheehy's aggressively laconic tones.

Malone didn't let up until he had pulled in by the checkpoint at Harcourt Terrace. Beads of rain flew off the car when Malone slammed the driver's door. He looked over the roof at Minogue. The same look an opponent would get as the bell rang to start the round, Minogue decided.

"I'll wait here," Malone said. "Polish the car or something while I'm waiting."

"Don't start up this again, Tommy. For the love of God, man."

Malone held his coat tighter.

"Hey, don't get me wrong, boss. I like the variety, et cetera. But I'm not a fucking gofer here."

"It's part of the case here, man."

"Oh yeah? Isn't the whole idea to get out of our way, let us do the job?"

"'Couse it is. We get the staff, the OT. The lab priority, the carryovers from the other branches, Intelligence —"

"Then how come we're heading up to talk to the Big One here?"

"Call it an education then, Tommy."

"Me bollocks. We're on a leash, I say."

"Tell him then. Don't be annoying me."

Malone cleared his throat, looked around, and spat. He followed

Minogue at a distance. O'Leary met them by the door to the commissioner's office. He ignored Malone's glare.

"Poxy out," he said. "Isn't it?"

"Good for the greens, Tony."

"Ah. A sign you're finally coming around?"

"I can't take it seriously, Tony. Sorry and all. It's the clothes basically. Himself is free now?"

"In a manner of," said O'Leary. "He's with those people."

O'Leary's face betrayed nothing. Minogue understood again that he couldn't help liking this how's-it-goin'-drop-dead Garda sergeant. Wasn't shy of a dust-up; loyal, quiet. Still waters, etc.

Tynan had told Minogue about several incidents involving O'Leary while he was doing his stint with the UN. O'Leary had knocked down a fellow UN policeman, a Dane he had become friendly with, for coming the heavy when a food riot was feared in a godforsaken village in Ethiopia. Self-preservation had been O'Leary's explanation. A mob had been restless and then angry after a badly parachuted mess of supplies had fallen on fresh graves where mostly children had been interred. The golf course that O'Leary had made was rumored to still exist and be maintained. It had been play a bit of golf or go off the deep end, he had told Tynan. The Dane visited Dublin almost yearly. O'Leary was said to know every bar in a particular part of Copenhagen.

"So," Minogue said. "Leyne. Who else is in there?"

"Billy O'Riordan. There's a handler too, a Yank. A lawyer fella, I think."

"Freeman?"

"The very one."

"Tony, I don't want to be giving you grief, now. But we don't work for Foreign Affairs or Industry and Commerce. Much less Bórd Fáilte."

O'Leary glanced over as Malone crossed his arms and leaned against the wall.

"I know, Matt," he said.

"So I want a word with himself before we're dropped into this whatever you call it. This, er, cabaret."

"I'll tell him."

Malone stared at the door after O'Leary closed it behind him.

"Fucking golfer," he said. "Paper boy."

"Give over, will you, Tommy. He's holding his nose too."

Malone strolled down the hall toward the lift. Tynan's head and shoulders appeared leaning out of the doorway. For a moment, Minogue didn't recognize the face sideways. What was the name of that header from Monty Python years ago?

Malone came in from the hallway last. Tynan sat on the edge of a secretary's desk. O'Leary stood by the door to a conference room. Malone began to take a keen interest in a postcard on a partition wall.

"Long day for you," said Tynan.

"It is that," said Minogue. "But there's plenty more of it left."

Tynan nodded toward the door by O'Leary.

"There's Leyne, Billy O'Riordan. A fella by the name of Freeman. You met him earlier on the way in from the airport."

Minogue nodded. Malone folded him arms again and leaned against a wall.

"I asked them in," Tynan went on. "They'd phoned earlier."

Minogue rubbed at his nose. It was getting sore from wiping and blowing.

"Can we park the badges a minute here, John?"

"Certainly."

"How much do we have to deal with these people in the near future?"

"As you need them. They're here to talk. It's information and it helps."

"Talk about what?"

"The deceased."

"Why are they in here, and not down at the squad?"

"They could and would if I'd told them. If I couldn't have raised you here on the phone while you were in town and handy to here, they'd have been dispatched there. He wanted to get my advice first."

"The deceased," said Minogue. "Our case."

"There's history to him," Tynan said.

"He has form?"

"It's not a criminal record," Tynan replied. "He's dirtied his bib. It goes beyond police files, so we can use it."

"Police files from where?"

"The hat holder, Freeman, has copies of files from Boston police. There's even an FBI mention. State police too."

"There's nothing in over our fax," said Minogue.

"Right. Leyne steered this stuff in here. Technically he shouldn't have access to this information, but he got ahold of it. So he wants us to use it, if it helps at all."

Minogue stared unseeing at the wall panel behind O'Leary. Malone shifted his weight to his other foot.

"The deceased related poorly to members of the opposite sex," said Tynan.

"He's gay?" Malone asked.

"Gay men don't go around beating up women," said Tynan. "Do they?"

"A woman is missing," said Minogue. "She was seen with Shaughnessy."

"That's why Leyne's here — so don't be giving me the eye. Tell me about her."

Minogue sat on a desk and related to Tynan what he had learned about Aoife Hartnett. Malone filled in bits about the photos at the dos.

"So," said Tynan. "Good career. High up in her job. Socializes. 'Networks.'"

"We're waiting for word of her passport or travel stuff from her place. A brother-in-law of hers let us in."

Tynan studied Malone's shoes.

"Well now. Mr. Shaughnessy: four charges, three from one incident. There are arraignments related to assault, both on women. One was in a club or a pub. The other was his fiancée. She dropped the charges then, upset the prosecution."

"Shorthand for bought," said Minogue. "Or did he say?"

"Leyne admits to a settlement. 'A matter of conscience.' So, his son has, had, no criminal record."

"Well whaddya know," said Malone. "Ain't life strange." Tynan gave him a glazed look.

"The father weighed in to save his neck," he said. "Leave the hows and whats aside a minute. The father has been detailing the son's troubles with the drink. And drugs."

Minogue rearranged his seat.

"Recent?"

"He thinks the son went clean this last year. We'll see soon enough with the toxicology?"

"Tomorrow," said Minogue. "A preliminary."

"Cocaine, the father's talking about, but highbrow. He was part of a set."

"What," said Malone. "Rich prats?"

"That's right," Tynan said.

"Out of control, was he?"

"The father says no."

"The father covered up before."

"I daresay," said Tynan. "But fathers will do that, I hear. An only child."

"All his ducks are swans, is that the story."

"You don't have to be the Holy Family to take that line."

There was no sting to it, Minogue realized. Tynan's gaze lingered. So he had seen the article on Iseult then. Tynan stood and tugged at his sleeves.

"So are you ready to go in and have a go at him for a proper statement?"

Minogue nodded.

"Another thing then. Leyne appears to be half-cut."

Lucky man, Minogue almost said.

"So give me a minute," said Tynan. "And we'll bring ye in?"

CHAPTER 12

ARMS FOLDED, MALONE PACED up and down the hall. Each step seemed carefully considered, as though where he so precisely placed each foot was a matter of delicate planning and balance. Minogue asked O'Leary where Shaughnessy's mother was.

"No contact. Leyne said they'd talked it over and agreed he'd come to us."

What us, Minogue wanted to know, but O'Leary excused himself. Malone kept up his carpet patrol.

"What if we get tired of sitting here pulling our wires, and just split the gaff?"

Minogue looked at Malone's back as the detective passed.

"Ballyhaunis," he murmured. "Bicycle patrols, Tommy. Rain. Culchies."

Tynan yanked open the door. The commissioner waited for Malone before pulling the door closed behind them. O'Riordan rose from his chair first. Younger than he imagined, Minogue realized. Maybe it was because he was used to seeing O'Riordan in a suit on the business pages. A slight smile set off by thick eyebrows raised high in greeting, but something puckish, even adolescent about the face too.

Leyne's greeting was a raised hand quickly dropped back onto the table. Minogue took in the watery eyes, the open shirt, the ashtray half-full in front of him. Fianna Fáil, he thought: bagman, fixer. Leyne waved at a half-standing Freeman.

"You met Jeff here," he said. He looked up sideways.

"What are you now, Jeff? What do we call you?"

"On our good days, Director, Management Support Services."

Minogue noted the attaché case on the floor behind Freeman. Leyne tapped his cigarette on the ashtray.

"You may know Billy O'Riordan."

Minogue nodded but O'Riordan extended his hand. Minogue turned to Malone. His colleague had jammed his hands in his pockets.

"Garda Malone here's a principal investigating officer on this case."

Tynan was first to sit down. His thumbs and forefingers joined and slowly separated over the table. A glance at Tynan's face confirmed Minogue's suspicions: wound up, calmly annoyed — a manner that Kilmartin mocked and feared.

"So, what's the news?" asked Leyne.

Nooz, Minogue heard. He flipped open his notebook and let it rest on his knee. Malone had pulled a chair out from the table. He sat almost behind the inspector. Minogue took out the bag of paper hankies and separated two.

"You took the words out of my mouth, Mr. Leyne."

He watched Leyne draw on a cigarette. Freeman sat the way only Americans sat: the ankle over the knee. Minogue blew his nose, crumpled his hanky into a ball and slipped it into his jacket pocket. Now he could smell the sweet sour-whiskey breath.

"Okay," said Leyne. "Patrick screwed up plenty of times. There."

"Could you be more detailed, please."

Minogue noted that Tynan's finger and thumb motions had stopped.

"I'm on the level here. Whatever he did or didn't do, he didn't deserve this. Dumped at an airport in the trunk, in the boot, of some rented car."

Minogue turned several pages back in his notebook. He looked up at Leyne.

"Your last contact with your son, Mr. Leyne?"

"A phone call the day before he left."

"He phoned you."

"That's right. I hadn't heard from him for weeks. I was in Palm Springs. We, I, have a place there. A friend of mine. Patrick was barred from visiting."

"Barred."

Leyne gave Minogue a glance.

"I kicked him out last year. He got mouthy, rude that is, with Pauline. Pauline and I are what you call an item. We've been friends for some years."

"Pauline's surname?"

Leyne's look fixed on Minogue for several seconds. The inspector did not look up from his notebook. He heard Malone shifting in his chair.

"Olson. Pauline Olson."

"O-L-S-E-N?"

"O-N," said Freeman. There was a tint in the glasses, Minogue decided. He returned Freeman's fleeting smile with his dull stare.

"Your ex-wife, Mr. Leyne. Her residence currently?"

"Geraldine lives in Boston," Leyne said. "We get along fine. We've gone our separate ways. I go to Palm Springs five, six times a year. Pauline's there most of the time. She's trying to be a movie star. She wants to do screenplays too. Her and a hundred million other people. Anyway, Patrick phoned. He came by the office pretty regularly, I'd have to say. Which was fine. I didn't want to have to guess what the hell he was going to do there. In the office I could deal with him."

"Where did he live again?"

"Well he'd had his own room with his mother, Geraldine. She kept it for him. In Boston. That's where he grew up, well from age ten anyway. When we split up. But he has . . . he had, his own place, since, well he was nineteen or twenty. His own apartment, I mean. That's how he wanted it. He'd call by Geraldine's a lot though. She's tremendous. She's a hundred times better parent than me. No secrets on that score there, er, Mike."

"Matt's fine."

"I'm an open book here, Matt."

"That conversation you had, the phone call. What did you talk about?"

Leyne coughed and lit another cigarette. He spun his lighter several times on the table.

"News, that kind of thing," he said.

"News? Does anything stand out? He told you he was going to Ireland?"

"Oh sure. Was there anything I wanted. As if there was no other way I could get it, you know?"

"Being . . ."

Leyne grabbed the lighter and stood it up.

"Christ, who knows? A souvenir or something? Ah, he was trying to make himself useful, I suppose. What's that word, ingra . . . ?"

"Ingratiate?"

"That's it. To make up. After his carry on. Trying to, well I suppose you'd say, be considerate?"

Freeman too was studying Leyne's work with the lighter. Leyne suddenly stopped.

"Trying to suck up, is a way of saying it too. Right, Jeff?"

Freeman opened his hands, shrugged, and looked at the lighter again. "Doesn't sound very nice, does it?"

"Your son had been through a bad patch, Mr. Leyne?"

Leyne snorted and he drew on his cigarette. He squinted at Minogue while he sucked on it. Never the patrician, Minogue decided, for all the money.

"That's what I like about here," Leyne said. "About coming home. No, not home. There's no going 'home.' It's hearing the way things are said here. 'A bad patch' or 'I'm sorry for your trouble' or 'God bless you.' It's not that they're beating around the bush or trying to pull a fast one on you — no. It's just that way of *saying* things. A 'bad patch' — and you're the cops too, the real McCoy too, the tough guys. Right, Jeff?"

Again the shrug, and a perfunctory smile, from Freeman.

"I'm only standing in for the boss," said Minogue. "He's on leave."

"Huh. A bad patch . . ."

Leyne sat forward, his elbows pressed hard into the armrests, and stared down at his cigarette. Minogue wondered if he was trying to keep from crying.

" . . . a bad patch. Right. Well, it was more like a fucking quilt. He'd been to Brentwood. That's a clinic, a treatment center down in New Jersey. A kind of last resort. That was last year. He'd kicked, he told me. Even the booze, but he could take a glass of wine and then stop. According to him anyway, he'd beat the whole thing."

"Is that true?"

"Not sure," said Leyne in a quiet voice. He let the smoke out slowly.

"The clinic tested him for drugs. I made them. Jesus, I paid them enough. One of the conditions I put on Patrick, we put on him, was that he get tested every week at the very least. Last I heard it was good."

"A condition, you said."

"Geraldine and I worked it out. The fiancée thing was the last straw. We decided to cut him off if he didn't get serious about his, his problems. Tough love, do people say that here in the old sod?"

Minogue nodded.

"The deal was he'd go to the clinic," Leyne said. "He'd take the cure, however long it took. Move to a new place — whatever. I told him I'd stand by him, get him started up. He knew Geraldine would too, of course. He had to shake off that bunch of bastards he'd been running with too. They were the problem. They were taking him for whatever they could. And he used to talk it up, you know, play the big shot. The name."

"Your name, is it?"

"Right. He signed things, he promised things, that could have gotten him time in jail."

Leyne took a long pull on his cigarette. He coughed and waved away smoke.

"Maybe I should never have bailed him out," he croaked. Minogue watched the color crest in his face and then fade. Brick red.

"How was he doing then?" Minogue asked. "After this treatment center."

"Seemed to be okay," Leyne said quickly. "I got him a start with a company near Boston. Denis Coughlan, property development. Denis'd get him trained and running, then he'd send him south. The Sun Belt. A lot of business is moving south. Patrick wouldn't be running the show."

He spun the lighter again, stopped it, and glanced at Minogue.

"Patrick wouldn't be able to run a bath. Denis would keep him on a short leash. Denis said good things about him actually. I was beginning to wonder, well, you know what I'm saying."

"So your son just wanted to have a chat. Nothing else?"

"He wanted to meet me."

"Did you?"

Freeman pushed at his glasses. Leyne stared at the tip of his cigarette.

"No, I didn't."

Minogue looked at the cigarette rolling between Leyne's fingers.

"I was busy," said Leyne. "I'm always busy. Christ."

He looked from face to face around the table.

"Look," he said. "I don't have that kind of patience. I worked my ass off. I started from nothing. You know, when I went to people here first with the idea that people would want to go to their fridges and take out frozen french fries — well, whatever . . . Marriages don't come with guarantees. But that doesn't mean that someone can go around blaming his parents for being fu —, for being a loser."

"Is that what he did?"

"He tried to. Any time I'd go after him, you know, show him reality, well he'd pull that one. But I'd have to say he hadn't been doing that for a while. No."

Minogue looked down at his notebook. Leyne rubbed his eyes with his knuckles and sighed. He sat back and looked over at the window.

"Did I want anything," he muttered. "That's what he asked me." He held his cigarette close to his chin and fixed his gaze on nothing.

"Guff," he murmured. "Bullshit, you say here now?"

"Both, Mr. Leyne. As a matter of fact I hear both terms used with frequency."

"Ah," said Leyne. "The political crowd here never changes, does it."

"It was my daughter actually I was thinking of."

Freeman allowed himself a smile. Leyne chuckled again. He eyed Tynan.

"Nice to see there are still some of the same Guards doing the job as I remember, Commissioner. The old guard."

Minogue didn't look for Tynan's reaction.

"Do you put much stock in the psychology stuff here? Patrick did. It's a bloody industry back in the States. He told me stuff about Ireland that he thought I was supposed to know. The Irish. Did I know any of the legends and that. Finn MacCool. Christ, as if we'd gone to school together. If I did, I don't remember him."

"Did he always have that interest, your son?"

"We brought him here on visits when he was a kid, but back then he couldn't get back on the plane quick enough. It was cold. It rained all the time. The people talked too much. Other kids here were out of it — all that. But then he started talking about things. I put it down to another shot at getting on my good side."

Put it down: the phrase circled in Minogue's mind. He thought of Daithi, how he still seemed to need to make him dispute, argue.

"Ah, some therapy thing there," Leyne was saying. 'Discovering your family' or somesuch. Victim shit. 'Reinventing your parents' was one of the things he blathered about once. Jesus wept. I mean, I had it explained to me by the people who ran it. The bottom line was, Patrick could get out of this habit he was always falling into if he learned more about us, about Geraldine and me. Figure that one out. Twenty-eight hundred dollars a week for that."

"If he understood you as people, more than just parents, is it?"

"I suppose. He thought if he'd do all this reading about Ireland that this would sort it all out. Ancient Ireland, for God's sake. Me and Finn MacCool, right?"

Leyne pulled his chair tighter into the table. Minogue eyed the bald spot, the once curly hair. It reminded him of some strange silver decoration on a Christmas tree, that light-as-gossamer stuff you pulled out of a ball and threw at the tree.

He spotted the top of the scar on his chest as Leyne straightened up. As though aware of the inspector's interest, Leyne tugged at his collar. The gap closed. A glance at Freeman told Minogue that he too had been watching.

"So there," muttered Leyne. "The Celts. Brian Ború. All the stuff I'd forgotten about fifty years ago. Talking about looking around for some university he could study it in. God, as if he had the marks to get into one. At the time he started this, I was just after getting into the foundation thing. I got talked into it a few years ago. What's it now, Jeff, the scholarship bit?"

"The Leyne Foundation," said Freeman. "Scholarship to study in Irish universities and four for Irish students to study in the u.s. The Visiting Lecturer Chair will start up this year."

"So," said Leyne. "I thought, well, Patrick saw an angle here. Sour, aren't I?"

"Let me go back to your son's situation just before he left for Ireland. He was holding down a job?"

"Yes. And he still had his own place too."

"He lived alone there."

"That's what he told me. He stayed over with Geraldine the odd time."

Minogue looked down at the page. Next time there'd be a tape, damn it.

"Eight schools," said Leyne. "Eight different schools. But he just didn't find that aptitude, whatever you call it. That focus. We worked and we worked, Geraldine and me — Geraldine and I. You'd think we'd be bitter, but we weren't. We're not. Geraldine dumped me, Mike."

"Matt."

"Matt. Sorry. She did. Geraldine is a lady. How I blew it was I had no discretion. I didn't have those smarts then, patience. Why would I? I wasn't born with a goddamn silver spoon in my mouth. I was hungry to make it. I went at a lot of things with the head down."

Minogue eased another tissue out of his package. He glanced at Leyne's shirt collar again. It remained closed.

"We don't play the blame game," Leyne said. "Geraldine and I. That's why I came to offer you what I can. To ask your help. For the second time."

He stared at Minogue. The inspector looked around the wall. The print of the mountains must be Rachel Tynan's.

"You're steamed, aren't you?"

Minogue glanced up from his tissue. Tynan began flexing his fingers again. "You think: who's this fucking tycoon sitting in here, going around your back, pulling strings. Leyne Foundation, money to the university here — what's the title?"

"The Leyne Chair in Early Irish History," said Freeman.

"This is not about special treatment here, Matt. I'm here to help. So's Geraldine. Patrick grew up with Geraldine. She did everything she could. She got him counseling and everything when he screwed up. It was her idea to start the private eye stuff."

Freeman began lifting three-ring binders from a bag on the floor next to his chair. They had a faux-marble finish. He slid them one by one down the table.

"This was after the first one. We settled that. It took nearly two years. The lawyers made a killing. The two-year thing was good because he had it hanging over him. She was a hooker, I don't care what anyone says. I still say he was set up. Her and that bastard who represented her at the hearings and all that."

He grunted as he slid the stack. Minogue made no move to take them.

"How does this help our investigation, Mr. Leyne?"

"I don't know if it does or not. It's my way of saying, of proving to you that I'll do anything I can to help you find out who killed Patrick."

"What does this cover?"

"There's three and a bit years. The full time was on for six months after he got stuck with that bitch."

Minogue looked at the logo on the spine of the folders.

"Shawmut's a small agency," said Freeman. "But it's done a lot of corporate stuff. Has a very good name."

"They did great stuff for people I knew," said Leyne. "They were trying to figure out how their competitors were always two steps ahead. They couldn't nail this Alison one on anything for us but they kept us clear on Patrick. It was to protect him. Us too, of course. There were people who'd like to have worked him and run one by us, I'm sure. Like that first one."

Minogue glanced at O'Riordan. He hadn't uttered a word. Sitting there, with a grave expression all through this.

"It's not pretty," said Leyne. "And I hate damn near every word of every fucking page in here. That's my son in there, but it's like he's a specimen. I paid for this, you know, and it kills me. Isn't that something?"

Minogue saw his eyes well up and he looked away. O'Riordan pursed his lips and patted Leyne on the shoulder. Leyne rubbed at his eyes, he took a deep breath and set his jaw. Mingue thought he heard a sigh. O'Riordan's hand stayed on Leyne's shoulder and he looked at the faces around the table. It was over then, was it, Minogue registered. The urge to sneeze had gone. Tynan pushed his chair back and slowly stood.

CHAPTER 13

Great," said malone. "Fucking great. A ton of books telling us who or what he did three thousand miles away. What a load of crap, for Jases' sake."

Minogue flipped by dividers. Patrick Leyne Shaughnessy had been a restless man. Maybe he should be cross-referencing these to phases of the moon. He stopped on a page that described a club called Coasters. June last year. Patrick had stayed for an hour. Left with a patron named Laura. Stayed at her apartment until exited at eleven-fifteen the following day. What was NCR? An adding machine?

"Talk about hopping the ball, boss. Mind if I puke?"

No Criminal Record — of course. She worked in a fitness club.

"What?"

"He's trying to steer the case, boss! Wake up, will you? You with me now?"

To the Exchange, lunch. Exited three-thirty with Karen Weiss to 301 Hyacinth Boulevard. Exited five forty-eight on foot to street. Taxi to apartment . . . Nice work, this property development job.

"Twenty-four hours a day, this crowd," he murmured. "That'd cost."

"Huh. To get him whatever his oul lad rigged up for him."

Exited apartment in car, 328 BMW convertible. Minogue closed the folder and stacked it on top of the other two. Malone examined his nails.

"We're thinking he flew over on his own," he said. "But maybe he'd arranged to meet someone."

"Who?"

Malone looked over his fingers again.

"This Hartnett one. We could start in on whether he phoned her."

"Say he knew her," said Minogue. "Knew *of* her anyway. To do what?"

"I don't know. Whatever screwed-up millionaire brats do. Hang around with cool people. 'The scene'? There's probably a southside thing over there in Boston too, wait'll you see. Losers and bollockses on the south side —"

"The usual hardworking salt-of-the-earth laboring men on the northside?"

"Exactly." Malone nodded at the folders. "And we're going to look for leads in this mountain of stuff? Huh. This is a screen, boss. It's to buy time for something. What do you think, someone followed him here from the States to pop him here? Oh that'll be great for us. Bleeding marvelous."

Minogue stood and stretched. The longtime companion ache in his lower back was announcing itself clearly. He looked around the meeting room. He wouldn't mind an office like this looking out onto Harcourt Street.

"He's dirty, boss. Clattering women and that. A druggie. Come on, now."

"Yes, Tommy."

"Record or no record. Don't get me wrong — I'm not out to nail him just because his oul lad's loaded. Stuff doesn't square up, yet anyhow. Look: he got clobbered for something here. Someone saw him in action, decided, well, here's a hit: rich, stupid — pissed even. Maybe he dropped the hand on someone's 'mot."

"You don't put much on any roots thing, do you?"

"What, the ancient Ireland stuff, all the glory?"

"Yes."

Malone cracked his knuckles.

"Ah now . . . ! Robbing and killing's the main event, boss. It's like Kilmartin says. Them's the stats this past twenty-year here on the squad, right?"

Minogue began counting pigeons prowling the footpath below.

"Tell me what's missing, that's my approach," said Malone. "You want to bet he was carrying? Cash, I mean. Maybe the American Express routine. Yeah, don't leave home without it — someone else's like. Jases, boss, there's hundreds of gougers walking the streets here who'd have a go at the likes of Shaughnessy if they thought they could get anything. Someone could be swimming in Margaritas on the Coasta Brava pretending to be Shaughnessy right now."

Minogue turned back from the window. He lifted the folders. It'd be a couple of days at least before they'd have any track of someone using stolen cards in Shaughnessy's name. A week even, if they were smart how they used them.

"Here, hard chaw," he said to Malone. "You carry them. We have other things to be thinking about at the present time."

Minogue held the door open for Malone. The hallway was empty but the door to Tynan's office was ajar. Minogue looked through the crack in the doorway.

"You're off then," Tynan called out. Minogue pushed the door open.

"We are. We have our bedside reading."

Tynan looked over Minogue's shoulder at Malone.

"You know what he's after, don't you?" he asked Minogue.

"I think so."

"What about yourself, Detective Malone. Are you wised up?"

"Me ma says no. But she'll always say that."

Tynan pushed his Biro into his tunic pocket.

"John Leyne wants us to prepare for the worst," he said. "Mrs. Shaughnessy would not be party to that last visit we just had. You know why, do you?"

Malone shifted the folders against his chest.

"She'd be in denial," he said. His voice had a tart edge to it.

Tynan nodded and looked up and down the hall.

"Did your ma ever tell you you should get on with your sergeant's exams?"

"Yeah she did. Sir."

"So are you?"

"No."

"Why not?"

"Too busy fighting crime. Sir."

"Get a bigger stick then. Stripes, Garda Malone: we need you."

•   •   •   •   •

"Another brick in the wall," said Malone again.

He turned the Nissan off High Street. He managed to find the largest of a series of potholes first. Minogue listened for new hums and noises from the car.

"What wall?"

"Mr. Excitement. Tynan. Throwing things at you out of the blue. His MO."

"He wouldn't prod you if he didn't think you could handle it."

"There's a pair of you in it. 'What about yourself, Detective Malone?' Jases. 'We need you.' Is he gay or what?"

"I've seen him merry, Tommy."

"You know what I mean."

"You told me once that denial was a big river in Egypt."

Malone stood on the brakes and swerved to avoid another pothole.

"Very funny, man. So very funny. I can be the gas-man Dub if you can hide behind being the Clare culchie."

"I am a Clare culchie. Ask Kathleen."

"You are on your bollocks. Am I blind or what? You and your shagging Magritte postcards all over the kip. Jases. The books — them snaps of those oul rocks there on the wall next to your desk."

"They're not oul rocks."

"What are they so? Houses the Martians built on their last trip here?"

"You win, Tommy. How did you know?"

"No wonder Kilmartin does be looking over his shoulder. That frigging carry-on of yours."

He knew the Nissan's speed wasn't a good gauge for Malone's annoyance.

"We're not going back to the Squad to be sitting and reading this stuff."

"Do you hear me fighting?" asked Malone. "But we keep the head straight."

"Aoife Hartnett, you're telling me."

"Right."

"Do you think she's hiding, Tommy?"

"No I don't," he said. "I think she's dead."

.   .   .   .   .

The rain started in earnest at eight. It kept going until nearly nine when Minogue went out to the car park to retrieve a box of Anadin from the glove box of his Citroen. It wasn't any one particular thing that had given him such a clanger. Not the call from Serious Crimes to tell him that so far their informants had come up dry on gang activity at the airport. Nor was it the call to Eimear at the lab to tell him that Shaughnessy had no booze in him, that the whiff Donavan had noted must have been decomposition effects.

He sat in the passenger seat and listened to the radio. He played with the fader and the balance and the presets and the idea of Patrick Leyne

Shaughnessy as a killer. He stopped a search when he hit upon something orchestral. It turned out to be a rather stiff rendition of Handel. The rain on the sunroof had almost stopped now. He looked across the deserted car park. He imagined the gush from a nearby gutter was keeping time with the music. He'd ask the bland Freeman how long ago his boss had had the heart surgery. Interesting to see if Freeman balked.

He slipped out of the Citroen, locked and alarmed it, and hot-footed it across to the door. He had forgotten the new dip in the tarmac left after last summer's heat wave. He managed to splash right up to his chest and even flick drops on his chin. He was in the foyer using a lot of bad language when Malone found him.

"That's desperate language. Who're you hanging around with?"

"Get away from me. I should have stayed in the damned car and driven home, so I should."

"Why don't you, so?"

Minogue shook two pills into his palm:

"Because I've nothing to sleep on, that's why."

"Oh here we go. Are you the one preaching the Watch and Wait stuff at me awhile ago? The black art and the Zen thing? 'The devil's in the detail, Tommy'?"

"I could have said anything by closing time in Willie Ryan's."

Malone followed him to the kitchen. Minogue half-filled a mug with water.

"We're firmed up on Donegal, at least," said Malone. "Those two places he stayed. One of the statements is in already. They have Guards doing the rounds in the pubs to ferret out more tonight."

Minogue let the water wash the pills off the back of his tongue. He stared at the chipped enamel by the front of the cooker.

"What's the link between the places he stayed?"

"Who knows," Malone said. "Except they're B & Bs, not the Hilton."

"If we could find her car," Minogue muttered. He drank the rest of the water and turned to Malone.

"We'd be clued in as to whether our man was acting the maggot. Prior intentions, plan. He must have said something to someone. 'Touring the west'?"

Malone leaned against the countertop and stretched his neck. Minogue heard a crack.

"She drove somewhere to meet him," Malone said. "That's where her car is."

Minogue's eyes felt like bruises now. Even when he closed them, they felt they might pop out and roll down his cheeks. The flu maybe?

"Hey, boss. Go home. We're all right."

"Phone Fergal at the airport again, Tommy. We really have to get a time — *a day* even — for the love of God."

Minogue trudged back down the hall to the squad room. The splashes on his trousers made the fabric cold and gritty on his skin. He rubbed his toes around and felt the itchy slip of wet socks. He stood in front of the boards.

Shaughnessy had started in Donegal, that's how it looked. He'd spent at least a day there. He'd been with Aoife Hartnett. They'd been in her car. Why? He wasn't scrimping: he was keeping his head down, out of sight. Shaughnessy had, as Minogue had heard so many times in the dry language of the books of evidence being quoted in court, formed an intent. He imagined him sitting in the Micra while Aoife Hartnett did the dealings: buying petrol, meals, booking a room.

He squinted at the map and let the names slide around in his mind. Ardara, Falcarragh, Gortahork; the Glengesh pass down into Glencolumbkille. Up again along that mountain road, out to Killybegs, and on to Donegal town. Down by Bundoran the marker's blue line went, through Sligo, and out to Collooney where it stopped by the question mark. He took the marker and uncapped it. He found Ballina and then the village of Cahercarraig. He drew the dotted line slowly and put his initials by the question mark.

John Murtagh yawned loud and long. He stood and groaned and stretched and groaned again and ambled over to Minogue.

"The guidebooks, you're thinking," said Murtagh. "Aren't you?"

"The crease on the page for Cahercarraig, John, yes. Right by these fields they're going to open up. The Carra Fields."

"And the interpretive center thing, right. She's the boss —"

Minogue's sneeze caused Murtagh to take a step back.

Murtagh was still poring over the list when Minogue finished blowing his nose. The phones had been silent for half an hour. Murtagh pointed at the eight-by-ten of the group at the museum party.

"She's the head honcho on that place, right?"

"The photo there, John. Yes. The unveiling of the exhibition."

"What else is marked in that guidebook from the car?"

"Just Glencolumbkille."

"Nothing for Mayo?"

Minogue shook his head. He stepped over to the photos. Wine glasses, panels with pictures and columns of words behind the group. Aoife Hartnett: a fairly public smile, if he had to find a word for it. Shaughnessy standing off to the side. Garland mightn't have realized who he was if it had been a big enough do.

Murtagh was back at the map with his finger in Mayo.

"Cahercarraig then," he said. "Five or six miles?"

"About that, John. Is it time we got our hardworking colleagues in County Mayo out on the roads too?"

"You were promised the world, I heard," Murtagh said.

Minogue looked over at Pat Curran, the lone remaining Guard on the call-in line. Curran had turned out to be a rower. Minogue had forgotten which Garda rowing team had gotten into a drinking spree at the Garda Boat Club two years ago and started throwing one another into the river.

"Thanks, Pat," he called out. "Go home, like a good man. We'll call you for follow-ups if we get inundated here."

Curran smiled and nodded. He stared at the phones for several moments as though to reproach them for not ringing. Then he rolled back from the table.

"John," said Minogue. "We can't sit on our hands waiting. You'll make the call to Galway. I'll call Mayo."

"Feed them the Micra, and this monument stuff too? Vague, isn't it?"

"The car for sure then. And tell them there'll be overnight faxes on Aoife Hartnett. Call us if they haven't received them by ten tomorrow morning."

Murtagh exchanged a look with the inspector.

"He or she, he and she, went on west to Mayo," Minogue muttered. "Every member, patrol schedule or not, has to have her picture and the details and Shaughnessy's too in their fists by dinnertime tomorrow."

He looked away from the map again. Murtagh hadn't moved.

"Go on with you, John Murtagh, and don't be looking at me like that. I know it's nine o'clock at night. We would have moved to an active search soon enough anyway. Any duty officers humming or hawing, or bellyaching, refer them to me."

Minogue used Kilmartin's office to phone Tynan. He hung up when the voice mail took over and dialed the cell phone number. O'Leary answered. He had dropped the commissioner home an hour ago. Did Minogue have the home number? Minogue pretended he didn't.

He was too bewildered to frame a witty reply to Rachel Tynan when she said his name.

"He said you might call."

Minogue heard music grow louder, a door close.

"Quite the statement," she said. "Did it surprise you?"

"The, er, case I'm on is it, er, Rachel?"

"The *Holy Family*. I really like it."

"Thanks — I mean I'll tell her."

"Had you seen it before?"

Tynan broke in on the extension.

"— Well be sure to tell her," said Rachel Tynan. "Don't forget, now."

He told her he would. He didn't know if he was fibbing.

"Excuse the hour, John."

"No bother. What's the news."

"Nothing stirring from the appeal yet."

"You're concerned?"

"I am. I am that. It's time to move. Let me cite your go-ahead for an active search in the western counties, starting tonight. The biggest they can mount. Overtime and leave canceled even."

"Tonight? It can't be in the morning?"

"Tonight. I'm the boss, remember?"

"There's no sign of her beyond what you had earlier, is that it?"

"Nothing. We're looking over lab results again, trying to pin anyone he seems to have had contact with here while he was in Dublin. The events he was seen at."

"You can place him until when, again?"

"There's not a sign after Sligo. The fine town of Coolooney. I'm juggling the possibility that he dropped out of sight on purpose. At least he wanted to avoid being noticed. I'm thinking he went into Mayo. There's the Carra Fields there. He might have had a particular interest in it. Aoife Hartnett is one of the nabobs on it."

"This Carra Fields thing, this site. What exactly is it?"

Minogue looked at the badges in Kilmartin's display. He hadn't noticed the Arizona one. No doubt he'd be coming home with a half-dozen more.

"Well it's by way of being an organized set of holes in the ground," he began. "They've been at it for six or seven years. A few prefabs and the like. European money came through last year to build an interpretive center. A half-million quid with more later. New roads going in around the place to get the buses, et cetera, in."

"A lost civilization in Mayo, then — or Ireland."

"Maybe, John, I don't know. I'm a stranger here myself."

"You'd better explain that to me someday."

"It'll have to be in a pub."

"Uh. Mayo — any word from our man in Boston?"

"Fame eludes him yet. Not a word. It must be a very intensive conference."

"If he calls, tell him he's doing great — keeping to himself, I mean."

"He'll get the hint I'm sure."

"He'll need to. They've thrown more into the stew, I'm afraid. Gemma O'Loughlin says she'll definitely lead with that nonsense about hit squads in the Guards. The Larry Smith shooting. She's got the Smith family all roused too."

"She knows that we're reviewing it? Purcell's crowd is, I mean?"

"She thinks that's just window dressing. 'Smoke screen.' I found this out an hour ago. I had an otherwise unremarkable chat with the editor."

Minogue stared at the framed picture of James and Maura Kilmartin and their son at the boy's graduation. The Killer's eyes were set in deep, the brow lowered, even when he tried to smile. The son's grin was a mix of bewilderment and relief. Kilmartin hadn't once in their years of friendship let slip that he'd considered retiring to Mayo. "Stick it out in Dublin," Minogue had heard almost daily from him.

"John. I've got to go. I'm going to phone Mayo Division and get a search of this Carra site first."

Tynan hummed.

"The Escort got rough treatment somewhere," Minogue said. "The underside of it had dings galore. Rocks and stones, I don't know, but something banged a hole underneath, where the spare is."

Minogue wondered why Tynan was keeping him. He heard a door close in Tynan's house. Rachel Tynan, he wondered, or one of the security squad coming in for a leak. Tynan had insisted on the squad members using the kitchen and toilet when they needed, instead of sitting for hours in their cars manufacturing piles.

"Matt?"

"Yes . . . ?"

"Smith . . . do you think it's — No, no. Forget that. Yes — forget I said it." Minogue stared at the badges again.

"All right, fine," said Tynan then. "Issue it tonight. And make it public too with a release tomorrow afternoon."

"I'll phone you in the morning."

CHAPTER 14

She had kept walking until the water reached her chin. He couldn't catch up with her. Worse: he couldn't make out what she was saying to him. The sea off Killiney was like glass, the surface dotted with the heads of swimmers. And no one on the beach or in the water seemed to notice that his daughter was trying to walk across the seabed of the Irish Sea in the general direction of Wales, toward the continent or even the coast of Africa.

Malone's eyes were baggy. Maybe he'd had forty winks and didn't realize it. He rubbed at his face. It felt blubbery. His nose was blocked solid again. He wanted to rest his head against the cabinet again, doze off. He shivered instead.

"Cuppa tea?"

"No. Thanks."

He looked around the squad room. The screen saver on the computer irritated him. Why was it left on anyway? Kathleen had said that Iseult and Pat could have come out tonight. It wasn't a conscious reproach, he knew, but her resigned good-night at ten felt like a dig: why, at your age, are you not delegating more so you can be at home in bed at a decent hour?

Two detective units from Castlebar and eight other Gardai were at the Carra Fields, walking around in the dark. It was lashing rain there. A Chief Inspector Noonan was continuing to have trouble with blackout areas on the walkie-talkies. Search teams had to relay messages to a farmhouse a mile from the site where there was a phone. Why not wait until morning, from Noonan. Minogue had prevaricated: it was a time thing; the squad would need to move quickly if they found the car there.

Malone stood and began stretching exercises.

"What's the big deal," he grunted. "It's always pissing rain out there, isn't it?"

Minogue didn't answer.

"They have a map of the place, haven't they?" Malone went on. "All they have to do is folley along any tracks you could get a car up. What do you call them, boreens? Couldn't they get the lowdown from any watchman type of a fella there?"

Minogue rested his head on the panel of the cabinet and stared at the clock. It was Murtagh who had taped up the newspaper ad for the contest to design a new friendly logo for the Guards that kids could fall in love with. Teddy the Safety Bear. Garda Jim, the Friendly Giant. FIDO, the Garda mascot from rank-and-file entries.

"It's all closed up, Tommy," he murmured. "Since they finished their digging and called it a day there after Christmas."

Malone rose from his toe-touching, his face flushed. He cracked his knuckles.

"What, before they got the money from Europe to build the place?"

Minogue wondered if he should phone Kilmartin in the morning. He always had the pretext of telling Kilmartin how the case was running: there are about three dozen very wet, very annoyed Guards here, Jim, with a dozen and more very bloody-annoyed Guards. What Malone could be whistling about at ten o'clock at night while he filled the kettle, Minogue couldn't imagine. Couldn't do it without a cup of something, but there was only instant coffee left.

The phone seemed unusually loud. Minogue picked up the extension on Murtagh's desk. Noonan wasn't irritated this time.

"Are you sure?" Minogue asked.

Noonan said he was. One of the Guards had actually gone down a part of the cliff to get a better look. They had a quartz searchlight from the car. Minogue stepped across to the boards and pulled the thumbtacks from the top of the site map. He spread it out on Murtagh's desk.

"Sorry, er —"

"Tom. Tell me, how'd you know it'd be there?"

"Well, I didn't," Minogue said, "to tell you the God's honest truth."

"But listen now, it'll have to wait until the morning. Get fellas down the cliff or a boat in."

"The cliff is . . . ?"

"It's like the side of a wall, sure," Noonan said. "There's a bit of a ledge there near the top. The lights can make out the wheels, they think."

"And it's on its roof."

"Upside down. That's how it looks."

Minogue ran his finger along the dotted lines to the cliff.

"So the car was driven up this track and over the top? Can't you get a squad car up there?"

"I might be able to get one up," said Noonan, "but I wouldn't be sure of getting it down again. Bucketing down here, the rain."

"How far is it from the site?"

"A quarter mile or so. I won't be risking anything or anybody here tonight."

Loud and clear, Minogue almost said. Couldn't blame him.

"What are the tides doing to it?"

"Well it's low tide now, so it's half submerged. There's rocks there below."

Minogue didn't want to ask Noonan again.

"So it'll be tough enough getting down there in the daylight," Noonan went on, "to see if there's anyone inside the car."

"Work well done. I'm obliged to you."

"We'll seal up the place for you now, will we?"

"If you please. And a Guard at the site. I'm a bit anxious now about evidence. If we can make sure to preserve any tire tracks and the like — shoe prints too if the car was pushed, now."

"Good luck to you there — it's muck entirely. Have ye rain up in Dublin?"

"Oh enough, but intermittent now."

"Bucketing all the long day here, yes."

Minogue waited.

"So will this be from Dublin?" Noonan asked. "Whoever's taking this over?"

.   .   .   .   .

Minogue didn't much mind the acidy aftertaste of the tea bags. Malone tapped his finger down on the dotted lines that led to the cliffs.

"The spiky bits are the cliffs, right?"

Minogue nodded and traced another path in from Cahercarraig Road.

"Boreens," Malone declared.

"You're coming on great with the languages since you started here."

"Bogs. Boreens. Bogmen. Sheep. More bogs. Sheep that look like bogmen. Bogmen that look like sheep."

He squinted at Minogue.

"Answer me this: how in the name of Jases did you figure on looking there?"

"Police science," Minogue said.

"No: how?"

"Ah, Tommy, I don't know. It's, ah . . ."

Malone shook his head and turned to the map again.

"So there's the places they were digging."

"About a quarter of a mile, yes."

"Bog roads. Turf and that, right?"

"Correct."

"Culchie priests and nuns they sell / Nightmares, fear and holy Hell."

"Is that Public Works?"

"No it isn't," Malone scoffed, "it's GOD. Culchie is from Kiltimagh, right? That's Mayo."

Minogue nodded. He studied the faint vapor rising above the rim of his cup. He wondered but didn't much care if the tea would keep him awake. If they had to go to Mayo tomorrow, it'd be five hours sitting in a car, thank you very much.

"See what turns up in the morning," he said. "There's trained site staff in Galway can go up and work it."

Malone swilled the remains of his tea in his cup. He belched behind his fist.

"Say she's in it then," he said.

Minogue sat down on the edge of the desk.

"Do you see him doing it?" he asked Malone.

"His oul lad would, I'll bet. If we asked him, straight up."

"Maybe his mother knows him better."

Malone placed his cup on the desk, and looked at the pins on the map.

"Or, the same crowd who did her, went after him too. Caught up with him here or there and — boom."

Minogue yawned. He thought of the pictures soaking in on Dermot Higgins's computer screen. Point and click. Malone was counting on his fingers.

"One: he's killed her," he said. "Two: a double — whoever killed her killed him too. But what's he doing in Dublin Airport in the boot of a car?"

Malone held on to his index finger and began gently waving his arms.

"Try again: a double murder. He wasn't topped at the same time as she was. Okay, say he doesn't know she's been thrown off a cliff. That's why he's not running to the Guards. They catch up to him and he's gone. But where? Here in Dublin?"

Minogue had had enough. He got up to go.

"You're a veteran now," he said to Malone as he passed him. "Last thing you think about before you go to sleep, first thing you think about when you wake up."

"Listen," Malone said. "Here's what I can't get me head around still."

Minogue gave him a knowing glance.

"If he killed her, is it?"

"Yeah. If it wasn't people robbing, or some half-arsed effort at extortion or kidnapping your man, even: who folleyed him somewhere? Who made it quits?"

. . . . .

"You should have seen them," Kathleen said. "Or maybe not."

Minogue tied his other shoelace. The morning had started with a bit of sun at last. He felt groggy from the blocked nose, but not as shaky as he had predicted when he fell into bed last night.

"The Smiths, love?"

"Glaring right into the camera," she said. "God, like animals. 'The Guards murdered my brother' — the exact words. Can't he be taken to court for that?"

"An interesting suggestion."

"'An interesting suggestion.' Aren't you even the slightest bit concerned that you might be one of those Guards he'd be referring to?"

Minogue looked up from his laces.

"No, love. I'm not. The Smiths are chancers, and liars, and thieves. They'll try anything."

"Well, did a Guard kill him?" Kathleen asked. "I can't deny the idea has some appeal, God forgive me, when I hear about the things Larry Smith did."

Minogue let his gaze drift out the window. It wasn't the subject or even the timing. It was something about Kathleen's tone that was getting to him. He thought of Damian Little, Trigger Little. Why had Little's wife walked out on him?

"We can thank Gemma O'Loughlin for stirring things up," Kathleen said.

"Well she's playing into the hands of the likes of the Smiths."

"Gave me the creeps, I tell you," she said. "The hate in his eyes, and the finger out, pointing. I thought he was pointing right through the telly at me. Ugh. 'They'll pay for this, the Guards,' says he, *snarling* — I mean to say, are people allowed to talk like that?"

Minogue shook the paper open. Kathleen sat back.

"All right," she muttered. "All right."

Minogue closed the paper again.

"Iseult phoned last night, you said."

"She did," Kathleen said. "You'd think it was me going to have the baby."

"Worrying, are you?"

"'Course I am. Aren't you?"

Kathleen did not need to hear of their daughter stalking his dreams. Water, daughter . . . fought her. Iseult and her imprinting. A Mozart composing right there as he was delivered.

"I am and I amn't," he said.

"'It's just her personality,' is that what you're going to say?"

"It's just her personality, Kathleen."

"You . . . !"

She put the lid on the margarine. He studied the tendons by her knuckles.

"I just wonder," she whispered, "if it's triggered something, like."

He turned back to the paper again.

"She's going to have a baby, love. A fine, big, healthy, good-looking, and decent child from day one. Like its grandfather."

Kathleen waited until he looked up.

"Well now," she said. "You remember your uncle Miko, don't you?"

"What? Give me a chance. I'm only after getting —"

"Schizophrenia, Matt. Let's not mince words here now."

"Miko? Miko Minogue?"

"Your uncle Miko Minogue. And what about the aunt you never met: Mary, the one in America, who died in the looney bin?"

"Ah, Miko was quare. He never married. So maybe he was gay."

Kathleen gave a breathy chortle.

"Denial."

"Heard that before. And very recently, as a matter of fact."

"Oh, did you now. Well at least you know what you're good at."

"Kathleen, it's, it's exuberance. Temporary state of being off her rocker. Come on now. You were dotty enough when you were expecting. You should hear Jim Kilmartin on the topic, let me tell you. He got stuff heaved at him."

"You're not listening. You don't understand."

"'Men.'"

"Yes it is! She's seven months, Matt. The ups and downs with the hormones should be gone now."

"Oh, just steady fear now, is that it?"

"No! More, more . . . serene or something."

"Iseult? Serene? Love —"

"Genes, Matt, genes! Stop trying to cod me here! I know you think about her morning, noon, and night. That's how you are. Don't be elbowing *me* because *I* worry! I read up on it at the library last night."

"What?"

"Schizophrenia strikes young adults —"

"She's twenty-three —"

"— but is frequent statistically in the twenties. Freud called it the Irish disease, did you know that?"

"Freud? The same Freud who declared that the Irish were the only crowd who couldn't be helped by psychoanalysis?"

"Did he? If you say so. I didn't know that, isn't that interesting."

"Freud's a gobshite."

Kathleen stared at him. He let out a breath and sat back.

"I beg your pardon. Barrack room talk. Slipped out. I'm sorry."

Her voice was softer now.

"Look," she said, "your uncle Miko 'went quare' when he was in his twenties. He was in and out of the mental hospital then all his life. Mary was hospitalized for years at a time there in Philadelphia. As I recall, she went that way after she had her first. Her first and only."

Minogue stared at the want ads. They seemed stupid now. Why did he read them every morning anyway?

"I don't know anything about it, Kathleen. Sorry. Maybe I think it's *mí ádh* to be talking about it. So there. I am primitive."

She touched his knuckles. He unclenched his fist. She fenced with her fingers before twining his in hers. Miko, the uncle singing in the fields, talking to himself at night, wandering the roads. They'd found him in his garden curled up like he was asleep by his beloved rhubarb, a smile on his face.

"We have to face it, Matt," she whispered. "It's nobody's fault. Genes."

"I'm not a nutcase, Kathleen. God knows I could be, easy enough. The job."

"We carry things though. Transmit them."

"Look at Daithi, then? We're opposites, aren't we?"

Kathleen rubbed at his hand.

"We'll see when he's older. When he gets to be himself."

He made to protest but she yanked on his hand.

"Come on now," she said. "I hear it often enough from you in bed."

Minogue studied the ingredients on the margarine lid.

"As cracked as her oul lad," he murmured.

"You know that's not what I meant now."

"She thinks she's God, Kathleen. Creation. Isn't that what a woman thinks when she's pregnant?"

Kathleen's laughter turned to whoops. She let herself back in the chair. He watched the tear work its way from the eyelid's edge down to her ear.

"Oh you're a scream," she said. "A panic entirely!"

"Are we quits then?"

She nodded and dabbed at her eyes. Minogue poured her more tea. She was somber now.

"God but she's taking the hard route, Matt. What's the matter with her?"

"Her baby will be the first baby in the world. She always starts from scratch."

She sighed.

Minogue read an ad for piano lessons. Rates reasonable. Iseult had been going to the Wednesday recitals in the National Gallery for months now. He tried to ignore the phone ringing.

"That's for you," she said. The phone rang again. He rose from the table.

"You're sure, are you?"

"I told him to phone back a half an hour later. John Murtagh. I turned the phone down after I got up. You dozed off again after the alarm."

"Kathleen . . . !"

"I know, I know. But I decided. He told me it could wait, that's why."

CHAPTER 15

Fergal sheehy slammed down the boot lid. Raindrops flew up as it rebounded. He swore with little fervor.

"Are those your wellies there?" he asked Malone.

"I don't have any shagging wellies. Wellies are for culchies."

"Is that your considered opinion?" Sheehy asked. "You're an iijit then."

"What else did your wife's latest fella tell you after that?"

Sheehy pushed Minogue's overnight further back in the boot. The car stank of cigars. Sheehy, smoking after winners, Minogue wondered. He turned down the radio. Sheehy closed the boot lid with a massive slam. Malone sat in.

"What's the matter with him?" he asked.

"We're going down the country," Minogue said. "He's not."

Minogue tugged out his seat belt. Sheehy sat in heavily behind the wheel.

Minogue still believed that the sergeant took grim satisfaction in being given the headbanger parts of an investigation.

"I hope you're not after breaking our duty free," Malone called out.

Sheehy cocked an eye at him.

"Take me drunk lads, I'm home," said Malone.

Sheehy crunched reverse twice before finding it. The suspension bottomed out when he sped out the gate onto the North Circular Road.

"Well shag this," said Malone. "I'm walking,"

"Some day's work this'll be," Sheehy grunted, "if this is how it's starting."

"The airport follow-ups," said Minogue.

"The passenger lists," said Sheehy. "The car park. The lookouts for stuff being fenced. Trying to trace your man's camera and such. But that's only the half of it."

Minogue flicked at the zipper handle on his briefcase. Had he reminded Murtagh to phone again, see if the bank cards had showed up active yet?

"Setting up to work on Aoife Hartnett, is it?"

"God, no," Sheehy grunted. "That's police work. That I don't mind."

He accelerated around a bread van through the amber light at Cabra Road.

"Ferrying you and Head-the-Ball out to fly off to Mayo, now *that's* work."

"Hey, Fergal, me oul son," Malone broke in. "Does there be a lot of muck and stuff out there? Down the country like. I don't want to get me new Nikes dirty."

Sheehy didn't take the bait. He worked his way through Glasnevin and turned down Griffith Avenue. Minogue tried to pin a name on the jig that Sheehy'd began whistling. Sheehy produced a cigar at the lights by Swords Road. Minogue rolled down his window. Sheehy affected not to notice. The air was damp, with an edge to it.

"Knock International, is it?" he asked.

"That's it. Look, Fergal. We were only codding about the duty free."

"Ah, well that's all right, so."

"We're on expenses," said Malone. "We don't need the duty free, like."

Sheehy shook his head and settled into top gear for the start of the motorway.

"See how cocky you are after falling around the place there a few hours," he said around the cigar. "In the bog. In the pissings of rain. You jackeen."

Minogue allowed himself to be drawn into a conversation about whether Mayo was wetter than Clare. Sheehy maintained that Dublin people were climatically deprived. Malone offered that Sheehy hadn't been crouched in a tent with the wind howling and the rain lashing the other night. Sheehy offered to exchange places with Malone on the trip to Mayo. Malone replied that he had finally been convinced that country people were far better educated than Dubs so the file work and searches would be best left to them. So, no.

Minogue tuned out more often. He thought about the Carra Fields and the bog roads around them. Five thousand years ago, Garland had told him, but it had returned to bogland by the time of the Bronze Age. With the forests down, the rain had leeched away the soil in no time at all.

"*Cad a dhéanfaimid feasta gan adhmad . . .*"* he murmured.

Sheehy cocked an ear. There was warmth in his voice now.

"*Tá deireadh na gcoillte ar lár,*
Níl tracht ar Kilcais ná a theaghlach . . .
I forget the last line."

"*S'ní cluinfear a chluin go brách,*" Minogue said. "You're good, Fergal."

"I bet you went through the Christian Brothers."

"It was a truce mostly, as I recall," Minogue said.

Traffic by the airport roundabout was light. Minogue studied the faces in the tour bus that had pulled over. American, he guessed. A maple leaf on the front window told him otherwise. Hard to tell. He looked over the fountain at the hangars on the north apron.

Sheehy was waved through the checkpoint. He pulled up by the taxi rank. Minogue blew his nose again and stepped out. Malone was pulling the bags out of the boot. A jet engine was warming up somewhere.

Sheehy looked around the roadway as though he had dropped money on it. Tired, Minogue knew, chasing leads all evening and another twelve hours of it ahead of him.

"Back tonight, do you think?" Sheehy asked.

"Might be, Fergal. Are ye all right?"

"Ah, we're in good order. As well as starting up background on the woman, I'm going to go after the people in those photos today. Start in, anyhow. See if Shaughnessy told anyone anything about what was on his mind."

"Good, Fergal. The calls might come better today too."

"They better. There's nothing."

"He'll show up. So will she."

---

* "Kilcais" (Kill-cash), a poem written anonymously in the early 1700s, was a staple of school learning until very recently. It laments the destruction both of Ireland's native forests and nobles' houses such as Kilcais. It became generalized as a somber comment on the loss of the past and its treasures.

> What shall we do for timber?
> The last of the woods is down.
> Kilcais and the house of its glory,
> The spot where that lady waited
> Who shamed all women for grace
> When earls came sailing to greet her
> And Mass was said in the place . . .

Sheehy looked over at Malone holding the door with his knee as he dragged the bags into the building.

"Seems to me now they were keen not to be noticed," he said. "I mean, people down the country don't miss much."

Minogue nodded.

"Good man yourself. And you stuck in Dublin, Fergal."

"Deliberate," said Sheehy. "Some class of planning went on. But that's for you to be thinking about."

·　　·　　·　　·　　·

Malone had his head glued to the window most of the time. There was low cloud coverage soon after Dublin but there were gaps. The constant noise bothered him more than the vibration. Why hadn't he brought a flask of coffee?

He looked out at the propellers again. Patches of land appeared through the clouds and were swiped away again. He checked his watch. They must be getting close now. An hour's drive from the airport should do it, an hour and a half at most.

He remembered Caty's disbelief when she and Daithi had returned to Dublin after their week in the west last year. Where were all the people out here, Caty wanted to know. Such a sense of isolation in such a small country. Et cetera. She had talked about the Famine over dinner in the new Chineser on George's Street. "Romancing" was Kathleen's predicable closer on Caty's talk of a huge weight of something in the air — but a lovely girl. She'd really wake up Daithi, really liven him up.

The copilot leaned around the doorway.

"About five minutes now," he shouted.

Minogue folded the newspaper. He unfolded it again to look at the picture of Larry Smith on the third page. He wasn't going to let it distract him. Why no pictures of all the addicts and the maimed people who'd run through Smith's hands before someone shot him? Inner-city families knew that, at least. His ears popped. Was it raining below? The nerve of the Smiths: "demanding" a public inquiry into why the murderers hadn't been caught.

The plane dipped, and droning louder, it rose sharply. Minogue's stomach followed the tilt. Fields and hedges came into view below the wing now, far-off hills and mountains. The high peak of the shrine passed under them.

"Will we be stopping in for a dose of holy water?" Malone called out. Minogue glared at him: a pilgrimage to Knock wasn't part of the plan. He wondered what Malone might say at the sight of barefoot pilgrims and penitents climbing Croagh Patrick: where do you get a hamburger around here?

The engines slowed. The hills to his left slid by and arranged themselves as the plane settled on an approach. Jumbos landed at Knock, didn't they? There was talk of several planes booked from the States direct to Knock for a commemoration of something. Coffin ships from the Famine, was it . . . ? He stared at the seat back ahead of him as the plane closed on the runway. The wings' sudden tipping caused him to glance back. The wheels bounced back once, settled, and the nose of the plane eased down. He was surprised how little runway it needed to slow to a brisk walking pace. He spotted the squad car by the terminal as the plane turned.

Minogue slipped on the ladder but Malone shouldered him back onto the step.

"Watch the moves there," he said. "You wouldn't try that back in Dublin."

The tarmac was wet in patches. Farm, he smelled. Over the hedges rose the hills of East Mayo. He eyed the canopy fluttering feebly by the runway. A turboprop was parked near the terminal and, beyond it, two light planes and a minibus.

"A bit like Heathrow," said Malone. "Except there's no people. Or buildings."

The squad car made its way at a leisurely speed from the terminal. Minogue took his bag from the pilot and squinted at the windscreen of the Vectra.

The driver was an affable, droopy-eyed Garda McGurk. He had the tonsured look of a monk and a bushy, Gallic mustache. The passenger was a Sergeant Ryan.

"Pat," said Ryan, and shook hands. His eyebrows were black, as were the few hairs high up on his cheeks, but his hair was a well-maintained ash-gray thatch. Folds of loose skin swelled against his collar and lapped over when he nodded. Would they mind stopping in at the Ballina station to have a chat with Inspector Noonan before heading up? No bother, from Minogue.

Minogue sat in the back with Malone. McGurk took the Vectra across the Claremorris Road and settled onto a narrow lane. The windscreen was filthy at the margins. There was a pig farm nearby, Minogue knew. The smell comforted him.

"The back way up through Kiltimagh," Ryan said.

Minogue looked out at the passing hedgerows.

"I thought ye'd go on to Castlebar," Ryan tried again. "The airport there."

"Ah we couldn't pass up Knock," Minogue had to say. "Pilgrims, we are. Or refugees, from Dublin. But does there be a high season for the shrine at all?"

"It's steady enough," replied Ryan. "There was a plane in from England Monday. Irish, the most of 'em, but. It was part of a bus tour thing."

Minogue shifted his knees against the back of the driver's seat.

"Have we news yet?" he asked. "Up at Cahercarraig there. The car."

Ryan scratched at the back of his head. Minogue tried yet again to guage the territorial quotient. The Dublin Experts: right. Sure. The car wallowed and jerked as it hit a dip in the road. Ryan unhooked the transceiver, checked the volume.

"I'll check for you now."

Malone kept up his study of the countryside as they left Kiltimagh.

"Lots of rocks and things," he said. McGurk glanced over his shoulder.

"How much would you pay for, say, a ticket to a concert up in the Big Smoke?" he asked Minogue.

"What type of concert, now?" Minogue asked, half-listening to the radio transmission. Ryan repeated that they were on their way to Ballina.

"Groups," said McGurk. "Big name."

"Traditional stuff, like?"

"God no. The big ones. What do you call the place, the Point."

"A fair whack," said Malone. "Depends, but."

"Okay. The Works. Them, say. What would you pay?"

Minogue looked at McGurk's bald crown.

"Twenty," said Malone. "Just to get in. Fifty if you want to get a look at 'em."

McGurk shook his head.

"Holy God," he said. "I told herself. She wouldn't believe me."

McGurk couldn't be far short of forty, Minogue decided. He studied the points of his mustache in profile. Was this corpulent Guard an off-duty rocker and general satyr? The rural Irishman at his simple, unfathomable best.

"They're deadly though," said McGurk. "You have to admit."

"They're all right," Malone said.

"*Bless the virgin, meek and mild; cruise the strip and save the child.*"

Minogue found himself trying to suppress a smile.

"Yeah," said Malone.

"I don't know what it means," said McGurk. "But I keep thinking about it."

"They have a way of throwing words together, I suppose."

Trowen, Minogue thought. Dee english language trowen on the fukken shoals of a Dubbalin — man's ideas, loike.

"You're not mad about them, are you?"

"Since they went big, I don't know. The edge is gone offa them. Washed up."

"Do you think? Who's on the edge then, now like?"

Malone studied a tractor as the squad car finally moved around it. He waved back at the driver.

"GOD. Now they're the business."

McGurk looked around at him.

"GOD? You're joking me."

"Why am I joking you?"

"They're head cases, aren't they? I heard two of them are lezzers, man."

Malone cracked his knuckles.

"What's the story on the drug scene these days?" asked Ryan. "Up in Dublin."

"Bad," said Minogue. "Been bad a long while now."

"It's all over now, of course," Ryan said. "Isn't it?"

So this was a territorial nark coming out. Minogue sensed that Malone had picked up the dig too. Drugs were an obvious plot by Dublin to defile rural Ireland. As well as Murder Squad luminaries landing on them here to tell Guards how to do their business. Being flown here, for the love of God, because they were so high and mighty. McGurk began to take a keener interest in negotiating the turns. They braked for a stop sign. Two articulated lorries swept by on the Castlebar Road.

"Another bit of a jog and we'll come up near to Foxford," said McGurk.

"They've brought up the drug squad to seven in Castlebar," said Ryan.

All Dublin's fault, Minogue was ready to agree.

"Terrible, isn't it," he murmured instead.

"Five years ago, there wasn't one."

Why was it taking so long to get a call back from Ballina?

"At this rate —"

Ryan didn't get the chance to finish. Malone too looked away from the window to listen better. They had floated the Nissan Micra off the rocks just a half an hour ago at high tide. A body had been recovered. Female, matching the description of the missing person. McGurk half-turned in the seat. He offered the mike to Minogue. The inspector shook his head.

"Ask him where they're taking it," he said. "If you please."

·   ·   ·   ·   ·

Chief Inspector Noonan was well over six feet. He had an odd bump at the bridge of his nose and fine, dark-red hair that reminded Minogue of a horse. Dyed, he wondered, but decided it couldn't be. The chief inspector had sandwiches and a pot of tea waiting for his visitors. Minogue wondered if he'd already struck up a liking for Noonan before he'd been offered the sandwiches. The expression maybe, the one eye open slightly more than the other, the quiet tones.

"Floats," said Minogue again. He glanced at the edge of the tomato slice peeping out from between the slices. Yellow more than green.

"Quite something, I tell you," said Noonan. "One fella went down from the boat, made two or three paddles back to the boat, gets enough for four points, and that's that."

"As easy as that."

"Child's play," Noonan said. "They inflated them open when they were ready. Up comes the car. The boat took it out from near the rocks and it's up on a winch and the boat's back in the harbor. You sort of forget how strong air is."

"Isn't that something."

"Tell you the truth, we were lucky," said Noonan. He pushed the second plate of sandwiches toward Minogue. "The fisheries crowd and the recovery gear were handy in Belmullet."

Minogue took a long sip of tea. The female removed from the car was in the morgue of the county hospital. The female: well who else could it be. The Micra was wrapped and headed to Castlebar in a lorry. "Jurisdictional," Noonan said flat-out. In the spirit of decentralization. It was Divisional HQ, and the forensic work was usually done there. Minogue glanced at the photos on Noonan's wall. There were two former commissioners among a group of smiling officers.

"Isn't it though?" Noonan asked again.

"Which now?"

"The means. Give us the tools. Sure, isn't that what's going on in Dublin?"

He had missed whatever preamble Noonan had given.

"I, er, well, there's always some new initiative, isn't there?" he managed.

"Law reform is the tool," said Noonan. He looked from Malone to Minogue.

"The whole Smith thing, sure, how come he was ever out on the streets at all? He should have been behind bars for life."

Minogue returned Noonan's quizzical smile. So the chief inspector wanted to chew the fat about Larry Smith, did he? He declined Noonan's offer of more tea.

"Sure it's the wild west above there isn't it? Gangs, the whole shooting gallery? Something has to be done."

The gentle smile lingered. Noonan inviting a confidence, assent: *Ah, you're right, the law's an ass. We should take the likes of Smith out ourselves if the law won't.* Noonan tilted his cup and rubbed it around the saucer. The Old Guard, Minogue thought. Noonan, with the countryman's innate hospitality, but the two former commissioners he was proud to display himself standing beside had been renowned as wallopers.

"How best can we get to the site?" he asked. "The cliffs . . . ?"

CHAPTER 16

Noonan drove. He waved at people. He rolled down the window and slowed to greet an old man laboring with a walking stick and a shopping bag.

He pulled in beside a railing that Minogue took to be a sign of a national school.

"Now," Noonan said. "I'll bring out our guest. She'll give us a bit of a background."

"Who, now?"

"Mairéad O'Reilly. Her father was the teacher out by Cahercarraig these years. It was Peadar, the father, who got the whole thing started — but sure let Mairéad tell you all about it."

Minogue studied the bars on the railing, imagined the headlong dash of the schoolchildren at the bell, charging through the gap in the wall and pushing off from the railing, scattering down the footpath.

Noonan returned smiling and talking to a thickset woman with large glasses and a three-quarter length suede coat. She carried a bag in one hand and a set of Wellington boots in the other.

"Maybe they're for you, Tommy," Minogue murmured

Malone tugged at the door release. Minogue caught the tail end of Mairéad O'Reilly's quip about the Guards taking the principal away in a squad car. Noonan took her wellies and dropped them in the boot.

A brisk, keen handshake as she sat in beside Minogue. She smiled and made no rebuttal to Noonan's joke about the pupils having the rest of the day off. Minogue introduced Malone.

"Mairéad's father was a legend," said Noonan. "Peadar O'Reilly. He died last June twelve-month. A great loss. If it wasn't for him now, well, Mairéad'd tell you all about it if she wasn't so modest. She and I go back a long ways."

"Not that far back now, Tom."

Minogue obliged with a grin. A schoolmistress not averse to being coy? She turned to Minogue.

"I've a brother a Guard in Roscommon," she said.

The squad car passed a dilapadated garage at the junction of the Cahercarraig Road. What was it about teachers, Minogue wondered. Self-assured from years of being up in front of others, he supposed: authoritative, complete, custodial. Always wanted the last word.

"He started before the war, didn't he, Mairéad," said Noonan. "The Fields?"

"In the thirties," she said. "Well, ever since he heard about it in school, I suppose, so earlier yet. He was always interested in the folklore and the history. He'd be walking the roads and talking to people. Of course sure he knew everybody. With the sports and the music and everything."

"A Renaissance man," Noonan said.

"Well now, he amassed a lot of information that would have been lost otherwise, I suppose."

"So your father discovered the Fields basically," said Minogue.

"He did that. He'd been out in the bogs one summer cutting turf. Some of it was for home and some of it for the school. Can you imagine? You're not Dublin, now are you?"

"I'm not. Clare, but bygone days."

She smiled.

"You had the one-room school, did you?"

"Indeed we did. A crowd of us, all shapes and sizes. I don't know how the teacher did it."

"Well how far we've come. I wonder what Da would say if he took a look at the Internet we're getting into the school next week. My God, I stare at the screen there when John Doyle's banging away on it and my mind, it goes, well I don't know. Connected to the whole world. I can't believe it. Satellites, signals flying through the air. From Mayo. Isn't it wonderful?"

The sun broke through as they slowed for a blind bend. Noonan drove in a puddle to leave room for an oncoming Harp lorry. Sunlight flooded in Minogue's side, caressed his neck and shoulders. Noonan steered over a narrow bridge.

"He was in Cahercarraig until they closed it," she said. "In 1962. The same year Kennedy came. The end of an era, I suppose you'd say. But we were reared out by Bruach. Seven of us. Oh, many's the Saturday we were out on Carra. I always think of those times as sunny days. Up on the bog — sure Ma must have been martyred with us, so she must. While Da was doing his digging."

She looked back at a boarded-up house.

"I remember once he dug a trench," she went on then. "It must have been nearly ten feet deep. Ma was petrified it'd fall in on him. The bog, you see. And she persuaded my uncle Ger to go up with him so's he'd not fall down a bog hole. Comical it was, the way Ger told it. 'I'll go up there no more,' Ger would say, 'for fear of meeting all the crowd he was telling me about.' Da couldn't work with Ger of course. Ger was always pulling his leg, d'you see. Da was very serious."

"Crowds of people, is it?" Minogue asked.

"Ah, God, no," Mairéad O'Reilly said. "There was no one there ever. Da would be lecturing Ger, getting carried away with himself. 'That layer there now, Ger, that's Rome being founded.' An amateur archaeologist."

"But sure he wasn't far off the mark now when it was finally excavated," said Noonan. "Was he?"

Minogue watched her eyes roam the hillsides. Her smile faded a little.

"'Tis true for you," she said. "But Da would have had you believe that this was where civilization started."

"Paradise lost," said Noonan, and he threw his head back once.

The few trees and hedges were behind them now. The views to both sides were across roadside ditches to bog. Minogue tried to figure north from west but the twisting road drove the sun across the roof of the car too often for him.

The road rose to a plateau. Minogue caught glimpses of the turns and dips as the road wound its way toward the coast ahead. They passed rusting forty gallon barrels, mounds of crushed rock.

"This road's going to be widened now to go along with the site," said Noonan.

"Hard to imagine fifteen or twenty thousand people living up here, isn't it?"

"That many," was all Minogue could manage.

"There's Carra Hill beyond," said Mairéad O'Reilly.

Minogue followed her pointed finger. Rising ground culminated in a gently rounded hill.

"There'd be the crowning there," she said, "with all the goings-on over by the road. That all died out of course. But it started up again after the Famine for a few years. It never caught on again after that. The people emigrating . . . ? I don't know."

"Your father had all this researched?" Minogue tried. She shifted in her seat.

"He did, he did," she replied. "But some of it turned out what you might call fanciful. Or at least that's what the ex — well, the history people thought. Da was an amateur, you see. And proud of it too: the Latin root, he'd always say — *amo, amas, amat* — to love something is not necessarily to carry a degree from some university around with you as authority. Those were his ways."

Was it the warmth of the sun, he wondered, or the pleasure of being away from Dublin that made him dreamy. Maybe it was the idea of this country schoolteacher for decades doggedly unearthing a forgotten history. He imagined O'Reilly in the classroom, singing, conjugating obscure Irish verbs, dependably clattering the odd dunce, roaring at one of his charges errant or lackadaisical with a hurley stick. Quite a breed, the country schoolteachers then, and some lost genius in many. He remembered the books given to him by his own teacher, McMahon, as a parting gift: Chekov and Gogol, Maupassant. McMahon, run over by a car at midnight on a road ten years later. Asleep in the middle of the road, drunk.

"People thought he was mad, of course," she was saying. "But sure everyone loved him. The kids adored him. Oh but he was strict! I get people writing me and telling me about Da. Universities, heads of companies, even people who ended up in Australia. A man sent us a thousand pounds from Sydney. He'd had Da as a teacher back before the war, but he hadn't forgotten. 'A habit of mind for learning,' Da would say, 'A cast of mind for truth.' The old school, I suppose some would say."

Minogue suppressed a yawn and tried to smile at her.

"Well of course the world caught up to Da," she went on. "But do you know, it didn't interest him much. He went on about his business after retiring, gathering the stories and the poems and the songs. He was going to buy a computer, he told me a week before he died. So as he could do the things he'd collected. He had eyewitness stories of the Famine, sure. People who were children when it happened. All that way back. He'd taken them down when he started teaching. His first notebook is 1928, when he was in school himself. A born historian. So there."

"Here we are," said Noonan, "up ahead."

Minogue saw the roof lights of the Garda car above the heather. Next to it was a sign. They rounded a bend and came in sight of a cleared graveled patch joined to the road by a makeshift bridge. Noonan took the car slowly over the ruts. He parked by a granite boulder sticking out of what looked to Minogue like an abandoned turf bank. He took a walkie-talkie out of the glove box. Minogue felt the anticipation worm in his stomach again, his chest grow tight.

"We'll go up now and introduce ourselves?" Noonan was asking him.

• • • • •

Minogue savored the give, the juicy sponge of the bog underfoot. His wellies sucked as he drew them out of the muck where he'd been standing. He held the edges of the map tight. Mairéad O'Reilly ran a finger along the line.

"That's us there," she said. "And there's tracks and boreens here. And here."

How the hell could you get a car up here, he wondered. Malone was hunkered over a track fifty yards away with Noonan pointing to something. Minogue looked beyond them to the parked cars by the Office of Public Works sign.

"So the site here is wide open really, you'd have to say," he said.

She pointed over to the fence surrounding a pit.

"That'd be to stop people falling in," she went on. "Liability, I don't know. This is all rock here up on the left and . . ." She looked down at the map again. "I think it's here they'll put in his plaque and what have you. A seating area too."

She looked over again.

"Da wouldn't be one for all the fuss. But he'd like it, I know. A nice touch."

Minogue looked from the map up onto the bog again. The only road most likely to have been fit to bear the weight of a small car was somewhere behind the other fenced-off place, the court tomb.

"Am I right now for that road here?"

She looked at the map.

{ 175 }

"Yes indeed now. That definitely leads over to the cliff. Unless now they've added a road of their own. There's going to be some kind of an observation spot up over the cliffs there, I suppose."

Minogue folded the map and looked around. There were no ancient peoples striding through the heather toward him. There was only Carra Hill, heather, clouds like candy floss, the softest of breezes stirring the heather. He looked down at his boots. He hadn't been mistaken: the mud was over his ankles already. He pulled each out in turn. Mairéad O'Reilly gave him a sympathetic smile and tucked her hair in under a headscarf. Henna, that was the name of the stuff, he remembered now.

He realized that his nostrils were no longer blocked. He tested the Velcro on the video camera grip and wondered if he'd get through this excursion into this sodden and desolate hinterland of Mayo without passing some remark to Noonan about the plodding boot prints of the Guards last night. All over the damn site, it looked like. He imagined Noonan's reply, and it'd be the correct one: wasn't my idea to send fellas in here in the dark. What did you expect would happen?

"Will I carry anything?" she asked.

"No thanks, Mairéad. No."

The breeze freshened closer to the cliffs. Malone changed films in the Polaroid. Minogue looked back at the white sticks he'd left stuck into the side of the track. Though blurred and worn away by the rain there were traces of vehicle tires in two spots.

Noonan was a man who liked marching through heather, it seemed.

"A week, do you think?" he called out. Minogue nodded. The hush in the background must be the sea. The edge of the cliff was but a hundred yards ahead.

"We have to get a fix on the last time anyone was up here, Tommy. If the car has been at the bottom of the cliff for a week . . ."

Malone bent over to shield the film as he inserted it.

"Who'd be up here, for Jas — I mean, do people go walking and hiking up here? In the pissing rain, like?"

He looked up over at Noonan and Mairéad O'Reilly. She was explaining something to him. He followed her outstretched arm as she swept it in short arcs from the tomb site to the large pit. A good five hours before the light would fail. An hour to get the search team lined up and ready.

Noonan seemed to have guessed what he was about to ask.

"Well are we set to go over the place now?"

"If you please. How many staff can we expect?"

"Sixteen or seventeen. A few in from Castlebar."

Noonan nodded. Minogue wondered if the chief inspector was holding back a smile. Minogue faced Carra Hill while Noonan radioed the squad car. They'd have to go to the farm again to phone in. Noonan pocketed the walkie-talkie.

Minogue pointed at the cliff edge on the map.

"We'll start there," he said to Noonan. "Tommy and myself."

Malone shrugged his leather jacket and zipped it higher.

"If ye'd split into teams," Minogue added, "pairs say, one covering the other so there's overlap and start in from the road. Mairéad would be with me, please."

"All right," said Noonan. "Mind yourselves. It's dodgy enough by the edge."

Noonan glanced at Malone's mountaineering boots. The muck had already come up to his calves.

"Those alpine jobs will come in handy there."

Malone looked down at his encrusted shoes.

"You're oney slagging 'cause you don't have any," he said.

●   ●   ●   ●   ●

"It's bleeding slippery here, boss."

Minogue looked over. Malone's head appeared between tussocks of grass.

"Anything?"

"Nothing," Malone replied. "And I'm not diving off the bloody cliff and poking around underwater."

Minogue looked across at the ragged, distant line of Guards coming in from the Cahercarraig Road. Mairéad O'Reilly was sitting in the squad car now. He felt he should say something to her. Thank her for coming out to help them sort out the paths and holes. He decided to see how the identification crew in from Castlebar was managing with lifting casts of the wheel ruts.

"Go over to the identification crowd there, Tommy. See them right, will you."

He picked his way back across the clumps of frockins and heather to the graveled area. There were three Garda cars there now beside the van from the Castlebar section. Noonan had made his way in from the line that was moving north toward the fenced-in excavation.

"Does she be needing to get back to school?" Minogue asked.

"Ah no," said Noonan. "She knew it might be the whole afternoon. If Mairéad can help, that's what she wants to do. Bred into her, and all of them."

Minogue smiled in at her. She let go her folder, rolled down the window.

"I hope we've not stolen the day on you now," he said.

"Not a bit of it," she replied. "I'm in a grand spot here, the bit of peace and quiet. It's like old times, so it is."

Minogue glanced down at the folder. The pictures were amateur looking. She lifted it.

"This?" she said. "It's just something to be reading. Again."

"It's the digging your father did years ago . . . ?"

"It is. It's old now, of course, but sure it was never meant to be the final word. More folklore now, they say."

Minogue tried to get a better look at the open pages.

"Here, by all means," she said.

He took it through the open window. Noonan stepped to his side.

"There's the man himself," Noonan said. "God rest him. When would that be, Mairéad?"

"Nineteen forty-eight."

Minogue glanced over at her.

"After that terrible winter of '47. A hundred years after the worst times of the Famine, he never stopped telling us. He's standing where that court tomb is opened up now. Well I can't say now that he knew then what he was standing on. He says he did."

Minogue read down. It had been poorly typed, and the copy was patchy.

"Well he added in the bits of stories and reading he'd done there. The whole locality. The Carra Fields, all that. Those roads there he put down to try and map things out. Twelve feet down he had to go."

"A court tomb now," said Minogue. "They're scarce enough, aren't they?"

"You're right," she said. "It'd be the well-to-do, the chieftain, being put in there, you see. Interred."

Minogue looked up from the page.

"Would there be any class of comforts sent along with him?" he asked. "Like our friends beyond in Egypt?"

"The cruiskeen lawn," said Noonan and grinned. "Poteen?"

"There would," said Mairéad O'Reilly. "But there was nothing found here at all. That tomb, now, it was all done by the museum people and the OPW. Two years they were at this part, as I recall."

Minogue returned to the folder. He turned the pages slowly in reverse order. Mairéad O'Reilly stepped out of the car and buttoned up the collar of her coat.

"That's yours truly there," she said. "In the middle. I was four years old."

Minogue grinned back.

"Don't be asking me if it was before or after the Carra Fields were inhabited."

Noonan laughed.

"There's the whole slew of us there," she went on. "Mam, God rest her, Eileen, John. That's Finbarr. Uncle Ger with the eyes rolling back in his head . . ."

She tugged her scarf tight and watched the Guards searching the heather.

"Take that back to Dublin with you," she murmured.

"Thank you. Are you sure?"

"Indeed and I am. I have other copies made. You can go home and spread the fame of the Carra Fields."

He watched Malone get up from his hunkers.

"That's rain," said Noonan. "By God, you could depend on it."

Minogue noted the few flecks on the car roof. The casts should be up by now, for the love of God. He'd have to get in touch with Galway to see what they could get up for recovery of bits from the seabed where the car had landed. Frogmen working in close to rocks and cliffs, if the wind rose? He checked his watch. No wonder his feet were like lumps, his fingertips clumsy: they'd been here two and a half hours. He'd been up and down by the track five times, all the way to the cliff. His shoulder ached from the chafing of the video camera.

Malone's whistle was piercing. All the search teams looked over too. Minogue waved them on.

"A bit of rain won't harm us," said Noonan.

"Let's try the hospital again, see if the doctor's showed up for the PM."

·　　·　　·　　·　　·

Noonan chewed spearmint gum. The windows were fogged up. Mairéad O'Reilly shifted in the seat next to Minogue. Malone unzipped the carry case for the cameras, looked inside, and zipped it up again.

{ 179 }

"Ah, we'll go on," said Noonan. "I don't know what's —"

The radio came alive. Minogue remembered the voice from the conversation earlier. He rubbed the glass and looked out at the puddle he had been using as his gauge for the rain. Steady drizzle, small drops. Two of the other Garda cars had their engines running now. The Guard at the Keogh farmhouse had just received the call back from the hospital. There was a pathologist, Kelly, up from Galway. When would there be an officer attending?

Malone shifted and looked back at Minogue. The inspector asked Noonan how long it would take to get back to the hospital. Under half an hour.

"Will you get word then, if you please?"

Minogue waited for Noonan to finish on the radio. He turned back to the page he'd kept his thumb on.

"Don't take that now as gospel," Mairéad O'Reilly murmured. "That's legend. Da wasn't shy of adding his own bits of conjecture."

He nodded. The search teams had met by the track just before the rain had turned into the monotonous, steady drizzle that would be down for the evening.

"If you could, leave a car here by the road," he said. "And ask them to step up the questioning. Stop anyone going along by the car park and see if they can fill in anything this past week or two."

Noonan got out of the car and walked over to the squad car. Minogue rubbed the back window and took in the car park. A hundred yards in on that track and a car would be out of sight of the Cahercarraig Road.

Noonan sat back in and started the engine.

"Thanks, Tom, yes," said Minogue. "The hospital."

The tires spun gravel as Noonan steered over the culvert. Better not forget the casts, Minogue thought, along with the faded, washed-out cigarette boxes, the illegible pieces of newspaper already almost a soggy dough. Some would doubtless turn out to have been used by one of the workmen to wipe his arse.

The car took the bend and began its descent back down from the highlands that formed the Carra Fields. He stole a glance at Mairéad O'Reilly. Sitting there with her thoughts away off years ago, it looked like. Was she too still wondering how the thousands of souls had lived here so contentedly, had left so little trace beyond the stone walls of their houses and a solitary, empty tomb? Or was she remembering the days of her childhood and youth trekking up with her father and family to dig and to picnic and to play in the heather?

He returned to the page, with the car bouncing and dropping as the bog road leveled out. Conjecture, was it, all this love of heroes and chieftains her father had had. A *geis*, like the jobs dished out to Hercules, to build a hill for the king so he could survey his lands and people, take his last earthbound breath and die happy.

"Some job of work," he murmured. Mairéad O'Reilly looked over.

"Building that hill, Carra Hill. And then to heft that boulder up to the top."

"Ah, don't forget we had giants to do it back then," she said.

"They'll make much of that when the center is made and opened up then."

"I doubt it," she said. "But what of it."

"Isn't it important, like?"

"Well Da thought it was. To him the stories got to be more important than the actual turning up things in the dig. What use was a collection of oul stones, he'd always say. Stones don't do much talking. It's the people we want to hear."

Minogue looked out at a passing house, a cottage tucked in under rhododendrons and scruffy firs. He sometimes forgot how rain in the west left you thinking you were cut off from the planet. Noonan beeped the horn as he passed the short laneway where a squad car was parked.

"Your father believed in the stories then. That they were there in history."

"Oh, yes," she said. "And he'll be proved right, maybe. That gave him great satisfaction to see how he was able to turn them around. The museum people."

"They were skeptical?"

She smiled wanly.

"Oh, they were," she said. "They didn't put much stock in the dowsing. Sure why would they? They're scientists really."

"The museum people were a bit slow off the mark then."

"They were that. But this was back after the war — long before they had the money and the staff. They didn't begin to cotton on to the Fields until, well, twenty years ago, really. They kept coming up with more, everywhere they put down the rods. Well, they've come around. It turned out to be a city, just like what Da said."

"How did he know?"

She smiled again.

"Well now. He didn't really, I suppose. He believed it was, so it became one."

Noonan met Minogue's eyes in the mirror.

"Teachers have a sixth sense," he said. "Did you always do your homework?"

Mairéad O'Reilly laughed.

"Oh, we're still the same," she said. "The sixth sense. But it works."

Minogue recalled a long and wandering and sometimes humorous chat with Tynan a few years ago: what makes good cops. Dowsing without the stick, Minogue tried, being a chancer too. Intuition, was Tynan's take: unconscious expertise.

The car hit a dip, wallowed, bounced back up. Minogue went back to the pages on Carra Hill. The last crowning stone was to be the throne for the king to retire to and to take his leave. O'Reilly allowed that the practical truth of the hill, if it were built by people at all, could have been something as prosaic as a keep, a retreat in time of war or battle, a place where a king could stage his heroic last battle and die gloriously, surrounded by his enemies.

"Your father allowed that there could be more to the Fields than a crowd of easygoing and well-behaved farmers."

She looked away from the window.

"The hill," he said. "Maybe a defense?"

"Oh, yes. After the son and heir had finished the job. Yes indeed."

The wipers creaking, the car's hissing passage over the wet roadway, had made Minogue fierce dopey again. The rain was lighter in town. He took in a new housing estate built by a deserted and crumbling ball alley, a new shopping center. A half mile further was a new plant making plastic bags. Noonan radioed in. There was a call in for a Chief Inspector Minogue, to call back Dublin. Who, Minogue asked Noonan. An O'Leary. Minogue exchanged a look with Malone.

"Thanks," he said. "Thanks, Tom."

CHAPTER 17

MINOGUE WATCHED MALONE working a stone out from between the cleats of his Nikes with a large version of a Swiss army knife. Seventy, eighty quid for the boots. Thirty-odd quid for the knife. Where the hell was O'Leary? The earpiece irritated his ear. An attendant wheeled a toothless man by on a wheelchair. Minogue eyed the drip feed on a stalk. Malone wiped the knife, watched the pair move down the hall.

"Sorry," said O'Leary. "I was on another line."

"You're all right. We're indoors here."

"What's the story with this woman's car? I'm asking for himself, like."

"Hard to say, tell him," Minogue said. "There's an identification going on the body."

"But it's her, is it? Unofficially?"

"It looks like it, Tony. The body's going to Dublin tonight for the next of kin before the full PM. I'll phone it through to the squad as soon as I can get positive here. We have the photos to match. John Murtagh'll pass it on. Now: is that enough to do you?"

"Got that," said O'Leary. "And thanks. I have to pass on something to yous. The boss is busy until about seven. He was talking to Leyne's minder. Freeman? Well, he phoned us. They'd heard the car was found. It was on the radio news."

Minogue watched the wheelchair heading back his way. Skin and bone: eyes vacant, inward turning on . . . nothing, maybe. He nodded back at the attendant.

"They'll hear in due course," he said to O'Leary.

"That's 'go to hell and leave us to hell alone to do our job,' is it?"

"Approximately, Tony. Look, it's tough enough."

"Okay, I'll translate that. Any help knowing himself said the same to them?"

"Nice to know, I suppose. The same phrases, I wonder?"

"You must be joking," said O'Leary. "He gave it out in theologian mode."

Minogue had to smile. Tynan's code when he resorted to the biting irony and the endless clauses would be harder to take than a clear FO. That it would have been over Freeman's finely coiffed American spin-doctor, legal-minder, courtier's head might have made it even funnier to witness.

"Here's the thing though," said O'Leary. "Why I had to call you now. Leyne took a turn. He's in the hospital, the clinic out in Blackrock."

Minogue thought of the scar tissue he'd seen in the open-necked shirt. An unconscious thing with Leyne, he had wondered, displaying his wound, exposing it to the healing of the light and air. Or an I-don't-give-a-damn?

"He's had bypasses and open heart," said O'Leary. "He's not out of the woods at all. He took dizzy or something, said Freeman, so he's signed into that clinic."

"Before or after he'd heard the news about Aoife Hartnett?"

"Two and two makes five," said O'Leary. "You decide. He's 'comfort-able,' says Freeman. Cohm-foht-abbel."

· · · · ·

"Well, they worked," Malone declared. He left his mountaineering boots by the wall, picked up their trailing laces, and dropped them inside. Minogue tugged on his change of socks. He noted half-past four look-ing back skew-ways at him from his watch.

"Dry as a bone, man."

Minogue looked at his own wellies.

"Bet you it was the shock," said Malone. "Maybe he knew all along."

Minogue looked up sideways at him.

"You say Leyne knew the son murdered her?"

"Capable of, I'm saying. Want to bet the son phoned him from here, from Ireland, I mean?"

"How will we know that until he gets out of the hospital, is the question."

"Ah," said Malone and threw his head back. "What they call diplo-matic flu, boss. The timing?"

Minogue looked up at his colleague. The scorn was plain enough.

"What," he said to Malone. "He's putting moves on us?"

Malone rested his chin on his knuckles and stared at the boots.

"Why'd he bring the handler with him? Covering up for the son, boss."

Malone brushed his hair with his fingers, ran his palms around his face and breathed out heavily. He shook his head once. Minogue reached down to zip his bag tighter. Then he stood and moved his toes around in his shoes. There'd been no offer of lab coats or even aprons. He and Malone had been steered into this changing room and left to themselves. He glanced down at Malone, still immobile.

"Are you any better now?" he asked.

Minogue had known straightaway it was her. He'd heard Malone gasp at the bloated body. Whatever had been feasting on her legs and her belly had seemed to be methodical. Dr. Kelly, a man so like Minogue's dentist that the inspector had asked him if he was related, had made two pages of notes. His hands had been shaking, Minogue had noticed. He looked down at his own notes. He'd been studying his own hand-writing too long not to notice the dropped endings of the letters and even the words, the scattered look to the page.

"Looked like she was pregnant," Malone murmured. "The bloating, like."

He lifted his head and squinted at Minogue.

"Crabs, is that what he said?"

"I think so, Tommy. A guess."

"Jesus. If I had a known that."

Minogue closed his notebook and slid it into the pouch in his carryall.

"I didn't write a bleeding word, boss. Sorry."

"It's okay. Do you think you'll make it?"

Malone looked around at the lockers and the stacked boxes.

"Well, Jases, I'm not staying here and that's a fact."

An orderly came in and began taking his clothes out of a locker. Minogue exchanged the greeting with his own estimates of the weather and quick agreement with the orderly's scorn for forecasts. Malone wrapped his boots in a plastic shopping bag and closed his travel bag.

Malone didn't look much better by the time Minogue finished his call from the phone at reception. Noonan would have a car over for them in five minutes.

"Cup of something, Tommy?"

"Not in here."

They watched an elderly woman inch her way down the hall using a walking contraption. Is that in his own near future too, Minogue wondered.

"Well that was the worst yet," Malone said. "She must have broken every . . . Ah well, what's the point of talking about it."

At least five days in the water, was Kelly's estimate. The marks of the string or rope had gone maroon. The X rays showed a broken spine and a fractured skull from the impact of the drop. Her lungs did not have enough water in them to suggest drowning. Minogue had welcomed with relief that numbness that had come over him when he had looked over Aoife Hartnett's body for the first time. His hands had made notes, while some other part of him had issued the questions of Kelly. He remembered his repeated queries for clarifications, the patient fencing with Kelly's irritated and defensive reluctance to say anything conclusive about how long ago Aoife Hartnett had been killed.

"Hoey told me he never got used to it," Malone said. "It's why he walked."

The drive outside was wet but it had stopped raining again. Minogue was pleased to see the expansively mustached and double-chinned Garda McGurk of the drooping eyelids and the rock concert query driving the squad car up to the door.

"There's our man," he said.

"Are they looking after you?" was McGurk's greeting. Minogue sat in beside him and sized up the face offering the gently mocking glances.

"In a manner of speaking now, and thanks."

"Back to the station, is it?" McGurk asked.

"To be sure. CI Noonan's in residence still?"

"He is, he is. Ye'll save the barley sandwiches until later on, will ye?"

"For a while, I'd say."

"Six months or so," said Malone.

McGurk leaned over the wheel to check traffic by the entrance to the hospital.

"Bad, was it?"

"As bad as you'd expect," Minogue said.

"The poor woman," was all McGurk said for the rest of the trip to the station. Minogue noted the frown settling over this affable, overweight rock fan he had taken a liking to. A Romeo, he wondered, charming them into bed with drollery and consideration.

Noonan had tea ready. He finished a radio exchange with a patrol car about registration numbers on a traveler's van. He ushered them into his office.

"There's a long day's work done," he said. "Terrible, isn't it?"

"It is that. It is."

Noonan slid out a sheet of photocopy paper from under a tray.

"I phoned about the car," he said. "Here's a partial list so far. She was in the backseat."

"There's no key in the ignition?" Minogue asked. Noonan shook his head.

Malone looked over Minogue's shoulder at the list.

"A tent, bejases," he said. "Sleeping bags . . . no stuff that'd be worth robbing? Didn't she have a camera or stuff?"

"No wallets or valuables yet," said Noonan. "Now isn't that something. What was the story with the American's car up in Dublin?"

"Nothing there either," muttered Minogue. "No."

"There could be stuff down in the rocks there," said Noonan. "At the bottom of the cliffs. It must have hit a right wallop."

Minogue looked up, met his eyes.

"I daresay. Yes. We'll need to look into that."

Noonan refilled his cup from the teapot.

"You'll be wanting to make calls here, is it?"

Minogue watched Noonan fill his own cup. Bony fingers, sinews: a townie. Minogue tested the chairback and crossed his legs.

"Thanks," he said. "Will you release the remains to Dublin for the PM?"

"I will indeed."

"I'll be wanting the car to be loaded on and sent up too."

Noonan nodded. Minogue looked down Noonan's list again.

"They had a bad time of getting her out of the car," Noonan said.

"Well you're ahead of us there, er, Tom."

"Ah, there was talk. The fellas taking the car in off the boat there."

Minogue nodded.

"Car's rightly smashed up now after that. A straight drop so far as I can see."

"I imagine so," Minogue agreed.

"The remains would be, well . . . sure I suppose it'd be the same as a head-on. Without the seat belts maybe?"

Noonan looked from Minogue to Malone and back. Malone jiggled his mug and took a mouthful of tea.

"I'd be obliged for the use of the phone for a while."

Noonan sat back and then stood.

"Fire away. It's all yours."

"We can —"

"Not a bit of it. Go right ahead and use the office. I'll be outside there."

Minogue took out his notebook and flipped to his telephone list. He looked around Noonan's office again while he tried to muster his instructions and queries for Murtagh to relay to the teams in Dublin.

The photos of Shaughnessy at the dos, the call-ins from Donegal needed mining properly. He lingered on the wood-framed photo of the group by a door somewhere. Noonan's broad smile, the uniform, sergeant's stripes on the ceremonial gray uniform. The hair looked wispy and soon to be departed even then. Ten years ago maybe? Minogue fingered the number for the Castlebar Garda station from the photocopy he taped into each of his notebooks. He turned the phone around and found a line out.

"I'll try Castlebar, Tommy. See if there's anything from the Micra before they wrap it."

A Sergeant Gerry Murphy handled scenes of the crimes. He had bagged the loose items and wrapped the car again.

"Thanks very much, now. Do ye have transport for it to the state lab up in Dublin?"

Murphy replied that they did indeed. Had he time to go over a preliminary with Minogue? He did.

Minogue added to the list Noonan had given him. Accordioned: was that now a technical term? Passenger compartment had been severely crushed. All seats out of their anchors. Anchors, Minogue wondered. Roof down at the front. Impact seems to have been on the bonnet, shared with the edge of the roof. The weight at the front, Murphy tried to explain. Minogue drew what he hoped looked like a hatchback. It had gone over nose first then? Most likely forward, yes. A bit of momentum seems to have carried it over the ninety degrees as it fell. Maps, carry-all bags with clothes, a rucksack, women's shoes. He waited for a pause before interrupting.

"Still no effects, Gerry? Handbag?"

"None, no."

"How much have ye done?"

"Well, we've emptied the car in actual fact."

"The boot too?"

"We have."

Minogue looked down the list again.

"Is there something we should be maybe have an eye out for, er, Inspector?"

It wasn't sarcasm, Minogue realized. He breathed out and rubbed at his eyes.

"Bits of string," he said. "A rope maybe?"

"No sign."

"Ashtrays?"

The dashboard had been shattered but the ashtray had stayed in place. There had been a gap and the water had worked in. Some fibers from the filters floating free had been bagged for the lab.

"I'm surprised there's not more. Stuff belonging to a man — shoes, clothes?"

"No," said Murphy. "Not yet identified, I'd better say, I suppose."

Had he come across that pushy, Minogue wondered.

"We're not playing paper chase here now, Gerry. Say what's on your mind."

"Well," Murphy said. "We don't want to make a slip here now, being as, well, it's tied in with the thing up in Dublin. The American?"

How could they not know, Minogue heard the voice mock him within, Murphy and Noonan and McGurk and half the bloody country, and it on the radio and telly?

"It's a tin opener you'd be needing to get at some bits," Murphy added.

Pushed up that track, Minogue wondered. Shoved off with another car? The keys could be anywhere off the cliffs too.

"The ignition was definitely off?" Minogue tried. "No bit of broken-off key?"

"No. We have the steering column in one piece."

Minogue let his Biro drop on the paper. He had drawn a box with a circle inside, and another box inside the circle. Put Shaughnessy in the damn car for us, he heard the voice again: that's all we want. Make one thing easy for us today, for the love of God. He looked down the list again.

"Rubbish in the car, Gerry? Tins of Coke or that?"

"Pepsi, actually. Two empties, one torn up in bits — by hand. You know the way people do it with the aluminium ones?"

"Not from the smash?"

"No. Peeled, one of them."

"Pepsi," Minogue said aloud. Malone looked over and raised his eyebrows. A sign of nerves, the shredding of a can during a row, to keep the hands busy?

"I wonder what we could lift off them after a few days of seawater . . ."

"Depends," Murphy said. "Ask Eimear above at the lab in Dublin. Alkaline deposits and brine . . . could be. They're bagged and ready to go to the lab in anyhow."

As in: don't be asking things we can't deliver. Minogue wondered if he had missed other hints earlier. He thanked Murphy and remembered to ask for his phone number again.

McGurk was sitting at a desk by the door to the public office of the Garda Station pretending to work. Minogue paused in the doorway. Noonan again told him it'd be no bother to set him up in the Western Hotel.

"Thanks, now, but we'll go along tonight as soon as we have the items from the car and the remains."

Noonan looked skeptical. Minogue couldn't tell if it was annoyance.

"Sure there's expertise already over the site now," Minogue added. And ye're doing a first-class job of it over at the Fields."

"An oul newspaper," said Noonan. "Cigarette packages. That's not much."

"You have a driver who'll do the run to Dublin tonight?"

"I do," said Noonan, and made a shy smile. "Beamish, the undertaker, will do it. 'There are no complaints about Beamish,' as they say. Will you take a lift with him?"

Minogue didn't know, as he thought about it later, if he'd done it for a dare, or because Noonan had said the driver was fast and knew the routine. Malone muttered something about the culchies looking for a chance to slag them, sending them back to Dublin in a hearse. Minogue shrugged that off.

McGurk led them out to the yard. There was a break in the clouds to the west and beams of light had broken through in the distance. The air had gone cooler. Malone still had no appetite.

"A bit of cake before we hit the trail," said Minogue. "And brewed coffee?"

McGurk piloted them to the Western Hotel. Vivaldi was playing in the foyer. They sat at a table across from the reception desk. Malone walked around, stopping to eye the goings-on in the street outside. Then he went wandering.

McGurk ordered a piece of cheesecake. He asked Minogue about prices in Dublin: the pictures, a dinner for two — not an all-out type dinner now, just a good one — a flat in Donnybrook. Minogue almost smiled. McGurk had heard there were new nightclubs in Dublin, really quite the thing. Had the inspector heard of them?

Minogue was about to try an answer he'd heard from gossip with Éilis and John Murtagh about prostitutes setting up in those new apartments when Malone reappeared from the lounge. He flicked his head toward the doorway. Minogue followed him into the lounge.

There were a half-dozen men at the bar, some couples at tables. The television was high over the bar, ignored. Beside Kilmartin's face were some kinds of charts. Another one slid out. Direct quotes and the date prominent — "no developments in the case . . ." Four months ago. Larry Smith's brother walking with his widow down a Dublin street. Another clip of a taped scene: the sheet over Smith out in Baldoyle with the blood from his pulped head soaked in. Minogue caught a glimpse of his own back and the bald spot Kathleen had taken to tickling after a few jars had made her frisky, as he stood with Kilmartin by the sheet.

The news reader reappeared. Gemma O'Loughlin's name, a columnist with the *Irish Times*. Papers turned over, the next item the camera slid left: a European Union meeting of agriculture ministers.

"Shite, meet fan," said Malone.

"What did I miss?" Minogue asked.

Malone looked around.

"'Allegations of a cover up,'" he said. "And Christy Smith sitting there with Larry's wife. He has a leg up on her, I heard. Tough talk. 'Hold them responsible.' Finger pointing. 'Public inquiry.' Shite like that."

"Names mentioned?"

"No, I didn't hear them. They mentioned the squad all right. But no names. 'Senior Gardai' aware of it, it said."

Minogue made his way back to the doorway into the foyer.

"Any reply from us?"

"Something about Garda sources denying it. And saying that we'd been bollocked by the family when we'd gone looking for clues anyway. Jases, the nerve."

•   •   •   •   •

The coffee had been too good probably. Minogue adjusted the seat belt again. Malone sat woodenly in the middle next to the driver, O'Callaghan.

He looked over his shoulder several times through the tinted glass. Their carryalls and evidence bags weren't moving around.

Minogue looked at the air-conditioning controls again. O'Callaghan noticed, started an explanation. The thermostat was always set low, he said. There was no need for it to tell you the God's honest truth. But people wanted to know you had it. Why? They'd heard about it, that was all.

He'd made the Dublin run before, but not in this direction. A lot of people living in Dublin even fifty years wanted to be buried at home. Home sweet home. Or people coming in from the States. There was a man of ninety-seven flown home from Los Angeles to be buried and two fellas from a funeral director's there came with the remains, if you don't mind. The money involved! No place like home. First thing they looked for, would you believe it, was an air-conditioned hearse.

It was dark by Foxford. The roads were dry here. Did they mind if he smoked, O'Callaghan asked. Minogue hadn't the heart to refuse. Swinford, eight miles. The inspector looked down at the clock. They'd be lucky to be back in Dublin by eleven. A signpost by the bridge over the River Moy sped by. Fishing, he thought, there's a thought. Couldn't you read and fish at the same time? O'Callaghan smoked heavily, savoring it. The smoke was yanked out the sliver of window by O'Callaghan's ear into the dark wake of the car.

What the hell did Shaughnessy get himself into here? Minogue listened to the changing notes of the wind from the window. *Éist le fuaim na habhainn, mar gheobhiadh tú bradán:* If you want to catch a salmon, you listen to the river. He'd phone Kathleen from Longford. A pint with Malone at Ryan's by closing time.

"Will you make it to Dublin before eleven?" he murmured.

No bother, from O'Callaghan. Something in the brash assurance told the inspector that he knew the reason the question, that he wouldn't mind being included in the arrangement for the pint. Strange isn't it, he began to talk in a monotone, how people are about certain things. Minogue rested his head on the headrest and leaned harder against the door. How people wanted to be buried and where. Tells you a lot about people, doesn't it? I suppose, from Minogue, a maybe, from Malone. O'Callaghan warmed to his subject.

Minogue watched the speedometer stay steady on one hundred. He wondered how well O'Callaghan knew the roads. He looked out at the dark shapes falling behind the headlights' glow. Not three feet behind him, through the glass, in a chilly space being driven through the Mayo night was the body of Aoife Hartnett.

O'Callaghan was beginning to annoy him seriously. Home, he was saying, sure home is only where you come from these days. And that's about it, wouldn't you say? Malone said he didn't know. The States, Europe, said O'Callaghan, we were only catching up. Mobility is the future. God knows where we'll end up with that stuff, hah? They'd have computers the size of a book soon and you could talk into them. Minogue let his eyes close. The monologue moved to cars.

Minutes passed. He had to talk to Mrs. Shaughnessy. She must know something of the son's recent shenanigans, for God's sake. He thought of the tracks out over the bog, the one that led to the cliff where Aoife Hartnett's car had plummeted to the rocks and water below. Bog holes, ponds, loughs of water even. But that track had been passable. Who'd know that? Noonan's reply last night on the phone — you'd get a car up there maybe but you wouldn't get it back down again too easy.

"Plane?" said O'Callaghan again. "From Dublin down to Knock Airport?"

"Right," said Malone. "A plane."

"And now ye're heading back in a hearse. A howl or what?"

Malone didn't answer. Did they mind him turning on the radio, he asked instead. Minogue opened his eyes: anything, *anything*. Malone found a live chat show from Galway. The question was: Had GOD sold out to the recording industry? A caller argued that women were still treated like shite in the rock industry and GOD had definitely sold out. She'd never listen to GOD again. Ever. Were they allowed to say words like shite on the radio now, Minogue wondered. O'Callaghan had to stop for a leak and a package of cigarettes. Did they want anything? Fishing about to see if they'd frown on having a few pints.

"The blather out of him," said Malone. "Be better off in the back with her."

Minogue fiddled with the radio. Not a gig out of it until the key was in.

"I can't figure it out," muttered Malone. "What am I missing here?"

"Who drove the car," said Minogue and yawned. "That's the key here now."

"Yeah. Right."

Malone turned to face him.

"I can see them driving out there," he said. "I can even see them — or him or her or whoever — driving up that track a bit. Why? To keep the car out of sight, say. They don't want people knowing they're around. Why? She's dead already? He plans or they plan to dump the car somewhere 'cause he doesn't want to be spotted on the road. I mean it sort of fits, being as what we're seeing people who kept off the beaten track on purpose."

"They had a tent, say."

"Well, yeah. But would you actually want to rough it out here? The bleeding rain and everything?"

Minogue surveyed the dashboard again. Blaupunkt, electric windows; the climate controls for the back: invincible. Who won the war again?

"Was she the outdoor type? I don't know, but I don't think so. Him?"

"Don't know, Tommy. We'll have to get better background. You're right."

"She was done there though. Yeah?"

Minogue nodded.

"You think he raped her? That was it?"

"The thought crossed my mind," Minogue said.

"Huh. How does he get out of there and wind up in Dublin, then? Unless he's dead too, with her. A double. But who'd kill the two of 'em, then take him off to Dublin in a car? Unless he's an outsider himself, heading out of the country too."

"This third party," said Minogue. "What's the point of trying to bring Shaughnessy back to Dublin?"

"Okay: he's alive then, say. Kidnapped."

"No. There's no sign of that, Tommy. Notes, calls. No PM signs."

"Okay. He's in cahoots with someone they meet on the road. Another Yank, say?"

"That's open, yes."

"But we can't even start on that until we get to place him — them, I mean. Or get through all the airline and boat lists. Back to Shaughnessy being the killer. Unless he's Mister Cool, he's out there in the bog freaking out entirely. Yeah?"

Minogue nodded.

"He's got a dead body," Malone went on. "Her car, it's dark say . . . Where's his car, the rental one, all this time? Parked off in Dublin? No. He's gone on his drive a day before she takes leave. So he's gone in his own car. But there's no sign of the car at all, the rental car."

"Wait, Tommy. We can't be sure. The B & B people couldn't put a definite make on their car."

"You'd have to wonder about them checking in at night and leaving early. Want to bet they parked their car away from the B & B? There might have been separate cars all the while."

Minogue shrugged.

"Yeah," said Malone. "That'd fix the business about how did he get out of the place handy enough. He has his own motor, like, so dumping the Micra is the thing to do. It buys time. A lot of time if it's done right."

"We'll be needing a blue Escort on the roads around there, Tommy, for this to hold. A clear, dependable sighting."

Malone yawned now.

"There had to be times he parked his somewhere though, I mean," he said. "They'd want to be together, wouldn't they? I mean what's the point of . . . ?"

O'Callaghan opened the door. Minogue caught him halfway in. Would he mind letting him get something out of his bag in the back, he asked. He followed O'Callaghan around the back, wondered if he had downed more than one pint.

"Is that peppermint you have?"

O'Callaghan gave no sign he'd picked up on the sarcasm.

"It is," he said briskly. "Would you like one, there . . . ?"

"Matt. Thanks."

Minogue took out the folder Mairéad O'Reilly had given him. He sat back in.

"Peppermint, Tommy?" Malone's reply was just as leaden.

"It's all right. I'll wait till we get to Dublin for me, ah, peppermints."

CHAPTER 18

MINOGUE WONDERED IF O'CALLAGHAN had been daring him to say something. The Mercedes had been doing one hundred and forty coming in the Lucan bypass. Malone had been dozing. He'd opened his eyes when O'Callaghan braked for the end of the motorway.

"Turn left there, if you please," said Minogue.

O'Callaghan left them by the door.

"Technical Bureau," O'Callaghan said. "Is that like a lab?"

"Adjacent," said Minogue. "We moved from across the river two years ago. Will you give us our bags now, and thanks very much."

It had rained recently. Malone stretched.

"Only half-ten," he said. Minogue took the bag from O'Callaghan.

"You know how to get to the city morgue, do you?"

"I have it here. Down by the Custom House."

"You'll wind up there yourself if you keep driving like you were." Minogue looked down at the evidence bags.

"Sign them in, Tommy, will you. And drop in the cassette for duplication."

He nearly dropped the videocassette taking it out of his carryall. He shoved the folder into the carryall and zipped it up again. Malone watched him.

"Do you want to go over anything before we knock off?"

"No."

Minogue fingered his key ring and pushed the remote. The lights on his Citroen flashed and the alarm chirped once.

"It'll wait until the morning. I'll drop this in the car and do a quick check of what's come in."

Malone followed him over. Minogue set the video case on the bonnet.

"The airport," Minogue murmured.

"Yeah?"

"Any closer on when the Escort was parked. If any of Shaughnessy's stuff has turned up. Her effects too. Call-ins from outside Dublin. See if we can find Aoife Hartnett too on any of those days."

Malone cleared his throat. He was about to spit, but he turned aside instead and gently let it go on the tarmac. Minogue looked around the night sky and listened for trains in the tunnel beneath this city end of Phoenix Park where Garda Headquarters was housed. His mind wandered back to the empty hills, the cliffs.

"With her," said Malone, "can we wait till the morning, like? The news?"

"We can," said Minogue. "The crowd she worked with. Garland. After the next of kin. I'll phone her brother-in-law at home first thing in the morning. There'll be nothing on the news until tomorrow. Let 'em sleep if they can tonight."

· · · · ·

Minogue slowed when he saw the thumb out. He'd at least drop a hint to this gawky, bedraggled teenager that standing on the side of the Bray Road after midnight thumbing a lift should have a health warning.

The girl noticed him slowing. He had almost stopped the car when he spotted the two fellas sidling out from the gateway behind her. He didn't hear much after the first shout. It was the girl doing most of it. Maybe they were too drunk to try to chase him. Annoyed and disheartened, he sped up to eighty passing Belfield. He thought about phoning them in. Or worse, go back and pick them up and speed off back to the Donnybrook station. Sit across the table from them and give them a bit of grief. Drugs, he wondered. No: he was overreacting.

He imagined Kilmartin in a swanky conference facility retailing war stories from the squad. Profiling: when, in the name of God, would the squad ever be using FBI profiles? He thought of Larry Smith, the brother finger-wagging at the camera, the dark warnings to the Guards. How the other drug gangsters must be laughing. The Citroen wavered only an instant as he turned sharply up the Rise. It was enough to alert him. He geared down. Why the hell was he driving like a madman? He was still thinking of Kilmartin's junket when he turned into the driveway.

He pulled out the key and waited for the Citroen to settle. The edges of his keys felt like teeth against his thumb. Vegan, that was it. Iseult was a vegan, according to Kathleen. Iseult mightn't be getting some vital vitamin or something. Unhinged her, couldn't think logically. How could he check? He stepped out onto the driveway but he turned instead and walked back to the gate.

The pillar had never been straight. The gate had always scraped even in the days when he'd made a point of closing it. Iseult, wouldn't you know it, had found a way to unlatch it soon after she had learned to walk. Meat is murder, wasn't that one of the slogans? Drisheen, eggs, sausages: the Holy Family though? Low.

The lamplight from the road showed patches of wet on the driveway. The faint bass thumping came on the breeze from the neighbors. Gearóid, Una Costigan's youngest, the one giving her the willies, no doubt. Still at it in the middle of the night. Shaved head, history graduate, unemployed. Nice lad; bone lazy. Or just unwilling to head off out on a plane somewhere? Gearóid thought he'd had a break at Christmas with a concert in the community center, but it didn't come off. Gearóid wore sunglasses, the insect-eye models, nearly all the time now.

What was Aoife Hartnett trying to do for God's sake? Did she and Shaughnessy have a thing going? There were no stars that he could see. The breezes barely stirred the hedge. Park the damn car in Cabinteely tomorrow evening no matter what, by God, and walk up by Tully, sit awhile, down Bride's Glen and . . . Inveigle Iseult out too. Try and get her to drink milk at least. Was that music getting louder?

The hedge should really be cut back. Why hadn't he? Only the hall light on. He and Kathleen had a house to themselves. Stuff forgotten about was turning up: Iseult's carving behind the lawn mower. Yes, Iseult called home her dacha. It had been months since she'd stayed overnight with them. The sudden ache reminded him of a paper cut.

Maybe that's why Gearóid Costigan's comings and goings had set his teeth on edge. It wasn't the smell of dope drifting in over the hedge last summer. It was the fact that Gearóid was at home. He'd never actually left. His own son, Daithi, was on the American express, going wherever his training and job took him. There were twenty-two years of his son's life upstairs in boxes and drawers. Lately he had found Kathleen's mantras of when Daithi comes home again unbearable. At least he wasn't the prodigal son.

Had Mrs. Shaughnessy written off her son? Johnny Leyne greasing the wheels and paying off predators to keep his one-and-only out of jail. Minogue ran his hand along the top railing of the gate, flicked off the drops of water. Remorse, that's what had them there. They knew they'd messed up. What could he do, sit Mrs. Shaughnessy down in back at an interview room at the squad and work on her to give him the true story? Would they try to offer money to Aoife Hartnett's family if it turned out that way, her mother, her sister, her nieces, her nephews . . . ?

He stared at the area carved out by the light over the hall door. He followed the sharp lines between the light and shadow by the garage door, the weakening ambit of the light as it lost out to the darkness by the hedge. When Daithi comes marching home again. The sharp stab over the heart stopped his thoughts. Football games, swimming down at Seapoint and Killiney, meeting him for a pint after he started college. He'd loved going up in the woods at Katty Gallagher before it had been turned into a managed park. But that was when he was eleven or twelve. His friends still phoned: Barney; Lorcan; Sarah, who'd finally given up on trying to hook Daithi but wanted to stay a friend. The bent for mathematics, the indifference and even exasperation with English. At least he'd stopped smoking. Caty had put him right. She'd look after him.

Minogue squeezed his thumb harder on the key and stared at the hall door. Maybe that's what Iseult had been doing those times he'd found her standing out on the bloody road staring at the house, sizing it up. No place like home. No place. Is that what the *Holy Family* came out of?

Before him was the step up, the mat underfoot, the key sliding into the lock. The Burren print on the wall then, the hello from Kathleen. Home. He'd been hearing that there was no place like home all bloody day, it seemed — Kilmartin knew something. The thought froze him there. No, he thought; it was pub talk, spoofing. Close ranks though — the Old Guard. He swore and pushed the hall door.

He closed the door and headed for the kitchen with the folder under his arm. The light over the counter was on. Kathleen had left a copy of the newspaper there. He could make out the photo of *The Holy Family* from across the room. He wondered if Kathleen had tried to get in touch with Iseult.

The cupboard door creaked. He reached in before it opened enough, felt the neck of the bottle, drew it out. He ran the tap slowly, took down a glass, and filled it. He downed three-quarters of the water, then he sized up the remainder and poured in as much Bushmills. The edge of the countertop bit into his hip but he didn't shift. He took another mouthful and eyed Mairéad O'Reilly's folder again.

It looked odd with the yellow stickies skew-ways sticking out of it. He lifted a chair out from under the table and sat. What was the name of that outfit in Africa . . . in Kenya? Tall, very tall — He just couldn't pin it. Tall, very tall — no, not the Bushmen. They measured wealth in cows too. A cow people. No wonder the Carra Fields had turned to bog. He opened to the sticky he'd scrawled "legends" on.

"What's messy?"

Sleepy-voiced, Kathleen pushed open the door. He'd said it aloud?

"Masai, I meant to say. Did I wake you?"

"I thought you heard me," she said. "What Masai?"

"I was thinking."

She nodded at the bottle. He gave her the eye.

"Thinking, I said, love. I'm only in the door."

"Give us a sup, will you?" she murmured.

He stared at her. She stared back at him.

"What are you looking at?"

"Well, I'm not sure," he said. "You want a sup of this?"

"Why not?"

"This is whiskey, Kathleen."

"Well my oh my. All these years and I didn't know that."

"But I'm going to hell and damnation with it, amn't I?"

"I never said that."

"Well why is the bottle hidden under the sink all these years?"

"It's not hidden if you know where it's kept, is it. Pour it, can't you?"

She sipped at it, grimaced. He studied her expression.

"When's the last time you took a drop of whiskey?"

"I phoned, you know. Éilis told me."

"Told you what?"

She held the glass out, turned it, and watched as it swilled.

"We had a grand long chat. I didn't know she was so clued-in, like."

"Éilis is away with the fairies sometimes now, Kathleen."

"No wonder she's a match for you. Tell me again it's the job that does it."

"It's the job that does it."

He looked from the glass to the bottle to Kathleen's face.

"Did you have a chat about Iseult? The thing in the paper?"

"I saw you outside, you know," Kathleen said. "I heard the car. You standing there staring at the place. That's what Iseult used to do. Una Costigan saw her late some nights, or Gearóid did. A half an hour, she said. Staring at the house."

Minogue slid the glass back to the folder.

"What's the folder? Work, is it?"

"To do with it, yes. What did Éilis have to say?"

"Nothing. The way girls talk, women talk. You wouldn't understand."

"Is this going to be a men-are-toxic thing?"

"You expected me to hit the roof, I'll bet you. The *Holy Family* thing."

Minogue stopped pouring.

"You're right. Did you?"

"No."

"Will you? In the near future?"

"I don't know," she said. "I don't know what came over me. I think it was talking to Éilis. She said to go with it. That Iseult needed me, needed us. And always would. She said that Iseult's stuff was part of a conversation with us. That she couldn't do what she had to do without us."

Minogue let more into the glass. Kathleen stared at his hand on the bottle.

"I don't get it," Kathleen murmured. "Do you?"

"No."

"I already had the article, you know. From the paper. I got it this afternoon when you were jet-setting it out in Mayo or wherever."

"God, if only you knew."

Kathleen rubbed at her upper lip.

"But Iseult makes some things sound really terrible, Matt. Going to mass, for God's sake. Fifteen-year-olds trying to make themselves miscarry. Hemorrhaging to death. The body and blood — I had to tell her to stop. It wasn't the hint of blasphemy either. Then there's your job, with killers. People'll begin to wonder."

Minogue took a measured gulp of Bushmills.

"People don't really wonder much, so far as I can see, Kathleen."

"I think it's the pregnancy. But I'm not going to admit that."

"She's always been heading in this direction. She's coming into her own."

Her eyes darted from the bottle to his face.

"Are you getting slagged over her at work?"

"No," he said. "Not that I noticed in anyhow."

"Oh right, Jim's off in the States. I nearly forgot. Good timing."

"How'd you mean?"

She shivered.

"Larry Smith and his crowd," she said. "Don't be talking to me about them. I saw the news. That family . . . God, they give me the creeps. Do you know what one of them said? 'This isn't over yet, not by a long shot.' Isn't that a threat?"

"They'll hide behind something, I don't know."

"They shot up that squad car out on Griffith Avenue last month, didn't they?"

"Prove it," he said. "Anyway. We're going to have Internal Inquiries look over how we've handled Smith."

"But what if they're serious, Matt? That they really will follow up on it, with the squad? You're in the hot seat now."

Minogue looked around the kitchen. He lingered on the shadows, the dull reflection of the light on the kettle, the dark corners. Would she know that Tynan wanted them to carry pistols now? She was staring at the calendar.

"People'll think she had a terrible childhood or something," she murmured. "You know how the jokes go around."

"Ah, it doesn't matter, love. I'll laugh it off."

Her frown returned.

"You think you can?"

He looked over at the window.

"It's either that," he said, "or I'll knock them down in the street. She's my daughter, isn't she? Ours. She's telling the truth. As she sees it. And that's that."

Kathleen sat back and folded her arms.

"So: how is our daughter then, after your chat?"

"Thrilled," Kathleen murmured. "Says she knew we'd understand."

Minogue sighed and shook his head. Kathleen let out a sigh.

"She says she won't preach about us still eating meat though."

"Good of her. Tell her I'd compromise on the black pudding. But the rashers stay. Did she give you the lecture on carnivores and violence . . ."

Kathleen searched his face. He kept staring at the sink.

"Are you all right, Matt?"

Meat and milk had made those Masai tall, strong.

"I am," he managed. "Yes."

"You must be tired after the gallivanting."

"I was just — Anyway. There were a few odd things lying around at the back of my mind. I think I just fell over them."

·   ·   ·   ·   ·

Dowsing, that's what Mairéad O'Reilly's father had done to find the buried walls. And it worked, didn't it? In the right hands, it was said. Maybe his own job wasn't far different. He put down the anniversary Shaeffer and rubbed at his eyes. A quarter after two, for the love of God. Fire with fire: he poured more Bushmills.

Next to his glass the photo of Peadar O'Reilly, done badly on an old photocopier, holding his forked stick, with the bog-cut below. The copy was good enough to see O'Reilly's pride in the direct stare, his staged grasp on the divining stick. The long poles he could understand. There had been hundreds used to plumb the bog. The excavations had laid bare thick walls under eight feet of bog.

He turned to the beginning of the folder again, looked down at the drawing of the Carra King. It had been done by a talented amateur with plenty of the heroic. It reminded him of a comic book of years gone by. It was probably one of O'Reilly's pupils. The Carra King? The Richly Imagined Carra King, it should be. The embellishments were as obvious in O'Reilly's version as they were in the drawing. The artist had slapped in a heavenward look on the dying king, as well as elaborate Celtic patterns on the hero's outfits. O'Reilly had dropped in gems like "weighing as much as the king's finest bull," "sacred hazel groves." Hardly science: a storyteller.

Minogue sipped at the whiskey again. He tried to imagine a country schoolmaster toiling away in a remote part of the west of Ireland. Postwar Ireland, asleep and detached, a man rearing a large family in a place being stripped of youth and history by emigration. O'Reilly, like so many of the teachers Minogue remembered, probably had an appetite for heroism and drama thwarted by making a living. This teacher had done much and worked in obscurity. Separated from those who were official custodians, no wonder he let his imagination fill in the gaps.

The stone was to crown the hill, Carra Hill. A signal, O'Reilly claimed, that the king was dead but that the new king was already installed. Maybe carrying the stone was practice for carrying the king up by himself when the time came.

The Bushmills still had bite. He flipped to where O'Reilly had thrown in stuff from the more widely known legends. It was common in legend for a man to be given a *geis,* a task, to fast or go out on the hills and live off berries and watercress. And it wasn't just poets and holy men like the mad poet Sweeney, lovesick and off the rails entirely, walking through hawthorn thickets like an iijit. Purification for the *geis:* to devour no creature, to abjure meat and milk, to abandon the sustenance his civilization had grown strong on.

Minogue held a sip of whiskey on his tongue. He looked over at the bank calendar open on a picture of a lake in Connemara. Wind, the curlew's cry, wild: he should go back and read those translations of the ancient poems again.

So: after three days of steering clear of meat, this candidate was purified, light-headed, and weighted down with a boulder, "an effigy of the king." But was there a stone carved for every succeeding king? Twenty thousand people in a well organized, peaceful settlement: there must have been craftsmen, ritual. Loaded down, your man was pointed toward the hill: off you go, son, find your way up there and you can unload at the top. Had many made it? If the chosen one didn't make it, what happened? O'Reilly didn't have a go at that. Wisely, probably. Nor had he much to say about a revival of the thing back in the 1840s.

He let the pages fall back to the one of O'Reilly standing over the exposed wall in 1952, the start of him being taken seriously: definitely a told-you-so look. He would continue for another fourteen years after he'd handed it over to the museum, or rather the museum had moved in.

He brushed the yellow stickies with his thumb. Where was the section on Donegal again? Carrick, that village on the road in to Glencolumbkille? Every second town in Ireland was Carrick-something. He opened the guidebook again. Wasn't there a Glen Road to Carrick song? Donegal: Dún na nGall, literally the Fort of the Foreigner. Shaughnessy had been over that road not two weeks ago. Looking for . . . ?

Minogue was getting addled now. He let the guidebook close. He took up O'Reilly's folder again. "A chieftain to the North . . ." — he'd seen it two or three times on one page. Cattle raids and knocking heads were part of the folklore epics and mythology. Taín bó Cuailgne, the Cattle Raid at Cooley. The North: couldn't mean the Vikings, they came a thousand years later . . . there. O'Reilly had it that the settlement went into decline when they had to give too much heed to guarding against northern raiders carrying off maidens and cattle and possessions.

There was nothing about the people of the Carra Fields just wearing out the pasture with cattle. Maybe that's why O'Reilly was held at a distance by the experts. They could spout about rainfall patterns, erosion, and nutritional decline in grasses and social dislocation. That was science, those were facts. O'Reilly, the obsessed amateur, would wander into the *béaloideas*, the oral tradition that still came through by the open fires and in the twinkling eyes of the aged, the stories O'Reilly would have listened to and rewritten later.

Minogue squinted at the words: the customs among the *dreams*, the tribal groups. Ransom perhaps, forced marriages, local wars. He yawned and slid back in the chair. He sat listening to the fridge and surveying the empty glass and the books and notes scattered on the table until he couldn't take the pain from the chair back grinding into his shoulders anymore.

He closed and stacked the maps and folders, shoved them to the wall. He probably wouldn't be able to sleep. He fought off the thought of another half-glass of whiskey. The list he'd made might look downright stupid in the morning. So what: he'd make time somehow. He wondered if Geraldine Shaughnessy was sleeping in her suite, wherever that suite was. Was her husband — her ex-husband — awake himself, in his hospital room?

He paused by the door and laid his hand on the light switch. And Aoife Hartnett coiled up in the water for days, that band around her neck where she'd been choked turning brown as the tissue decayed. Pieces of her torn and chewed by whatever lived at the bottom of the Carra Cliffs.

Kathleen grunted and swallowed as he lay next to her.

"Are you all right?"

Talking in her sleep. He clamped his eyelids shut. It wouldn't be the first time he fibbed.

"I am," he said.

CHAPTER 19

"FINE BY ME," Minogue repeated. "Honestly."

One coffee wasn't enough. He studied the edge of the carpet by the hall door. Anne Boland had a Cork accent. He wanted her to keep talking, about anything really. She was explaining how Geraldine Shaughnessy, her sister, was so nervous about going to an interview in a police station.

"It's not that she's trying to, well . . . She's what you might say a bit phobic. She may be trying to keep some hope alive, you know, now? Going into a barracks now would be a real trial for her, I'm thinking. She doesn't know I'm phoning now. I stayed with her last night. Sure she hardly slept a wink."

"I understand, Mrs. Boland. There'll be no bother. But at some point we'd be needing to get an interview."

"She'd never phone yourself now . . ."

"So you'll steer her over to Grafton Street then?"

"I will indeed. I'll wait for her too. I have my eldest, Gráinne, here too. We'll all be driving down to Mallow when ye're finished, please God."

Minogue said good-bye and put down the receiver. Anne Boland had suggested the hotel but Minogue had said Bewleys. He finished his coffee and packed the folder in his briefcase. He set the house alarm under the stairs, quickstepped out the hall door, and turned the dead bolt.

He tilted the sunroof and cursed the return of that rubbery ache behind his eyes. Ranelagh was all right for a change. The traffic lights by the canal were out of kilter. A cyclist tried to pull a stunt on the footpath as Minogue worked around a bus with a foot of space to his left. The cyclist came close to taking a header across the front of the Citroen.

Minogue stared him down. The man slapping tickets on windscreens on Molesworth Street needed more coaxing than Minogue thought fair for a senior Garda detective with a hangover.

He skipped across Dawson Street with his eyeballs jiggling up and down in their sockets in a way that surprised and appalled him. He arrived on Grafton Street almost in time to be crushed by a milk delivery lorry. He hadn't a leg to stand on when the driver called him a fucking yob: the street wasn't pedestrian only for another hour. Bewleys offered him no comfort this morning. The nod from Kevin Kelly, an enormous, sweaty, and good-natured ex-soldier turned floor man, seemed guarded, solemn even.

"What's the story there, Matt."

"This is an awful town, Kevin. How're Theresa and the kids keeping?"

"Top form. Thanks. Jasmin's into the art still."

Minogue hammered on the lift button again. Kelly's face turned grave.

"Saw her looking at her dinner the other day, but. Very strange look on her face."

"That a fact now, Kevin."

"Yeah. Asked me if we have any pictures of the Holy Family anywhere."

Minogue knew better than to expect any trace of humor on the Dubliner's face.

"Go easy there, Kevin."

"What are you hammering on that button for? The lift is bollocksed."

Minogue sighed and looked up through the metalwork.

"You better not be having me on, Kevin."

"Where are you off to in anyhow? You're a Main Floor man."

"The museum."

"Well you're late then, aren't you."

"I should give you another dig for that. What are you saying?"

"Party of five gone up ahead of you. Two women, a teenager, a girl. Looked important enough. Even without the two heavies."

Minogue put his foot on the first step. Four flights, a sore head.

"Two of ours, is it?"

Kevin nodded.

"Unless everyone in town is walking around with radios and shooters tucked in the back of their trousers."

Kevin Kelly cleared his throat and tugged at his shirt cuffs. He had risen to corporal before jumping ship.

"Tell them not to look so shagging shifty, Matt."

Minogue stepped aside to allow a wheezing bedraggled man down the steps. Kelly moved in and grasped the elderly man under the arm.

"Heard a strange thing."

Minogue looked away from the busker setting up across the street from the restaurant. He noted the excessive care Kevin was taking with the old man.

"You're being fitted up for something."

Minogue looked around at the passing faces.

"Your outfit I mean. The job."

Kelly had a big smile for a young woman carrying an armful of books. He spoke out of the side of his mouth.

"Well, am I right?"

"Kevin, I can't be doing business here now."

"Don't be so bloody contrary, will you. Bernard, my lad, well one of his mates was in a pub there last week. Some of the Smith crowd were there; hangers-on."

Kelly's face suddenly gave way to a smile and a wink at a couple. Minogue remembered that it was Kevin Kelly's size and charm that had allowed Bewleys to stay open late for several years now.

"Anyway. He overheard some talk. There was something mentioned, something about 'quits.' Oh sure, pub talk. But he's in tight enough with the Smiths, Bernard says."

Minogue glanced at Kelly's beefy hands adjusting his tie. He must work hard to keep the belly in, he decided.

"What kind of 'quits'?"

"Something serious."

"Like using a Garda squad car at Griffith Avenue for target practice?"

"Might be connected, I don't know. I'm only passing it on."

"Any name?"

Kelly shook his head.

"A friend of a friend — and all that. There's no comeback on it. Just something I heard thirdhand."

"All right, Kevin. Thanks."

"Now I'm not a tout, for Jases' sake. Okay? But if I hear more, I'll let you know. If it's the Smiths, you better be wide awake, that's all I'm saying. They're bigger than even the Guards know. I'm telling you. They don't care, some of them. You know?"

Minogue took his time on the stairs. He waited by the hallway leading to the museum café for a minute to get his breath. Kilmartin couldn't have picked a better time to be on a fortnight's jaunt in the States. Had he known? He thought of Tynan. The commissioner had spoken to him more in the past few days than in the past six months. Chess, moving pieces to gain advantage. He rubbed hard at his eyes to try to clear the suspicion and anger surging up into his thoughts.

·   ·   ·   ·   ·

"You'd qualify as a prominent person, Mrs. Shaughnessy," he said. "'It's better to be safe . . .' is the approach, I imagine now."

Minogue looked at the detective who had been eyeing the doorway, the bored-looking one with the skimpy beard and the polo shirt under his leather jacket.

"Could I trouble you to set us up with a cup of something here?"

A pause and a blink before he nodded. Minogue exchanged a look with the older detective.

"You won't mind if Mrs. Shaughnessy and I were to chat alone there over in the corner?"

The coffee was too hot. The detective slid the change onto the table. A fifty-penny coin rolled to the edge and fell to the floor. He took a seat near the door. Minogue picked up the coin. The only other clients, a couple with wire-rimmed glasses and hair so blond Minogue believed it could be dyed, were exchanging maps and sheets of paper at a table by the counter.

"They're certainly different from the Guards I knew," Mrs. Shaughnessy said. "Hard to tell they're Guards at all really."

"That's the idea, I think."

"Are they armed?"

Minogue nodded. She looked away.

"On bicycles, I remember," she murmured. "Armed only with their tongues. Little enough for them to do back then of course. How things change."

From what airy suite Geraldine Shaughnessy had been summoned to be told of her son's death, he wondered. He imagined a city skyline at night, all glass and pastel carpet, a piano —

"I do appreciate all that you're doing," she said. "Especially this now. I dreaded the thought of going to a Garda station to . . . I'm embarrassed, really."

Minogue smiled. Fifty, looked thirty-five — if even. Girlish yet: coltish, was that a word? He couldn't tell if she had makeup. The freckles were scattered sparsely along the back of her hands. Her eyes were bloodshot, the lids pink and tight-looking. He wondered if she'd tell him that Johnny Leyne was in hospital. Maybe she didn't know herself. Hardly.

"Can you tell me if you have anything new on, what's happened?"

N-oo: nooze. Her native Cork accent clicked handily with American.

"I can tell you what we know, but it's far from being anything we can seize on as a solution."

She studied the tabletop while she listened. Her eyes didn't rest on Minogue when she looked up. He noted her hand shaking on the cup. Her eyes were glassy now. She didn't reach for a handkerchief. She wasn't going to try drinking the rest of her coffee. The German or Dutch or Swedish couple decamped. That could have been the real color of their hair, he decided. He watched the bearded detective adjust something under his arm. Surly young fella: like to pin him someday, wise him up to manners.

A woman with a stream of white hair down her back entered the restaurant. The two detectives exchanged a glance. Mrs. Shaughnessy asked Minogue to repeat words. Place-names and people. Did she want to take notes maybe? She thanked him but no. He began to feel terrible for her. Alone she seemed, composed and dazed and polite and refined. She began to roll a thin silver bracelet up and down over her wrist. He took a delicate line on the cause of death. She stopped tugging on her bracelet.

"As a result of . . . ?"

Pale enough to start with, he believed she seemed to have shrunk since they sat down. He lowered his voice.

"There'd have been blood loss. I think the doctor would describe it as shock."

"But the beating," she murmured. She began rolling the bracelet again.

"Severe. Not many blows but, well, a lot of force applied."

She closed her eyes. Minogue saw her chest heave.

"Your sister," he said. "Would you prefer . . . ? She's waiting below, isn't she?"

She opened her mouth and breathed out through her mouth. "Hah," Minogue heard.

"No. I asked her not to come up with me. John, of course, well he couldn't."

She picked up her handbag and took out paper hankies.

"Are you married? I suppose you are."

She blew her nose. She paused, stared at something on the table, and dropped the hanky into her bag.

"I am."

"The person you marry is a different person than —"

She caught herself and looked at Minogue.

"I'm sorry," she said. "It's you need to get information from me, and here I am blathering."

"It's all right. Don't be worrying about that."

Her eyes went to the white-haired woman. Surrounded by a pot of tea, cakes, and books, she had begun to write in a copy book.

"John and I got along well. Odd, isn't it? But we married different people — when we married, I mean. He's not well, you know."

Minogue nodded.

"He asked me on the plane coming over. I knew he couldn't sleep, that he'd been thinking about it, that it hurt him so terribly. He asked me if it would have made a difference to Patrick if we'd had more children. Oh, it wasn't sniping or blame or anything."

She dabbed at her eyes with a fresh hanky.

"Without going into detail let me just say it wasn't medically possible back then. It was me, not John. Things didn't go well. Patrick was premature. The delivery didn't go well even. I was left with complications. We would have liked more kids. Patrick had difficulties. That was clear right from the start. This was before they had all the lingo they have nowadays. ADD — do you have that over here?"

"I'm not sure."

"Hyperactive kids? Attention Deficit Disorder?"

"I think I've heard of it."

"Learning disabilities?"

"Oh, to be sure. Now I'm with you. Plenty to go around here."

"Good health though, that was Patrick. Nannies came and went. He'd be up all night as an infant. I had no idea kids could be like that. He couldn't sleep sometimes. And he had a tough time of it dealing with other kids when he went to the nursery — the only child thing now. It was more than he couldn't really manage everything that was going on around him . . . One specialist thought it was a kind of manic depressive thing, even."

"He lashed out at people?"

She let down the rolled up hanky on her saucer.

"Yes."

"It carried into adult life, did it?"

Her voice was low when she replied.

"I think you know that by now. John and I agreed we could hide nothing."

Minogue watched the white-haired woman cleaning her glasses. An albino — of course. Albina?

"If he brought it on himself we must face up to that," she said.

Minogue wondered if Patrick Shaughnessy had struck his mother.

"The thought occurred to me, Inspector, that my son —"

He saw her bite her lip. He wasn't ready for the glimpse of her contorted face as she lowered her head. He stood and drew his chair around beside her. The detective with the beard was watching him. Her words came out in the squeezed and bitter whispers Minogue had heard so often in interview rooms from innocent and guilty alike.

"He wasn't a psychopath, you know. He wasn't."

He nodded at the older detective and mouthed "sister" at him. Her shoulders were bony, he realized. He didn't know whether to hold her arm instead. Why had he thought her so remote?

Geraldine Shaughnessy's sister arrived out of breath. A small enough resemblance, he couldn't help thinking, between Anne Boland and her. He let go of her shoulder and stood up. Behind the lenses, the white-haired woman's eyes were enormous. Still she squinted. Minogue stared at her but she seemed not to notice. He headed off the older detective in the doorway.

"I don't want her leaving town now," he said. The detective scratched at the back of his head.

"There was talk of them going to Cork today. There's two escort cars set up already, I know that much."

"Tell them no can do then, if you please. I didn't get to recent stuff with the son at all. We have to have her here in Dublin until she can talk."

"Fair enough. I'll pass it on. Who do we call if there's a scrap over it? All we have is 'do what the family wants.'"

"Call Tynan."

The detective's eyelid drooped a little.

"Tynan, you said?"

"That's the one. Have your scrap with him."

•   •   •   •   •

"You're probably right," he said to Malone. "She just realized then that he wasn't coming back. Ever, like."

Minogue leaned around the partition.

"Anyone call in about Mrs. Shaughnessy, Éilis? Is she sticking to some plan to go to her family below in Cork?"

Éilis shook her head. Minogue returned to the table. Murtagh tapped his Biro on the duty schedule again.

"Farrell took that APF fella's statement. Murphy, Michael — Mick. Murphy leveled with him. So the car could have been there all through those shifts."

"Are the others still playing holy?"

Murtagh shrugged.

"They don't want to get kicked, boss."

"Tell Farrell to go after them in earnest. Round two."

Minogue looked down the list again. Murtagh was eying him. Something he'd said?

"Just pretend I'm Jim Kilmartin for a while, John," he murmured. He turned to see Murtagh's reaction.

"Still nothing solid on phones? People who used the car park?"

Murtagh shook his head.

"Tell me about the photos then, how they're coming. The, er, celebrity mob he was cozying up with."

Murtagh stood, tugged at his belt, and waved at the photos pinned to the side of the map.

"This fella's a stockbroker. He made a killing on the markets there a few years ago. That's down at the auction place, what do you call — Goff's. Doesn't remember Shaughnessy at all. Nobody does. Oh, this one here, the fat fella, Kavanagh, he remembers being introduced to 'an American.' That's all."

Malone strolled over. He held out a bag of crisps.

"Those are the horses there, right," he said.

"Good for you, Tommy."

"Is that O'Riordan there?"

"That's him, yes."

Hard to match this beaming face with the reserved, diplomatic companion to Leyne and his ex-wife Minogue remembered from the hotel.

"Have we set him up for an interview?"

Murtagh let go the crisps he had drawn from Malone's bag.

"He'd be, er . . ."

"It's all right, John, I'm not going to bark."

"You see him knowing much about Shaughnessy? 'Friend of the family'?"

"Try anyway. Get hold of him. Tell him we'll be wanting a statement. If he fights shy, I'll talk to him. Eventually. Shaughnessy must have had at least a chat with him. Even if it's only a how-do. There he is — and again — two places they're in the same crowd."

"He's a big deal, boss. You see the picture in the papers a lot."

"The ponies, the castles for the Hollywood mob, yes, I know."

"More to him than that, isn't there? He put money in films here at the right time. Remember that one that got it all started there about ten years back, *Leaves Are Green,* was it?"

"*Leaves of Green,*"said Minogue.

"You saw that?" from Malone. "The drug one and the IRA? Shite wasn't it?"

"Never got around to seeing it."

"Well the Guards look like iijits in it," said Malone. "Shaughnessy was in on the music scene too, when it took off, right?"

Minogue nodded.

"The Thicks were the first. I remember them. Then there was God-damnitohell, remember the ones used to piss on the stage? Then came the Works, managed from day one. But where's whatshername, this Aoife Hartnett, in this?"

Minogue searched the eight-by-tens.

"That's her next to the sculpture. There's the side of Shaughnessy. Looks like he's smiling at someone. Nothing in his hands there — look."

"Put it on a table," said Malone.

"Maybe. Or maybe he went on the wagon," said Minogue.

"Huh. She has something. Wine."

Minogue stared at the shots of Shaughnessy in a group next to a banner about film.

"Is she in the Film Museum thing?"

"Don't know yet, boss."

Minogue searched the half-turned faces, even the ones in shadow behind Shaughnessy. The hairdos were so short now, shaved almost.

"Will you look at all the black in that," said Malone. "Artsy-fartsy crowd. What's the story there, with them always standing around looking pissed off?" Minogue stepped over to the shots of the Carra Fields.

"There's the Taoiseach, God be good to him," said Murtagh. "The back of his head in anyhow. The good side of him. The minister — there's Garland. Hard to miss him, with the dickey bow — the size of him."

"O'Riordan again," said Minogue.

"Shaughnessy's talking to someone there, that's all I can tell you."

"Damn," said Minogue. "Your man, the cameraman, can't remember?"

Murtagh crunched a few crisps.

"'Do you know how many people were there?' says he. 'Everyone.'"

"Ask him who then."

"What, a list?"

"A list, John, yes. We've lots of paper."

Malone crushed the crisp bag slowly. Minogue turned back to Murtagh.

"What are our sources on Aoife Hartnett?"

"Well she had friends. Pals at work. Had a social life too. She played squash at a club. She knew a lot of people, it looks like."

"Who, like?"

Murtagh glanced over at Malone.

"Well the sister says she knew a lot of people in the art scene. The exhibitions were a thing for her."

"Who have we been drawing on here, John?"

Murtagh began counting.

"First, the sister, now she's in a bad way. Her husband, Nolan, well he's gotten over being a pain. The sister felt sorry for her lately, the past while, says Nolan."

"Why so?"

"Well it's a bit thick really. I mean, who's to say here. The sister stays at home. Nolan's a solicitor so they're okay for the few shillings. She left Telecom after they started having kids. Anyway, Nolan says that the wife says that Aoife wasn't that happy. Especially the last while, like."

Minogue leaned against the wall.

"She couldn't settle. A let-down with a fella, Whelan. He's a Eurocrat type. In Brussels now. No hard feelings, it just didn't work. Nolan thinks — and the wife too — the job might have been losing its appeal too. 'She'd only complain the odd time though.'"

Minogue looked around the squad room. Malone was trying to dislodge a piece of potato crisp from somewhere in his lower back teeth. The inspector couldn't settle on a question to ask Murtagh.

"Go on, then," he said.

"The money thing was okay. She had her own place and that, paid her way. Got to go to conferences and that. But said there wasn't much elbow room left. That, well, she's kind of hit a level. All the jobs are filled like."

"A plateau," said Malone. "The roof like."

"Nolan says he thinks the oul biological clock thing was getting to her too. Things passing her by."

"Kids?"

"Yes. Family, he says."

"That was all over the phone to you?"

"Yep. I told him to phone us as soon as the wife was in shape to interview. Ah, I was on the phone to him for half an hour. He's shook now. The wheels fell off the solicitor bit when he got the idea maybe something bad's after happening to her."

"Who's doing her apartment?"

"Driscoll. They started the search just after eleven. Said he'd phone us at four, whether or which. I fed him pointers we were keen on: any sign Shaughnessy was there, like. Travel stuff."

"Her car, the Micra?"

Murtagh nodded at the clock.

"I phoned at half-nine. It's somewhere between Castlebar and Dublin."

Minogue slid the fax paper out from under the photocopies of statements from the airport. The list of contents, bagged and boxed and also en route to Dublin, was two tightly written pages. Minogue rubbed the paper between thumb and forefinger.

"At the museum, John. You've put in for interviews with the staff there?"

"I have, to be sure. One of her mates is on holliers in Kilkenny since Tuesday but he's checking out sound anyway. Him and the wife and the kids visiting in-laws. She had a secretary who's very shaky now. Eileen Brogan. I got her to go through the desk for us, appointment diaries, messages, and that."

Malone was tapping his Biro on his knuckles now. Minogue watched it hop. Malone stopped.

"Phone Garland, John," said Minogue. "Ask him to free up the people she was closest to there. I'm going over there myself."

CHAPTER 20

GARLAND STARED OUT THE WINDOW of Aoife Hartnett's office and rubbed at his eyes again. Minogue could hear Malone's tones in the adjoining room, a meeting room where staff were now coming in one by one, some in tears, to tell him what they could of Aoife Hartnett. Minogue was waiting for Eileen Brogan to return from the toilet so he could interview her.

"But they must be connected," said Garland finally. "I don't remember seeing this Shaughnessy character at those things, but there he is in the picture. There were loads of people there."

"Aoife went on leave the twenty-eighth, I have here?"

"That's it," said Garland and blew his nose. "I checked."

"And the sick leave was in April. Two weeks, was it?"

"The seventh to the eighteenth. Yes."

Minogue fixed the eight in eighteenth. His Biro wasn't putting out. Garland slid one across to him. April is the cruelest month; who wrote that one?

"We'll be needing to know why."

Garland squirmed, laid his hands on the table.

"Well, is that not confidential information still?"

"I don't mean why you didn't tell us the other night about her sick leave," Minogue said. "I mean the reason for her taking the leave."

"Well, you'll be consulting with Aoife's doctor, maybe?"

"When we need to. Her apartment's being investigated as we speak."

Garland looked down at the desktop. He made a table setting of two Biros and a pencil.

"As much as I'm allowed to divulge, now, I suppose," he whispered.

"Aoife's dead, Mr. Garland."

Garland swallowed. His eyes darted to Minogue's.

"We're all on the one side here, I'm thinking," Minogue added. "She's being examined today here in Dublin. There's not much privacy left in the process now, if you follow me."

Garland leaned to one side of his chair and rubbed at his nose. He sighed and ran his hand down his face. He left his eyes closed for several moments.

"Well if you can talk to her doctor. She was getting treatment this last while."

"For what, now?"

"Depression," said Garland. "I think it was more burnout. Aoife needed time away from the job. I think she finally realized that."

"Was there something that helped her realize that, something specific?"

Garland held his breath for a moment while he sized Minogue up.

"Yes." The breath rushing out seemed to make him suddenly tired.

"Remember that Aoife and I worked together, God, nine years now. She's a first-class scholar and archaeologist. None better, let me tell you. Single-minded, dedicated — always the one to go the distance. Very, very dedicated. I still, well . . ."

Minogue watched Garland swallow and pinch his eyes. The dickey bow had gone askew. Garland took out another paper hanky and turned away. Minogue studied the postcards and photos. Columns: Greece, Rome? Turkey, it turned out.

"Mr. Garland. Is there something you're leaving out? Out of respect for Aoife?"

Garland's face was blotchy now. He stared dully at Minogue.

"Do you always look for the dark side?"

Minogue held back his first answer. He raised his eyebrows instead.

"I'd hope I could persuade you that I'm not trying to dig up dirt," he said. "I can think of no other way to say it at the moment. So: sorry. Help me, help us. That's what's needed."

Garland cleared his throat.

"All right, so. The leave was for Aoife to think over what she wanted to do. Where she wanted to go. In her career, her life, I mean."

Minogue thought of the group he had detached Garland from the other night at L'Avenue. He'd heard the phrase so often lately: What I want to do with my life.

"Was it an ultimatum to her?"

"God, no!" said Garland and sat back. "We all liked Aoife. She lived for her work, you know, but things hadn't been going her way or at least she'd maybe forgotten the knack of adapting."

"Give me a for instance, can you."

"Well the job itself: on the one hand we have fewer staff and more responsibilities. She took them all on, to be sure, but there were weeks on end that I know she was here until ten or eleven at night. She managed great until a few bumps in the road came along."

"Which, now?"

"Well, to be blunt, there were things disappearing. From sites."

"Monuments, do you mean?"

"Yes. There were three gone in April of last year. They were set into walls even and Public Works themselves thought they'd be secure against anything. But these people were determined and up to the job it seemed."

"Stolen? Did they turn up?"

"Not here they didn't. Oddly enough it died down this year. It'd be an impossible job to keep them all safe, short of bringing them in here. We took in several after Crom Dubh below in Kerry. Did you hear of that one last year?"

"I seem to remember something."

"Fifteen hundred years old. But pre-Christian to be sure. No trace."

"Is there money in these?"

"I don't rightly know. No one does. But I'll bet there is."

Minogue looked down at Garland rearranging the Biros.

"What does this have to do with Aoife?"

"Well technically the assistant keeper would be responsible for securing sites — along with the OPW, of course. The Office of Public Works, sorry. Aoife was up to her eyes already. She wanted a lot of them taken down and brought in here for safekeeping. But there were other interests, local groups wanting things kept, for the tourism thing, it came down to really. But Aoife's idea was to put all these things out to the world internationally. That was the project she got funding for, the computer stuff you had a look at there . . ."

"Oration?"

"Ovation. The logic was sound: the pieces would be seen by millions, and they'd be secure. Irish culture would reach around the world. A bit like the missionary work the monks were doing in Europe all those centuries ago. Funny in a way, isn't it?"

Minogue's hands remembered the feel of the stone cross at Tully, the centuries of weather and other hands coming through his skin to entrance him.

"Oh, something like that," Garland was saying. "But without leaving your home. Yes, it's cheap — oh, there are umpteen perfectly good, rational reasons . . ."

A redundancy, Minogue thought. Too reasonable maybe, too well thought out.

"And she got some European funding," said Garland. "'The past is the future,' do you get it?"

The words were out before he'd thought about it, and Minogue regretted them almost immediately.

"You don't mean Bosnia, I take it," he heard himself say. "Or Belfast."

Garland stopped wiping his nose and fixed a look on Minogue.

"By God," he murmured and started rubbing again. "You'd fit right in with the crowd up in L'Avenue, my crowd: 'The past is a nightmare from which we struggle to awaken' and all that. My overeducated generation, far from bare feet now. Dublin intelligensia, with their mental theme parks."

"I take it you have a different point of view then."

"The past is real," said Garland. Minogue saw the keenness in Garland's eyes. "It's with us. It's not a nightmare. Stephen Daedalus was a bit too precious for my liking."

"It was Nietzsche," said Minogue. "Mister Joyce didn't invent it."

Garland sat back. A smile began to break through.

"You're serious," he said. "I don't believe I'm hearing this from a, a Garda."

"Don't be fretting now. I do be reading a lot when I can't sleep."

Garland's eyes took on a new light. He sat over the desk again.

"You, you would know about the past more than anyone," he said. "Of course — yes: when you go trying to solve a . . . ?"

Minogue wanted out. He kicked himself for drifting into this.

"Maybe," he said. "I —"

"Exactly! We both try to extricate something from the . . . I have to think this out . . ."

"Computers," said Minogue. "We strayed off talking about Aoife's job?"

The frown slid back down Garland's forehead.

"Yes, yes," he murmured.

"Bringing ancient Ireland to someone in a library in say, Milan?"

Garland hadn't completely left the other conversation yet. Minogue took to staring at him. Garland suddenly saw Minogue's eyes, blinked.

"Virtually, like. Yes . . . Point and click, isn't that the expression?"

Minogue was suddenly back in Ryan's pub. A crowd in from Fraud celebrating, Kilmartin too of course. Who had said that there? It was about the Smiths: point and click.

"Wizzywig," said Garland. "That's another paradigm we hear."

"Pardon?"

"Oh, it's more of the jargon," said Garland. "What-you-see-is-what-you-get. Pictures, little film clips. Next will be virtual reality, Dermot told me. Someone in Japan could 'log on' and go around the museum here. All electronic of course, but they could even pick things up and turn them around. Makes the mind go quite giddy on me, I have to say."

Minogue wrote "Ovation" in his notebook.

"Did this computer thing get in the way of Aoife's other duties?"

"Well now," Garland began. Minogue detected the quick slide into caution, the clear signal from the considered pause. "Ovation began to take up a lot of time. Very taken up with it, she was. Yes, I had to speak with her about that project. Yes."

"By way of being a row, would you say?"

Garland nodded.

"It turned out to be. She was insisting I sign an approval in advance for the funding renewal that was to come up six months down the road. I just, well, I couldn't really. She needed to show what the project had done so far, I told her."

"How bad a row?"

The pause was longer now. What food for thought Garland was considering in his study of his own thumbnails, Minogue didn't much care to wonder about. He felt his own impatience turn to annoyance.

"Well, I haven't seen too many like it in my career," said Garland. "But I knew in my heart that Aoife was not getting personal about it."

"Personal. Could you fill in the gaps there a bit for me?"

"Ahhh . . ." Garland's gasp surprised Minogue. The words came out in a hoarse whisper. "What a strange and terrible thing to be sitting here, what kind of a day is it or world is it . . . that I sit here with a policeman talking about someone I've know and . . ."

Minogue looked away while Garland cried. His annoyance ebbed. It was the recall of the bunch at L'Avenue which had been worming away at him all the while, he began to understand. Some vestige of his irritation with them had made him want to fence with Garland over some stupid philosophizing about what the past meant. Navel-gazers, chatterers, intellectuals. The men who lost Ireland: Garland had the wit all right. He thought of Leyne again, the self-made battler, grasper, and fixer, his derision for experts. But both so familiar, so Irish, Minogue had to agree as the muted sounds of grief and the sighing between sobs flowed around and through his thoughts. Don't worry, you're all right, was all he could say to Garland's choked-off apology as he tried to regain some control. He rambled by Tully Cross again while he waited for Garland, and then slipped away to the waves at Fanore.

"You've been in these situations a lot, I suppose," from Garland finally.

The inspector nodded.

"You cope?" said Garland. "You have to, I suppose."

Minogue had to let go of his wanderings down the lane to Gleninagh Pier.

"It's always bad," he said. He met Garland's blurry eyes. "Tell me what she said. When ye had your disagreement, I mean."

Garland sighed and wiped his eyes again.

"Oh, I hadn't the vision. The vision — me. Aoife could put her case very well. Did I not see the implication for the future of the new media, et cetera. Ecotourism came into it somewhere. Distributed learning, walls coming down . . ."

"Is there a book of less than twenty pages where I could figure out what any of that means?"

Garland smiled briefly and blew his nose.

"Maybe she was right," he resumed. "That's the hard thing to take right now. That we — that I — thwarted her, God forgive me."

Garland had more hankies in his pocket. Minogue jotted down "medication?" in his notebook. She must have confided in someone.

"A catalyst it was," Garland said, " when you think about it now. The artifacts being stolen, I mean. We very quickly saw the need to bring in some of the vulnerable pieces. There was no doubt about that. There was good agreement there in committee, I mean. But the computer stuff available all over the world, well it seemed to be an answer for some time in the future, maybe."

"But not from your point of view."

"I'd still have to stand by that. It's not just that these things should be kept in their area, the indigenous area, for tourists to spend money getting there in their rented cars and eating their dinners in the local hotel and that. It's that these things belong there. The vernacular. I don't know if that makes sense now to the man in the street . . ."

He stopped wiping his eye and eyed the inspector.

"Do the Guards speak MBA now? 'Reengineering?' 'Vision statements' . . . ?"

"I don't know," Minogue said. "We get odd memos at times, to be sure."

Garland took a breath. Minogue heard it escape slowly.

"Well, it was my idea she take a leave. I only hope now I didn't do wrong. Putting time on her hands then."

"April," Minogue said.

"Yes."

"And how was she since?"

"Oh, good. Everything running smoothly. The project ready . . ."

"Did you know her socially, like, would she be in your milieu?"

A flicker on Garland's face gave Minogue a pleasant twinge. Garland didn't know whether this Guard meant it sarcastically, and he wouldn't ask.

"No. She liked the arts. Well, obviously. Her ex was an opera fan, I believe."

"She didn't discuss her personal life with you?"

"No. We'd chat, go to dos together, but nothing of a personal nature, no."

"Who did she mix with, relate most to, here at the office?"

Garland eased back. Minogue listened to the chair back taking the weight.

"Well, she was friendly with everyone really. Eileen, her secretary, would be in there now. Dermot Higgins, she had a lot of time for him."

"Was she involved with him?"

"No. I mean, I don't know. I don't think so. I never heard anything to . . ."

"She had a job to come back to here when she left on leave?"

"Of course she did." Said like a retort, Minogue registered.

"And she knew this?"

"Absolutely. I told her. We'd stand by her, without a doubt."

"She didn't mention resigning, did she?"

"No."

"Or moving? Departments, jobs?"

"God, no. There'd be no place really, well that I can think of. Her expertise and all, you know?"

Minogue fell to staring out the window. Garland blowing his nose brought him back.

"Thanks," he said. "You'll be here for the afternoon? In the office, I mean."

Garland said that he would. Minogue watched him leave. He waited for several minutes. He couldn't very well go out and drag in Eileen Brogan if she was so upset still. Maybe he should leave her until the afternoon. No, he couldn't.

He looked around the walls of Aoife Hartnett's office again. There were pictures of kids, the niece and nephew, he guessed, on the corkboard by postcards. The Algarve — she'd been, the writer thanked her for steering them to the best hotel — Moscow, Paris. Milan. Thirty-eight, that wasn't old. Smart, hardworking. She worked late, she did her homework. She took on loads of work, more than she should have, probably. Had she reached the top in the job and then found there was nowhere to go? Where did she want to go anyway, and who with? Shaughnessy? Christ, he thought, and the weariness fell on him. She'd had a nervous breakdown, big or small — that's what pushed everything off the rails.

Minogue heard shoes on the carpet outside. It was Eileen Brogan who tapped on the open door. Already, he thought: things might go his way at last.

"Mrs. Brogan? Thanks now."

She stood in the doorway.

"You're great now," he said. "I'm wondering if you could give me some of your time first to go over her messages. Voice mail and that too, if you can?"

She glanced back toward the main office.

"We won't be long now," he said. "Tell me, are you long here?"

"Three years," she said. "I was at home but then I did a job training thing. Word processing and that."

"You're well ahead of me then," he tried. "I'm an iijit still in that line."

She tried to smile but a tear dropped from her eyelash.

"I saw you on the telly the other night," she whispered. "Asking about the man at the airport."

Minogue looked around her freckled face.

"It was your good self who alerted Mr. Garland to phone us, Mrs. Brogan. I'm obliged to you. Thank you."

She stared at him, the surprise winning out over the frown or wariness.

"Oh . . . well," she paused to clear her throat, "it'd be hard to miss him. The Am — you knew that he called himself something else here?"

"Leyne, I was told. Did that name mean anything to you?"

She shook her head.

"How'd he strike you?"

In the moment their eyes met, Minogue understood that she had picked up on his clumsy phrasing.

"Well, I only saw him the once. He arrived in asking for Aoife."

"'Aoife'? 'Ms. Hartnett'? 'Dr. Hartnett'?"

"I think he said Doctor."

"Was that all then?"

"Well, yes. I went off to tell Aoife. She was in with Dermot, I think. He stood there, but by my desk there, waiting."

"Smoking? Say anything?"

She frowned and scrutinized the hanky she had been twining slowly.

"But I, well, maybe I'm just putting ideas on it now."

"You lost me there," he said.

"Ah, maybe after hearing about Aoife, that he was with her."

Her lip trembled.

"An impression you had maybe?" he tried.

"Maybe I'm not being fair."

"Go on, you're all right. It's not a statement now. We're chatting."

She looked at the window as though it had some irresistible appeal for her.

"Well, he, ah — eyes on him — ah, it's not fair."

Minogue waited.

"Eyeing people," she said. "Women. His eyes would be on you, you'd feel them. Like, sizing you up. Maybe all the Americans are that way."

Minogue looked down at the lists she'd made, the hanky crushed tight in her fist now.

"Cup of tea?"

She let out a sigh, sat back, and opened her hand. She seemed surprised to find the hanky there.

"No thanks," she murmured. "I was told to go home after you're finished. I'll pick up Rónan from the minder's and —"

Minogue studied the list for several moments.

"This message there, you have it under voice mail."

"I know," she said. "It's just force of habit. I'd take Aoife's messages off her voice mail and put them on slips. I'm in the habit of dumping them as soon as I have them on paper. The paper version — well, you can see yourself."

"It's just a question mark," he said.

"Oh, I know, I know. Don't talk to me about it. I feel so *stupid* about it. I remember saying to myself, God, you iijit, how will Aoife even know if she can't hear the voice herself! The things you do!"

"You say it was a man. Irish?"

"Definitely."

"Heard him before?"

"It sounded familiar, you know? But like a lot you hear, I suppose every accent . . . Sorry. It's just a stupid thing."

"Ah, you're all right. Would you recognize it again?"

"Oh, I don't know. I could try, I suppose."

"Do you recall the exact words, the phrasing maybe?"

"No. But he'd have been bouncing from Aoife's voice mail. If you wanted to speak to someone in the office itself you'd hit a three."

"Is that announced?"

"It is."

"Is the date right?"

"Definitely. At least I did that part right."

Minogue looked up. A kid really, face full of freckles under a red mop.

"Don't be so hard on yourself now," he said. "We'll do the best we can and that'll be good enough."

He returned to the list of her appointments in the days before she left. When he looked up again, tears were rolling down her cheeks.

"Here, will you change your mind about the tea? Ah, do — come on now."

She shook her head.

"That was Aoife," she whispered. "Just like what you said."

"Not the tea, is it . . . ?"

"No, no. That kind of attitude, that you're all right. That your best is good enough. That they accept you for what you are. Old-fashioned, maybe."

{ 226 }

Minogue smiled. He waited.

"Maybe it's country people, I don't know," she said. "Always the good word for people under her. But she could be so hard on herself . . . ! She knew what way I'd come up. With Tony in and out of jail, I thought I'd never get anywhere — and Tony a mechanic making good money until it all went in his . . ."

"Your husband?"

She nodded.

"He's off in England or somewhere. I got a barring order and all. There's just me and Rónan now. Things are so bad nowadays. Like they say, 'giving your baby a shot in the arm . . .'"

"You think they're better than the Works?"

Her brow lifted.

"What? GOD? You know about them?"

"'Course I do. What do you take me for, a middle-aged culchie Guard?"

Her eyes twinkled. He kept the put-upon look, but allowed a smile to creep in.

"They're the best," she said. "GOD. They're *real*, like."

She frowned then and her eyes went dully to the papers on the desk.

"Larry Smith," she murmured. Minogue tried to hide his surprise.

"His mob," she went on. "Tony used to fix cars . . . Yous probably know more about Larry Smith than I do."

"I haven't had to live with the results of his doings."

"Don't get me wrong — I'm no big fan of the Guards. But I don't have it in for them either, the way some people have. And if it was a Guard who did away with . . ."

Her eyes went to the window again.

"Dublin's changed, so it is," she murmured. "Like you wouldn't believe." His eyes went from studying her profile and trying to finish her sentence to staring at the window himself now. Where would Iseult and Pat and the baby live? They couldn't stay in that kippy flat. He wrenched himself back.

"If you're ready to lead me through your list there . . ."

She seemed equally surprised to be back in the present. He took few notes. He was aware of her watching him write. He let her ramble several times before drawing her back to specifics.

"She seems to have been a busy person lately."

"Oh, she was," Eileen Brogan said. "Even after she came back from the time off. She always . . ."

Minogue watched her rubbing more tears from the corners of her eyes.

"Sorry, I can't seem to stop it."

He stood and walked to the doorway. It was Garland who caught his eye.

"Where would we get tea, if you please?"

He turned back, looked around the room when he heard the phone. His own, and he'd forgotten where he'd put it. Eileen Brogan pointed it out to him.

It was Tony O'Leary: could he phone Tynan's office from a desk phone. Minogue framed a reply and quickly squelched it. Tynan picked up the phone before the first ring finished.

"Can you tell me anything, Matt?"

Minogue waited for a count of three.

"Hello, John," he said, "and how are you and yours this fine morning?"

"Excuse me. I have a call waiting, that's the hurry. Can you talk?"

"I can. I'm following up on Aoife Hartnett."

He turned back to Eileen Brogan.

"A moment while I get a quiet spot."

Eileen Brogan obliged. She closed the door behind her.

"I'm here in Aoife Hartnett's office on a follow-up. I think she and Shaughnessy might have been an item."

"Who killed her?"

"I don't know. I can't see a motive yet, even with the background."

"Could Shaughnessy have done it?"

"Without a doubt. But it's wide open yet."

"What else?"

"She'd taken sick leave not so long ago. She'd been given it."

"Impropriety?"

"The opposite, I'm hearing. Burnout. I'm getting the upstairs, down-stairs versions sorted out here."

"Is that it so far then?"

"Well, I'm finding out about culture on the side. Heritage."

"Spare me, Matt. What I'd like to know is if you can connect anything. Or where you're headed with both cases."

"Too early. Sorry, but."

"Is the PM on her done yet?"

Minogue found dust in the corner of a window sash. Maybe Malone had the right approach with bouts of bad language.

"I'll phone you when I know, John."

"She was a higher up. Right?"

"Yes. Hardworking, a lot of responsibility. Knew her stuff. She mixed, 'networked' — all that."

"How does she, how did she, connect with Shaughnessy?"

"Still don't know," said Minogue. "Maybe we can put him in her apartment. There's a team collecting there. An affair, I don't know. A few things seem to be coming through. They seem to have traveled together. They didn't want to attract attention, maybe even to the extent of sneaking into bed-and-breakfasts separately."

"The lack of stuff coming in from the appeal, is it?"

Minogue wondered how Tynan knew.

"I'd be thinking they went to some trouble to avoid people."

He heard something rubbing over the mouthpiece at Tynan's end. Muffled voices in his office. The rubbing stopped.

"You're sure?" he heard Tynan say to someone else.

"Excuse me," said Tynan then. "Two conversations going here. So I'll be hearing from you later in the day on this. Even if you're annoyed."

"Fair enough."

"No word from James?"

"No. Am I to pass on a message if he does phone?"

"You could. We may shortly be getting information which would allow him off the stage here with the media. In relation to Mr. Smith."

"Is it solid?"

"I don't know. It happened a half hour ago. This fella has been known awhile but didn't stand out for any particular reason then."

"Do I know him?"

"It's not a Guard, that's what I want you to know. A certain person started asking his barrister some very odd questions today at the Special Criminal Court. He's facing a third conviction for an armed robbery a few months ago. He's looking for a soft spot to land on."

"Does anyone know about this outside the Guards on the court yet?"

"No," said Tynan. "I'll be phoning an editor in a few minutes. If they're smart they'll hold fire on the first article until we get a proper look at this fella."

Minogue pushed the top of his Biro harder into the paper and let it go. He didn't realize how annoyed he had become in the past few moments.

"So it'll be okay again to have a few jars and wild blather with our colleagues above in the club?"

"Was it ever otherwise? Listen, now. There's something you need to know. This Freeman character phoned me."

"Leyne?"

"Yes. I asked to be kept informed. It's to be kept quiet, but Leyne had told him to keep me up if anything happened. Very confidential."

Minogue looked at a break in the clouds over the south city.

"You won't be able to talk to Leyne, Matt."

He thought of the old man grasping his arm: anything, he'd said. The yellow skin, the scar reaching up to his neck. Had Leyne known?

"This Freeman character, his potboy," said Tynan, "he phoned. They have Leyne on a machine. The consensus there is that he won't be coming back to us."

CHAPTER 21

Eileen brogan looked up from the page at him. Minogue had been thinking of a hospital room. Machines, tubes, wires.

"Sorry," he said.

"July," she said again. "That was the end of that stage. There was a do here, a reception. We went over to Sheehan's pub after the approval was confirmed."

"Then it passed on to the construction phase, did you say?"

"Yes. All the approvals were in, I heard."

"The exhibition was the launch of the actual building for the center?"

She nodded.

"I don't recall seeing any building work started there," he said.

"I only know what I read from typing up letters and minutes and that or what I'd hear. But I did I hear her complaining here not too long ago. There was some holdup with one of the tenders for drainage work or something. The County Council there weren't doing their job fast enough."

Her voice began to quiver again.

"She was so meticulous, so . . . She worked so hard. I'd go at half-five and I'd tell her, Aoife, go home would you, for God's sake. I'd feel guilty, and me only a clerk typist really."

She was trying to stop shivering.

"I'm sorry," he said. "I hadn't realized."

"No, no," she said with an edge to her voice now. "I want to do the best I can here now. For Aoife."

She stared at the Biro Minogue turned against his thumb.

"She wasn't the kind to talk about home life much. Maybe that's because she wasn't married or that. She'd talk about her niece now, or about people she knew."

"Did she maybe mention things that were on her mind? Upsetting her?"

"You asked me that earlier, I know, and I've been trying to think. I didn't know anything about that few weeks she took off until the afternoon before."

"You got no impression she resented it?"

"No. I knew she was tired. She wouldn't complain and she'd just carry on, but there was something missing. I'd never have asked her. I used to ask myself well what would Aoife want, like. Me — I'm just, well, there's Rónan and me. Not much room for anything else. No holidays or car, not even a house for God's sake, but me ma and da are great. They're my family again, sort of. Since Tony and that. Aoife hadn't been lucky well in the marriage stakes, I suppose — I thought."

"You knew something about that?"

"Not really," she replied. "I mean, nobody told me. But I saw her here — right over there, by the window. I knew she'd been crying. This is months ago. And I kind of knew — well, there was a feeling — it was a letdown with a fella. I didn't want to be putting me foot in it. Aoife had her own sort of territory. What would I say?"

"Reserve, do you mean?"

"I suppose. Not snobby now or that. The way a good boss is, not trying to be pallsy-walsy or that. Some people found her cool because of it, or they were a bit put out by her being so smart and all. I liked that about her. But I felt so bad for her then. 'Plenty more fish in the sea,' I remember saying to her. Stupid things you say, you know? She sort of smiled. She knew, I think. That I knew, like. Do you know what I'm saying?"

He waited for several moments. She frowned and looked at her hanky.

"What else did you know of that side of Aoife?"

"That's it. There should have been someone for her, that's what's been getting to me this last hour, yes."

Her eyes went to a corner of the ceiling.

"What about Dermot Higgins, maybe?"

"Dermot here?"

Minogue nodded. Her lips twitched.

"Ah no, that wasn't on. You'd easy fall for him though, wouldn't you? If you were a girl, like. No. Dermot doesn't make a big deal out of it. Everyone knows."

"What, now?"

"Dermot's gay."

Minogue tried not to let his bewilderment show. Didn't gay men all have short hair and earrings these days? The giveaway voice and mannerisms?

"She did say something that day, now," Eileen Brogan began again. "Now, if only I can remember it. I thought it was a person she was talking about. Her ex maybe, but I didn't ask. It was like she was making a crack about it, I don't know, a fish or something. It was something else though, I suppose."

"What did she say, can you remember?"

Minogue watched her face as she seized on some recollection, met his gaze, then frowned again as she lost it.

"Oh God, if I could remember it . . . it was just that I thought of it when I said fish. Something that sounded like a sissy. I was thinking to myself, what kind of a fish is that, a piranha or something? You're no sooner at the top of a hill than you're right back at the bottom again, I think she said. Back where you started. A sissy . . . ?"

She dabbed at her eyes again. Minogue didn't push it. He began to arrange the pages. He looked over the poster of the Carra Hill. How many people, how many centuries had it taken to make it? The size of the rocks, how could one person — he looked up at her then.

"Sisyphus?"

Her eyes widened. She nodded once.

"That's what it was, yes. How did you know that?"

.   .   .   .   .

Malone leaned against the doorjamb. Minogue looked down at the files he had scanned already.

"Well," said Malone, "not one of them worth getting a proper statement out of. How do you like that?"

Minogue sat back.

"Well-respected," said Malone. "Not a bad word about her. Bit of a workaholic. Is that what you're getting too?"

Minogue nodded. He closed the folder on the pages from O'Reilly's booklet about Carra Hill and the stone.

"Here, that's the book your woman had down there yesterday," said Malone. "It's another copy, Tommy."

Malone sat on the edge of the desk and looked up at the pictures.

"What's that?" asked Malone and pointed at one. "It's like a giant soccer ball there. That big rock."

"That's the Burren."

"Who put that big boulder there?"

"God. Some giant. Finn MacCool maybe."

"You were there when it happened, were you."

"It was always there. The weather did that to it."

"Don't you just want to put the boot to it, like? Give it a little shove, watch it rolling — hey, wait a minute. Haven't you got a picture of something like that back at the office? That Magoo, Magray . . . ?"

"Magritte," said Minogue. He'd phone Mairéad O'Reilly.

"There was something at the place, Tommy."

"What? She was strangled, and her car pushed over the cliff, yeah."

"Something at the place . . ."

"Like?"

Minogue looked up from the cover of the folder. He thought of O'Reilly's decades of digging, the patient, stubborn mind refusing to give up its belief. Maybe he needed to believe in things to keep going.

"I found these inside that book."

Malone picked up the photocopies.

"What are the numbers there — wait. They're measurements, yeah. This is part of her job, isn't it?"

Minogue didn't answer. He watched Malone turn some sideways and return each to the back of the sheaf.

"Seen some of 'em before," said Malone. He dropped them on the desk and looked at Minogue. "In pictures and that."

Minogue plucked one out and put it on the desk in front of Malone.

"Seen it."

"Boa Island."

He dropped another.

"No," said Malone. "Don't know it."

"Drumlin. County Roscommon. This one's in the museum already."

"Okay," Malone said. "But so what?"

"I don't know."

Malone gave his boss a long, slow blink.

"So we'd better get back to work then."

Minogue gathered the pages again and slid them into the folder.

"They're all heads, Tommy."

"Good. Try tails next time."

"She knew the Carra Fields stuff inside out."

"Right," said Malone. "That was her job, yeah?"

"That history, the one O'Reilly wrote, the one I took home the other day. There's a page and a half on a description of the stone, the one they say had to be carried up the hill."

"For the new fella to be crowned? The next king, like?"

"Yes. Why has she all these pictures from all kinds of books and magazines and even tourist brochures in next to that page?"

Malone rubbed his palm on the short hairs over his crown.

"It's her job, boss. Same as we'd, I don't know, make points of comparison with statements or MOs. Scene summaries?"

"There's more to it than that, Tommy."

Malone stood away from the doorjamb.

"Well, let me ask you something, so," he said. "How much of what your man wrote is true? I was there yesterday. Even the daughter knows there was stuff made up. Your man was into it all his life, you know. All the legends and stuff — well, I mean, how much of that is just his own inventions? Like, bullshit . . . ?"

Minogue made no reply. He looked at his watch instead. Half-two. Well? he heard from Malone. Still he said nothing. He let his cuff over his wrist again. O'Reilly had no sources for what he'd written. A stone the weight of a bull, carried up a hill? Heroic entirely, but best left in myth. Damn. Why hadn't he heard what they'd turned up in her apartment? Phone Murtagh.

Murtagh went slowly down his list.

"Spell that again, John. What's it for, do you know?"

"Antidepressant. It's just the label bit you get from the chemist. She probably took the stuff with her."

"Current, is it?"

"It is," Murtagh said. "There's other paraphernalia. Old antibiotics too."

"Can we put Shaughnessy at her place? Visiting even?"

"No answer on that. Yet, like."

"Cigarettes — what did he smoke again?"

"I'll pass it on to them, boss."

"Any life on the phones?"

"Nothing."

Minogue released the Biro he'd been bending.

"When's the PM scheduled, John?"

"Hers? There was a phone call in from Donavan's office to notify for attendance. He can do it this afternoon or early tomorrow. Who will we send?"

Malone, that's who, Minogue had to conclude.

·   ·   ·   ·   ·

"By the way," said Malone. "Now that I think of it, when are we ever going to pick up your hardware?"

"What hardware?"

"Come on, you know. We were issued, remember?"

"Not now, anyway."

"Why not? Didn't you tell me that fella Kevin Whatsisname passed on something, something about the Smiths?"

Minogue stared at the clock on the dashboard, willing it to change its numbers. He shouldn't have mentioned what Kevin Kelly had told him in Bewleys.

"Is it the Smiths blathering has you thinking about this again?"

"Maybe," Malone said. "What about back when you and the Killer were up against a crowd down from the North? When was that, seven or eight years ago? There was bullets flying then, wasn't there?"

"Seven years, yes," said Minogue. "The time of the Christmas bombings."

"Did you then?"

"No."

"Why the hell not?"

Minogue studied the tips of his shoes. More than scuff there now. They'd go in a few months.

"Well, I wouldn't have one in the house, Tommy. That was all."

Malone jammed the gearshift into second and floored the accelerator. Minogue heard him swear under his breath.

"I don't get paid enough to try to talk sense into you," Malone said. "Why don't you just sign it out and park it in the cabinet then?"

"It's still optional, Tommy."

"They should make you."

"They can't make me bring a gun into my home. And that's that."

"Even if it went to compulsory issue?"

"They've never made us. We call in the heavies if we think there are guns."

"You think Larry Smith's mob doesn't have guns?"

Minogue studied his shoes again.

"There's seventeen holes in that squad car," said Malone. "I'd say that's a serious message."

Maybe they should really send the bill to Gemma O'Loughlin, Minogue thought. Printing that drivel about the Larry Smith solution from a lubricated, giddy Kilmartin showboating for his cronies at the Garda Club.

"They'd know where we live, you know," said Malone.

Minogue couldn't disagree. He'd heard enough over the years of the open threats delivered one-on-one to Guards by the Smiths. The names of their children, even; where their parents lived.

"Hold the horses there," he said. "Are you going to tell me it's at home I should be strutting around with a gun in me apron and me doing the dishes?"

"Apron is right," said Malone, and looked away. Minogue let the silence hang.

"I can't win this one, can I," said Malone at last. "You get that thick culchie head of yours down and you won't budge."

Minogue let the silence hang. He thought of Mick Fahy's halfhearted attempt to convince him when they were signing out Malone's at the armory. It's not the old days, Matt: they all have them and they use them; there's no respect for the uniform anymore. He thought about Trigger Little, the heaviness in the air around him. Wife and three kids, separated. Did Malone himself actually like guns, he wondered. And why did he not know this about a man he'd worked with for over a year? Driving around Dublin with an automatic pistol in the back of your pants, now that was progress.

"Back to the case, Tommy."

"What about it?"

"If the airport is beginning to dry up, well, that's not the end of the world. We have a couple traveling together and two cars waiting to give us leads. It takes so long though, that's the frustrating part."

Malone turned into the Coombe. Minogue returned the stares of two nattily dressed men leaning on a silver BMW. One of the men looked away.

"Want to bet how that was paid for," Malone said. "That Beemer, with the two music video charlies lying up against it?"

He rolled down the window and spat out a piece of a nail he'd been nibbling on. The air smelled of decaying fruit and exhaust smoke. A pound shop was playing "Only Starting" from the Works' first CD. One of the speakers seemed to be blown. A tweeter.

Malone seemed to be changing gears just for something to do now.

"We might be getting out from under Smith and Company," Minogue said.

"What, a gouger who's going to cough up the fells who did for Larry Smith?"

"There's a chance," Minogue said. "Just today, it came up in a court recess."

"Huh. Jases, I'd sell anyone, anything, if I was up against a ten-year term. And if I was a junkie? If I was a junkie with bills that could get collected the wrong way in jail, I'd rat on Mother Teresa, so I would."

There'd be no pleasing Malone now, Minogue decided. He studied the half-built apartments beyond Christ Church. Bow windows, wasn't that something. Cubicles for yuppies. Then it struck him that Malone could be edgy because he'd been told to attend on the PM for Aoife Hartnett. Minogue decided to waive preliminaries.

"The PM's not going to be that bad, Tommy. Pierce knows you don't need the full chapter and verse during."

"It's all right," Malone said.

"I can phone him, leave a message."

"It's okay, boss. No big deal. All right?"

Minogue gave up. He though about putting more life into tracing the missing stuff from Shaughnessy's car. Somebody doing their job right in Dublin Garda divisions had to have an ear with fences and gougers. Her purse was gone. Access card at least. Shaughnessy's cards, his camera. Other paraphernalia. And what about all the people at the dos that Shaughnessy or Aoife Hartnett had been at?

.   .   .   .   .

Full of questions, Minogue strode into the squad room. He was dimly aware of, and indifferent to, the fact that he was annoyed. The job, he thought, osmosis of Kilmartin's personality. Maybe it was Malone nagging him about signing for a gun.

Murtagh kept his head down for most of the questions. There were still eighteen cars that needed following up at the long-term car park. Minogue told Murtagh to phone the family of whoever's name was on the car and find out when the hell he or she had parked their bloody car there.

If Fergal Sheehy was down to the last few interviews then he'd better start finding more: widen the net. A weapon — search the whole damned airport top to bottom. Get Farrell to start right away even. Decide on the motorway even — maybe the weapon was fecked out the window in a panic. And warm up the appeal and put it out again. Specifics: roads in Mayo, person missing. Did Shaughnessy have a camera when he'd arrived in Ireland, or did he bloody-well not? Still trying to figure that out, was Murtagh's reply. Where were his credit card receipts then? Murtagh pointed to a copy pinned on the boards. Minogue saw Murtagh's eyes dart to Malone's as he walked over.

"He paid the hotel here on, what's this, Mastercard?"

"The last one they have is for the hotel, yes."

"Are they saying that he didn't use it afterward or that they don't know yet?"

"My new pal, Debbie, in the States says that's it. They'd have it recorded inside of two days now."

Minogue looked up from the copy at Malone.

"Other cards?"

Murtagh didn't quite carry off the southern accent on the vowels.

"She done told me she'd run a credit check on heem. He was done flagged bad for priors."

"What kind of prayers?"

"Naw," said Murtagh. "Pr-i-ors. He went to hell on an American Express and some other cards a few years back. They nixed him. He only got back on the books a few months ago. There's a low limit on his new one too."

"Cash then," Minogue declared. "Bank records. He must have been carrying, for the love of God."

Murtagh chose his words carefully.

"I'll put priority on it, so, boss."

Minogue couldn't miss the tone. He turned from the boards again and gave Murtagh the eye.

"Thank you," he said, just as deliberately.

Murtagh closed a folder and looked up brightly at Éilis.

"Any word from our leader beyond in Boston, Éilis, oul stock?"

"Not yet," said Éilis. "Quiet for him, isn't it now?"

"Be nice to get him back," said Malone. Minogue wasn't going to ignore this.

"I'll maybe phone him tonight," he said to Malone. "I'll tell him you were asking for him. He'll like that."

"Me too," said Éilis. "Tell him I miss him. His quiet ways. The subtle wit."

"He'll be touched, Éilis. It'll be news to him too, I'd venture to suggest."

"Don't forget me," said Murtagh. Minogue turned his glare back on him.

"I suppose Sheehy and the crew too?" he asked.

"Yeah," said Malone. "Definitely. They asked me to tell you."

"He'll be deeply moved, then."

"All the mob in Serious Crime too," said Murtagh. "I was at a do there and they were asking after him."

"Did the president send her wishes too, Éilis?" Minogue asked.

"Oh," she murmured. "I forgot to write it down. Thanks for reminding me."

"What about filling in for him over at Keagh's Pub?" Murtagh asked. "He foots the bill for a few rounds. Did you forget?"

Minogue pinned the copy of the transaction record back on the boards.

"Enough," he said. "I hear ye. Loud and clear. Wait till I get paid, at least. I'm skint."

"Ah, you're always skint," Malone said.

"Mine's brandy then," said Éilis. "Brandy'll make up for it."

"I'll go easy on you," said Murtagh. "Three pints."

"One for each day since Jim left, right?"

Murtagh beamed.

"What about you, Tommy?"

"Same as John Boy there. Fifteen pints or so."

· · · · ·

Minogue looked over at the message board. The slips were green this week, were they. Where the hell did Éilis dig up those memo pads? He gave Malone a thoose on the arm as he walked by.

"Just gimme the money instead of the pints then," said Malone.

Minogue saw that his partner was losing the battle to hold back a grin. Malone dropped his head, pushed out his elbows, and jabbed at the air with open hands.

"Won't work," Minogue warned him. "I have the reach, pal."

"You better reach into your shagging pocket when payday comes, so."

Minogue put his arms out but Malone was on him too fast. He felt Malone's arms clamp his as he was shepherded to the wall.

"Yous culchies," muttered Malone. He feigned a left hook.

"Corner boy," Minogue said.

Éilis shook her head and lit another cigarette.

"Men," she said to no one. "The more they begin to cop on how use-less they are, the more of a bloody racket they make."

"Heard that," said Malone and parried Minogue's attempt at a shove.

"I give up," said Éilis.

"Nail him one in the chops, there, you," said Murtagh.

"Who?"

"Any of yous. I don't care who."

Malone let Minogue push him away.

"That'll learn you," he grunted. "Fifteen pints and the hiding of your life, you sodbuster."

"Do you want your messages," Éilis called out, "or do you want an-other round to knock the shite out of one another?"

"Éilis!" said Murtagh. "The bleeding language . . . !"

"Not you," she said. "His honor here. A personal and a call from the quare fella what's with Leyne. Freeman. He's a Yank."

Minogue straightened his shirt collar.

"Whyn't you tell me on the cell phone, Éilis, when I was over beyond at Aoife Hartnett's crowd?"

"He phoned a quarter of an hour ago only. I told him I could raise you and conference you through to him if it was urgent."

"What did he say?"

"He asked if it was a cell phone. I said it was. He said he'd wait, so."

Malone exchanged a frown with Minogue. The inspector took the slips from Éilis's outstretched hand. Kathleen first. Today was her half day. He'd forgotten.

She was eating something when he phoned her. Iseult had a plan, she told him. She had consulted her conscience before phoning with the news that she'd be going out for a swim in Killiney Bay. Orla's father had a boat, remember. Iseult didn't want them worrying, that was all. Wasn't that nice? He rubbed at his eyes and held in a sigh. His knuckles ached when he tried to switch the receiver to his left hand. The office had gone quiet. He turned to see where Murtagh was.

Purcell had come out of Kilmartin's office. He'd nearly forgotten about him being here, Minogue thought as he listened to Kathleen's arrangements. Iseult didn't mind him coming out in the boat with

Orla's father. In fact she wanted it. Didn't things work out well there? Minogue nodded at Purcell. Then he stared at the phone cord until his eyes went sandy. Purcell had sidled over to Murtagh, who was ignoring his questions.

Minogue said good-bye to Kathleen and let the phone down slowly. Purcell tried again with Murtagh. Murtagh looked him up and down.

Minogue studied Purcell's face. Curious, suspicious.

"Heard the news on the Smith thing?" Purcell tried. He looked from face to face. Malone stopped rubbing his nose and looked over at Purcell.

"It might be the clincher," he said. "Home free. That'd be great."

Minogue studied the phone number Freeman had left.

He stood and stretched. Purcell fingered his lip and watched his approach.

"Matt."

Purcell had scaly skin, redder when he was bothered.

"Matt. You know I think the same thing. I'd only be delighted to walk out of here. We're only here to assure administration that the case is gone as far as it could go for now, that the Smith file is jammed for good reason. We can't have people thinking that the squad's just sitting on it."

Minogue searched the sparse hair Purcell had recently combed down.

"That's as far as it goes," Purcell said. "We all agree on that, I think."

"Smith's file is active, Seán," said Minogue. Purcell nodded, looked at the wall. "We review in short every month, going back eight years to a stabbing in Fairview even. We reassign in full every three months to get the new eyes on it. It's always moving. Always."

"You know that, I know that, but it's been reviewed independently."

Minogue looked at Kilmartin's clock.

"You know," said Purcell. "I never get pally when we go in like this. Never. I shouldn't even be talking to you probably. It's just that, well, this isn't some hooligan getting his arm broken in a squad car, this is a case of the best we have here. No one seriously believes what that bitch said in the paper. She parroted anything the Smiths said just to sell papers."

Bitch, Minogue reflected. Well, now. Purcell should move on to a different department. A different job, maybe.

"Nobody in their right minds could believe what she was letting these gangsters say through her column. Really, I mean . . ."

Minogue said nothing. Purcell finally shrugged and looked away.

CHAPTER 22

MINOGUE WATCHED MURTAGH checking the levels on the cassette recorder by the phone. He lifted the phone and got a line several times, listening.

"Go ahead," said Murtagh. "Anytime now. It's line one, don't forget."

Minogue glanced down at the phone number for the Aisling Hotel. The receptionist had an odd accent. Like the ad for that new detergent. He didn't get a chance to thank her before he was switched. Two rings. Gone, was he —

"Yes? Hello?"

"Jeffrey Freeman?"

"Yes. Hi. Is this Officer Minogue?"

Officer, Minogue thought: that'd do nicely.

"It is indeed. You phoned me."

"Can we meet? Soon?"

None of this Thank You For Returning My Call? He let the pause linger. "Why?"

"It concerns the Shaughnessy case."

"The Shaughnessy case. You better explain where you fit with that now, like a good man."

"Okay. I can give you background, but we really should meet, personally."

"Talk for now, Mr. Freeman."

"You know about Mr. Leyne, right?"

"What have I been told about Mr. Leyne?"

"I understand you were informed he's on a life support system at the . . ."

"The Blackrock Clinic, yes."

"Your commissioner, right?"

"He didn't put him there, Mr. Freeman. He only told me about it."

"And that it is absolutely confidential?"

"Words to that effect, yes."

"You haven't told anyone about it, have you?"

Minogue looked across at Malone.

"Mr. Freeman —"

"Jeff, please —"

"Jeff. I have two phones here on my desk. Tell me why I shouldn't lift the other one and call in a squad car to go to your hotel room and drag you out here?"

"What? I mean, excuse me? Is this some kind of, *intimidation*, I'm hearing?"

"It's notice of intent."

"It sounds like a threat —"

"It's not a threat," Minogue broke in. "Threats are about the future. What I'm keen to do would take all of about seven minutes."

Malone had made his way over. He raised his eyebrows at Minogue, held up his hand, and clamped his fingers on his wrist. Minogue shook his head.

"You're serious, I do believe you're being serious. This is unbelievable."

"If I believe you are a threat to public order or you're trying to obstruct a murder investigation, there'll be a half a dozen coming through your door."

"Well let me relay that news to the embassy. They'd be interested, I'm sure. Then your commissioner."

"Good day to you, Mr. Freeman. You'll be coming here in person in about a half an hour to see for yourself just how mistaken you are."

"Wait! Look — let's take a step back from this. I'm a visitor here. Maybe I haven't come across the way people here are used to."

"You're going to be a resident here if you don't get smart. You've got about ten seconds."

"My client here —"

"Your employer, you mean. Play by the rules. To me you're a person obstructing a murder investigation."

"Okay," said Freeman, "say what you like, but I have a legal obligation to my client. I'm telling you that I have to respect it. I can only do that by meeting you in person. And I don't want any police, Garda I mean, tail this time."

Minogue sat in tighter to the desk.

"What do you mean, this time?"

"Let's not waste time on that one. Please? I was told you were in on everything. So: we don't need the 'escort.'"

Minogue said nothing.

"Okay? So we can get together on this? I'll hand over what I'm supposed to and then we can proceed whatever way you like."

"Take a taxi here then. Or I can have you picked up."

"Please. Mr. Leyne directed me to deal with you. You only."

"Me?"

"Mr. Leyne doesn't have confidence in the authorities here," Freeman said. "You're known. So is your boss, the one on vacation. He was very specific."

"Was?"

"'Is,' 'was.'" Freeman's voice dropped. "I need your assurance that what I tell you stays confidential?"

"Why?"

"I have to execute Mr. Leyne's instructions," he said. "When he becomes, well, when he becomes incapacitated."

"I'm a policeman, Mr. Freeman. Get serious now, or —"

"Do you know much about Leyne's Foods? How stock markets work?"

Minogue's Biro broke through the paper.

"Look," said Freeman. "Mr. Leyne's son telephoned from Ireland. I have a signed statement from Mr. Leyne here stating the substance of their conversation."

"What did he say?"

"I'm afraid I have to repeat that my instructions are to contact you in person and deliver the material to you."

Minogue caught Malone's eye.

"Enough of this trick of the loop playacting. I'm bringing you in."

Malone pointed down at Freeman's name. Minogue nodded.

"Wait," said Freeman. "This won't help. It's a goddamn mess already."

"Do you think so, now," Minogue said. "Well it's only starting for you. You're about money, mister; I'm about crime."

"If you give me a chance," Freeman said.

"You should have handed this over when your boss dragged in those reports, the private-eye stuff on Shaughnessy."

"Believe me," Freeman said. "We're acting in good faith here. Please."

Minogue let down his arm, held his hand over the mouthpiece.

"Throw him out the window, boss?"

He looked up at Malone. Murtagh was slowly nodding. But Freeman didn't need to phone, he realized. And this "You're known"? Leyne's bluster in the car coming in from the airport, he'd known all about Minogue all along. There had been a broad enough hint, with Leyne's happy disdain for the "researchers" he hired. How Leyne got himself those copies of police investigation records involving this wayward son of his back in the States, that said something about his reach too. The personal touch, insiders. Now this Freeman fella was holding his nose, for a fine fee too no doubt, and trying to engineer another inside track for Leyne to get to Inspector Minogue.

He closed his eyes for several seconds. He saw Leyne's sallow face again, the strain as he labored out of the car. Damn! He shoved the phone back on his ear.

"Listen," he said, "I'm coming over."

"I really appreciate it, and so will, so would —"

"Well I don't, let me tell you. Give me everything you've got. I want a statement from you; I want whatever documents and records you have. I want your utter and undivided attention. I don't want to hear name dropping or flag waving or client privilege talk. Leyne picked you for something, I don't know what, but I hope for your sake he picked right. Are you with me on this now?"

"I hear you. It's all aboveboard."

"Fifteen minutes or so."

"Fine. Oh, you can tell your guy in the lobby or wherever he is, that I'm not going anywhere."

Tynan, was Minogue's first thought: he had left him in the dark on purpose.

"I don't know anything about that," he said.

·   ·   ·   ·

Malone glanced over before racing from the lights at the head of Dame Street. The Audi he had raced kept beeping.

"How much again?" he asked Minogue.

"I heard two hundred million."

"Dollars or pounds?"

"I can't remember."

Malone turned sharply around two cyclists.

"So he says one of ours or some of ours are on the prowl."

"He, she, or it is not one of mine, Tommy."

"You don't care? I still think you should check with C3."

Minogue bit his lip. He really should get advice on how to give Freeman some serious grief. An American lawyer executing a brief for his client in Ireland. He doesn't trust the authorities . . . Had Leyne known he was on his last legs?

"'Cause you'll find out Tynan has us on a string."

"Be quiet, can't you. I'm thinking."

"Collar him," Malone declared. "The whole shebang: drag him out of the place, shove him into the back of the car, and bring him around the corner to Pearse Street. Take him apart. What's the big fu — what's the big *deal* here, like?"

Minogue didn't answer. He'd been thinking about the computer screen, the pictures fading and returning, the drums and the talk of time before the pharaohs.

"Like, what made you change your mind and tell him we'd go to his place . . . ?"

"I don't know. We'll burn that bridge when we get to it. Don't be asking me any more."

"Come on now, boss. He *killed* her. The da knew, because your man phoned him. And this fukken Freeman dude is trying his best to bury it. Share prices, all that's bullshit. Freeman's following a plan. Tynan's after pouring cement on us somewhere too. We'll be lucky if we even get told what the hell happened."

Minogue looked up to see the restoration work being done above the facade of what had been a tobacconist shop by Cuffe Street. Dust drifted away from a sandblaster overhead.

Malone pulled hard on the hand brake and stepped out onto the roadway, in one fluid movement.

"Jases, will you look at the doorman," he said. "The hat on him. Jases."

Minogue checked his door was locked and looked over the roof of the Nissan at the front of the Aisling Hotel. All glass, brass, and crass.

"Gardai," Malone said to the doorman. "Won't be long."

Minogue quickstepped through the foyer. Carpets up to your ankles, flowers, marble. He looked into two alcoves. Empty except for a group of three elderly women. Hardly C3.

The lift was all tinted mirrors. Minogue didn't much like the look of the middle-aged cop looking back at him. Annoyed-looking, a bit tired. Malone was trying to get some shape on his hair. The back of his jacket bulged as he leaned forward. Had he been carrying the pistol yesterday, Minogue wondered.

"This better be good," Malone said. The lift jiggled and opened onto a maroon and gray carpet. The two policemen stood by the door for several moments.

"Someone with him, boss. What do you think?"

Minogue couldn't make out the words.

He knocked. There was a burr as someone's shoe slid on the carpet inside. The spyhole darkened, and the handle was turned.

Freeman was a very different kettle of fish now. Denim shirt open two buttons. Minogue declined the hand. He stepped in and stared at Kieran Hayes. Kieran Hayes, as in Mr. Slick from C3, as in fixer and golden boy trailing glory and the glamour of Special Branch intrigue in his wake. "Works out of Harcourt Street," did he? Angry as he was, Minogue kept trying not to look stunned.

Hayes stood up slowly.

"Matt," he said. "How are you keeping? And Tommy?"

Declan King was standing by the window. He nodded at the two policemen.

"Anyone else?" Minogue asked. "Under the bed here maybe?"

"Not that we know of," said Hayes. "Cup of tea?"

Minogue waved off the tea. He nodded at Freeman.

"Mr. Freeman?"

"Yes?"

"I am arresting you for obstruction of —"

"Whoa, there," said Hayes. "We have a big misunderstanding here now, Matt. Let's talk this out. That phone call you made here, well —"

"Out of me way."

"What?" asked Hayes.

"You going to obstruct the investigation too?"

"Enough now," said Hayes. "That's not going to help."

"Enough is right," Minogue said. He took out his phone.

"We'll fill you in on the gaps now," King said.

"What are you doing?" asked Hayes. Minogue ignored him. Murtagh answered.

"John? Yes. We ran into a bit of a barney here at Freeman's. Get's a wagon and two or three uniforms. Large size."

"Wait a minute, hey!"

Minogue turned away and plugged his other ear.

"No, no trouble," he said to Murtagh. "Yet. And place a call to Tynan's office. Tell O'Leary I'll be phoning later on. Tell him the show's over. We're tired of the routine. We want our man."

He closed the phone and dropped it in his jacket pocket. Hayes looked from him to Malone and back. Minogue studied the curtains and the carpet. Let them eat cake up in Ballymun; this is the real Ireland. Someone should tell Colm Tierney that Ireland had reappeared. It was high class, European, and it smelled nice.

"Did I hear you right?" from Freeman.

"I don't know. Tommy, give Mr. Freeman his rights and bring him in."

King was up now. Hayes had taken out his phone now. Comical, Minogue was thinking, the phones being pulled out. The Wild West, but polite.

"Mr. Hayes," Minogue began. "Or is it Garda Officer Hayes? I'm placing you under arrest on a charge of —"

"Oh, for Christ's sake," Hayes said. "Where do you think you are?"

Minogue took a breath and sighed.

"Conspiracy to prevent —" he resumed.

"You're out of your mind," Hayes said.

"Resisting arrest is number two — oh, shut down that phone there —"

Hayes turned and walked to the window, dialing. Minogue gave Malone the nod.

Malone came around the table and grabbed Hayes's arm. Minogue heard Hayes swear as he shoved hard against Malone. He kept his eyes on King, watched the mouth open. Freeman looked over Minogue's shoulder at the door. The inspector shook his head.

"Put your phone away there, Hayes. And sit down and shut up."

Hayes had turned away from Malone. He began shouting into the phone. Minogue recognized the name: second in command in the branch. Malone pulled Hayes's arm and made a grab for the phone. Hayes elbowed him hard. Minogue heard Malone's grunt, saw his knee come up, and then Hayes stagger back. The voice on Hayes's phone kept on saying hello. Minogue picked it up.

"This is Inspector Minogue," he said. "Your man is all right, or will be. Except for resisting arrest. You'll be able to get hold of him at the Pearse Street station."

He held his thumb on the end button. Hayes got to his feet. Declan King began making his way along the wall to the door.

"Stay put, Mr. King," Minogue said. "You're in the pot along with these two clowns."

"You stupid fucking iijits," Hayes said. "Give me the phone back."

"No phone," said Minogue. "Sit. And stop the language. Mr. Freeman here is a visitor from America."

Freeman looked very pale now. His hands were wavering.

"I have no idea what this is," he began. "I'm not going to be arrested, am I?"

"You are arrested. So are these two."

"But Mr. Hayes is a police officer," said Freeman. "A Gar-da officer."

"I understand that too, yes. But he's also a considerable pain in the arse here."

"And Mr. King here has been my main contact with the government." Minogue glanced at King.

"Inspector, I have to butt in here," King began. The house phone began to ring. Minogue waved Freeman away.

"Yes?"

"Mr. Freeman?"

"No. He's busy."

"Who's this?"

"I'm a Garda inspector. Who's this?"

"Front desk — you're not filming a movie or something and we weren't told?"

"No."

"There are five Guards on the way up. One of them stopped by to check the room number."

"Why are you phoning here then?"

"Well, Mr. Freeman asked us to."

"Asked you to what?"

"He said he was wondering if there was someone following him, but I told him, I says, if you think that you should be talking to the Guards, I told him . . ."

Freeman and his cloak-and-dagger stuff, was Minogue's first thought. Maybe Leyne had been telling him everyone in Ireland was crooked, chancers at least

"Okay. What's your name, like, a good man?"

"Liam."

"Okay, Liam, listen. Everything's all right here. There's no one hurt, there's no property damage. We're all in fine fettle here. So: a piece of advice. Never, ever phone up ahead of a Garda who's on his way to apprehend someone."

"I just thought — okay. Is this a sting, like?"

Minogue glanced at Hayes.

"A sting?"

"Yeah, like when, you know . . . ?"

"Good-bye, Liam. And remember what I told you."

Minogue nodded at Freeman.

"Get all the stuff."

"What stuff?"

"Are we going to carry on like this all day? The stuff you should have given me the minute you stepped off that plane at Dublin Airport."

Freeman exchanged a look with King.

Minogue walked to the table and flicked open the folder. A signed affidavit or something, signed by Leyne and Freeman and some Villani, same name as the firm on the letterhead. He heard murmuring from the hallway now. Malone opened the door. A tall Garda had one arm raised to knock.

"You come with us," Minogue said to Freeman.

Hayes began arguing with the Garda. The tall one inspected Hayes's photocard on both sides and glanced at Minogue several times.

"It's these two bloody lunatics you should be taking in," said Hayes. "I want him on assault too — him: Malone."

"They've had the caution," said Minogue. "Hayes there belongs to the cell phone there."

Hayes pointed at Minogue.

"You are talking your way out of a job," he said.

"Give him his call at the station," Minogue said to the Guard.

He paused and eyed Hayes.

"Unless you have reason to believe, as I do, that that call might further hinder the prosecution by police of a serious crime —"

"That's a load of crap —"

"— or to the commission of another."

The Garda pushed his hat back, and studied the photocard again. Then he motioned Minogue over to the door.

"This says C3, you know," he murmured. "They're the tin gods aren't they?"

Minogue gave him a glazed look but said nothing.

"The highfliers," the Guard murmured. "And he's a sergeant. Are you sure about this?"

Minogue nodded toward King.

"That's nothing compared to the other fella here," he said. "He's up in the stratosphere in Justice. But he knows enough to keep his gob shut there now."

"Both of 'em?" asked the Garda. Under the wariness, the skepticism, Minogue was sure he saw a smile begin.

"Take them in," he said. "Obstructing a police officer. I'll follow up with a call within the hour. This Freeman fella is the same but he's going to the squad for a chat first."

CHAPTER 23

Minogue had noticed the tic on the left side of Freeman's face first. A quick blink of both eyes, a tilt of the head, and then his nose would wrinkle. It was usually followed by an intake of breath which Freeman seemed to hold on to for a long time.

"It's not withholding," said Freeman. "Mr. Leyne would never have suggested that."

"Me bollocks," said Malone.

"What?"

"He doesn't believe you," Minogue said. He looked up from the statements.

"Whose idea was it to produce these?" he asked Freeman.

"Mr. Leyne got advice from our firm."

"Before or after the news that the son had been found?"

"Does this matter at the moment?"

"It matters," said Malone.

"He never said directly. The date here is after you found him."

"How do we know it stayed sealed until he was put on life support here?"

"He's my client, and I'm an ethical lawyer."

Malone snorted. Minogue watched another tic. He was almost ready to feel sorry for him. Cruising around Dublin with two detectives who had just busted an arrangement he'd thought was official, high level, wasn't in a day's work for him.

"Mr. Leyne knew he was taking a risk coming here," Freeman went on. "You saw him. You heard him. He wouldn't take a physician, a doctor, with him. 'I don't need a doctor anymore,' he said. Is that nor — I mean, is that the way people are here, usually?"

Malone turned down Ship Street, down toward the back gate of Dublin Castle.

"Where are we going?"

"We're taking the scenic route back to our office," said Minogue.

"You're buying time, to stay out of touch so no one can reach me. That's illegal."

"Listen," said Minogue. "It's in your interests here to put all your cards on the table. What did Leyne tell the son to do in those phone conversations?"

"I don't know. Nobody knows."

"You're covering for Leyne," said Malone. "Or the business, or something. You've got two hundred million reasons to do what you're doing, right?"

"Ridiculous. Shield him from what?"

"Liability," said Minogue. "Accessory. That's what."

"Wait a minute: are you accusing him of counseling Patrick to commit a crime? Or to cooperate in one?"

"What did he tell the son on the phone then?" Minogue asked. "To go ahead and take this stone?"

"Of course not!"

"He collects this kind of stuff, doesn't he?"

"What's on the open market at auctions, yes," said Freeman. "Where ownership is established. And legal, of course."

"Did the son tell him he'd killed someone to get his hands on it?"

"Oh, come on!" said Freeman. "Don't even think of pushing this. I'm a lawyer, for God's sake. If this is the way you intend to carry on here —"

"What happens now to the company?"

Freeman sat back against the door. He stared at Minogue. Another tic. Minogue knew that Freeman had seen it noticed.

"And his foundations here?" Minogue added. "His family?"

"There's no way I'm even going to reply to that," Freeman said. "Much less speculate on this, this innuendo. Anyone can see what you're leading to."

"His will," said Minogue. "Have you seen it? Did the son know something about it?"

"I can tell you this, that he never wanted anything from Patrick except to be left in peace, to see out the rest of his days."

"Changed his will after the operation, did he?" Malone joined in. "So a lawyer was more important than a doctor to have with him on the trip here? In case he had to make some change to the will in a big hurry —"

"This is getting more and more bizarre —"

"What was it?" Minogue asked. "Bypass? They found cancer?"

Freeman shook his head and looked at the traffic.

"Book me," he said, "and give me my call. Anything's better than this."

"Two hundred million," said Malone. "That's a lot of jack, man."

"Was Leyne behaving erratically?" Minogue tried. "According to shareholders or directors, maybe?"

Malone had to slow down for the cobblestones. Freeman surveyed the high walls, the graffiti on doors long sealed.

"Why are we going along here?" he asked. Minogue looked in the envelope where he had taken the documents from. No, nothing more.

"Is this your idea of sending me a message or something, cruising by here?"

"This is an historic part of the city," Minogue murmured. He took another look across the covering letter. "So don't be complaining just because it looks like a bomb hit it."

Malone pulled in to let a taxi and a lorry pass. Minogue looked out at the line of parked cars, the steering lock contraptions so prominent in the windows. People still willing to take a chance and park here instead of paying through the nose for car parking. He noted the leftovers of a shattered window on the roadway, a relic of a recent break-in, no doubt.

"If it's any news to you, Mr. Leyne didn't exactly have confidence in the police here. He was right."

Minogue cocked an eye at Freeman.

"Whatever he has or had, Mr. Freeman, whatever he decided to **do** with his company, his foundations, his family, his will — all that, these are things others would be very keen to know about, can we agree?"

Freeman kept his stare on the headrest.

"Patrick Shaughnessy in particular would be one who'd have a stake."

Still Freeman said nothing.

"Who else, then?" Minogue went on. "Who else would get burned if Leyne did something like turn things he had into some class of charitable foundation? Or if he was to liquidate a company, sell off a bit of one? Stock prices, would they drop, would they catch fire?"

"I don't play the market," Freeman muttered. "And from the sound of things, you shouldn't either."

Minogue studied Freeman's face.

"Ah, don't feel so bad there now," he said. He glanced at Malone, met his eyes for a moment. "You're probably not the only one who's been set up here."

"Is this how you treat people here?" Freeman asked. "Then maybe Mr. Leyne was wised-up years ago. I heard you were friendly, easy to get along with. Oh sure, awkward maybe, but decent. I actually used to turn a deaf ear to him when he'd go into his, his, they weren't exactly tirades, but — 'They'd cut your throat behind your back.' There — an Irishman saying that about an Irishman?"

"No news there," Minogue said.

"And still he was — he is — so proud of being Irish. You probably can't understand that, can you? And after this episode, let me tell you —"

"Shut up a minute," said Malone. "Boss?"

Minogue turned.

"You see it?"

"Which?"

"A green Mondeo sitting back there? A boom-boom version. Fancy wheels?"

"Might be one of ours, Tommy. Turn on the radio."

There was a two-way about a stolen van being followed through Finglas.

"He wasn't there when we came onto the street," said Malone. "He must have come in after that lorry, and pulled in."

Minogue strained to see along the parked cars.

"Naw," Malone murmured. "He pulled in at an entrance to some place there. I can still see a bit of the side of him there. . . ."

Minogue turned up the radio a notch. There was a traffic accident somewhere near Rathmines. The stolen van was now speeding through red lights in Finglas village.

"If it's someone Hayes's mob has put on us, they'd have their own band," said Malone.

Minogue weighed the phone in his hand. Freeman wasn't going to tell them anything. Time to show up, probably. Whatever about Hayes and company, Declan King would be trouble. Tynan might blow a gasket over this.

"Let's move on, Tommy. Let them play if they want."

"I think he might have been with us a few streets back, boss."

"Are we close to your place?" asked Freeman.

"He's coming along with us, boss," said Malone. Minogue looked out the back window. He wondered if there was a pick-up car, a tandem, somewhere ahead.

"Who's following us?" Freeman asked.

"I don't know," said Minogue.

The dispatcher's voice had a different tone now, Minogue believed. He repeated the message. A gray Nissan, a Technical Squad car, thought to be in the city center, perhaps heading for headquarters in the Phoenix Park.

"We're famous now," said Malone. "Bet you it's the Iceman. He's gotten an earful from King already."

The dispatcher repeated the request to get in touch with CDU section 3 by phone immediately.

"There goes the promotion," said Malone.

"You'd better tell me what's going on here," said Freeman.

"Huh," said Malone, his eyes on the rear mirror. "Hayes's mob. James fucking Bond cha-cha tango gobshites. With their souped-up shitbox Mond — Jesus!!"

Malone stood on the brakes and yanked the wheel. Minogue's belt bit into his neck. Freeman's shoulder hit hard on the seatback. It was a white car, a Golf, but Malone had managed not to stop in time. Tires shrieked somewhere behind. Freeman was trying to right himself in the backseat. Son of a, he was saying.

The passenger door of the Golf swung open. Minogue was surprised: how could a driver so blatantly in the wrong want to leap out and start shouting. In the split second before the man turned, Minogue had taken in the covering on his head, the bomber jacket, the thing in his hand, and he had registered all this somewhere as trouble. Planned, he knew instinctively as he realized that he was watching a man with a nylon stocking over his face carrying a gun.

Malone had already found reverse. He jammed the pedal, shouting. The man with the gun hesitated, took a few steps, and stopped as Malone accelerated. The Nissan began to waver as Malone overcorrected but he kept it going. Minogue looked out the front. Someone in the Golf was waving and shouting at the gunman.

"Oh-oh," from Malone, and then a shout as the Mondeo blocked the roadway behind.

"Hang on," Malone called out. "I'm going to have a go at him!"

Malone didn't slow down. Minogue put his head down as the Nissan hit the Mondeo, but the impact threw his head against the headrest. Freeman came forward, his hands over his head, crashing into the seat. The Nissan was stalled and beeping. Minogue heard something metallic rolling away outside on the roadway. Malone leaned over the wheel now, grabbing at the small of his back.

"Out," he shouted. "Get somewhere between the parked cars!"

Minogue saw that the gunman had begun to run toward them now, the Golf following. He looked around for Freeman, and then slipped as he came around his open door and went down on his side. The pain from his hip and his elbow stunned him. He heard Malone was calling his name, shouting something about over here. The roadway was greasy under his palms. A slicing pain from his palm came to the fore now: some piece of a light from one of the cars was embedded there. He got up to a crouch, called out Freeman's name.

There were hissing sounds coming from somewhere, grinding too: the front of the Mondeo. The driver was trying to start the engine again. Malone shouted something about Freeman, he was over here.

Minogue ducked when he heard the crack, like a stone being split, then another. He ran blind on his hunkers to the parked cars. Malone grabbed his collar as he put out his hands.

"Get down here, boss! Boss! Down!"

He saw Freeman's leg as he dropped down between the bumpers. Malone leaned around a bumper and fired off three shots down the street. There was a quick squeal of tires and a shout. Minogue thought he heard "gun." Maybe they hadn't expected them to be armed. Freeman was half on the footpath now. Minogue called out to him. Freeman's face appeared by a taillight, his mouth slack with the shock. He was bobbing on his hunkers.

"Don't," Minogue called out.

The driver of the Mondeo gave up. A car door opened. Minogue crouched lower, heard footsteps scrambling. Oh fuck, he heard Malone curse. Someone began shooting steadily now. He couldn't tell what direction it was coming from. There was a whirr in the air close by. Malone bobbed up, fired a shot toward the Mondeo, and dropped down.

Minogue turned when he heard the scrambling behind. Freeman was gone. There were more shouts, some from himself, Malone. Two shots rang out in quick succession, then two more. The running footsteps stopped and he heard something hit a panel, scrape on the cement of the footpath. Malone began shouting Freeman's name now too.

There was another shot and then Minogue heard someone running. Minogue tried to get his feet under him better for a sprint. One of his knees wouldn't bend enough. A car began to rev high — the Golf, he thought. Someone was shouting, "Let's fucking *go!*" More shots now, a steady, measured volley from one gun. A car window went out with a pop nearby, pieces hesitating and then cascading in bunches to the roadway. Malone fired: to keep them at bay, Minogue knew. How many were in a clip on those new automatics, he thought. Did Malone carry — The revving gave way to tires squealing and a door being pulled shut.

"Freeman, are you there?" he heard himself call out.

"Stay down," he heard Malone shout. The driver of the Golf made a racer's gear change into second.

"Are they gone?" Malone called out. Minogue peered around the bumper. It was a Peugeot he'd been hugging, he realized. Behind him, a Starlet, close to being a clapped-out banger. His palm was beginning to sting. He looked down at the cut. And there was a rip at the knee of his newish trousers, bought in that shop in . . . The weakness flooded into him in an instant. Was he going to faint now?

"Are they gone?" Malone was asking.

"I don't know," he managed. Malone, his face red and contorted, was backing toward him on his haunches, his gun trained on the gap between the cars.

"Where's Freeman?"

Minogue's jaw seemed to be locked. He shook his head.

"Where's Freeman?"

Still Minogue couldn't find the words. Tires squealed one street over. The hum and background hush of the city seemed to come back louder than ever. Malone began to take quick looks around the bumper at the two cars in the middle of the road. The driver's door on the Mondeo still hung open.

"Did they take off in the other car?" Minogue heard him ask. There was a sharp smell in the air that Minogue recognized all too well. Malone was standing in a crouch now, looking through the window of the Starlet. Minogue heard him talking but couldn't hear the words. Malone hunkered down again, gasping.

"He's over by the footpath," Malone said and gasped again. "Boss?"

Minogue scrambled on his knees over to the edge of the footpath. He put his hand out on the bumper to steady himself and took a quick look down the path. Those boating shoes Americans seemed to be in love with, he thought first, not wanting to take in the sight. There was something dark on the footpath beside where Freeman lay. A line led crookedly out from it to the edge of the footpath.

Malone's hand grasped his upper arm but he hardly noticed. He looked up to where Malone was crouched above him now.

"They went after him," Malone said in a whisper. "They went after Freeman. What are we going to do?"

·   ·   ·   ·   ·

"There he is," said Dolan. "The boss man himself."

Minogue turned his head slowly. Even at this distance, he recognized O'Leary stepping out. Tynan was out then, putting on his hat. Something about the way he put on the hat seemed ridiculous to Minogue. He watched the television crew pushing forward by the cordon at the end of the street behind. Tynan stooped to get under the tape.

Minogue shifted in his seat and exchanged a glance with Malone. Malone sighed and stared at the fluttering tape, the small crowd milling behind the squad cars drawn up at the end of the street. Minogue tried again to stretch. No go. In the half hour since Sergeant Malachy Dolan had shepherded them into the unmarked car at the far end of the area, his neck and shoulders had gone stiff.

Dolan hadn't annoyed them much with questions, especially after Malone's angry reply to a question asked more than once: he didn't know if the other fella or fellas had all jumped into the frigging Golf, because he was busy ducking bullets from one of them to cover their getaway, for Jases' sake. Dolan didn't seem to take this badly at all, and had sat behind the wheel, monitoring the radio for news of the Golf with them. Nothing was showing up.

Minogue fingered the plaster on his palm and tried to flex his knee again. It wasn't swollen, but it had gone warm and numb. He watched Tynan study the footpath, incline his head to listen to Murtagh.

"Let's have our say, Tommy," he said, and opened the door. "And get out of here."

The handle felt odd: tight, well-made, too springy maybe. The strangeness of everything now. He felt the beginnings of a laugh, then panic. Dolan looked over when he didn't step out.

"Are you all right?" he asked.

His chest was still full of that airy, swollen feeling. Maybe he should have gone in for observation for a few hours. Malone was waiting for him to step out too.

"Boss? We're not carrying the can for this, right?"

Minogue was up now. Tynan had spotted them, and had ducked back under the tape and was heading toward them.

"They knew," Malone went on, "they *knew*, there was something else going on with all this. Right? And they didn't say a fucking word to us, so they didn't. It's all up to them then, isn't it? The bastards."

Minogue nodded. Malone's bastards were Hayes and company, he supposed. Tynan covered ground quickly, he thought. The handshake, unexpected, reminded Minogue of the loser in a close bout.

"Matt?"

"Well I'm on me feet."

"Tommy?"

Malone shrugged, took the handshake. Tynan stared at Minogue.

"At least get a lie down, will you?"

"No. I'm okay."

Minogue stared at the crowd standing by the tape. Dolan had followed them from the car. He stood back now.

"No."

Tynan looked back at the sheet covering Freeman, Murtagh writing something.

"You knew straightaway?" he asked. "After the shooting?"

Minogue nodded.

"Can you tell me what happened? The lead-up."

"The fella behind was tracking us," said Malone. "He was good. I only spotted him later on."

Minogue shivered.

"But they definitely went after Freeman," he said.

Tynan frowned.

"You don't think they put him as one of yours? Ours, I mean. A Guard?"

Minogue waited for Tynan to out with it.

"Smiths?" he murmured finally.

Minogue shrugged and looked over at Malone, who shook his head once.

"They'd know us," he said.

"I'm still going after each and every one of the Smiths' crowd," Tynan said. "Every last little hanger-on and gofer, every little worm that ever had anything to do with them."

Tynan turned to Dolan.

"Can we clear these two to go?"

"Yes, sir," said Dolan. "We can get a car in for them soon's we get the word."

"Please," said Tynan. "And would you go into that bashed-up Nissan there and take out an envelope, a big one, with some fancy letterhead printed on it, and get it for us?"

Tynan watched him quickstep it back to the car. Minogue looked over at the Nissan and the roadway beyond. The chalk circles around the bullet casings looked like eyes.

"Did you sign over your pistol?" Tynan asked Malone.

"I did. To John Murtagh, he bagged it."

"Good," Tynan said. He threw a glance Minogue's way. "I won't bother asking you. Have you changed your bloody mind after this, then?"

Minogue said nothing.

"Now," said Tynan. "We need to clear the decks sometime soon here. We're going to sit down very shortly and sort out, try and sort out, what happened in that hotel room."

Minogue tugged at the edge of his plaster again. He was aware that Malone was standing very still beside him. He didn't want to look over at him for a reaction.

"Because that's when things started to fall apart," Tynan added. He waited until Minogue looked at him.

"What were you doing in this part of town, with Freeman in tow?"

"We were headed for the squad," said Minogue. "An interview."

Tynan looked from Minogue to Malone and back.

"Those papers Freeman had for you," he said. "I know what's in them. So did King, and so did Hayes."

Tynan looked at the two site technicians by the Mondeo. Callaghan, one of them.

"Aren't you surprised?"

"I am and I amn't," Minogue said. "I thought we were first in."

"So did Freeman," said Tynan. "He had called Boston to get the go-ahead after our Mr. Leyne took a turn and was put on the life support. He got the go-ahead to go to you. But we received a phone call here from the principals too."

"Who, you?" Minogue asked.

"No. Justice. Mr. Declan King."

"Hayes?"

"That went around me completely," Tynan said. "That's why you and Head-the-Ball are not being given the treatment here at this very moment. At least your contrariness was out in the open —"

"They were running us, John. They were trying to turn the case."

Tynan set his jaw and looked over at Malone.

"Are you picking up on all this, Detective Garda?"

Malone nodded.

"Your CO here arguing the toss with the commissioner? At a murder scene? Right in front of a detective Garda, detective Garda from Dublin?"

Malone darted a glance at Minogue. Tynan's blank stare went back to Minogue.

"I only heard of these calls after you two clattered King and company down at the hotel," Tynan went on. "They'd come in on Freeman, and they were going to set you straight when you showed up for the meeting. That didn't happen."

"Set us straight how?"

Tynan gave no sign he'd heard Minogue.

"Oddly enough, Leyne seems to have formed some . . ." he paused to consider his choice of words. ". . . some *attachment* to yourself, Inspector. Seems to think you were all you were cracked up to be — and he checked, let me tell you, I found out. So he wanted to rely on you with this affidavit about the son phoning. But the lawyers beyond had their own ideas, and one of them was to notify the Department of Justice here that you were going to be given these papers. An insurance measure, you might say."

Tynan looked down the street at the cordon.

"In my book, it's that meddling made this come about. But now look: Freeman . . . There'll be moves over this after the dust settles, let me tell you. Clean house, and sharpish. But this, this mess hangs on King and the others."

He turned back to Minogue.

"You asked what King knew, and was going to let you in on?"

"Money, I'd be thinking," said Minogue.

"Always a safe guess."

Minogue gave him a hard look.

"Okay then: when do we get some real answers?"

Tynan looked around once, nodded at O'Leary.

"Right now, if that's what you can handle. But not here."

Minogue exchanged a look with Malone, who shrugged.

"Let's go, then," he said to Tynan.

"Fair enough, then," Tynan said. Minogue didn't mistake the new edge in his voice. "But, before we start, know this: you're standing down from the case for now, the both of you. No arguing here about it either."

O'Leary held up the cordon tape but it was Dolan steering them to Tynan's Grenada, brushing off a man holding out a walkman. He insisted on shaking hands with Minogue and Malone as they sat in. Minogue's knee gave him a stab as he pulled in his leg. He looked over at Malone. His colleague looked like he'd just been pulled out of a carwash.

Someone shouted Tynan's name from the small crowd around his car. Tynan paused to answer a question. O'Leary shifted in his seat.

"A right mess," he murmured. "Are you okay?"

"Not so great, Tony. Thanks. A mess is right."

"You should have heard the boss," O'Leary said, "when he found out what they'd done. Declan King and them. Never heard the like of it before. Ructions."

Outside, Tynan broke away away from two reporters. O'Leary started the engine. Tynan sat in and pulled the door hard behind him. Minogue winced when the flash went off by the window. Tynan half-turned.

"The both of you could be going off for a bit of observation, you know," he said. He looked at Minogue. "Especially you. Haven't you blood pressure or something?"

"I'll be all right. For now."

"Have you phoned Kathleen yet?"

"No. I will in a little while."

Tynan took out a notebook.

"Really, now," he muttered and he crossed something out. "Do you think a small Jameson would help the proceedings here?"

"Only if there was a pint to go with it," said Minogue.

Tynan closed the book with a snap

"Go to Quinn's," he said. "They have a snug there."

CHAPTER 24

TYNAN PUT DOWN THE ENVELOPE. He laid the sheets on top of it.

"So that's it," he said. "There's nothing here about Leyne's response to the son's phone call."

Minogue studied the countertop by his glass. The light coming through the whiskey fanned golden on the wood. He eyed Tynan.

"Leyne collects things, doesn't he?"

"What do you mean?"

Minogue had to wrench his eyes off the play of the light.

"What I mean is that the son was here to get this damned stone and smuggle it back to Leyne, John. To get back in his good books. To get his name in the will."

Tynan poured water into his empty glass. Further down the bar two old men had engaged the barman in a discussion about farmers. It was a poor enough pretense at not eavesdropping, Minogue decided.

"That's a fair take," said Tynan. "The son mentions that this stone had been verified by an expert."

"This 'expert' being Aoife Hartnett," Minogue said.

Minogue became distracted again by Malone's hands. He hadn't let up rubbing them, squeezing them until it seemed the knuckles would burst through the skin. O'Leary's phone went off. He listened, nodded, and ended the call.

"No sign of those fellas yet," he said to Tynan.

"Not even the car?"

O'Leary shook his head. Tynan turned back to Minogue.

"Well I don't see the son telling him over the phone that he's killed someone," he said. "There's no point. It'd poison things for him entirely. Yes?"

Minogue shivered. The whiskey was working against him now.

"I just don't know," he managed. "Panicking?"

"Does it sound like panic to you?" Tynan asked. "Not to me. The gist of the conversation is the son telling him this stone is a genuine find, this Carra stone. That no one knows it's been turned up, so no one's going to miss it. And on he goes into the some story about it."

Tynan waited for Minogue to look his way.

"It's also clear to me from this flimsy statement that Leyne has doubts about the whole thing anyway," he said. "It's what he doesn't put in the affidavit is what's got me wondering."

Minogue thought about Eileen Brogan crying. Garland biting his lip as he tried to explain the leave of absence he'd pushed Aoife Hartnett into. He saw Dermot Higgins pointing and clicking, heard his distracted murmurs, the pictures dissolving and sliding off the screen. He rubbed his eyes. It didn't help: his thoughts were slipping away.

"Okay," he tried. "The call is made 'just outside Dublin.' The son is in a hurry. Has he a means of getting this stone out of the country at this point, a plan? Contacts? We don't know."

Tynan shifted on his stool. Wanted to get going, Minogue registered.

"You read up on this Carra place, didn't you?" Tynan asked. "What about this stone anyway? Is there such an item?"

"Legend says there is. Or there was."

"It's never been found though?"

Minogue missed with his glass as he was returning it to the table. It tipped, rolled, and fell on the floor, intact. Tynan lifted his feet to place them away from the spilled whiskey. Minogue reached down and brought up the glass. He fixed Tynan with a glance.

"Okay, let me throw in a question now," he said. "Declan King was at the airport to meet Leyne. So was Hayes. What did they know, how much, and how early?"

"King reports to the minister, not me. Hayes, I'll be getting to."

"They colluded in keeping information from us. What's your view on that?"

Tynan began to stack the coins on the counter. He placed the last coin, a five-penny on the top. He looked up suddenly at O'Leary.

"Tony. You and himself here give us a bit of room, will you."

O'Leary waited for Malone to rise. Tynan watched the door of the snug being pulled tight.

"Listen here, Matt. No more noises for now, about Hayes working behind your back. King, I can't do anything about."

"I had two connected murders on my hands," Minogue said. "Three, now."

"You don't. The squad does. You're off the case, for now."

"We've been led. Now we're being shoved aside. And Leyne or his fixers are papering over the cracks all the time."

"Leyne's in a coma. He has brain damage."

"He knew something was up. He's been throwing bones to us. The private-eye stuff on the son, now the affidavit — but I say he knew all along."

"He had his own interests," said Tynan.

"Two hundred million of them, is that it? Is that what concerns the likes of Hayes and King? Or you?"

"Did Freeman tell you that?"

"No. I asked him about the will and he got into a dander."

"Well you'd just arrested him, driven around the streets, growling at him."

"Why did Leyne have a lawyer with him? He was expecting the worst."

Tynan lifted the coins in groups from the stack and began dropping them back on the stack.

"Two hundred million, I heard," said Minogue. "Am I wrong?"

Tynan released the coins and rubbed his hands.

"It's not two hundred million," he said. "It's fifty. It's part of what he's worth."

He looked up from his palm at Minogue.

"Leyne made contact with people in the last government," he said. "He had a proposal, to donate fifty million dollars to the development of Irish culture. It was to go into history, heritage centers. Like the Carnegie libraries years ago."

Heritage, Minogue thought. He watched Tynan examining his palms.

"Let me guess," he said then. "There's a deal involved. An amnesty for stuff Leyne had, stuff he'd bought that was smuggled out of Ireland? Goddamn it, John, we give amnesties to tax dodgers and drug barons here every day, so why not Leyne?"

Tynan let the seconds pass.

"That was the deal until the son got himself jammed in the works," he said then. "Leyne would never have to divulge who or where or how these pieces ended up in his possession. And that the fifty million would be very welcome, thank you very much."

"Hush money," Minogue said. "A half-step up from extortion."

"Look at the results," said Tynan. "A lot of money for heritage here, re-covering missing — stolen — artifacts too. Call it restitution if you like. That would be a good day's work. Yes?"

Anything you want, Minogue was thinking: the hand grasping his arm.

"I think that Leyne actually tried to make me an offer," he said. "Ex-cept that I was too thick to get it."

"For all your work, you're still a bit of a gom, I'm afraid."

Minogue gave him a hard look.

"Well here's how I see it then," he began. "Or does it matter, at this stage?"

"It matters. Fire away."

"King was in touch with Freeman on a regular basis. King would be doing the trick-bicyclist routine, the deal maker with the delicate stuff. Hayes, maybe the gofer to shadow Leyne or Freeman while they're here. Fits, doesn't it? Except that Aoife Hartnett is murdered. And Shaugh-nessy himself."

Tynan turned on him.

"Listen," he said to Minogue. "The clock has moved on. You have to come in now. The case proceeds, but you need to step aside for a while at least."

"Why? Because now Freeman's been murdered? Because we weren't shown the menu? Because we crashed the party?"

"Among other reasons, because the minister has requested it."

Minogue put down his glass. He studied Tynan's face.

"John," he said. "Wait a minute here now. You bought me a cup of cof-fee the other day. A nice cup of Bewleys white coffee. You asked about Jim dirtying his bib at the club. Fair enough, I thought. It's wise to be on guard with this newspaper article, the Smiths stirring up trouble again. And Gemma O'Loughlin is out to sell papers. And then you talked about Shaughnessy, how you want to be in the know every day. Still fair enough, I said to myself again: a visitor, tourist, well-known family, profile — whatever. It has to be done right. Fine and well."

Minogue paused to get Tynan's eyes back from a study of the glass.

"But today, out of the blue, there's a murder. It's a well-planned mur-der. How well planned? They knew there were Guards there, and maybe even that the Guards might be armed. But they were determined enough, desperate enough . . . or maybe they were so well paid, so afraid of failure, that they followed through anyway."

He leaned forward. He could feel the muscles at the back of his neck quivering now, his head beginning to shake.

"There's part of me knows that those two fellas were only after Freeman, John. The poor iijit panicked and ran for it. That's when they got him."

Tynan nodded once and looked down at the floor.

"Now they were nothing to the Smiths, John, were they?"

Tynan raised his eyebrows.

"I say they were there for Freeman."

Tynan picked up the coins again.

"There's something you're not telling me here," Minogue said. "And if you don't tell me, I'm going to find out myself. If you won't let me at King or Hayes, I'll go after them myself."

Tynan let the coins drop into his other hand. His voice was soft when he spoke now.

"The last person who spoke to me like that was an assistant commissioner," he said. "Was, I say. Now he hadn't been threatened, or shot at, like you have. So you're going to make it. For now. We'll let that last remark go by."

"The suits went around you," Minogue said. "But they're not going around my case. We have three murders, they're related, and I'm not going away. A bunch of robbed antiques and fifty million notwithstanding."

Tynan let the coins slide over one another in his palm. Minogue wondered if O'Leary and Malone could hear him on the other side of the partition. Tynan glanced up from his palm.

"Okay, then," he said. "It's not just the money. Or even these, what can we call them — artifacts — he says he's going to give back 'to the Irish people.'"

The commissioner looked at the distorted glass in the partition of the snug. That head could only be Malone's, Minogue decided.

"You talked with Leyne, didn't you?"

"In the car," replied Minogue. "At the press conference, a bit."

"Well, did you ever hear him hold forth on the state of the nation here?"

"A short, sour few words, yes. He was still back in the fifties. I kind of switched off."

"You remember 1969, Derry?"

Minogue searched Tynan's face for a clue.

"What about it?"

"The riots in the Bogside, when everything was going up? How it looked from here? Nights of burning houses, riots, and petrol bombs? Remember?"

"Yes, of course I do."

"The B Specials and the RUC? The black outfits, like storm troopers?"

"What's this . . . ?"

"You remember we were considering sending in the army, over the border into Derry?"

"Yes, there was talk —"

"Talk?" said Tynan. "You know well there was more than that."

"Why are you bringing this . . ."

He left the question unfinished. He stared at the commissioner. Tynan looked and sounded as though he was reminiscing about a clumsy prank as a schoolboy. Minogue knew the expression, the tone to be signs of a quiet fury.

"Where is this coming from?" he tried.

"Didn't I tell you I had a chat with the Minister of Justice this morning?"

"Wait," said Minogue, "I'm not on board here. First I'm thinking smuggling, then pay-off so Leyne can get his shot at immortality here, then cover-up for his son, but now . . . ?"

"I had several questions to ask of the minister," said Tynan. "At least the conversation ended on a civil note. Can I get back to this history lesson now?"

Minogue nodded.

"The North, the sieges around Catholic areas, the barricades. The arms that we didn't officially notice being sent into the North from here."

"Leyne was part of that?"

Tynan looked at the empty Seven-Up O'Leary had drunk.

"NORAID, the Americans — that was the start of that," he said. "There was big money involved. You got caught in the tail end of a bit of the worst yourself."

For a moment Minogue was back at the border that night, his legs beginning to give out as he tried to reach a car already rolling into the ditch, the bullets still slamming into it.

"What are you saying here?"

Tynan opened the snug door and asked O'Leary to phone a Hogan, tell him he'd call later. Through the doorway Minogue eyed a customer, an elderly man with a gaunt face and a long tongue, which he kept flicking around his lips as he hauled himself onto a stool. The knuckles were misplaced, jammed together. Tynan closed the door again.

"We heard a rumor a few years ago," he resumed, "that Leyne had been involved back then. Yes — the self-made entrepreneur still with the politics of a Republican. It surfaced when he made his approach about giving back these artifacts, and donating all the money. He's no stranger to donations, by the way, I learned: do you want to know how many millions he's given to the Democrats over the past decade? Anyway, that was before the IRA went shopping in Moscow and Libya, and doing their deals with the other slime in Amsterdam and Prague and the rest of it."

Tynan gave Minogue a quick survey.

"Even before the business phase kicked in," he resumed, "with the robberies and the rackets and the drug trade. He believed, or he wanted to believe, that the IRA was the same IRA as had fought Black and Tans. Remember where he came from, Matt: small farmer, pushed around here. He walked away when the politics went way left. That's history now."

"History," said Minogue. "But plenty stayed in, people that Leyne would know still, then?"

Tynan looked at his watch.

"Probably," he said.

"What if the son knew that, had a name . . . ? Or what if he'd told the father some of what he'd done here and Leyne pulled out some old contacts here to get the son out of the mess?"

He tried to arrange his thoughts but they kept going sideways on him.

"The son, Shaughnessy . . . ," he began. "He was trouble, that we can tell. Would he have put the heavy word on people here, how he could spill the beans on something from way in the past, so's they'd have to help unglue him from whatever he was up to here?"

Tynan nodded slowly. Minogue didn't know whether he was agreeing with him or just placating him.

"More to the point," Minogue went on, "if Leyne began to suspect that his contacts here had gotten fed up fast with demands the son was making in his name and then gotten rid of Shaughnessy, maybe even Aoife Hartnett because she was in the wrong place at the wrong time . . . Leyne might put them to the wall too?"

Tynan didn't nod again. He had resumed fiddling with the coins.

"Freeman had access to Leyne," Minogue resumed. "Even to his will maybe. Leyne might have let slip what was on his mind to him. So Freeman would be an unknown quantity here if people thought he could pass on something to the Guards. . . ."

Minogue let his words drop away. The soreness in his knee came back to him.

"So that's where your case goes off the map," Tynan said then. "This is not just about smuggled stuff from old churches and graveyards down the country."

"Shaughnessy, he lit the fuse, didn't he?"

"Could be," said Tynan. "But those gunmen today were part of something a damn sight bigger than you and your partner, and even your squad, can handle alone."

"This is a squad case first and foremost," Minogue said. "We can't sit on our hands at the door here."

Tynan eyed him.

"Seems like you have inherited Kilmartin's selective hearing here," he said. "Safety's number one: get through this, what just happened. And you can't have an edge after this. You're also going to have to take stock of the situation at home, get a break after this. Kathleen?"

"I'll handle that. But we can't walk away from this though."

"There's no disgrace," said Tynan, his voice rising slightly. "We messed up because we were kept blind. You did the best job possible. Stand down for now, let me get Intelligence in with some of the old hands on the paramilitaries, going back to whenever. This won't be buried any more."

"We're okay, Tommy and me," Minogue said. "We have to keep a hand in, or we could lose momentum here, could bury the case even. It's asking too much to walk at this stage."

"No, it damned well isn't."

Tynan's murmur drew Minogue to check the anger in the commissioner's dull stare.

"Everything costs something, Matt," he said after a few moments. "Eventually. Sometimes a lot more than it's worth. What I have from the minister is that you and Malone walk from that mess back at the hotel."

"It was obstruction," said Minogue, "whatever way you want to dress it up."

"You should have listened," Tynan said, "before you bounced them and whipped this Freeman off in the car. So. Hear me out now? You standing down means there'll be no comeback from King or the minister, even. As for Hayes, I'll deal with him myself, but part of the horse-trading on the phone this morning saves Hayes's neck. If he wants to work for the minister, then he gets out of the force. And I'm going to see that he does within the week. Now, that's what's been happening this morning in my little world."

Tynan's stare returned to a gaze at the glasses on the countertop.

"This started as politics," he said. "Or culture. Or heritage, whatever that is anymore. But it's going to end as justice."

CHAPTER 25

O'LEARY DROVE THEM DOWN the quays after he had dropped the commissioner at Harcourt Street. The giddiness was gone but so was the panic: Minogue just felt more jittery now. O'Leary didn't try any small talk.

"I have such a bleeding headache," said Minogue at last.

Minogue knew that Kathleen would be at the squad by now.

"What are you going to do then?" Malone asked. "Go home and put the feet up?"

"Maybe."

The Four Courts slid along the top of the quay walls. It looked ragged today.

"Hey," Malone said to O'Leary. "Were you ever shot at?"

O'Leary nodded.

"Where, in Dublin here?"

"No."

"Where?"

"In a small town in the middle of nowhere. Near the border with Sudan."

"And what was it like? Not the place, but what did you do, like?"

"I ran the other way," said O'Leary. "They were robbers. I was on leave with another UN fella. We probably shouldn't have been there."

"You weren't a basket case after it though?"

"I don't remember really."

"Well, I thought I'd be a basket case by now. After this, I mean." He turned to Minogue. "But I feel, like, *up*. I'm actually very fu — , very *annoyed*, like?"

Minogue shivered. O'Leary had them in the car park in short order. Minogue looked over at his Citroen. It looked damned fine. He longed to sit in and coast off, away out to the west in it. Himself and herself, the Galway road, no hurry. He returned O'Leary's wave. There was a bite to the breeze now. He looked around the sky.

"So, are we going home or what?" Malone asked.

Minogue wondered what Kathleen would say. She hadn't freaked entirely during the phone call, but she was damned if she wasn't coming in to see him. How could he fight that off without hurting her.

"I'm going to do a bit of reading and a bit of thinking," he said. "Maybe a bit of talking. I don't care where I do it. But, I'm not sitting and waiting."

Malone looked around the yard.

"Plans, have you?"

Minogue nodded.

"Was that an order from Tynan or a suggestion?"

"An order, Tommy. He has to answer to people to, as well as we do."

"There's no way this was the Smiths' caper then. Is that what you're telling me?"

Minogue nodded. Kathleen appeared in the doorway. Minogue went for her. She dug her fingers into his shoulders, hugged him tighter. She was fierce annoyed. She let him go and held him at arm's length. Her eyes were red but the anger made them bright and steady.

"They were after the other man," he tried.

"How do you know?"

He shrugged.

"And does that matter anyway?" she insisted. "Does it?"

He gave her another tight squeeze when he felt the tremor in her chest. She sniffed and detached herself. She turned to Malone, his hand on the door.

"You look after this iijit, Tommy Malone," she said. "You hear me?"

"Yeah, Kathleen. Sure all the culchies need hand-holding up here."

They followed Malone in. Farrell and Éilis met them in the hall. The squad room was quiet. Kilmartin's door was shut. Minogue wondered but didn't care where Purcell was. Éilis drew on her cigarette and studied the boards.

"It has to stop," Kathleen declared to no one in particular. "The place is being run by gangs and mur —"

Her voice broke. Minogue smelled shampoo from her hair, felt the folds where her strap had dug in a little tighter over the years. She had asked him out of the blue if she looked fat the other day. He hugged her tighter and listened without much interest to a two-way about a man who had collapsed in a pub. In his twenties, he thought vaguely. Overdose, he wondered.

Minogue felt her relax. It was Kathleen who pulled away this time. Éilis slid a box of paper hankies across the table. Farrell looked up from his study of the floor.

"Cup of tea," said Éilis at last. "Or a smathán from the cupboard?"

"Tea's grand, thanks," said Kathleen a little too quickly. "You're a star, Éilis."

Éilis stubbed at her cigarette and looked up warily at Kathleen.

"Tell us about Iseult, will you," she said Éilis. "I'm dying to know how she's going on."

Kathleen sat back in the chair and closed her eyes.

"Sacred Heart of Jesus, Éilis. Between Iseult and your man here . . ."

"I'm going to make coffee then," Minogue said. He waited in the kitchen for Malone.

"Worse, are you?" he asked.

"It's got to hit me sometime. But I'm still so bloody wired."

Minogue took down the kettle and began filling it. Malone was fidgeting with a fork.

"Boss? If we'd stayed we'd a been in Hayes's pocket, or King's. Wouldn't we?"

"Probably. Hard to say. I don't know, Tommy."

"Well that's what I need to think right now. You know what I'm saying?"

Minogue glanced over. The tremor in Malone's voice was quickly disguised. He plugged the kettle in and leaned back against the counter. Malone breathed out between pursed lips several times.

Was that laugh he heard from the squad room Kathleen? He toyed with the filter as he drew it out. Malone was staring at Minogue's coffee jar.

"Well?"

The kettle ticked. It was Kathleen's shriek of laughter he'd heard. What was Éilis talking about? A man's voice, could only be Farrell, derision; more hoots of laughter. He opened the lid and shook the jar of beans.

"Well what?"

"What's the story now?" Malone asked. "We sit around this kip chewing our nails, is it?"

Minogue was not really surprised to realize that he had made up his mind a lot earlier. Maybe it was even when Tynan had led the way leaving the pub.

"The story is this, Tommy."

Malone stopped hopping the fork off the countertop.

"Sooner or later I'm going to try my hand at a bit of, what would you call it, treasure hunting. Looking through haystacks, you might call it."

Malone's eyes narrowed.

"Still the job, like? This case . . . ?"

"That'd be it, Tommy. Yes."

"You're not too pushed that he'll be dug out of you, Tynan?"

"Well, no. In a word."

He eyed Malone.

"I have three murders to solve," he said. "We can't stop the clock on them."

He poured the beans into the grinder. One by one he picked up the half-dozen that spilled onto the counter. The laughter was louder. He cocked an ear. Éilis, that gift for making people laugh.

"Would you be considering going a bit of the road with me, Tommy?"

"Am I going to get a sudden attack of lead poisoning if I say yeah?"

"Doubtful."

"Who minds the shop here?"

"John Murtagh. Farrell too. We'll pull Fergal Sheehy in here to do his interviews."

"Will I be on the dole if I survive the lead poisoning?"

"There's always room in the dole queue, I suppose."

"You're not much on the hard sell here, boss . . ."

"Do I need to be? Give me a couple of hours to get started."

"Started on what though?"

He closed the lid and looked up at Malone.

"It's out there somewhere, Tommy. It exists. Whatever it is."

"What the hell are you talking about?"

"He had it in the boot. It's heavy. It broke the panel over the spare wheel, it was so heavy."

"What is? The thing you were telling me about on the way back from Mayo?"

"He had it. He told his da he had it."

"This stone?"

"He wanted his da to tell him how to get it out to the States."

Malone took a step back. He spread his hands on the counter.

"Leyne had it done before, you're saying. The robbing. Right?"

Minogue nodded.

"Or he knew someone who could do it."

"Lookit," said Malone. "What if this goes all the way to gang stuff, paramilitaries? They're crossed over anyway, half the time. Hey, I'm not stupid. Tynan could be kicking us off the field for a good reason. Jases, you can see that, can't you?"

"See what, now?"

"If they're all tied in, boss. Scratch one and it all goes back. To the IRA, their outfits — we'd be in the ha'penny place if we found ourselves, just the two of us, up again them."

Minogue pushed down the lid. He held the grinder, shook it. Malone stared at it while it spun. Minogue lifted the lid and sniffed the ground coffee.

"I'm in then," Malone said. "But just so's you know: I'm not going up against the IRA or their fucking partners."

·　　·　　·　　·　　·

Kathleen sank into the front seat of the Toyota. Minogue wondered where he'd seen the driver, a detective from Store Street, before. She wound down the window.

"Look at those trousers," she said. "The rip there at the knee. You look like a tinker, God . . . !"

"I'll be all right. Thanks."

"But your knee . . . !"

"It'd be locked up by now if it was serious, love."

Kathleen began to say something but stopped.

"And you'll phone Iseult, won't you?" she said instead. "Tell her she could come over with us to Daithi's at Christmas."

"I will."

"And we'll pay, of course, right?"

"To be sure, love."

He nodded and stepped back. The driver took the hint.

"You'll stay well away from whatever commotion has come out of this? Nothing more than the stolen property case you were telling me about?"

"Exactly. The best thing is to be busy, they say. I'll phone you."

"Think about Iseult," she said as the Toyota pulled away. "And the baby."

Malone accosted him in the hall on his return.

"So Kathleen sorted you out, then?"

"I'm to stay out of the way of trouble, and work only on, er, stolen property cases."

"Fair play to her," said Malone. "Now you have to sign on to my contract."

He wiped away a dribble of water from his forehead. Why did this gurrier keep running water on his face and on his hair so much, Minogue wondered.

"What are you on about, man?"

"Here's what: you sign for a gun. So's I don't have to worry about you."

Minogue looked at Éilis and Murtagh poring over some files. Malone pointed a finger at him.

"Start arguing and I'm walking," he said. Minogue looked back at him.

"A gun? For tracing stolen property around the airport, Tommy?"

"Don't try that on me. It worked for the missus, but I know what's going on. Get the equipment. And don't roll out the excuses. This isn't Dear Oul Dirty Dublin any more. Wake up, man."

Minogue said nothing. He returned to his desk and opened the file Mairéad O'Reilly had given him. He couldn't remember where the part about the stone was. There was a page and a bit at least, though. How could O'Reilly ever know anything about the Carra stone except what he'd made up in fancy? Éilis was standing by the desk when he looked up.

"So you're staying, your honor?"

"For a while, Éilis. Yes."

"I'm to phone Purcell to tell him when you're gone."

"Who says, a stór?"

"I says. We asked him to absent himself when we got the news you were on the way here, John Murtagh and I. In the event there might be friction. Emotions running high, your honor."

Minogue watched her light another cigarette.

"He's away off in C Wing. He took some files with him. Smith and that. So: I'll be phoning him . . . ?"

"Would you phone Firearms Issue for me first, please."

"Firearms, you said?"

"Exactly, Éilis. Firearms Issue. We're still on alert. Tommy needs a replacement. His was bagged at the scene, the shooting."

"Fair enough."

"And I'll be wanting one."

She drew on the cigarette. Minogue looked up at her. Her face remained impassive.

"Then we'll be off," he said.

·   ·   ·   ·   ·

Malone backed the Opel out of the parking spot. He drove slowly, adjusting the mirror. Whoever had used the Opel last had smoked. Minogue imagined a couple of detectives on surveillance, smoking and eating and farting for days. Weeks, maybe. He rolled down the window more.

He couldn't get comfortable. He reached up under his arm to pull the strap looser. It was too much trouble to take off here. The Velcro was too far around to reach without taking off his jacket. He felt the aches as a clamp across his lower back and his shoulders now. He yawned and stretched. A faint relic of Kathleen's perfume came to him.

Malone's driving began to annoy him.

"Why are you driving like this?"

"Like who?"

"It's not 'who,' it's 'what.' You're driving too carefully."

"Jases, if it's not one thing with you it's another. I'm shook, that's why."

Malone passed Mountjoy Prison without a glance over. Anytime he passed it, Minogue had thought of Malone's brother. Malone made the green light at Drumcondra Road. A convoy of articulated lorries under plumes of diesel smoke awaited them. Malone swore and settled the car into second gear between the lorries.

"So we're looking for a rock," he said. "This 'stolen property' gig you told Kathleen about. And if Tynan wants to know."

"Right," said Minogue. "A stone."

"But there *is* no rock you're telling me. Right?"

"That's it."

"So when we *do* find it we'll know then that it's not there. Right?"

Minogue studied the patterns of dirt at the doors to the lorry ahead. "Now you have it."

Malone grunted and pulled around one of the lorries. Minogue eyed the Cat and Cage Pub over the passing traffic.

"Leave no stone unturned," said Malone. "Is that the idea?"

He had to wait until the lights at Collins Avenue to shake off the last of the convoy. Minogue thought of Leyne, the eyes set into those pouchy folds. Like a lizard. Tired of life was he. How many things had he collected over the years? Geraldine Shaughnessy must have known about them. The son too. He thought of the winding bog road up by Carra, the ditches. . . . He opened his eyes as Malone took the curve leading to the roundabout for the airport.

"Where am I going?"

"What?"

"You dozed off," said Malone. "Where am I going, I said?"

"Turn down the first chance you get to the freight end. The South Apron, it's called."

"Is it that we don't want them to know we're poking around here or that we don't care?"

Minogue was stiff. There couldn't be bruises everywhere, he thought. He moved his neck slowly. The strap for the pistol harness was biting across his ribs.

"The former," he managed and levered himself more upright. "Here's the routine. We're just looking around to double-check we didn't overlook anything in the area."

Minogue didn't expect a checkpoint just inside the entrance to the freight terminals.

"There's an unmarked over there," said Malone.

The Guard was brash, puzzled. Malone took his card back.

"It's a walkabout," said Minogue. "Just in case we missed something."

"The American fella? In the boot of the car?"

"Yeah," said Malone. "The pressure's on. To make sure we covered everything."

"Fair enough," said the Guard.

"Thanks," said Minogue. "By the way, are you permanent here? This checkpoint, I mean."

The Guard made a face as he tried to dislodge something from his eye.

"Ah no, we're only here for autographs."

He stopped poking and looked back down at Malone.

"Only joking. The Works are due in sometime this evening."

"So," said Malone. "No more scaring the shite out of some sheikh's wife for the fans."

"Right," said the Guard, a wry smile tugging at the corner of his mouth. "Ah sure, we'll be out here again in a few days to get rid of them again."

Minogue leaned over and looked up at the Guard.

"The band, you mean?"

"Yep. They go on tour in the States, I heard."

Minogue looked over at the freight buildings.

"The big time," said the Guard. "That's how it is."

"Is there an office out here with a layout of this end of the airport?"

"Go over there. That's the start of the Customs Hall. Shipping and receiving's down the far side of it. There's offices there, the Customs and Excise mob. Federal Express, other ones."

He stopped poking at his eye, looked down at his finger, and then at Minogue.

"Thanks," said Minogue.

Malone stopped tugging and pushing the gear stick across neutral.

"What's on your mind there?" he asked Minogue.

"I'm thinking how I'd get something out of the country in a hurry."

Minogue shrugged.

"I don't know."

Malone held out his hands over the wheel.

"Gimme. What's this? You're saying he gets to the airport, he's in a corner because he's got — but there is no Carra thing, for Jases' sake. *You* even say that. What's her name there down in Mayo, you even phone'd her again just before we left. Mairéad O'Reilly. Legends, man, all stories, bullshit. Yeah?"

"I said there's no 'The Carra Stone,' Tommy."

"Yeah, yeah? Yeah . . . ? Well try English, will you, boss."

"The indefinite article."

"The what?"

"There may be *a* Carra stone."

He tapped on the dashboard and pointed to a sign before Malone could start in on more.

"Park it over there, Tommy. Air Freight Storage. See if a walk'll wake me up."

· · · · ·

The Customs and Excise officer was a trim, black-haired Dubliner by the name of Paddy Mac. Mac-what, was not volunteered and Minogue didn't ask. Dyed or not, the pompadour hair and the thick sideburns impressed the inspector. A man who could so steadfastly cling to the fashions of his early teens was a man well chosen to keep track of things. Paddy Mac looked up at him.

"That mugshot must have been taken awhile back, chief."

"January."

"This last January? What happened since? No offense, like, but."

Minogue looked around the office. There were showband photos on the wall over his desk. He wondered if these were collector's items by now. Was it that long ago? The Hucklebuck, Kathleen and he went to the club on Harcourt Street. What were those photos of birds? A bunch of boxes, cages — pigeons, of course: a pigeon racer.

Malone tilted his head, studied the photos of the showbands.

"What?" asked Paddy Mac.

"Just wondering who they were," Malone said. He turned to Paddy Mac.

"No sign of the Works or any of them," said Malone. Paddy Mac put his hands on his hips. He studied Malone for several moments.

"Why would there be?"

"The next generation maybe?"

"They're nothing to me. Dossers, fakers, shapers. Along with the rest of them. Junkies."

"Do you think?"

"You'd know, wouldn't you? Your mob, I mean."

The sharp tang of cardboard that had stung in Minogue's nose had given way to an oily smell. He hadn't seen an ashtray.

"Wait a minute, but," said Malone. "Wasn't Elvis the world's biggest junkie?"

"When they killed him, yeah."

"Who killed him? He ate his way into the bloody coffin."

Paddy Mac gave Minogue a bleak look.

"You and me'd know better, I'd like to think. What do you say to that shite?"

"Well, I haven't really kept up," said Minogue.

"What's to keep up with?"

"GOD? I don't know really."

"GOD? Holy, crucified Jases. That bunch a —"

Malone shuffled, looked around the room. Paddy Mac glared at him.

"— and don't start in on Elvis again. They broke him, so they did. Did you see the Hawaii comeback? That's when I knew it was over. That's when I knew what the sixties had been all about."

Minogue exchanged a look with Malone. The weariness, the aches were like jet lag and a hangover combined. His eyes were beginning to signal the return of a headache.

"So," said Paddy Mac. "You want to look around. What are we looking for?"

"Anything," said Minogue.

"A murder weapon maybe?"

"Well, yes. Stuff that might have been robbed from a car. Rags, gloves."

"There were Guards all over the kip there the other day outside here. You think that someone came in here for dirty work? Airport staff?"

Minogue held up his hands, wiggled them.

"What, we're under suspicion?"

"Can we wander around?" Minogue asked.

Paddy Mac waited a moment.

"Okay," he said. "Suit yourselves. I mean, yous're the law. Wander all you like — but there's locked areas now."

Minogue studied the map pinned to a corkboard.

"Have you a plan of the place you'd give me, now?"

Paddy Mac tugged at his belt.

"Tell you what I'll do: I'll go around with yous. Stretch me legs."

He gave Malone the eye. Malone put up his hands.

"As long as hair-oil here doesn't start on musical theory."

CHAPTER 26

P ADDY MAC USED HIS RADIO antenna to point. Minogue watched him wave it about, jab with the antenna. A conductor of sorts, he thought.

"Air freight inspections start there," said Paddy Mac. "That's for outbound with all the papers ready. The customs broker's spot's there, see? There's the entry to the Customs Hall. Incoming, inspections."

Minogue turned the corner and looked down at the open door at the far end of the warehouse. Paddy Mac wheeled and faced Minogue.

"This Yank," he said. "What was he up to out here anyway?"

"Well, there you have me."

A forklift shot by the doorway and scooted out of sight behind stacks of crates. Pallets of tightly wrapped sacks rose to the ceiling behind them. The creases and the dull shine of the plastic wrap put Minogue in mind of shrouds. Pupae. He paused to yawn, and then followed Paddy Mac through a double door into what looked like another warehouse. He studied the heavy wire mesh on the cages they passed.

"Now," said Paddy Mac. "Here's a sight. Are you ready for this, are you?"

"What?"

"Over there, in that cage. Look at that gear, will you."

Minogue stepped through the doorway. He tried to count the boxes. Many of them were sheathed in aluminium. Others were made of black panels edged with metal bands and reinforced corners. Paddy Mac twisted and tugged the lock out of the holder and followed Minogue.

"That's the better part of a half a payload there," he said. "I saw it coming in. I asked what's his name what it was worth."

"Who?"

"Ah, your man — what's his name. He came out one day before they took the spot. The manager, with the pigtail."

"The ponytail," said Malone.

"Yeah. . . . Daly: that's him. 'Two hundred grand,' says he. So I says, why not rent it all there, like."

Minogue recognized none of the brand names on the boxes.

"'It's all customized,' says he," Paddy Mac went on. "Like I didn't know. What it is, is to cover 'em up. To drown 'em out."

"Do you think," said Minogue.

"What, do you think they can actually play their instruments?"

"Why would he be out here doing the loading and unloading? Is that common?"

"Well Jases, I don't know," said Paddy Mac. "He doesn't want slip-ups . . . ?"

Minogue strained to read part of a sticker. Mockb —. Moscow, of course.

"Shiny lights, smoke," Paddy Mac said. "Earrings, hats. Making a racket. Throw in a few big words, pretend they're philosophers. That's not your hungry kid driving an oul car up to Memphis, just him and his guitar, is it?"

Gih-tar, Minogue registered. Paddy Mac was in deep.

"Well what are they using in Germany then," asked Malone, "if their gear is all packed here?"

"Germany? For some video gig there on the Berlin Wall or whatever the hell they were on about?"

Minogue craned his neck to see over a box the size of a sofa.

"Ah, they'd be just standing there for that. Throwing shapes, that's about it."

Minogue turned to him.

"How do you mean?"

"Ah the video shite," said Paddy Mac, grimacing. "Hate to break it to yous now, but they dub everything. Didn't you know that? It's not the real thing at all, at all. Shapers, man. That's all."

"Go way," said Minogue.

"I'm telling you. It's not singing or anything. It's playacting."

"So this is their gear then, their real equipment?"

Paddy Mac snorted and waved his arm. The disdain came to Minogue as the genial, indulgent sarcasm that had baffled him for years after he had first arrived in Dublin.

"I suppose," he said. "I don't *know* what's in them. That's for someone to inspect in the States."

"Not here?"

"Right. Customs here don't touch these ones. They'll get the treatment over beyond when that stuff lands, yes sir. They don't be messing around over there, let me tell you. The electronics and sniffers and what have you. No messing there, man — Christ, they'll be all over the stuff for you know what. The dope."

Paddy Mac plucked a pouch from a hook on the mesh by the doorway. He rummaged and scanned a half-page document. Minogue studied the sharp, even lines on his sideburns.

"Goes out to the States day after tomorrow," Paddy Mac declared. He looked up at Minogue.

"It's common enough, if that's what you're wondering."

"Really."

"Sure it is. You have stuff brought out days ahead of time. It needs wrapping, tying up. Pallets and that? Organize the heights and widths for the plane doors. You don't want to pull a load of stuff out on the tarmac, hoist it up to the bay, and find it's three inches too big, do you? Jase, no. You have to shuffle stuff. Balance, weight, height. It's a science, I'm not joking you."

Minogue shoved against one of the boxes with his thigh. It didn't budge.

"That's what I'm saying," said Paddy Mac. "Weighs a ton. And it all has to be set and balanced, packed right."

Malone tugged at the catches on a box.

"Hold your horses," said Paddy Mac. "You can't be opening that."

Malone glanced at Minogue.

"It's restricted here," he said. "I'm only showing you around."

"Restricted how?"

"Well, first of all, we're responsible for stuff here. There's insurance, liability. But the big thing is we close it off so's no one comes in and tampers with outgoing freight. Security's the main thing. Then there's headers, obviously."

"Bombs, you mean?" Malone asked. Paddy Mac looked him up and down.

"Well, yeah. If you put it like that. Or there's people dropping little *items* in along with legit stuff going out. Contraband. Drugs — but that's all seat traffic for years, if it's not passenger baggage, like. If they're really stupid."

"So, not everything's inspected," said Minogue.

"On the way out? Who's asking?"

"Just a Guard," said Minogue.

"Like an inspector just-a-Guard?"

"Just-a-Guard."

"Shouldn't you be going through the APF mob for these questions? What happened to security, confidentiality?"

"Well stop us if we're putting our feet in it."

Paddy Mac tugged at his lip. He looked from Minogue to Malone and back.

"Okay," he said. "Okay. Only some stuff is inspected. But do you know what goes through here? Bet you don't. Microchips. Computers. Software by the ton. Not a lot of people know that. People think it's still butter and pigs and boatloads of Guinness. Not anymore, let me tell you. Exports, man. High tech."

Minogue looked at the boxes again.

"Drugs?"

"What? Drugs? You keep asking me that. Wouldn't yous know that?"

"Haven't a clue, to be honest," said Minogue. Paddy Mac took a step back.

"Wait a minute. Are we just having a conversation here? Or are we talking about this band and drugs, like?"

"Just a chat," said Minogue.

"In that case, then we'd better introduce some common sense then," said Paddy Mac. "Who'd be such a gobshite as to stuff drugs in here? Even a week's dope for one of them? Come on. Nobody's that thick — not even them. Sure they're millionaires, man. They'd have no trouble getting what they'd want on tour. Drugs. Free teenagers."

He gave Malone a wry look.

"Like the King?" Malone asked.

Paddy Mac put his knuckles on his hips. The dust and the acrid smell from fresh plastic was beginning to cloud Minogue's thoughts.

"Here, look. You can bet your bottom dollar the Yanks would be all over any stuff coming in freight for a rock band. They don't sit around over there you know. Customs, DEA, FBI. Do you know anything about them?"

Minogue stopped rubbing his eyes. He examined the reinforcing bands on one of the boxes again.

"No. Who gets in here? Into this cage, I mean."

"Staff," said Paddy Mac quickly. "It'd depend on the shift. Stuff'd be moved in and out, signed in by whoever's on shift."

"Other people, I mean."

"Nobody. We sign for stuff, we bring it in here."

"So say there's stuff brought here —"

"— drivers, freight forwarders, taxis sometimes, couriers, you're talking about, Chief. We get the paperwork, we see the bill of lading. We sort it out. We stick it on the right plane."

"Do you get break-ins?" Malone asked. "Stuff go missing?"

"A: no. B: it's happened."

"Recently?"

Paddy Mac studied some distant part of the ceiling for several moments.

"The last break-in was two and a half years ago," he said. "Yobs, total iijits. We had pilfering and that but two fellas were nailed for that. That was early last year."

He turned and pointed at two boxes by hanging lights.

"See them?"

"Yes and no," Minogue said. "What are they?"

"They're cameras. The union finally gave them the go-ahead last year. It was a do or die thing. The computer crowd as well as the big pharmaceutical companies here put the boot in and said they couldn't do business here if there was no watertight freight handling. Security and that."

Minogue surveyed the boxes again.

"Are all those boxes that heavy stuff?" he asked.

"What would you say now," said Paddy Mac. Minogue read the scorn plainly now. "The boys'd need their gear, wouldn't they? 'Customized,' oh yeah. Everything has to be just perfect. For *the boys*."

The sneer was for Malone, Minogue believed.

●   ●   ●   ●   ●

Malone looked at his watch. He held his hands out.

"I think I'm getting the shakes," he said. "Do you know that? I keep on thinking this last while I'm going to wake up. Is that how it —"

Minogue had his hand on the phone already. He pressed to receive even before the ring had finished. Éilis's voice brought him relief.

"What's with the warrant, a stór?"

"Not a word, I'm afraid."

"But didn't we have a judge lined up?"

"We do," she said. "Fergal and John Murtagh took it to Enright's chambers, what is it, now?"

"Over an hour ago, Éilis. What does Enright want, someone bigger than sergeant to sign it over?"

Éilis said that she didn't know. Minogue leaned against the window of the Opel. A breeze stirred a crisps bag and sent it scudding across the pavement. There had been steady traffic in and out of the terminal. He had given up counting the planes. Paddy Mac's shift was over in ten minutes. He thanked Éilis and closed the phone.

"Nothing on the getaway car even?" Malone asked.

"No. It's the search warrant we're chasing now still."

"Ah shite," said Malone and closed his eyes again.

Minogue studied his colleague's face for several moments. The patches around the eyes, already almost closed to slits, were new to him. Malone opened his eyes, and rolled down the window. He hawked long, and then spat once.

Minogue checked the battery strength.

Malone let his eyes close and settled back in the seat.

"Waiting," he sighed and yawned. "Sitting in a car, waiting. That's half the job."

Minogue felt the belt pinch his shoulders again. He shifted in his seat. He knew he'd be checking the gun, for the tenth time since they'd driven out to the airport. Completely neurotic, of course, but still he'd check: he had never loaded in a magazine.

He reached in and pushed up the strap. The Velcro gave a little.

"Are you going to load it or not?" Malone murmured. Minogue looked over. Malone hadn't opened his eyes.

"I should just take a bleeding walk and leave you to it," Malone said.

Minogue thumbed the Velcro down and tugged on the grip. Tight.

"Well?"

"Well what?" asked Minogue.

"Where's the clip?"

Minogue studied the scrawny shrubs wavering in the breeze. A small turboprop rose over the terminal.

"You need things called bullets to make it work. You know?"

"Tings," said Minogue.

"Come on," said Malone. "Show it to me, in anyhow."

"What?"

"The clip. So's I know you have one at least. Or did you throw it out the shagging window on the way out here?"

"No. I have it."

"Prove it. How do I know? Show it to me."

"I just didn't want to blow my arm off, Tommy."

"What, you want someone else to do it for you? Gimme."

"I haven't had one of these for years. Anything could happen."

"Anything will happen! If you don't show me the —"

"I'm an inspector, Tommy."

"Oh yeah, now you pull the regimental shite? Now all of a sudden you decide it's —"

Minogue lifted out the phone and waved it at Malone. Éilis sounded pleased.

"They're on the way, your honor."

"Who, Éilis? The both of them?"

"To be sure. They don't want to be in the squad with Purcell and company looking through the laundry here."

"But who's in charge there then?"

"I am."

"Éilis, much as I admire —"

"I have Purcell corralled in the palace. I think he's busy phoning people. Locksmiths or such like."

Minogue stared at the frayed tip of the windscreen wiper. Malone had shoved home the clip and had tested the safety twice.

"What in the name of God does he want a locksmith for?"

"We can't find keys to some of the cabinets, your honor."

"Éilis —"

"Whissht! I've enough on my hands. Farrell's here too. He'll cover the legit side of the staffing for the investigation."

"Should I be hearing this?"

"Decide that for yourself," she said.

"Is there anything coming in then?"

"Not a thing — wait. There's only seven cars left at the long-term car park unaccounted for. Three were claimed this morning, all holiday people in from Greece I think."

Minogue glanced at Malone.

"I take it Purcell has tried to contact me at home to get those keys then?"

"He has," she said. "And you're not there are you?"

Minogue closed the phone and checked he had switched it off.

"We're on," he said to Malone. "They got it. The warrant, Fergal and John."

Malone handed him the pistol.

"Take it," he said. "Remember the deal: I don't want to be a sitting duck like this morning."

Minogue waited until Malone had stepped out to greet Sheehy when he and Murtagh showed up ten minutes later. He drew out the pistol and shoved it under the seat before he stepped out.

Fergal Sheehy unfolded the warrant and handed it to the inspector.

"So we're investigating the theft of a bit of the nation's heritage then."

Minogue checked the Premises section again.

"That's right, Fergal," he said.

"You look like you're just after getting out of ten years solitary," said Sheehy. Malone leaned against the window. He looked from Murtagh to Sheehy.

"You look worse," said Murtagh. Malone grunted.

"Do you want us in then?" asked Sheehy. Minogue folded the warrant again.

"As long as you know you're only assisting us in a theft investigation," he said. "We're, er, standing back. In a manner of speaking."

Sheehy nodded. Minogue heard Malone's mocking snort.

"Here, look," said Malone then. "Here's our fella."

"With the hair?" said Murtagh. Minogue opened the door first.

Paddy Mac stopped and pulled his jacket tighter. Minogue almost smiled. Horsey people ended up looking like their horses. Why not racing pigeons? It must be the haircut.

" . . . Teddy boy, for Jases' sake . . . ," Minogue heard before slamming the door. He nodded at Paddy Mac and walked over.

"Well," said Paddy Mac. Minogue studied the white spots by his nostrils. The wind had picked up.

"We have a warrant here, Paddy," Minogue began. "But I don't want to just march in there and start in on it."

Paddy Mac eyed the three policemen in the Corolla.

"What," he said, "more of yous? That should be enough to overpower any resistors."

Rezizz-tarz. The gleeful scorn. How could he ever leave this damned city, Minogue thought. It was the whole bit: the stance, the jaw lowered,

Paddy Mac's slow-moving eyes that took in an imagined future which could only be comical.

"So what are yous waiting for?"

"It has to be done on the QT, Paddy. I need you."

Paddy Mac eyed the Corolla again and sighed. He began to sing between his teeth.

"*I ne-heed you so-o . . .*"

"The Commodores?"

"*I-hi wa-hant you so-hoo.* No."

"The Bachelors?"

"No. No Commodores, no Bachelors."

"Will you come over to the car for a chat?"

"What? Into that car with three, four cops? Are you mad?"

"No. I have that Opel there."

"Why on the quiet, if you have the warrant?"

"We need it tight so's no one knows we've been through."

"Do I look like James Bond? Yous'll have to do your own thing here —"

"Will you sit in the car and I'll tell you?"

Paddy Mac looked from the Corolla to the Opel.

"All right. Where's your butty, the musical know-it-all. The Dubb-al-in man."

"He's hiding in the car there."

Minogue waved at the Corolla. Malone sat up.

"Yous have a plan, I hear," Paddy Mac said.

Malone said nothing. Minogue led Paddy Mac to the passenger seat.

"We need to keep it clean," Minogue said. "It's not the time to waltz in and grab people yet."

"What people?"

"If what we're thinking is not there, then they'll never bring it if they know we're onto it."

"Who, though? Are you trying to tell me there's bent staff here?"

"I don't know who," said Minogue. "But if there's cargo going out —"

"Freight. Cargo's for boats."

"Freight. If there's something going out with a certain shipment — is *shipment* the right word?"

"I like payload: but shipment's okay for runners-in."

"Well then, it might not have been brought out here yet."

"What thing are yous talking about?"

"A rock."

"A rock? A rock band?"

"A stone," said Minogue. "It'd be like a kind of a statue."

"What, an antique, like?"

"Something like that, yes. Can I tell you what we'd need?"

"You can try, but I have to kick this upstairs. Someone has to know about it."

"No, Paddy. Sorry. No. That can't be done."

"Says who?"

"Let me explain it, then."

Paddy Mac listened, watching Malone fiddle with the keys, then the wipers, then the keys again.

"Okay," said Paddy Mac. "But maybe you weren't listening to a whole lot of things I told you earlier on. Number one, anything to do with the likes of the Works would be clean as a whistle. They wouldn't be stupid enough to smuggle anything."

"Intentionally, you mean."

"Any shagging way, that's what I mean. That's why they have managers and everything. Their stuff is under lockup here so's it doesn't get interfered with."

"It's not checked going out is it though?"

"What, that mountain of gear? No. How big a thing are yous looking for?"

"I don't know."

"Well I can tell we're going to have a grand time of it, so."

"But I do know it could arrive here as long as no one thinks we're onto them."

Paddy Mac took a step back. Minogue glanced down at the feet. Tiny, ninety degrees, like birds. The barrel chest.

"Well how do you propose to keep it all quiet here?"

"Number one is that you undertake not to say a word to anyone."

"What, including me boss?"

"Including your boss, your wife and kids, anybody. Then you get us in there, as employees maybe. A set of uniforms maybe? Overalls?"

"Four of yous?"

"Two of us, say."

Paddy Mac looked from face to face. Minogue wondered if the humor would win out.

"Let me have a gander at this warrant then."

Minogue handed it over. Malone met his eyes in the mirror.

"Never seen one before, tell you the truth," said Paddy Mac. "Except on the telly. Ha, ha. Looks real enough, but."

He folded the papers and handed them back.

"So," said Malone. "What's it going to be, Love Me Tender?"

The Dublinman's glazed and faraway stare gave way to a smirk.

"Well it won't be Heartbreak Hotel," he said. "This time, like."

CHAPTER 27

Minogue's overalls were too short in the crotch. He pulled at them, shoved his hands down hard in the pockets, but they still caught him. Malone looked a model. He leaned against the wall and watched Minogue try to stretch the overalls again. Paddy Mac arrived in from the hall.

"Jases, you look like you're choking in that."

"Have you nothing else?"

"No. Here's the list for that load of stuff."

Minogue gave up on tailoring and joined Malone looking over the printout.

"What's fei?" Malone asked.

"Freight Express Ireland. They're just the delivery agent. The number there is the day. The month comes first. It's American software."

Minogue looked down the dates. He tried to put dates to Shaughnessy. His brain wouldn't work. He searched for a Biro.

"The dates," he muttered.

"Dates for what?" Paddy Mac asked.

"Ah, I'm trying to match events to this stuff, this storage."

Minogue opened his notebook and tore out a sheet. He began with the last day of Shaughnessy's stay in Jury's Hotel. He half-listened to Paddy Mac quizzing Malone about murders.

"The American fella," said Paddy Mac. "You're not telling me anything about that end."

"Call out the dates to me, Tommy, like a good man."

Malone stopped when Minogue raised his hand. The inspector looked back in his notebook.

"What?" asked Paddy Mac.

Malone stepped over to Minogue. The inspector tapped on dates he'd put down after the PM.

"The last two there," Malone whispered. "That'd be after he was killed, right?"

Minogue looked at the boxes again.

"Is this all there is for them?" he asked Paddy Mac.

"You mean is there more? I don't know."

"What's the count there again?"

"Twenty . . . seven."

"And the latest stuff in?"

"Four days back."

Minogue stepped around Paddy Mac and pulled at the catch on one of the boxes. Bose — he'd heard of that. There were five pop-up latches. The third one wouldn't budge. Paddy Mac took out a tool from his belt and held it out to Minogue. The inspector didn't know which way to hold it. He looked at the screwdriver head, the jemmy edge next to it, the small hammer head.

"Here," said Paddy Mac. "Let me do it. You'd only break it."

Minogue helped him lift the lid. Coiled electrical wires as thick as his finger, knobs, a grille, sockets to plug in leads.

"Amplifying stuff," said Paddy Mac. "I don't know."

There was a hiss and a whirr outside the cage, a whistle. Minogue looked around Paddy Mac at the forklift operator. Paddy Mac stepped out. Minogue turned back to the boxes. He listened to Paddy Mac's drollery with the driver. A dry run for the new spot checks, Minogue heard: customs, an EU effort, no warning, such a fuckin' crowd, yeah? The forklift squealed away. Malone wedged himself in between boxes. He used his knees to lever two stacks apart. The squeak as they moved cut right through Minogue's ears.

"The most recent ones here at the front, Paddy?" Minogue asked.

"That's the general idea. Yeah. Hey, how are yous going to get into them without a lift?"

Malone looked up at the the top of the stack. Paddy Mac sighed.

"One a them'll fall on you and I'll wind up in the dock for it, or something."

"Jailhouse rock," said Malone.

"You're a scream. Here — I'm going to get a lift."

Minogue watched Paddy Mac's walk, the toes outward. The divinity that shapes our ends, he thought, and people became like their —

"Any of the lads come by," Paddy Mac called out over his shoulder, "give them the Customs and Excise spotcheck line. We're only starting them next year to fall in with the EU-regulations. Dry run, tell them."

Minogue leaned around a box to look for a label. He stooped and looked through a gap toward the boxes in the middle of the stack. Malone climbed on one and began trying to slip the cables on another. Minogue heard Paddy Mac's voice echo, the words of his call lost somewhere at the other end of the warehouse. Someone laughed. A door slid open, squeaked, and opened faster until it hit the end of its line.

"Wires," said Malone. "Big, fat leads. Speakers. Woofers. Tweeters. More wires."

Minogue squinted in at the cases. Malone closed the lid and clipped the catches. Minogue stood up when he heard the scratching as Malone shoved a box. He heard the forklift rattle and hum as it approached.

"Wait there, Tommy, will you."

Paddy Mac behind the wheel was a man possessed. Minogue stood outside with Malone watching. He wondered what Paddy Mac was saying to himself as he reversed and shot forward, swept in tight circles with inches to spare, dropped the boxes almost to the floor before braking, and then lowering the loads soundlessly to the floor. Minogue waved to him. Paddy Mac reversed over and stopped. Minogue pointed to the boxes that had been uncovered. Paddy Mac leaned his forearms on the rim of the steering wheel and watched as the two detectives edged their way through the cases toward the back of the set of boxes.

Minogue lifted the catches on a long box. Smells of rubber and dust rose around him. Lights? He lifted the edge of one and saw cables and filters. He remembered watching the goings-on at a film shoot in Kilmainham last year. The miles of cable, lights, everything up on stalks. He shoved the cable aside and examined the clamps and holders. One of them would be the bees knees entirely for holding joints to be glued on that bloody antique table Kathleen wanted.

"Here, boss. Come here."

Minogue laid the clamp down and closed the lid.

"Come up here and have a look."

Minogue worked his way around the lid. Malone had pulled out a console covered with sliding buttons. Minogue eyed it for an instant as he maneuvred around the cables. He heard Malone breathing hard in his nostrils from the exertion. He looked down. He felt no surprise. He wondered why: was he in some weird state, drifting along after the shooting, disconnected somehow? And when he woke up?

It looked so familiar. Maybe it was because he was so used to seeing pictures of things like this over the years. The outlines of the face were shadowed but he'd seen eyes like that before. It had struck him before that children drew eyes the same way as those forgotten and unknown carvers in ancient Ireland. And modern art, whatever that was, did the same. He followed the lines until they met. Whose hands had worked this so long ago, what efforts had gone into it, with their tools and their faith?

He crouched and pulled the cloth back further, tucked it down between the edge of the stone and the side of the box. He ran his hands across the lines. A collar, he guessed, a necklace maybe. Royalty? Malone was muttering something.

He glanced up at him.

"You're magic, boss," he whispered. "Fucking magic."

Minogue looked down again. There were sharp edges in places on the granite. He dropped to one knee and let his hand down the length of the stone. Something which could be excitement, or awe, or even some kind of fear began to leak into his mind.

"What in the name of Jases is that?"

He hadn't heard Paddy Mac walking over. His knee was locked now, but the ache from the graze was gone. He watched his own shadow stir on the stone as he labored to get up. Paddy Mac was scratching hard with his nails in his sideburns.

"A prop or something?" he asked. "All that stuff they haul up on stage, the oul plaster casts and the bits of cars?"

"No," said Malone. Paddy Mac turned to him.

"What's it, then?"

Minogue didn't know whether Malone had been waiting to get in the dig.

"That," Malone said. "That is the king."

•   •   •   •   •

Minogue had been dozing. The chimes and flight announcements had lulled him. Airports, waiting, dentists, hospital — they all made him drowsy.

{ 299 }

"Here they are," said Malone again. "Hey. Boss?"

He opened his eyes slowly. There were three dozen people or so by the arrivals gate, four Guards in uniform. He was locked up tight, from his shoulders down his back to his legs: stiff as a board. Malone watched him lever himself upright.

"Give Fergal the word then," he said to Malone.

He'd have to take the next bit handy, the getting to his feet. He ran his hand down to the rip in the knee of his trousers: wasn't that big, really. He had been dreaming of pigeons. It was a Magritte painting too, he was sure, the one with the birdcage in place of the man's chest, under a cloak. He should look for it in Hanna's bookshop. As well as getting some scientific answer for how pigeons, and other birds for that matter, found their way from so far off.

He stood slowly, made his way over to the railing. There were three girls arguing with a sergeant. One of them shrieked. The sergeant eyed her. She covered her mouth in embarrassment. He made a space for four photographers. Others pressed forward. A cheer started at the far end of the railing. The Guards walked to the glass doors. Minogue wondered how anybody could see anything. People began to drift over from the pub, glasses in hand. Malone pocketed the phone. Two of the girls were hopping now. The doors slid open.

First out were two APFs. Cortina Byrne came next, smoking and laughing. He threw his arm around a woman with a blond stubble on her head. She was somebody famous, Minogue realized. He couldn't place her. She wore one of those plastic, shiny jackets the ones that looked like they were made in a doll factory in 1962. The flashes began to go off.

Then Daly looked warily up and down the passageway the Guards had cleared. The shoulder bag was the size of a suitcase. Soft leather, and one of those purses —

"Jee-zuzz, *Jimmy!*"

Minogue recoiled at the scream and glared at the girl. The screamer had a white face and a lot of metal around her face.

"Come here, I want you!" she shrieked.

Two more girls came tripping over.

"Come on home to Artane, will you!" another shouted.

Daly looked over to the scream. His eyes settled on Minogue's for a moment and then returned to a darting survey of the crowd. Minogue elbowed Malone and took out his card. Daly eyed him again as Minogue moved around the sergeant. A chant started.

"*In the future . . .*"

One of the girls elbowed Minogue. He tried to get around her but she shifted and elbowed him again. She got by him to the end of the railing. The sergeant had seen her.

"*We'll have freedom.*"

She tried to wiggle by but the sergeant jammed his knee against the upright.

"*In the future, we'll have love.*"

"Mr. Daly," he called out.

Daly had heard him all right. He lifted the overnight bag on his shoulder and turned to look back at the band.

Minogue walked alongside him.

"Mr. Daly, I need to talk to you."

"What," said Daly. He looked at the Guards who had made way for Minogue to get to him. "Who are you?"

"I'm a Garda inspector. But I don't want to be waving me card here now."

Daly slowed and frowned.

"Yeah," he said. "You were here before, weren't you?"

He stopped and turned and called out to the band. Minogue looked at the outstretched arms, the pieces of paper waving. How could anybody hear anything back there?

"*In the future, we'll have freedom . . .*"

Two of the band began to grasp some of the papers and sign them. Malone edged by Minogue. He had his notebook open. He was flapping it gently on the back of his sleeve.

"I have to ask you a few things, Mr. Daly."

Daly turned back.

"What? Now? You can't be serious."

"I can wait until your outfit has gotten through here, yes."

"What? I can't hear you."

Minogue leaned in.

"I said I can wait a few minutes, but."

"Ah, come on, you're joking me," said Daly. "Look at this. This is all happening, Christ, this has to be done right. We came in the terminal, to try and undo the bad rap we got for sneaking out of the country there, you know? There's been enough fu — enough crap over the other thing. The scrap with the fans and those people from the Indonesian embassy . . ."

Minogue watched Cortina Byrne disentangle himself from one of the women leaning over the railing. She leaned back into the crowd, her hands over her face. Byrne spotted Daly and then the two detectives. His eyebrows went up.

"Just me?" Daly asked.

"For now, yes."

"Why, what about?"

"It's too noisy here. There's a quiet spot over there behind the pub. An employee lounge."

Daly turned away. He waved at a thickset man in a suede jacket by the door. The cheering was broken up now. The chanting was getting louder. Cleaners and restaurant staff were in the crowd now. Minogue watched Daly shaking his head as he spoke into the suede jacket's ear. Byrne had grabbed his girlfriend again. He was laughing and waving. He stopped by Daly and listened in. The girlfriend looked at Minogue. The inspector nodded. Wasn't she that actress one? Maybe not. Byrne was eyeing Malone now. He resumed his journey. Malone held up his notebook. Byrne hugged his girlfriend tighter. She looked like she hadn't slept. There was a tiny jewel in her nostril.

"I know you," said Byrne. Malone nodded and held out his notebook.

"This for the ma again?"

"Yeah."

Byrne let go of the girl and took Malone's Biro. The scribble and the droopy one-eyed smile up at Malone was almost a leer. Minogue looked at the girlfriend's face again. A flash went off behind Minogue.

"You're the fella with the sister's blouse thing." He threw his arms around her shoulders.

"These are Guards, love," he said to her. "Our police, yeah? This one here has a part-time job, a nixer. He's a comedian."

Minogue couldn't make out a *K* in the scribble but the *F* and the *U* were unmistakable.

•　　•　　•　　•　　•

"Is this like a slap on the wrist maybe?" Daly asked.

"No. Why?"

"You think I dissed you the last time? When we were trying to get our flight?"

Minogue glanced at Malone.

"Disrespected," said Malone. "Dissed, like?"

Minogue frowned.

"Because I made some calls," Daly added.

"God, no," said Minogue. "The head of the MCC, the fella in charge of the response, the Mobile Communications Centre, well he was annoyed. But that's history now, as they say."

"Okay," said Daly. "Well, should I be sitting here being polite or picking up a phone?"

"Your choice, Mr. Daly."

"If I knew what you seem to think is so bloody important that you can't wait until I get the lads on the road out of here."

The lads, thought Minogue. The chanting had stayed in some recess of his brain. *In the few-chur.* One of their anthems now.

"Oh, it's just that we were out here anyway," said Minogue. "We heard ye were coming in. So we thought, just a few minutes, you see."

"Go ahead then," said Daly. "Number one: what's this all about?"

Minogue let the pause last.

"We found a body here. The day you left."

Daly nodded and looked from Malone to Minogue.

"I heard later, yes."

"So we're trying to find out who did it," said Malone. "And catch them, like?"

The dry tone didn't seem to register with Daly.

"What," he said, "but why me? You want to question me?"

Minogue uncrossed his legs. So what if Daly noticed the rip in his trousers.

"Photographs have come to light, Mr. Daly. The murder victim appears in them, as do members of your band and yourself."

Daly frowned. He looked down at his cell phone. Malone wouldn't stop tapping the end of his Biro on his notebook. Minogue wanted to shout at him.

"You're nuts," said Daly. "The both of you. You're fucking nuts."

The tightness across his chest suddenly alarmed Minogue. He'd forgotten about the bloody gun again. He shifted in his seat and tried to ease the pinch of the strap under his arm.

"Go ahead and phone all you want," he said to Daly. "If you think you need to, like."

"I'll go one better," said Daly. "I'll get myself and my stuff and get to hell out of here."

"So you heard of the murder."

"I heard someone had been found, yes. I'm in touch two or three times a day with the office. They told me a bit about it. An American, I heard. Right?"

Minogue nodded.

"He appears to have had an in with your lads. The photo —"

"Wait there now. 'My lads'? This kind of dig, or innuendo, is this PI of the manual: 'provoke and annoy the shite out of someone'?"

"I'm asking you if you know this man."

Minogue slid the photocopy across the table.

"Is this the fella that was murdered?" Daly asked.

"Have you seen him before?"

"No. Or if I did, it didn't register."

"You attended an art exhibit," Minogue went on. "Óisin Hogan's, a fortnight ago. Along with Cortina Byrne and others."

"Sure I did. Óisin's one of the lads grew up around the corner from Cortina. They're pals. Yes, I went. Why?"

Minogue glanced at Malone. His colleague was now hopping his pen on his upper teeth. He seemed to be studying the top of Daly's head.

"Do you recall this person at all? Talking to you? Talking to members of the band?"

"No, I don't. Do you know how many people claim to be personal friends of the lads in the band? Long-lost cousins, friends of the family? Half-brothers?"

Minogue looked down at the phone. You could use these ones on the continent now. *Seamless service,* was that the term?

"I don't know what they told you," said Daly, "but you're barking up the wrong tree."

He raised his hands.

"I know yous have your job to do and all and fair play to you, but someone's been selling you a line. Sorry."

"I see," said Minogue. "We're being codded, is it."

"I think you have," said Daly. "And maybe it's someone just starting rumors or trouble making. Sour grapes, you know?"

"Oh, like people who'd not be pleased with your success?"

"Exactly," said Daly, with that light inflection Minogue remembered of impatient teachers. "Now you've got it. Begrudgers. The old story here."

Daly was looking from Minogue to Malone and back now. Lesson over, Minogue thought, even for the dunces who were slow to catch on. Plodders.

"Okay?" Daly asked. "I'm off, all right? Here, take this card."

He waited for Minogue to say something.

"Sorry now," Daly went on when he saw that neither detective seemed to have more to say. "I don't mean to come across too heavy on this but I've nothing for you. If you're really serious here, phone and I'll be happy to sit down with you."

Minogue smacked the tabletop lightly with his hands. Daly made to stand.

"You're headed for the States now in what, three days?"

Daly rose slowly from his crouch over the chair.

"That's right."

"The murdered man was American. You know that, of course."

Daly picked up his phone and began swapping it from hand to hand.

"Spell that one out, will you?"

"One of our lines of inquiry is that this person may have involved himself in illegal activity, here in Ireland."

"What illegal activity?"

Daly seemed to grasp an answer before Minogue had offered. He smacked his forehead with his palm and closed his eyes for a moment. He spoke slowly then, his gaze on the table at first.

"Come on, you can't be serious," he said. He looked up at Minogue. "You're not going to try a drug thing on us, are you? What is this, a shakedown?"

"Listen now, Mr. Daly," said Minogue. "That's exactly the wrong thing to say."

"Listen you," Daly shot back. "If this is a shakedown it's the lamest, stupidest effort I've ever seen."

He used his phone to point to the two detectives in turn.

"What do you know," he said. "If you had ever consulted with your pals back in Harcourt Street, you'd know just what's involved in running a phenomenon like Public Works."

"What's that got to do with Harcourt Street, or Guards?" Malone asked.

"This is an *industry*," Daly said, "a valuable export *industry*. Do you know how many blackmail attempts we get in an average month? Pregnant sixteen-year-olds? The most disgusting stories about drugs? Fellas phoning up who want ten grand so's one of the band doesn't get his legs broken? We've had it all."

"That bad, huh," murmured Malone

Daly glared at him.

"Yes, it fucking is. Excuse me. But I'm not complaining. There are gobshites everywhere. Let me tell you something: we have the best security in this country — well maybe not like the British ambassador or them but that's a different — ah, what's the point . . ."

Minogue watched Daly sling his overnight over his shoulder.

"Before you take your leave, Mr. Daly."

"What? 'It's a mistake'?"

"No," said Minogue. "Hardly that. We'd like to close off this, er, line of inquiry. The possibility that your band was being set up as transport for material being taken out of the country. Illegally?"

Daly said nothing. Minogue watched the scorn change to anger on his face. It quickly became bewilderment. Daly put the phone in his pocket and rubbed at his face. He let the overnight bag down on the back of his chair. His voice dropped to a whisper.

"Am I hearing you right, you're saying that . . . ?"

"Nothing is watertight," said Minogue. "The band takes pretty serious amounts of gear when they go on tour, am I right?"

Daly sat back. His frown deepened. Minogue rubbed at his elbow again and tried to straighten his arm.

"Jesus," said Daly. He sat down slowly, looked across at the detectives. "My God. Now I see where you're coming from."

CHAPTER 28

Mᴜʟᴇꜱ," ꜱᴀɪᴅ ᴅᴀʟʏ. "That's what you're getting at."

"How do you mean?" Minogue asked. He'd been thinking of Paddy Mac: the hair like a crop, his pigeons hurtling hell-for-leather through the air for home. Pigeons could hit sixty miles an hour.

"You know," said Daly. "Carriers? Dummies, who wouldn't even be aware of what they were doing."

"I suppose," said Minogue. "Yes. Mules."

"Drugs, then? Is that where you're leading?"

"We don't think so. Some stolen property."

"This American . . . ?"

Minogue nodded.

"Wait a minute now," said Daly. "Hang on there. I'm not going to let on I don't know who this guy was."

"Oh," said Malone. "You remember him now do you?"

"No, I don't. What I mean is that I know he's connected or was connected to a big shot. Something to do with Leynes, the food guy in the States. Right?"

"That's right," Minogue said. Daly sat back.

"I was curious," he said. "Maria — she runs the studio with Noel — she told me the next day. I was on the phone early before the first take. If this guy was well-to-do, what's he trying to move? Why would he be doing that, I mean?"

Minogue shrugged.

"There you have me now," he said. "That's why we're chasing down any small leads we have."

Daly looked down at his bag and back at Minogue. Then he shook his head and let out a sigh. Minogue eyed the capped teeth as Daly yawned.

"Look," Daly murmured. "I think I've made a bollocks of meself."

The face had turned boyish, Minogue realized. Maybe the smile was genuine.

"Ah, you're all right," said Minogue. "Pressure and all that. Maybe our timing's not the best here. I just thought, well, being as we're out here, we'd . . ."

"Ah, don't be talking about pressure."

Minogue managed a smile in return.

"Between yourself and myself now, Mr. Daly —"

"Call me Kevin, will you."

"Thanks, Kevin. Well, we have very little to go on, Kevin. The family want answers, and sure why wouldn't they. We have to chase down every lead. So there you have it now."

Daly nodded his head.

"I understand," he said. "The Guards have been taking a lot of stick this last while."

He glanced over and met Malone's stare for several moments.

"What with the gangs and that, the, er. Well, you know what I mean."

"The drug trade," Minogue murmured. "The paramilitaries? The open cases on two murdered Gardai. The flood of guns that hit Dublin last year."

Daly nodded and looked down at the floor.

"As well as the usual fucking losers," said Malone. Daly half-smiled at him. He doesn't get it, Minogue thought. It took practice to recognize Malone's anger.

"Joey — Cortina — mentioned you," Daly said. "'Funny fella.' Weren't you the one asking for your sister's blouse back?"

Malone chewed his gum several times.

"So let me ask you," Minogue said. "Are there places where your baggage, your equipment, I mean, could be interfered with?"

Daly stroked his neck, looked up at the ceiling for several moments.

"If someone could stash something in there, like," he murmured. "Maybe. Well, I mean, if someone really wanted to and it was small . . . I'd have to ask. I could find out for you, no bother."

"That'd be grand," said Minogue. "Yes. Thanks now. But tell me, wouldn't you be on the ball to such a possibility? With your security and that?"

"Oh, I think so. Yes. We have Coughlin, you know them? Worked for the Guards. Very thorough."

"Do they look after such things for you?"

Daly made a short huff and looked ruefully at the inspector.

"Well to tell you the truth, I don't actually know," he said. "So there. Doesn't sound too professional, does it? I don't know the exact detail, I mean. But Maria would."

Minogue studied the seams on Daly's overnight bag again. Daly chewed on his lip.

"Look," he said. "The business has its bad elements, sure. I mean, behind it all, these are ordinary lads who made it big — very big, yes. We all have our foibles, don't we?"

"To be sure."

"But I can't dictate to all the lads what they can or can't be doing. It's not like say, well, say the Guards. No offense now, but yous do what you're told, basically. Right?"

Minogue flicked a glance at Malone.

"Most of the time, I suppose."

"Tell you what," said Daly then. "I'll head back into town and find what's what. And then I'll phone you?"

"We'd prefer now that we be the ones going through the equipment now, Kevin."

Daly frowned.

"It might well be that the very staff supposed to be taking care of your lads' equipment might be the ones who'd be blackguarding."

"What, our staff? That's impossible — I mean, I just can't imagine that."

"Whoever handles your arrangements to get things packed and put on a plane. Your freight handlers, agents."

Daly took in a breath and held it for several moments.

"All right," he said. "All right. All I can say is I'd be absolutely shocked, I mean, totally. We've dealt with the same handlers for years."

"Would there be stuff already here at the airport that we could look through?" Minogue asked.

Daly seemed to be lost in thought. Malone had resumed chewing. An announcement on the PA came through as a resonance in the walls and door.

"What? Oh yes. I was just thinking that — well, I'm just totally gobsmacked here. I'm beginning to see that you might have, what I mean is, I'm beginning to think how you think. It'd be only logical from your point of view. This man, the photos — yes."

"There's stuff here at the airport in storage that we could take a look at?"

"No, not really. A few bits at most maybe. The real stuff is at the studio, in people's houses even, can you believe. I know we're headed out but I'm not sure at all how far ahead we are in putting it together. Let me phone Maria and I'll ask."

Minogue leaned against the wall. Malone began unwrapping a piece of gum. The smell of leather and leftover cologne was stronger now. Daly's jacket squeaked as he used his arms. Minogue studied his shoes. Maria wasn't there. "Shit," said Daly, and asked for a Noel. Minogue couldn't hear any of the other side of the conversation. He listened to Daly's rapid-fire questions, the impatience. Maybe they all talked like this on cell phones. "Are you sure?" Daly asked the Noel again. He folded his phone and tugged at his nose.

"'Don't think so,' says Noel," he said. "They're just putting stuff together and testing it at the studio before they're packing it tomorrow."

"Nothing packed and waiting that we could look at?"

Daly shrugged.

"There you have me. No. But I can find out pretty quick. How soon do you need to know?"

"Right away," said Minogue.

"Tell you what. I'll go straight to the studio, see if I can find out and I'll phone you. I'll look into it personally. How about that?"

Minogue exchanged a look with Malone.

"I'd know inside an hour maybe. Would that do you?"

. . . . . .

"'Call me Kevin,'" said Minogue. "I like that. Kevin: howiya, Kevin."

Malone snorted.

"Buy me a pint, Kevin," he muttered. "Have you any sisters, Kevin."

Malone kept his eyes on the monitor hanging from the ceiling. It was the same replay of Doherty's goal, the header against Spain last year.

"He can always say he didn't know," he said. "He knows what he's doing. The lying bastard."

"Maybe he genuinely doesn't know."

"What? There's a load of really expensive equipment out here ready to be wheeled onto a plane and he doesn't know that?"

"Could be, Tommy. He doesn't have to persuade us, you know."

Malone slid up from his slouch and stretched his neck. The queues had gone from the check-ins. Minogue thought over his determination not to come to this airport for a long time in the future if he could avoid it. The phone ringing confused him. He fumbled but Malone had it. He listened to Sheehy and then handed it to Minogue.

"Fergal, me life on you. What have you?"

"I've a pain in my side laughing at this fella you sat me with. Paddy Mac."

"Are you still there in the electrical room?"

"I am."

"Is Paddy Mac doing what he's told, but?"

"Arra God, no. He doesn't need to be told anything. Sure he's right into it. 'The man from UNCLE,' says he. James Bond — James Effin' Bond, I should say."

Minogue watched the arrivals list roll down the screen again. Something from Tenerife had landed. Sunburned, hungover faces would be drifting in soon.

"But has he covered all the items?"

"I think so," Sheehy replied. "He has the evening supervisor set with the story. The boxes and crates are stacked and ready. He even got a bit of dust on the them. A real pro."

Someone was singing in the pub. Minogue looked over. Two women were rocking from side to side, their glasses raised.

"He has it all worked out," Sheehy went on. "The minute anyone shows he'll be down there. He has a stack of crates and cases and God knows what else dumped in a cage opposite so's he can be in there beavering away and keeping an eye out."

"Any loose ends you can see, Fergal?"

Sheehy paused.

"I still think keeping an eye on the big one is a bit dodgy. The one with the stone in it. They all look the same to me, all them boxes."

"Well Paddy Mac has me persuaded, Fergal."

"Fair enough, but — ah, I'm not going to pretend I'm happy with it."

"It might be a long night, Fergal. It's gone to a twenty-four-hour facility since last year."

"Send us over a few pints and bags of crisps why don't you."

Minogue eyed the two singing again. They had lapsed into giggles. What he had thought were shorts on the one with the long hair was actually a skirt.

Minogue felt the vibrations on his hand before the ringing registered with him. His fingers slipped as he drew the phone out again.

"There's a fella here," said Sheehy. "Just arrived."

Something began in Minogue's chest. A glow, he had tried to explain it, some stirring: not really excitement yet, just a relief that something was on the go. He stood up, the aches at a distance now, and turned toward the back of a kiosk.

"Go ahead now, Fergal, I'm with you."

"Paddy Mac took it over. He's headed down to a loading door with one of those trolley things."

"Did you get a look at this fella?"

"He's a delivery man. Street clothes. Mid-thirties. Heavyset. Longish hair, fair, clean shaven. Sounds Dublin, but he's not saying much. Wearing fancy runners, a jean jacket over a sweatshirt, I think. He has a big van backed up at the door. Paddy Mac waltzed him over so's I could get a dekko at him. Trouble is, I don't know if he's coming back or what the hell's going to happen."

"We're coming over, Fergal."

"Are we sticking to the plan? Let 'em out? No transmitter?"

"Unless there's some big upset. John's waiting outside at the end of the service road with Jesus Farrell to tag them when they hit the motorway. We'll folley them out and go by them, pick them up in White-hall and let John out of their mirror awhile."

He heard Sheehy moving about the room.

"Paddy Mac might be overplaying this," he said. "I hear him halfway down the building, so I do, bollocksing away to this fella about flu and absenteeism and overwork. Christ —"

"All right, Fergal. Thanks very much."

Malone followed the inspector out to the car. Minogue glanced up at the night sky. It was brown. He sat in and grabbed the map. Malone drove by the checkpoint and pulled in behind a parked bulldozer.

"Well," he said. "Now, are you going to let the Iceman in on this?"

Minogue had no answer. He looked in the mirror again as a taxi passed.

"When's the last time you did any training in pursuits?" Malone went on.

Minogue pushed the phone charger harder into the cigarette lighter.

He clicked the light-on display. Malone shifted in his seat and tugged under his arm.

"What's he doing, for Jases' sake?"

Minogue checked his watch. Four minutes since they'd parked. He turned to Malone.

"Give John a poke, will you. Make sure."

Malone took the handset up off the floor.

"Tell me who we are again."

"Mazurka. John's Polka."

"What's a mazurka again?"

"It's what we dance to in Clare when we do be in a good humor. Now call him, Tommy, for the love of God and stop throwing questions at me."

Minogue watched a BMW brake to take the turn onto the roundabout. Skirts they called those low bits: cost a fortune, too. Murtagh must have been thinking along the same lines as Malone.

"'We're still solo on this,' he wants to know," said Malone.

Minogue gave Malone his reply in the same deadpan tone Malone had relayed Murtagh's question to him.

"For the moment, yes."

"He says for the moment yes," said Malone.

Minogue held his thumb off the button until the first ring elapsed.

"He's heading out," said Sheehy. "Just left."

"Are we sure he has it?"

"Paddy Mac went right out to the van with him, yes. He dropped off one box and took ours."

"No mistake now, Fergal?"

"For sure he took it. The one he left's a box just like it. Almost the same size, heavyish. That's a sign, I'm thinking."

"What's in it? Did Paddy chat him up at all?"

"He didn't push him at all," said Sheehy. "Just like you told him."

Malone started the engine.

"Any idea if there's other stuff in the van there?"

"Can't be sure at all," came Sheehy's reply. "He went out to the loading dock with him but your man didn't want any extras, help loading, I mean. He didn't give him the brush-off or anything but Paddy didn't want to drop a hint at all."

"Thanks, Fergal. You'll stay put and make sure there's no on else coming out of the woodwork for any of the stuff there?"

"This is him, I think," said Malone.

"We have him here, Fergal. I'm going to the radio now."

Minogue glimpsed the driver's face as the van passed. The antenna on the roof of the van glinted and shook.

"Did you get the number?"

He counted to five. He heard Malone licking his lips.

"Are we on?" came Farrell's voice now. Minogue tapped the dashboard. Malone pulled out.

"We are, Polka One. We'll go by him before you take over."

Malone slid in behind a station wagon which had come through the roundabout from the Belfast Road.

"Take bets," he said. "I say the van heads for the studio. Plenty of places to lose something there. Switch it too, very handy."

Minogue kept scratching at the rubber on the antenna.

"He's fairly shifting it now," Malone went on.

Minogue eyed the van edging into the fast lane. Sixty, already. He'd better tell Murtagh.

"Mazurka to Polka One."

"Go ahead there, Mazurka."

"Our friend is motoring. You'd better get a start there."

He nudged Malone.

"Pass him, Tommy. Fast as you like."

Malone didn't change into fifth until he was directly behind the van.

"There's Johnny Boy," he muttered. Minogue spotted Murtagh's Corolla ahead of an aged Renault 4. Jesus Farrell was slouched in the passenger seat.

Minogue looked down at the speedometer. Seventy-five.

"Oh, oh," Malone murmured. "He's on the phone."

Minogue eyed the headlights receding in the passenger mirror. The van pulled out to pass Murtagh now.

"I'm going to pull in the far side of the lights, by that church, what's the name of it. . . ."

Minogue let go the antenna.

"Stick with that for now, Tommy, yes."

"Polka One to Mazurka. I'm on. Over."

"Good enough, Polka One. You'll see us the far side of the lights."

Malone kept flicking glances at the mirror.

"He's still motoring, boss. He's damn near catching us."

"Take it handy, Tommy. Let him do what he wants."

Malone didn't touch the wipers after the first few drops hit the window. He swore instead. He finally jerked the stick as they came in sight of the traffic lights and the turnoff to Santry.

He spoke the same time as Murtagh came on the radio.

"Polka One. Is he turning? Can you see him?"

Malone geared down for the red light.

"He's five or six back," said Malone. "Can't see him."

"Stand by, Polka One."

"I think he's coming now," said Malone. "Yeah. Behind this Escort. Doesn't have his blinker on. What does that tell ya? Yep, he's going left."

"Can you take it, Polka One?"

"I can. Over."

"We're going with the original. Look for us in a minute."

Malone didn't stop swearing until he had made it across the road into the turning lane. The old Vauxhall ahead hesitated.

"We're bollocksed," he whispered. "Look. He's sussed us. He's done this before, let me tell you."

Minogue fingered the city guide to page twenty-four.

"What's in Coolock for him," he muttered. "Lives there, and he's parking it for the night? Hardly."

Malone jammed the accelerator as the light changed and came around the wrong side of the Vauxhall.

"Mazurka to Polka One. How are we doing?"

Farrell sounded harassed now.

"Steady here," he replied. "Are you with me? Over."

"Can't see you yet but a couple of minutes at most."

Malone let the Opel over the white line but the cars ahead were slowing.

"We've hit a red light here, Polka One. Keep us posted."

Malone slapped his knuckles on Minogue's arm.

"Byrne grew up around here," he said. "Home turf. But he doesn't live here now, I can tell you. He's up in some ranch the far side of Malahide."

Minogue studied the red light smear on the wet roadway ahead. Malone had to brake after he'd accelerated too quickly behind a Golf.

"He's going to dump us, boss. That's all he wants here. We're the gobshites."

"He's speeding," came Farrell's voice. "Over."

Minogue began to squeeze the base of the cell phone between his thumb and forefinger. He could phone Tynan and keep his head down when the shite hit the fan. Malone tried to pass the Fiat ahead but had to pull back in. He braked hard as the oncoming lorry's horn sounded. He glared at Minogue.

"Call him in, boss. We're going to lose him if we don't."

"Do you know Coolock and evirons well, Tommy?"

"Pretty well. Maybe. What's the plan?"

"If the fella in the van takes a runner, you're going to catch him for us."

"What, behind all this traffic? In this piece of shite? He's probably barrelling down the bloody Howth Road by now."

Minogue thumbed the radio.

"Mazurka to Polka One. Are you still on board?"

"We are," said Murtagh. "He's in sight, but he's flying. I think he's onto us."

"Go to Code One, Polka. We need the location."

"Confirm that, Mazurka. Over."

"Go to Code One. Start giving us the locations."

Minogue counted to eleven before Murtagh began. How could he be annoyed at him? Murtagh too must have been wondering about a scanner pickup, or what the hell Communications was making of the radio traffic on this band. Polkas, reels, mazurkas: the Clare dance card.

"Will I put up the lights?" asked Malone. "See if he freaks now?"

Minogue shook his head.

"Just wait for now, but," he said. He knew that Malone was eyeing him, but he didn't look over.

"And if we lose him? What's the plan then?"

Minogue wanted to tell his colleague to shut up.

"Boots up on the high road, Tommy. That'd be it."

CHAPTER 29

THE RADIO WENT HISSY. Minogue tried tuning it manually. It made it worse.

"He's going down . . ." Murtagh was saying. "Wait, I don't know the name yet . . . Over?"

Minogue heard Murtagh's car working hard in second or third gear.

"Have you gone by Barryscourt Road yet?" he asked

"I have," said Murtagh, but Minogue heard the uncertainty still. "He's turned. Coolock Avenue. Over."

"Christ on a crutch," Malone said. "It's a bleeding maze in there."

"Are you on him, Polka One? Over."

"Waiting to cross. No. More cars. Here we go."

Malone strained to see around the Fiat ahead.

"I can meet him if he's doubling back, boss," said Malone. "Kilmore Road?"

Minogue nodded.

Malone pulled hard on the wheel. The Opel's tires slid but he slackened his grip on the wheel and the car straightened.

"He's at the bottom of the Avenue," said Murtagh. "Gone right. Over."

"Gotcha, ya bollocks," Malone murmured. He punched the horn at two teenagers meandering on bikes by the curb.

Minogue brought the flashlight and the map closer. Tranquillity Grove? What kind of a mind had come up with that one?

"I turn here at Kilmore Avenue or Close or whatever it's called, and there we are."

Minogue put down the map.

"Come in, Polka One."

"Okay," said Murtagh. "He's slowing down . . . Over."

Malone took the turn off Kilmore Road.

"Pull in, Tommy."

"He's parking it. I'm going to carry on by him. Over."

"Go around the block, Polka One. Kilmore Close. And wait at the top of the road. Over."

"Are you caught up? Over."

"Look to your left as you go around," said Minogue. "Is he moving at all?"

"He's out. I'm going by him now. . . . I can't get a house number . . . Over."

Malone shook his head.

"He's gone home?" he muttered.

". . . gone around the back of the van. I'm gone by him now. Coming around the corner . . . No, he's out of the mirror. Over."

Malone flashed the lights as Murtagh and Farrell passed.

"I'm going for a walk, Polka One. Come around and wait at the far end. Over."

"Read you. Over."

"You're what?" Malone said.

Minogue already had his belt off. He buttoned the top of his coat and pulled the door handle.

"A quick walk by and we'll see what the score is. Fair enough, Tommy?"

"The rain, boss? You've no hat, have you?"

Minogue dropped the walkie-talkie in Malone's lap.

"All right, so," he said. He opened the coat again. "I'm going to be gargled."

Humming, loose limbed, Minogue stopped and swayed. The rain had turned to a drizzle. He fumbled in his pockets and groaned.

"Me fags," he said. "Me fags is gone. Aw, *jases*."

He hawked and spat and continued down the footpath. The van stood by a battered Dihatsu. He slowed to watch the glow and flare of an enormous television in the window of a darkened living room. There was some muscle-bound gobshite leaning out of an American sports car firing off a machine gun. The sounds came to him from the windows as grinding vibrations. He glanced at the van and then back to the carnage in the window.

A drip started down his forehead. He made a clumsy effort to wipe it off the bridge of his nose. He heard the scrape of a hall door opening, words.

He dragged his left foot a little as he moved on and let his elbow dig into the hedge. Raindrops sprayed up at him from the leaves as his elbow dragged on.

He started humming first and soon let words take over.

"There was a wild colonial boy,"

The van was new. The United pennant hanging from the mirror had gold lettering on it. He still couldn't make out the conversation from the doorway.

"Jack Duggan was his name. . . ."

The antenna on the roof was nothing special. Any delivery van would have one. A drainpipe gurgled somewhere ahead. One of the two men in the doorway turned.

"He was born and raised in I-er-land . . . "

He leaned against the gatepost and coughed.

"Hi lads, am I right for Bolands, am I?"

The driver he recognized from Murtagh's description. The other one had white hair and a Fu Manchu mustache. The denim waistcoat with the silvery bits put Minogue in mind of some country-and-western type.

"Am I right . . . ?" he called out again.

"What?" from Fu Manchu.

"Am I right for Bolands, lads?"

"Bolands?"

"Bolands Pub. The taxi man said go down here."

One of the men chortled.

"Ah, you're on the wrong planet there, man," said Fu Manchu. "There's no Bolands here."

Minogue allowed himself a gentle sway.

"But didn't I get a taxi here?"

"You were codded then, weren't you. No Bolands, pal. No pub."

"But your man in the taxi . . ."

"Where did you come from?" Fu Manchu asked.

"I'm up from Lisdoon, so I am. I came up tonight on the Limerick train."

"Lisdoonvarna? And where are you headed?"

"A nephew of mine says to come out to Fairview to meet a fella about a job. A watchman."

"Fairview?"

"That's it. Bolands Pub in Fairview."

The driver cleared his throat and pulled out a packet of cigarettes.

"There's a Fairview and there's a Bolands there too, pal," said Fu Manchu. "But you're going at it arseways, in a big way. Where did you get your taxi from?"

"Down the quays. I stopped off for a pint and . . ."

"Well I hope you like walking. Fairview's that way. Where's your bag?"

"What bag?"

Minogue took a step back and looked around the footpath. He backed into the gatepost again.

"Me bag," he shouted. "Where's me bag? I had it in the seat beside me there, I put it . . . ah, for the love of God . . ."

Fu Manchu blew out a volley of smoke.

"Jases," he said. "You weren't just codded there, pal, you were robbed. You'd be better off going home to Lisdoon."

"But what am I . . ." Minogue went on. "Where's me fags? I've no fags either."

The driver stepped out to the gate. He held out three cigarettes. Minogue let his eyes out of focus and grabbed at them. He looked down to where they fell and smiled.

"Holy Jases," said the driver. "I'm fuckin' throwing money away on a culchie."

"Ah, you're the decent man —"

"Look it," he said. "Go up that way there and go left. Find a bus stop this side of the road and go back and get your shagging train home to wherever."

The hand on Minogue's shoulder let go.

"Where . . ."

"Go on with you," the driver called out. "Before somebody catches you here and throws you into a fuckin' saucepan and eats you."

There were bars across the back of the bench seat of the van but the streetlamp showed the bottoms of the boxes. Two for sure.

He paused by the van and turned.

"Have you got a light, lads?"

"Get out to hell with you," the driver called out. "You'd oney set fire to yourself. Go on with you!"

·   ·   ·   ·   ·

"What do you mean you've no comb?"

Malone yawned. "I-have-no-comb," he said. He eyed his colleague. "No fucking comb. Are you with me now?"

Minogue shifted in the seat. He tugged at his collar again. The rain had gone all the way down his back. Malone had inched the Opel to the head of the street. Lights glistened on the wet hedge, the puddles, the dips in the cement roadway.

"What the hell are they doing?"

Minogue wondered if he'd overdone it. He looked down at Malone's notebook again. Fu Manchu was Kevin Halloran, an uncle of one of the band members. He'd been in the music scene himself thirty years ago. Listed as musician. A drunk and disorderly assault within the past five years. Receiving stolen goods seven years ago.

"Have you heard of this Tony Hackett?" Minogue asked. "The driver?"

"No. Has he any form? Wait, here they come."

The handcart came out the gate, hopping once as Hackett pushed it onto the footpath. Halloran entered the van by the sliding door. Hackett flicked his cigarette into the street and stepped into the van after him.

"Say when," Malone murmured. Minogue held up his hands.

The van shook and wavered as they moved about inside. Halloran stepped down on the path. Hackett joined him and began lifting down a box.

"That's it," said Malone. "So how do you want it?"

Minogue ran his fingers along the buttons on the walkie-talkie.

"Leave it," he said. "Wait. I want to see what happens with the van."

He could admire the dexterity with which Tony Hackett nudged the box onto the handcart, levered it up, and smartly turned back up in the driveway. He called Murtagh.

"Mazurka to Polka One."

"Go ahead. Over."

"Stand by," said Minogue. "We're waiting to see if our fella leaves."

Malone gave him a nudge. The driver, collar up now, strode out the gateway and stepped around to the driver's side.

"You think he's going to phone Halloran in a few minutes," said Malone. "To check?"

Minogue watched the vapor from the exhaust.

"Polka One," Minogue said. "He's off. We're going after him. Over."

It was Farrell answering.

"What about the house?" he asked.

"Stay put here. You might be going in. If there are any comings and goings, ye'll go in for sure, no questions asked. Over."

"Fair enough," said Farrell in a voice Minogue knew only too well. "Out."

Malone started the Opel. He waited until the van had turned the corner before he let out the clutch.

"Oi, boss."

Minogue didn't look over.

"I'd feel a lot smarter if we had company, boss, I have to tell you. If this Hackett's up to what you think he is, he might be ready to really lose us."

Minogue pulled his seat belt tighter. He checked his flashlight on the map again. Malone slowed and let the Opel freewheel.

"What's he doing?" Malone asked.

Minogue switched off the flashlight. The van turned on to Oscar Traynor Road. Malone pulled out after a taxi.

"Unless he's going out to the Malahide Road," he muttered. "And then taking that way back down to the studio. Why would he be going that way?"

Hackett's home address was Terenure, Minogue remembered.

"Any sign of him there, boss?"

The traffic slowed at the lights for the Malahide Road.

"There he is ahead. He's gone straight."

Malone glanced over at Minogue.

"He's headed out to Kilbarrack? Raheny?"

Minogue ran the flashlight over the street map.

"He's not hanging around either," said Malone. "Are we going to bust your man's gaff now, Halloran's? See what's in the box?"

Minogue took the radio up from his lap.

"Mazurka to Polka One. Over."

"Go ahead, Mazurka," said Farrell.

"Move in now. No calls, sit tight. Over."

"Are we expecting anything?"

"Our friend might be phoning or your fella might try to phone out," replied Minogue. "*Bí ullamh.* Over."

"Read you, Mazurka. Over."

Malone sprayed the windscreen. He left the wipers on full for several seconds. Minogue caught a glimpse of the van three cars ahead.

"*Bí ullamh,*" said Malone. "Last time I heard that one was the Killer, up with that lunatic in the South Circular, who was he. Mac something. The suicide. After he shot the wife's new fella."

It was drizzling like this then too, Minogue remembered. Kilmartin had gotten a call for a talker. There'd been a shooting and the gunman was still in the flat. He wanted some "serious cop," someone who knew their stuff, someone from the Murder Squad, not some fukken chancers trying to play shrink. Kilmartin had muttered the Irish boy scout motto as he and Minogue and Malone had pushed their backs harder into the wall to let the armed response team scurry by.

"I just got that feeling, boss," said Malone.

"What?"

"'Member I told you about the boxing? When you got hurt with a punch and you know you're hurt?"

Minogue looked over. Malone's somber tone was rare.

"And you know that he knows it," Malone went on. "And he's really going to let you have it now. The both of you know that neither of yous can stop it. You're hurt but you're wide awake. You know everything's out of hand but it's going to play itself out, and finish."

Malone flicked the wipers back to normal. He let out a sigh.

"Ah, I don't know," he added. "Maybe I'm only beginning to freak out after the mess this morning. The delay, like . . . ?"

Minogue waited. Malone shifted in the seat.

"It's just I can't stop thinking, well, we're headed in the wrong direction here," he said. "Ah Christ — forget it. Look, there's the DART."

Minogue caught a glimpse of the passengers in the train before the Opel bobbed as it came over the bridge. The van picked up speed.

"What's he doing . . ." Malone whispered.

"Polka One to Mazurka."

"Go ahead Polka."

"We're on board here," said Farrell. "No problems. Over."

"Have you had a look through?" Minogue asked.

"I'm in the garage now. Yours truly's got your man in the kitchen, him and his missus."

"No trouble getting in?"

"Not a bother. Made no run for a phone or the like."

"Do you think he expected us?" Minogue asked.

"Can't say. He didn't freak when I gave him the grounds, the receiving goods one. 'Go ahead,' says he. 'I've nothing to hide.'"

"What's the story then?"

"There's a big speaker and wires," Farrell replied. "That's it."

"Nothing?"

"Nothing. 'I been doing repairs for years,' says he. 'They send me stuff to fix. It's the nephew; I got him started a few years ago. Never forgot where he came from.'"

Malone smacked the steering wheel.

"What's he say about the driver?"

"Doesn't know him from Adam."

"That's all?"

"That's all. Over."

"You were right," said Malone. Minogue's thumb danced over the button.

"Will we stay put, Mazurka? Over."

"Stand by."

"Maybe he was given two drops," said Malone. "He could be blind himself, you know, a dummy? Is this the Howth Road already . . . ?"

The van wasn't indicating a turn back into the city center. Minogue watched the brake lights of the car ahead.

"Mazurka to Polka One. Over."

"Go ahead."

"Stay put," said Minogue. "Bring them in, the two of them, if he starts with you. Over."

"Good enough. If — hold on, I think I hear the phone."

Minogue squeezed the button hard.

"Listen," he said to Farrell. "Let him answer. I want every word. Over."

"I'm going in the kitchen door now. Read you."

"He's headed the other way," said Malone.

Minogue watched the streetlamps on the Howth Road slide along the panel of the van as it turned.

"I think he's on the phone," said Malone. "Look, will you. He is, isn't he?"

Minogue couldn't decide. The hand was up by his head. Headlights from a city-bound car came closer.

"He is, boss. I'm telling you. They're in on it."

Only a much-abused Mini Metro sagging at one side separated them from the van now. The van began to pull away. Minogue heard the breathing grow louder. It was his own.

"He's slowing," said Malone. "Look."

Minogue looked across at the speedometer.

"He's finished talking," said Malone.

"Polka One to Mazurka. Over."

"Go ahead, Polka One."

"Very short and sweet," said Farrell. "Nothing clear to us. Over."

"Did you pick up on it?"

"Only this end. And I think it was a code or the like."

"What did he say exactly though?"

"'Yeah,'" said Farrell. "And 'Not so bad.' Then, 'Buy me a pint.' Laughed a bit. Then he hung up after a 'yeah' or two."

"Nothing clear?"

Minogue's throat was tight now.

"Go after him," he snapped. "Take the missus in too. Aiding and abetting will do for a start."

The drizzle had eased. He stared through the drizzle on the window at the lights of the van.

"Look," said Malone. "He's on the phone again. I'd swear it. Look at the head going up and down. Let's take him now, boss."

Minogue's eyes were stuck on the lights.

"We take him, boss. Right?"

"Give me a minute."

"Look, he's talking. See him? He's got the phone on the seat 'cause he knows we're on to him."

Minogue flipped to Tynan's number and began to dial. One ring.

"Ah, *shite*," Malone cried and stood on the brakes. The belt snapped taut against Minogue's collarbone. Not again, was his first thought. He heard O'Leary's voice from the phone again.

The glow from the brake lights on the Mini flared across the windscreen. Minogue got his hands on the dashboard as the Opel slid. The Mini hopped as they hit. A shower of plastic from taillights flew up on the bonnet.

Malone was trying to reverse. The van was turning. Malone stabbed at his belt release, shoved open the door. The van's back tires spun on the wet road as it went by. Malone rolled back in and grabbed the gear stick again. The driver of the Mini was a bewildered middle-aged man with a woollen hat hanging off the back of his head. He placed his two feet on the road, paused, and elbowed himself upright. Minogue's fingers went to his pocket. Two cars had stopped behind.

"Out of the way!" Malone called out. "Gardai! Stay where you are, mister, we'll get a car out to you and sort it out. We're chasing someone. Out of me way!"

A lorry driver leaned on the horn as Malone began his turn. It slowed to walking speed as it drew alongside the front of the Opel.

"Ya bleedin' maniacs," Minogue heard. Malone leaned on the horn and began shouting. Minogue lifted the phone again. Dead: he'd hit the wrong button somehow.

The car swayed as Malone launched himself out, shouting. Minogue stared down at the pieces of colored plastic glittering on the bonnet, and he swore.

CHAPTER 30

MINOGUE REDIALED. He still couldn't get his thoughts to line up.

"Sorry, Tony, it's Matt Minogue again."

"Are you okay there?" O'Leary asked.

The lorry had stopped. Malone had grabbed the walkie-talkie and launched himself onto the roadway. He watched Malone waving the walkie-talkie and telling the driver to get the fuck out of the way or else. This driver, Hackett, knew what he was doing. If they couldn't catch him, Daly could walk away laughing behind a half-decent barrister. That was even if they could get the DPP to come up with anything that'd stick. Botched and bollocksed, a squad investigation that blew up because Minogue had kept it an inside job. Gemma O'Loughlin could paste this on readers' eyeballs to sell more papers too.

"I am, Tony, sorry."

"What's going on there? Are yous in a scrap or something?"

"In a manner of. I'm out on the Howth Road. We were in a pursuit but it's gone jammy. We're after walloping a car a bit here. We need a bit of help but no questions until the dust settles."

Over Malone's shouts of take your fucking complaints and stick them up your hole and the noisy revving of the lorry's diesel, Minogue heard a paper being turned at O'Leary's end.

"A pursuit?"

"Don't ask yet, Tony. We need a few cars out here. The van we were after made a run for it. He's carrying something from the airport. To do with the Shaughnessy murder."

"What, the American thing, Leyne again?"

"We were tracking this van, two of ours, but he made a drop-off. The other team stayed to cover that."

"What kind of a setup is this fella, a van you said?"

Malone sat back in behind the wheel and accelerated around the Mini before taking a U-turn. Minogue stared at the roadway ahead. All he could see were the lights of the center city and docks, the oncoming headlights.

"He seems to be wised up with the electronic gear," he said to O'Leary.

"Armed?"

"Doubtful," said Minogue. "But can't say for sure. I want you to call out for North Central cars."

"From the boss, like?"

Minogue listened to the ticks he heard from the engine as Malone took it to sixty in third. He couldn't tell if the headlights were still intact.

"I don't have time to explain, Tony. That's why it's you I'm calling. We need this van. Here's the registration."

Malone braked behind a newish Volvo, swearing. A horn from an oncoming car trailed off behind as it passed. O'Leary asked for the number again.

"The Howth Road, where?"

"Coming up to the lights where it goes up to Raheny."

"Decision time," said Malone.

"Give me a minute there, Tony. Sorry."

He strained over the dashboard to look up the Howth Road. Nothing. The Raheny Garda station was a mile up there. Was he trying to double back to the airport, to throw them off? He grabbed the map again and squinted at it.

"He wouldn't have many outs that I can see if he headed up to Raheny, Tommy."

"What," said Malone, "go along by the sea there? What do you think?"

Four cars waited on the red light to turn up to Raheny.

"Go the Clontarf Road," Minogue said. "Whatever it's called."

Malone pulled to the left. There were taillights in the distance. Minogue took his hand off the mouthpiece.

"Tony. We're heading down the Clontarf Road. Into town, like."

"Have you radio?"

"I was using a branch frequency. I'll switch over. I was using Mazurka. Will you feed us to Dispatch then?"

The slaps from the joints in the roadway came like a slow drumbeat up from the wheels.

"I'll get back to you," said O'Leary.

The thumping grew faster. Eighty miles an hour, Minogue saw.

"We've only the one headlight," said Malone. "Which traffic lights are these ahead? The park there, St. Anne's?"

Minogue turned the map.

"No," he said. "That's the road onto Bull Island. A golf club out there, isn't there?"

"Yeah. But it's a dead end though."

"But there's another bridge at the far end though," said Minogue. "Isn't there? Dollymount?"

"Yeah, but for cars, I mean," said Malone. "They blocked off the strand with them rocks to stop people racing down there. Years ago. How you go in is how you go out, see."

Minogue tried to shield his eyes from the glare of the streetlamps as Malone eased his foot off the accelerator. The lights of the south city, and the more scattered and dim points from the hills, were soon cut off by the dunes that rose from Bull Island.

Minogue looked at the streetlamps over the causeway and the darkness beyond.

"If he knows his stuff he's not going down there," said Malone.

Minogue saw the pedestrian light flashing ahead. This light must have been green for a good long while. The van would have been flying through, making for streets he knew. A straight road ahead, with plenty of streets to turn into now. "Go then," he said. Malone floored the pedal as the light changed.

"This shitbox, I'm telling you . . ." Malone said.

"Control to Mazurka. Over?"

"Oh-oh," said Malone and jammed it into fourth again. "That was fast. We're on the air now."

Minogue wondered if Tynan himself had made the call. He glanced over at Malone. His colleague shook his head once and swore.

"Mazurka here," Minogue said. "Go ahead, Control. Over."

"You have three units dispatched for your assistance, Mazurka. Over."

He eyed the map again.

"All right. Get them to call in and give location, if you please. Over."

Malone dithered as Minogue asked for one patrol car to come out the

Howth Road from Fairview. Alpha Bravo Two had what sounded like a Corkman handling the radio. They were coming out of Raheny. Minogue repeated the registration number of the van.

He waited for the third car to confirm it was turned around on the Howth Road by Killester. The bus ahead pulled out from the stop. Two, three sets of headlights were closing the distance from the city end.

"Ah, not this!" Malone shouted. "I can't . . . *Now* we're bollocksed for sure . . ."

"Pull in there," said Minogue. "Ask that oul lad with the dog if he saw it."

The Opel slid before it came to a stop, and the front wheel bounced off the curb. Malone rolled down his window as two cars passed. Minogue leaned down to see the man better. The poodle had a tartan jacket.

"Did a white van come flying by here," Malone asked. "Going like hell?"

The streetlamps caught the man's glasses. Seventies, Minogue guessed. He put his hand to his ear. Another car passed between them. The fine spray landed on Minogue's face too.

"A van," Malone shouted. "A white van going like bejases?"

The man shook his head.

"Are you sure?"

A few nods of the head. The shrugs didn't help.

"The fucking bastard," said Malone. "He did it. He fucking *did* it."

He looked down at the map, and followed the lines with his finger.

"He could go around the corner there and head back out. Ah *Jases!*"

Minogue turned. A steady row of headlights filled the rear window now. A car pulled out from behind them. The driver looked across with a raised eyebrow as it passed. Minogue decided he could at least have one of the squad cars roll down Vernon Avenue.

"Mazurka to Control," said Minogue. "Over."

He wondered if Tynan was listening in to the radio traffic. The driver would hear it anyway.

"Go ahead, Mazurka. Over."

"Put the van out to all units, if you please."

"North and south, Mazurka?"

"The both, yes. He's done a bunk on us for the moment. Over."

Malone drove the Opel up onto the footpath. The tilt made Minogue lean on his door. The two policemen listened to the radio traffic, the desultory reports from the squad cars trolling the area. A car going along Dorset Street called in inquiring the number of the van again.

Malone said nothing. He began a slow tattoo with the knuckle of his fore-finger against the window, shifting several times and tugging at his jacket.

Minogue switched off the light and rolled down the window. The smell of seaweed was stronger. He heard lapping against the seawall.

"We're fucked, aren't we," said Malone. Minogue rolled up the window again. He held the map up, turned it to face the streetlamp.

"Well?"

He held his thumb and forefinger on the scale and then tried to measure.

"We're waiting, Tommy, that's what we're doing. Waiting."

He'd been out here maybe twice in the past twenty years. That uncle of Kathleen's: Tony. Heart attack at fifty-eight; nearly twenty stone when he dropped dead on the floor. Got up to switch stations when his team were getting hammered in the FA Cup one year.

"Let's bring Daly in then," said Malone, "and take bits off him."

"Soon enough," Minogue said.

"How soon?"

"We're full of holes still, until this van turns up."

"Come *on* now, boss. Put this Halloran in the blender, at least."

Minogue held the map up to the window.

"You and Jimmy," he murmured. "Twins, you are, but born a genera-tion apart. A miracle entirely."

"Well what's your suggestion then?"

Minogue put down the map again. He radioed the Raheny car.

"'The causeway," came the Cork accent from Alpha Bravo Two. "Next to St. Anne's? Over."

"That's it. Station yourselves there and keep us up on it. Over."

"Are we conducting here, Mazurka, or just roosting? Over."

"Sit tight for now. You'll have company there if we can't turn up the van. He might abandon it down there on the island or that. Anything coming or going down that bit of road, you open it."

Malone ran the wipers. The grit scratched even with the fluid going constantly.

"Go down there to Dollymount, Tommy. The other bridge there."

"And park it?"

"For now, yes."

Malone drove off the footpath without slowing. He slowed a little as they passed the Dollymount Inn to eye the car park. No van there. He turned onto the bridge and stopped at the red light. The streetlamps from the Clontarf Road behind shivered on the waters of the channel below. Minogue rolled down the window to get a better look at four cars parked by the cottages attached to the old coast guard station. To Malone's side the lights of the city docks and Liffey Basin shone yellow and white over the blackness by the side of the road.

The light changed. Malone took it slowly. Minogue didn't remember the bridge being this long.

"Park it awhile, Tommy."

Minogue radioed their location to the squad cars. The car from Fairview had reached Clontarf. No van. Minogue told them to go around Castle Avenue and come back by Vernon Avenue.

The breezes came in short gusts around the car now. The road ahead was empty.

"You might get fellas coming and going to the clubhouse," said Malone. "Gargle and that. Couples coming down for a wear maybe. In their cars, like."

Minogue shoved his hands in his coat pockets. The strap around his shoulder began to bite again. Prickly heat under the leather. He shuffled in his seat, tried to move the lump under his arm better. The strap pulled at the hairs in his armpit.

"Enough of this," he said. "Damn it to hell. I'm crucified with this thing."

He slid the pistol out and laid it on the floor.

"Ah, Jases, come on, will you? Don't leave it there, boss. You'll forget it and it'll be robbed. Or you'll kick it and shoot someone's shagging foot off. Like mine."

Minogue held back the retort. They listened to a two way about a hit and run in Drumcondra.

"How long more?"

"How long more what?"

"Until we get out of here and start trying to pick up the bits? Until you make the call on Daly? Until we start pushing?"

Minogue was not surprised to feel almost indifferent. Sitting here listening to the wind rising, the dull lisp of the tide: not such a bad prospect at all. "Look," said Malone. "Is this guy going to drive onto Bull Island and sit there until the morning? You can't swim off it, and you can't walk off it or drive off it without coming this bridge or the other one. It's a no-go here, boss. Come on, park one of those patrol cars here and let's get back to civilization there."

"Who was he phoning," Minogue murmured. "That's the thing."

"Who? The driver? Ah, he's wised up. I can see him sitting somewhere, laughing his head off now, with his phones and his scanners and everything. Let's go, come on."

Minogue dropped the map in Malone's lap.

"Show me where these barriers are, will you," he said to Malone. "Here, on the map. Those big boulders you told me about, the ones the Corpo rolled out across the beach to stop the racing up and down?"

He called the car down from Castle Avenue. Malone placed his finger on a red line that divided the island.

"I don't know," he said. "There, maybe?"

"Let's have a look then. Come on."

Malone looked back down at the map.

"What, you want to walk out there, halfway into Dublin Bay, in the dark?"

"Can't we drive?"

· · · · · ·

Minogue nodded at the Guard behind the wheel.

"Good enough, so," he said. Malone turned the Opel back toward the dunes. Minogue looked back to see the squad car being reversed across the road by the lights.

"Do you know where you're going?"

"No," said Malone. "But I'll find a way out onto the bloody thing somehow. What if it's six-feet deep in water?"

"Does the tide come in like that?" Minogue asked.

"I don't know, but we're going to find out, aren't we."

The headlight slid over ash colored sand.

"That's the clubhouse there on the left," said Malone, "the Royal Dublin. If we go this way . . . Yeah, look: that's a sort of a car park."

The city lights slid into view as the Opel came around the dunes and onto the open strand.

"Turn off the lights a minute, Tommy. I can't see with them."

"What's this — you're coming out of the closet here, are you?"

Minogue rolled down the window further.

"I can hear the water, but I can't see it."

"Famous last words," said Malone. "Come on."

"Drive over there so we can see where the tide's in."

The waves broke gently in white, curling strips at the outer limits of the car's high beams. Malone slowed as they approached the water's edge.

"That's them up ahead, isn't it? The boulders."

Minogue couldn't make out anything. He followed the tire marks crisscrossing the sand ahead.

"There. Now do you see them?"

Like dumplings or something, he thought, or the rocks on the Burren. The beam of light wavered as the car bobbed in soft spots in the sand. The rocks seemed to move as they drew closer.

"Lawrence of shagging Arabia, here," said Malone. "But in the middle of Dublin Bay, like."

Minogue radioed in his position. Control asked him to confirm it.

"Boulders," said Minogue. "Out here halfway down Dollymount Strand. Bull Island."

Malone turned slowly. The headlight flickered on the sand in the spaces between the rocks. He stopped.

"Well?"

Minogue uncoupled his belt and pulled the door release.

"Keep your hands to yourself," Malone said. "Or I'll tell Kathleen on you."

"I'll be back in a minute."

"What? A leak?"

"A walkabout for a minute, you savage," Minogue said over his shoulder. He slammed the door behind him and listened to the sea.

He looked into the tunnel of light made by the beam ahead. The lights stopped at the foot of what he guessed to be dunes leading up to the golf club. The sand gave way slightly under his feet. Malone's voice carried over the dull thunder of the waves rushing up on the sand.

"Ah, come on," Minogue heard. He shielded his eyes and looked back. He could make out Malone leaning on the roof in the open door of the Opel. The grille was in bits, he could see now, the bumper sideways and marked.

"We'll head back and let them wait until daylight," Malone went on. "Then it won't be us walking up and down like gobshites here."

He turned back and followed the line of boulders into the water. No moon. He could make out spreading movements of the waves as they slid up and then retreated on the sand. He trod hard with his heel in the sand. It barely wiggled now. The breeze was yanking at his hair. He pulled his collar tighter, looked around the bay to the south. The boulders must run down right into the water, to stop traffic even at low tide.

He rubbed his eyes again. Sheer bloody vanity: he should get his eyes tested more often. The furthest rock he could see had a more regular shape. Cement, maybe, a final wall built to finish the job. He took a few steps, trailing his hand on one of the boulders. The dull vibrations coming from the car must be the radio. He glanced back. Malone was standing in the beam of light now. Minogue could make out the walkie-talkie in his hand. The lone headlight wasn't helping him at all: better off to let the night vision settle in for this.

He rubbed at his eyes again and waited for his vision to return. The dark shapes became sharper. The water was slapping the base of a boulder not fifty feet ahead. That one in the water had stright edges all right. He walked beyond the next boulder, let his eyes play to both sides. He shielded his eyes to both sides with his hands. The water lapped not twenty feet from him now. It slapped against the rocks and slid up the sand with a hush. He closed his eyes for several seconds and waited. It was no better when he opened them again.

He turned back to the car. Malone had switched off the headlight. Maybe he had gotten the idea. Now he'd the car around and pointing the one light out over the water, see what that thing looked like out there. The engine was off too. Out for a leak maybe. He saw that the boot lid was open. Something about that caused Minogue stop. He let go his collar. The gusts played about his scalp. He shivered.

"Matt?"

He turned to the voice. A figure detached itself from the darker shape of a boulder.

"Matt. Stay put now, or there'll be trouble."

The shock tightened his scalp. He struggled to remember something that was familiar in the voice, but it stayed just out of reach.

"Where's Tommy?" he managed.

"Tommy's looked after. Don't be worrying."

The odd quiet he remembered was gone from the voice, but the soft ah-huh, the clearing of the throat that had become a mannerism.

"Damian . . ."

"I'll drop you right here, Matt, if you don't shut up. I mean it. Hit the dirt there and I'll give you your chance."

Little stepped forward. He held the gun at arm's length.

"What are you doing?" he tried again.

"This is Tommy's hardware, Matt. Don't make me."

Minogue stared into the shadows. He couldn't see Little's face yet.

"I'll leave you here if I have to, Matt. Hit the dirt there. You know the routine."

Minogue felt the breeze work its way under his coat. He didn't try to stop the lapel of his coat flapping. Little cocked the pistol.

"He's in the fucking boot, okay?" he said. "He's going to wake up with a lump on his bloody head. Now move."

The sand under his knee gave way slowly. The rain and seawater soaked up his trousers. He hesitated, tried again to speak through the tightness in his throat.

"Damian," he managed. Little was standing over him, his hand working down his back. He stopped at his shoulder.

"You're carrying, Matt? Well, my Jesus. What's the world coming to. Where is it?"

"I took it out. Tommy —"

The cold metal pressed against his head made him stop. He held his breath. The hand ran under his arm, pushing at his armpit, tugging at his coat. The pressure of the muzzle began to ease.

"Where'd you put it then?"

Minogue started to talk but couldn't.

"You're a fucking iijit, Matt. Where'd you put it?"

"Locked it up. I didn't want to —"

"Put your hands on the back of your head — that's it, close your fingers. Now, roll over. Nice and slow."

Minogue used his elbows to maneuvre. Little kept circling him, doubling back, stopping, walking again.

"We have to do some business, Matt. The timing's not the best, I know. But you have some deciding to do. And you're going to do the deciding for himself there in the boot too."

The breeze made Minogue's eyes water. He'd been trying to keep Little in sight as he walked.

"You're too much, Matt. Things'd still be shaping up grand if Kilmartin wasn't away on his bloody jaunt. What made you decide to come down here?"

"We'd lost the van."

"You've got squad cars at both ends, haven't you?"

Minogue said nothing.

"Tell them to walk, Matt, the one at Dollymount only. The walkie-talkie's on the front seat. You and me and Tommy are heading back to civilization."

Minogue took a breath. He spread his hands. The sand was like wet cement. "I want to see Tommy first."

The flash and thump of the bullet as it tore into the sand beside him made his arms buckle. The ripples in the sand were like bones pushing up at his own. He covered his head with his arms. He felt Little's weight move the sand near him. The voice wasn't much more than a whisper.

"You're not doing so hot here," Little said. "Don't be leaning on me. By rights you and your pal should be out there floating by the van. Up."

Minogue stumbled once near the Opel.

"Wait a minute," Little called out. Minogue watched the boot lid fall, heard it catch. Little shoved the lid again to be sure.

"Take the walkie-talkie out the window," said Little. "Tell them."

CHAPTER 31

THE LIGHT DIDN'T GO ON WHEN Minogue opened the door. He hesitated.

"On the driver's seat," Little said. "Take it out with you. Go on."

"Mazurka to Alpha Bravo One. Over."

"Go ahead, Mazurka. Over."

Alpha Bravo One didn't sound impressed. The slagging would filter back soon enough: now they'd screwed up, the glamour brigade in the Murder Squad couldn't make up their minds what way to look.

"Okay," said Little. "Put it back. You're driving. Go on in."

Little had the passenger door open already. The smell of the upholstery came to Minogue over the smell of the strand and sea. His pistol was an arm's length away. He imagined its weight in his hand.

The Opel felt sluggish, too much travel in the clutch. The steering wheel wobbled as he crossed a patch of wetter sand. He turned away from the dunes.

"Do you know your way?"

"I'm not sure."

"Keep to the right of that light there ahead of you. That's the way through the dunes."

Minogue geared up to third for traction.

"What about your fella back there," he said. "The van?"

"He's not my fella," said Little. "And it was his lookout. He would've jumped ship sooner or later anyway."

Minogue tried to set the wheels back into the tracks ahead.

"Don't come the high and mighty here," Little said. "They're all bent, they're all gougers. You know that. I just hope you see a bit of sense. For Tommy too."

"As long as I know he's —"

"Don't start," Little snapped. "You don't even know how close you came. It was me kept you and that bullet-headed gobshite in the back in one piece, so don't start on me. Kathleen's the widow who's going to be in bits at the funeral, with the Killer and Tynan and all the fucking hoi polloi standing there — all because you couldn't see straight! Christ, Kilmartin and his big mouth."

"What does Jimmy know?"

"He doesn't know a damned thing! Jimmy's a gobshite. Blathering on there and making an iijit of himself there in the bloody papers. But you — I told them you could be trouble."

Minogue grasped the wheel tighter. Lights appeared in a gap in the dunes.

"I couldn't have stopped that mess this afternoon," Little went on. "Even if I'd wanted to I couldn't. I didn't know about it until later."

The line of sand looked like a sizeable bump. He let the wheel slide under his fingers. The car thudded as they hit. There was a squeak from the springs, a shuffling in the boot. He wondered if that had been enough to slide the gun back.

"Back over there," said Little. "Stick to those tire tracks there."

The dunes opened and streetlamps began to slide into the widening gap. The yellow glow from the center city grew brighter. Little shifted in his seat. He was soaked, Minogue realized.

"So, nice and easy, there. Get us out onto the Howth Road and we'll see what's what."

There were two cars parked by the wall. One had fogged windows.

"Same as ever," said Little. "Like rabbits. Tell me something."

Minogue's neck was beginning to cramp. He tried to ease it but couldn't. Had the bumpy drive across the strand done anything for Malone? He looked across at the lights of the cars on the Clontarf Road. He couldn't see any cars near the bridge.

Minogue let his hand rest on the gearshift. Not three feet away, he thought, but it might as well be three miles.

"Did you have any idea that there could be an insider?"

"I was sort of wondering," he said. "There were a lot of closed doors."

Little shoved the gun under his coat.

"Closed doors," he said.

Minogue slowed for the light. No patrol car by the end of the bridge.

"You ever get locked out, Matt?"

"I, well, I lost the keys of the car a few times."

"Not your car. Your house, your *marriage*. Your job, even."

He let the Opel roll to a stop. He pushed it into neutral and pulled up the handbrake.

"I've put away some real gougers, Matt. I don't mean just Saturday night pub champs, armed robbers even. I mean McGrane. Kennedy. Remember them?"

Minogue nodded.

"I wasn't looking for glory either. It was pretty simple. They were a threat to the state. I swore an oath, Matt, so did you. But Smith and his crowd were mental. We got phone calls at home. I've had a half-dozen numbers in one year — that's at home. She said it was for the kids and that we could talk about it. How can you talk when you're not even allowed in the door of your own house? The guns, says she. The *atmosphere*. Well she fucking conned the JP into getting the barring order. For about ten seconds I wanted to kill her. Right then, right there. But then I got real, I don't know, tired or something. I just walked away. And we haven't had a cross word since, the two of us. I meet her a couple of times a week. The kids, I see them every weekend. They're coming around. I knew they were frightened of me, I knew that. In a weird way it's worked out. Here — there's the light."

Minogue shifted into first and released the handbrake. He let the clutch in quickly. The car lurched.

"Hey," said Little. "Take your time."

There were no cars waiting for the light by the bridge. Minogue held his breath.

"You knew about that," Little said. "The wife and kids?"

"No."

"No?"

Little sighed.

"I wonder . . . Then there was the heat from some of the operations. Remember that?"

Minogue nodded.

"You know how they treated me with that bit, don't you? It was get out of active operations with the response crews or take a walk. Right?"

"I'd heard."

"Just because of a screwup on one job. One job. 'The public' they told me — 'the public can't countenance this.' Jesus. The *public?* Ah, what's the use . . ."

Minogue steered onto the bridge. The front wheels slapped on the edge of the planks. He let his hand slide down the handbrake.

"We're going to try Oz," Little went on. "The kids know. I wouldn't go to the States. I have a brother in Sydney. He has an in with a security crowd. Corporate business. It looks good."

"What else did Daly get you to do?"

Little looked over.

"Are you going to talk your way into the fucking grave, Matt? I have a lot of respect for you. That's why Head-the-Ball is in the boot, and not out there floating around belly up in Dublin Bay. What, you want to ask about the fella in the van?"

Minogue said nothing.

"Let me guess: you want to but you don't want to, is that it? 'Cause you're in too deep. Well he's dead. And yeah, I shot him. He was a gangster. Remember those guys, Matt? The bad guys, the gougers, 'the crims'? What else do you want to know? That I parked a robbed car the far side of the rocks? That I'm covered?"

The lights onto the Howth Road were red.

"Where was he taking the statue?"

Little's eyes were boring into him.

"Might as well be hung for a sheep as a lamb, is it? That's a dangerous fucking game, Matt. Well I'll tell you then. But consider this proof of what I'm going to offer you here when we get a bot of breathing space. You're going to get a deal you can't say no to. And you'd better do some quick thinking here for you and Tommy. Turn right here when you get the green. Out to Howth."

Minogue let out the clutch.

"To finish the job," said Little. "Delivery guaranteed. I want him to see what the sharp end of business looks like. The dirty work."

Little's voice had fallen to a murmur. Minogue glanced over.

"So's he doesn't forget, and so's he can express his damn gratitude in the appropriate manner. I'm going to dump it all in his lap, just like this bloody statue. And then we're going to discuss the future with him. Yours, mine, and Tommy's. Here, you've got the light."

Minogue searched the road ahead as he turned. No Garda cars.

"And Matt?"

He waited until Minogue looked over.

"There'll be no going back. For me, for you. O'Riordan knows that. Larry Smith knew that too, for about ten seconds, I'd say. He was headed up the same road, looking for his jackpot when *he* found out."

Minogue searched Little's face.

"That's right, Matt. When you do a job, you do it right. What, Smith? Smith was a lying, thieving little shite. He sold amphetamines to kids. He beat up women. He hurt people because he liked to, more than for money. He tried to put the heavy hand on Guards like me. He helped to fuck up my family. Then he thought he'd hit the big time because he had a hook on that moron, Byrne. Whatever his name is, I can never get the nickname right."

"Cortina?"

"Him, yeah. Smith thought he could put the fix in there. Blackmail. A piece of the band, he wanted, if you don't mind. Delusions of fucking grandeur or what. Not just a payoff, oh no. Or even a wage out of it. He thought he was a businessman. There's big money here. You wouldn't know how much. That's another story. Hey, you probably want the basics, am I right?"

Minogue looked over again.

"The basics are that I kept that prick Byrne out of jail. How about that. What he really needs is someone to take him out the back of his bloody mansion and give him a good hiding. Break his jaw for him. See if he can sing for a while."

"Smith went to O'Riordan, then."

"No. He went to Daly. Daly went to O'Riordan. And then . . . that's where I get hired."

Minogue strained to listen for sounds from the boot, if the motion of the car would bring Malone around.

"Come on, now," said Little. "Tell me you're not surprised. What, you think Smith didn't deserve what he got? It was a win-win thing. Dance on his grave."

Minogue waited for several moments before he spoke.

"What about Shaughnessy?"

"Ah, don't bring that up. That bloody — it came out of the blue. O'Riordan got this phone call. Do you know anything about him? That he was a headcase? An addict, he was. He was chasing some statue to give to his oul lad. Leyne. I don't know who put him on to this statue thing, but he ended up killing that woman out there in some godforsaken bog hole."

"How do you know?"

"Ah, he airs it all to O'Riordan. Phones up in a panic. This woman has put the arm on him, he says. She wants something out of him, to get his oul lad to do something. I don't know, some history thing. To set up an outfit here she could run. Computers, history, museums, I don't know. He made her these bloody promises he could never deliver on, that's what."

Minogue's fingers were down the side of the seat now.

"History?" he tried.

"History, right. Like we don't have enough. Like it matters a damn anymore."

His fingertips traced over grit trapped in the carpet, collided with the seat rail.

"All I know is there's some priceless rock out there under about four foot of water. A king something. Christ, there I was there by those big boulders waiting for this fella. I used to train out here for years, did you know that? In the sand. Endurance runs, you know? Conditioning. Anyway, there I was thinking: what's going to come out of all this tonight? The Battle of Clontarf was here, then I remembered — the Vikings. Brian Ború? The last high king wasn't he, finally putting the boots to the Vikings here, wasn't it? The Viking hordes. The barbarians, that robbed the monasteries. Plundered, all that stuff we learned in school . . ."

The Opel was gaining on a cluster of cars. Minogue didn't want to have to change gear. He let up on the accelerator.

"What about Shaughnessy, then?" he asked.

Little gave a short laugh.

"God, the things you ask. And me telling you, what's worse. Did you do those courses up at the Park, the Techniques course?"

"Back years ago," Minogue replied. "When they were starting out."

"One of the Interview ones, I'll never forget it. About an unconscious thing: wanting to unburden yourself. Wanting to tell, needing to tell, like the punishing parent thing. Guilt. Do you believe that?"

"I don't know."

"Well just remember this, Matt: there's two sides to it. The more I tell you, the more hangs on your decision. You aren't going to walk away from this tonight if you can't persuade me. And you're deciding for him there in the boot, you hear?"

Minogue let his hand rest, but Little was suspicious now.

"Get your hands up there on the wheel where I can see them."

Minogue geared down instead of braking for the traffic ahead.

"Shaughnessy: O'Riordan dumped it down on Daly. Tit for tat: after all, Daly owed him one for taking Smith out of the picture, didn't he?"

For a moment, Minogue was back at the scene by the Strand Road all those months ago: the Fiat van peppered with automatic fire, the gray and crimson bits of Larry Smith's head across the roadway.

"Daly knows everything about coming and going with the band," said Little. "This Shaughnessy is going to drop the works on O'Riordan, because . . . ?"

"O'Riordan and Leyne were partners in the old days," Minogue said.

"You've got it," said Little. "I told them you were going to come really close, Matt, to be ready. Christ . . . How things turn out. Yes, O'Riordan and Leyne were dealers. Years ago, but still too. There's high finance and something to do with O'Riordan moving stuff for this fella. I wasn't told exactly, but put two and two together and you can figure that O'Riordan had done stuff for Leyne under the table. The basics were that O'Riordan would be up the creek if the son started blathering. O'Riordan tells Daly to talk to him, see what can be done. At least buy time. But it looks bad. This young fella's off the wall, he's going to do anything. He puts the heavy hand on O'Riordan pretty quick, it ends up with me. So, it suddenly gets very simple. There's a conversation to which I am party to: if O'Riordan goes, everything goes."

He tested the elbows of his jacket. Minogue gripped the wheel tighter.

"You know what that would mean, do you?"

Minogue shook his head.

"I doubt that," said Little. "Whether you do or not, it was O'Riordan got that crowd of wankers started up, Public Works. He was the money man. He's in for half of them, what they make. Did you know that?"

"A half?" was all Minogue could think of saying.

"And here's you and me holding the fort for people like that. So they can do their thing. So that crowd of scumbags can do whatever comes into their addled little minds to do. Millionaires. While me and you, and that gom in the back, walk the streets, or argue with our kids why they shouldn't pay twenty quid to go to a concert where they're going to be hanging around with ten thousand other iijits who'll shove drugs their way. Ever thought about that, have you?"

"I'm not sure —"

"Ah, quit the pretending, Matt! The whole *duty* thing, the decency thing — what you and me grew up with as part of our bloody genes — the pay-your-way, rear the family, save your money, be polite — that it's all a fucking con?"

Minogue glanced at him.

"Keep going there. Yeah, through Sutton Cross. O'Riordan's is up Thormanbury Road there. His palace. Where was I? Shaughnessy. So yes, if that's what you're asking. I went out to get him. Outside of Lacy's Pub there in Kinnegad. He'd had the sense to lay low awhile there, but was up in a heap when I got there. He actually asked me if I could put him in touch with someone who'd sell him coke. Me, a policeman . . . ! And I knew this prick had murdered a woman. He'd promised her the sun, moon, and stars to get ahold of this rock. His da would pay this and his da would do that — and then he starts in on me, what he'd pay, what his da would do for me. I just about nailed him then. I got him out to a place the far end of Inchicore. A lockup there. Told him we had to hide it until I took care of his car and everything. That I had a fella waiting to bring it into the airport. I don't know if he believed me or not. Look: he didn't know what hit him. And the airport? I've been in and out of there a half a dozen times since Christmas. Training runs, we have to work up to the standards coming in from Brussels now, the new standards. Thank you, Eurocrats. Can you credit that, they have regulations on Civil Defense emergency communications, and we fall under that too. Anyway. I know me way around the airport. Happy?"

A fine mist began to glisten on the windscreen. Little reached over and flicked the wiper stalk.

"Get a move on," he said. "And turn up the radio, if they're looking for you."

The reflective stripes on the side of the squad car ahead were nudging out from a driveway ahead. Little stared.

"Who the hell are these fellas?"

"I don't know," Minogue said.

"Hey," said Little. He took the gun out from under his jacket. "You didn't call for checkpoints, did you?"

Minogue shook his head. The back of his neck prickled.

"What have you done? Did you call this?"

Minogue eased his foot off the accelerator. The ache he'd felt growing under his arms vanished.

"I didn't," he said.

"Two I can see," said Little. "There's one up there on a car. There must be more of them. What is this? Breathalyzers, this time of year?"

The Guard with the flashlight was decked out in the reflective coat for spotchecks. Two cars had parked the footpath the far side of the checkpoint. A Rover, it looked like; a Fiat.

"There was a — that woman was killed last month," said Little. "Out walking, her and her husband, the hit and run?"

He tugged his coat out from behind him to cover the gun again.

"Get out your card," he said.

For a moment Minogue thought the noise was the engine. Malone groaned again. Little turned.

"Shut up, Tommy!" Little shouted. "So help me, I'll blow your brains out!"

Minogue's fingers slid across the top edge of his wallet. His chest was locked tight. He had to remember to breathe. Malone seemed to be moving now.

"Not a word, Tommy!" said Little. "And don't move an inch. This is for keeps tonight."

"He has claustraphobia, Damian —"

"I don't give a flying —"

There was panic in Little's eyes. He lifted out his wallet and thumbed it open.

"Christ," Little hissed. "What's he waving us in for? Can't he spot an unmarked?"

He nudged Minogue's arm with the pistol.

"Don't play hero, Matt. There's a lot in this tonight — I've got them where I want them for this. All of them: O'Riordan, those fucking *stars* — There'll be no more after this, no need — and you can be part of this, you and Tommy. But I'll do what I have to do, no matter what. You hear that, Tommy? Did you? There's plenty for everyone in this, so think about that, you hear me?"

Minogue geared down to second. Little took two deep breaths and sat back. Minogue let his fingers off the card.

"Damn."

"What?"

"I dropped me card."

"You — where? The gearshift, where?"

"Let me see."

His fingers ran over the end of the handbrake and dropped to the carpet. Nothing. Little leaned against the door to watch.

"It's all right, just leave it," he said. "Give him mine! Stop it! Just leave it there, for Christ's sake. Come on, here he is."

The Guard had stepped out in the road. He stared in at the two. Minogue's fingernails slid along the carpet. Tiny pebbles, he registered, grit, a cigarette butt.

The Guard eyed the tax disk as he came around. Minogue's fingers stubbed the seat rails. The pistol must be right up at the front. Little elbowed him.

"Take mine," he said. "Quick!"

The Guard had a wispy mustache. The collar on his fluorescent jacket was high up alongside his cheek. He let the flashlight run across the interior.

"Are you aware you're driving with only one light, there?"

"We had a bit of a ding not long ago," said Little. The Guard took the photocard. He looked in at Little.

"I thought the car had the look of one."

"We're active at the moment," said Little. "I'm co."

"Right so, right," the Guard murmured. Minogue let his hand down the handbrake again.

"Take care, lads. Er, Superintendent. No comment on the belt situation, there."

"What?" Little said. "Oh, right. Thanks."

The Guard nodded. He nodded toward the backseat.

"You have something the matter with your seat back there."

Minogue stared at him. The Guard bobbed to look into the backseat again.

"Is there something loose maybe?" he added. "See? The back there, look."

"What," said Minogue.

"Let's go," said Little. "Sure it's falling apart, this heap. Come on. Thanks."

The Guard took a step back. His eyes finally met with Minogue's. The inspector let the eyes flicker toward Little.

"Let's go," said Little again.

"Damian —"

"Shut up! Not a fucking word!"

Minogue let out the clutch slowly. The Guard had backed off a few steps. He was speaking into his collar mike. The Guard by the Fiat looked over. Sergeant's stripes, forties; a wide, ruddy face, a hard stare. He cocked his ear and stepped out onto the roadway.

"Go around him," said Little. "Move!"

The sergeant's stare began to dull. His arm came up, his fingers spread out.

"Go!"

Minogue eased his foot off the clutch. The Guard held up a flashlight, waved the beam toward the footpath. Minogue turned the wheel more. The Guard said something. Minogue waited until they drew level, and stamped on the brake.

The Opel shuddered and bucked twice before the engine stopped, and they rocked to a standstill. Minogue lunged with his left hand and clamped it on the muzzle. The seat belt rumbled out of its drum and ran up to his neck as he followed up with his right hand. He shouldered Little against the door.

He felt Little's sinews strain under his grip, water oozing from the leather sleeve. He pushed the gun harder into Little's leg. Little's right arm squirmed behind Minogue's shoulder and slowly rose to his shoulder blades. The car began to shake. Minogue kept shouting for Malone. Little's right arm broke free over his shoulder. The first blow, more knuckle than fist, hit him in the neck. Something gave way in the car then and hit the back of his seat. He heard shoes scraping.

Little was suddenly gone. The light dazzled Minogue. A cold breeze brushed across his face as he came up, stabbing at the belt release. The chimes were slow and squeaky. Malone's face appeared between the seats. Someone was on the road just outside the door. Little was shouting. Malone was scrambling out the back door. He heard Little shouting for someone to get away.

The roadway was greasy under the drizzle. Minogue slammed the door but the light stayed on. Someone else was shouting now. A car door slammed.

"Where is he?" from Malone crouched behind him. Little was shouting at someone to get in the car.

"Damian," he shouted. "It's over! It's no use!"

Something hit the bonnet of the car.

"He's going to do it," said Malone.

"Leave it, Damian! It's finished, there's —"

The pop was followed by a small shower of glass on the roadway. Malone grabbed his arm.

"Shut up, will you, boss! He's going to kill someone!"

Minogue's eyes began a giddy slide. He got back on his hunkers. He held his eyes closed tight for a moment. Malone's white face, his contorted forehead stayed with him.

"That's my gun he has," said Malone. "Where's yours?"

"I slid it under the seat there earlier —"

"Did he get that one too?"

"I don't think so."

Malone pulled open the door and slithered in on the floor. A car door slammed. Minogue looked over the edge of the door. Through the glass he saw the older Guard, the sergeant, standing by the squad car with his hands out. Malone scrambled out onto his knees.

"I got it! Where's he gone?"

"He's taking the squad car. He has one of the spot-check fellas behind the wheel."

An engine revved and tires howled on the roadway. Malone edged around the back bumper. He shouted something and stood to a crouch. Minogue saw the taillights run across the rain-flecked glass of the Opel. Malone had broken into a sprint. The flashes from Malone's gun came quickly. He counted four. Someone began shouting again. He heard the change into second just before the Orion began to slide. The driver hesitated as the back of the car wobbled and began to bump. Malone's sprint slowed. The pasenger door on the squad car opened. Headlights coming in from Howth dipped. The car, a well-polished Nissan, came to a sliding stop fifty feet from the squad car.

Little slammed the door behind him and darted toward the Nissan. The driver's door was opening. Little ran across the headlights to the seawall. Minogue shouted Little's name. Malone was up again, advancing on the Nissan in a crouch. Flashes came steadily from his gun now. Minogue stood and moved around the back of the Opel. Malone was crouched by the front of the Nissan, waving someone away. There was a flash from the far side of the Nissan. Malone dropped to the roadway and reached around the front wheel with the gun. Minogue saw his hand twitch, the flashes against the seawall.

Neither rain nor drizzle, but that clammy, oily combination of the worst of both, began to settle on Minogue's face. The leftovers of the smoke stung in his nose as he lurched toward Malone. He held his ribs and huffed to ease the jabs from his side. He caught a glimpse of something on the path as he slid down by the door. Malone was breathing hard.

The driver of the Nissan was moving about.

"Stay down!" Malone shouted. "We're Guards. And turn off the engine!"

A siren in the distance was joined by a second.

"He's down," said Malone. "I think I heard the gun falling onto the road."

Minogue leaned against the Nissan. The driver was saying something.

"Shut up, will you!"

Malone's head was almost on the roadway by the tire.

"I see him," he said to Minogue.

"And I can see the gun. My one."

Malone scampered to the driver's door of the Nissan. He yanked it open, pulled at the driver, shoved him across the road.

"Over there — go on, the back of the Garda car!"

Minogue watched Malone stand, the pistol at arm's length, the slow zigzag walk he had seen parodied too often for it to be funny. Malone called out as he advanced. Minogue stood. The pain in his knee was a slicing ache now. His eyes wavered still. He rested his hand on the bonnet of the Nissan until the dizziness passed. He wondered if his colleague had noted the thick lines creeping away from the shadows under Damian Little.

CHAPTER 32

Orla mckeon's father looked younger than last year when Minogue had bumped into him on O'Connell Bridge. Orla had come back from six months in Italy. She and Iseult were going to get a studio together at that stage.

The hair was his own, that Minogue was sure of, but was it tinted or dyed? Why so long at fifty-something anyway. Transplants, maybe. Iseult had said that Orla found out her father was having an affair. He had moved from insurance some years ago and had done well in pet food for some reason.

"Great day for being out," said Tom McKeon.

Minogue took a step toward him. His knee was just as stiff today, but the pain had gone down to an ache that he sometimes was able to ignore. The boat breasted the wake of a smaller craft making for Dun Laoghaire Harbour. Minogue had quickly learned to keep his knees bent. His hair whipped back again. He narrowed his eyes.

"Pardon?"

"Great day," said McKeon. "Evening, I should say."

Minogue nodded. He looked back at the churning water behind the engine. A hundred and fifty horsepower? Half as much again as his Citroen? The water seemed to stand still by the railing, drawn up in a jagged crest that cast off drops and streams at the edges. Spume, that was the word. The engine turned slightly and Minogue looked back. Tom McKeon had the bow directly on the rocks by Dalkey Island ahead. There were lights on by Bulloch Harbour, but Minogue was drawn again to the pink-and-mustard sky behind the Three Rock Mountain. He felt a cold cylinder against his knuckles.

"Go on," said McKeon.

Budweiser. Would he get sick on it with the boat hopping on the waves?

"Thanks."

He sat down next to McKeon.

"Cold are you?"

"Ah, I'm all right."

"You look cold. Take that there."

Minogue picked up a nylon jacket with a woolly inside. There was neon green somewhere in the middle of the back, a fancy logo with a little wave in the middle. Drown in style. McKeon held his can while Minogue got into the jacket. He missed threading the zip several times. He steadied himself against the railing.

Iseult arrived on deck in an enormous T-shirt and a pair of football shorts. The breeze took wisps of her hair away from the hair band. Orla closed the door behind her.

"Your towel," he said. She had goose bumps already. There was an odd light in her eyes.

"What?"

"Your towel. You'll catch your death of cold."

"I'm going in the water, Da."

Tom McKeon was looking up at him with a mischievous look. Minogue wanted to drag him out of his captain's chair and pitch him into the sea.

"Here," said McKeon. "Go on."

Minogue didn't open the can. He stepped down to where Orla and Iseult huddled.

"Where's your life jacket then?"

"Do you want one?" Orla asked.

"Of course she does," Minogue said. "She'll go to the bottom like a stone. The size of her."

"Ah, Da! If I thought you were going to start this, I could have brought Ma."

"Here, Matt," came McKeon's voice above. "Come on up and take the helm."

He didn't want to take any bloody helm. Jack Tar, climb the rigging; pirates ahoy.

"Come on up! We're headed through Dalkey Sound out into the bay."

McKeon showed him the throttle, how to get to neutral, how not to mash the gears to porridge.

"Good man, yes, sit there. I have a few things to get."

"What, martinis?"

"What?"

"Nothing."

Minogue slowed the boat. It was all too easy, wasn't it? The moving shore, the sky cast up again from the water out in the bay took over his thoughts. How often he had walked there in the woods and now he was out here looking back to shore for signs of life.

"Aim to that side of him, Matt."

There was gray in the woods under Dalkey Hill already. The bay opened before him, silver and brown. He felt his chest easing, the glow, and then the rush of gladness. Fool I've been, he thought, never to have had a boat. Should have been a pet-food tycoon like Tom McKeon. He glanced over. McKeon smiled.

"Go on," he said. "Open it. It'll taste a lot better."

It did. He drank half the can in one go. He could have finished it too. McKeon pointed to Bray Head.

"Aim for there."

Not a bad fella at all, McKeon. So what if he was trick acting with someone, but — Iseult's laugh had a hollow sound to it. Orla whispered something to her. Iseult nodded. Minogue eyed her.

"Suits you, Da," she called out.

"Been to the States, er, Matt?" McKeon asked.

"No."

"Your lad is there isn't he?"

"He is."

McKeon was about to say something but he frowned, then smiled and waved his arm.

"Where else in the world would you have this," he said. "Isn't it only gorgeous?"

Minogue nodded. McKeon finished his can. He studied it carefully before tossing it below. He covered a belch with the back of his hand and then pulled hard on the rail. A plane was coming in over the Irish Sea.

"But you can be in touch anywhere," said McKeon. Minogue frowned. McKeon nodded toward a cell phone on the seat below.

"A fella in that plane there could phone me. Did you know that?"

Minogue nodded.

"Yous all have them now, don't you?"

"We've come to rely on them."

McKeon winked.

"All digital and all. So's ye won't be listened in on. It was in the paper the other day."

He looked over at the inspector.

"Along with the whole ball of wax with O'Riordan and them. The manager, the whole Larry Smith thing. Well, Jases, talk about scandal. You're a celebrity now, ha ha, along with herself."

McKeon winked.

"The *Holy Family*. Ha ha. Catchy though, isn't it?"

"No."

"Oh. Well tell me something — if you don't mind me asking. Did the Guards know about this Little, the one who — well, you know what I'm saying."

Minogue felt McKeon's eyes on him but he kept his gaze on the waves.

"No."

"Ah sure, what odds," said McKeon. "There's no place like home."

"Any way we can slip a life jacket on you know who there, Tom?"

McKeon looked over his shoulder at their daughters.

"Oh God, aye. Not sure it'd fit your one, but."

"Can we try?"

"What are you worrying about? They'll float. They're witches, sure."

McKeon stepped down to the lower deck and began opening hatches. He pulled out ropes, plastic boxes. Minogue looked up over Shankill. There were people on the crest of Katty Gallagher. The mountains had gone dark. He looked at his watch. Twenty minutes to here. How long did they plan to be in the water?

He looked back at McKeon. Gone. His head reappeared, turned up to look at Minogue.

"Slow it down, we're there."

"There where?"

McKeon was beside him then.

"Thanks. Nice going there. Are you warmed-up now?"

Minogue eyed the two shivering women. Orla bellylaughed about something.

"What do we do now?"

"I drop anchor, they jump in, and I play Jeeves with the gargle. For them, like."

"Gargle, for Iseult?"

"Oh God, no — under very strict orders there. It's nonalcoholic stuff. Pretend champagne."

He watched McKeon let an anchor over the side of the bow.

"Is Orla a good swimmer?"

"The best entirely."

"Yourself too?"

"Middling to good." McKeon looked up and winked.

He searched McKeon's face. The eyes on him. He'd had a few jars before getting into the boat in the first place. The rope was slack. McKeon pulled it tight and tied it.

"Now. We're going nowhere."

The boat gently wheeling, the rub of the rope as the anchor drew hard took Minogue's attention. Iseult shrieked with laughter. There were figures on the shore by Killiney, a dog running along the beach.

"Well, girls," McKeon called out. "Like they say, 'This is your life.'"

Iseult's smile faded. She looked out at the pale, oily water. Minogue took another mouthful of beer. Kathleen had persuaded Iseult that there was bacteria and rubbish by the beach that could give her an infection. Neither Kathleen nor Matt had expected Iseult to come up with fifty thousand quid's worth of boat as a solution, however. No pollution away from the beach, was Iseult's contention.

"This should be good," said McKeon.

Orla had turned serious too. She cupped water in her hand and rubbed her face. The boat rocked gently.

"Lezzers," said McKeon behind his hand. "What do you think?"

He looked over when Minogue didn't answer.

"Only joking."

Iseult looked up at her father. She nodded toward the cabin.

"Go ahead there, Matt," said McKeon.

He perched on the edge of a seat. Iseult loomed large in the doorway.

"Da. I want you to do something. I couldn't ask you back in Dun Laoghaire."

"I won't do it."

"Won't do what?"

"Whatever it is. All I want is a bit of a jaunt and go home. You're cracked."

"Come on. Don't let me down."

Minogue stared out at the horizon falling and rising in the window.

"Tell Orla's father to come in here. Cover up the windows for five or ten minutes. That's all."

"Why?"

"I want to go in the water in me birthday suit."

Minogue covered his face with his left hand.

"Da! Da — please! Look up there. You can see the trees by Tully. And the mountains . . ."

"You crackpot," he muttered. "I knew each and every one of those places long before you were even born."

"Yes, I know. So?"

"Who's going to be out there keeping an eye on you and dragging you out of the water then?"

"You will. I don't mind you."

"Orla? Is she in on this — Wiccan thing too?"

"It's not Wiccan —"

"Her father has ye as lesbians."

"Ah, he's a fucking waster. Orla could hit him with a bloody two-by-four as soon as look at him. She hates him. Come on. Orla says she doesn't mind you."

"What if I mind?"

"But you've seen lots of . . . well, whatever. She says it's okay. That's the main thing."

Minogue sat back and rubbed at his eyes. The beer had already started clawing at his bladder.

"See?" she went on. "All the stories you told me, that's part of it."

"What are you talking about."

"Tully, a sanctuary, for people sort of on the run?"

"Well there's a bit more to it than that, now."

"It doesn't matter."

"I was just trying to make those hikes a bit interesting for you and Daithi."

"The druids looking out from under the trees at us?"

"A definite whopper. Never saw even the one. Sorry."

"But this *gets* to be true, Da — you know what I mean, now. Come on."

"What does this have to do with us out here in the middle of the Irish Sea? Your mother is worried that you're gone mental, you know. A family thing — ah, I shouldn't be telling you."

"Did he give you a drink yet?"

"Yes."

"Ask him for another one."

"I don't want one. Off him anyway. He's a nice enough fella, but."

"Ah, he's a prick. He has money off in the Bahamas or somewhere, Orla says. Pays for his bit's apartment in Rathgar. Everybody knows. Orla's ma shops all the time and goes to spas in Germany. I'll bet you he brings his bit out in the boat here. Go on, get another drink. Let him blather away. He likes to talk. He thinks you're cool, you know. Dying to ask you questions — the job, you know?"

"You know I don't want the job at home Iseult, come on now."

"Just make sure the curtain things are pulled."

"Look —"

"Bring him down here and talk the face off him, Da — please! It's for Céline —"

"Céline who?"

"The baby. If it's a girl like. Even if it's a boy, sure . . ."

"You never told me this."

"Bring him down, Da. Please!"

She was out the door before Minogue could marshal his arguments. He forgot the low door. He stepped out with his jaw set, the pain over his forehead half-blinding him.

"Tom. Are you there?"

"I am."

He had opened another can of beer. Minogue kept rubbing at his head. The two women watched him. Lock him in the toilet — the head — maybe; mutiny.

"Tom, can you come down for a word, please?"

McKeon's smile told the inspector he knew something was up.

"Tom. Could you maybe show me the cabin and how things work in there?"

"Ah, go way. The jacks is up the front. It's called the head. Go on with you and look around yourself."

Minogue fixed him with a stare. Orla sniggered and turned away.

"The names of the different things, Tom? Maps and that . . . ? I've never . . ."

"Is this about the two mermaids wanting to do their ceremony in the nip?"

Minogue glared at Iseult. She shrugged. It could have been Orla.

"Not to put too fine a point on it, yes."

"You want me to show you how to draw the curtains is it?"

"I think I can manage that part."

"Another one of those Buds, Matt?"

Minogue crouched this time. McKeon Velcroed the curtains carefully. The yellow light overhead was weak. Minogue listened to the feet outside, felt the boat rock with the steps.

"As if I gave a shite, Matt. You know what I'm saying?"

Minogue nodded. The pain in his forehead was taking a long time to ease.

"Come on now. You'd have to see the funny side of it wouldn't you?"

McKeon took his can and popped it.

"Come on now, Matt, relax. Let them do what they want. Sure they're only observing their religion. That's in the constitution, isn't it?"

Minogue liked this second can of beer more than the first. McKeon eyed him.

"Gas, isn't it? Two oul geezers locked inside the cabin."

"It better not be locked."

"Only joking. But look at us, out in Killiney Bay, with their two so-called grown-up daughters —"

The yelp and the sudden tug on the boat had Minogue up even before he heard the two splashes. He was on the deck in time to see Iseult surface. Her hair was all over the water. He tried not to look at the huge white belly glowing, the enormous nipples. A whale, is right.

"God, it's bloody cold!!"

"Are you okay?"

"Go on back, Da! I'm fine."

He looked at the water for shark fins, and turned to the sky. Every pastel color was there, depthless, a seamless move to the sky, lilac, lemon —

"Go on, Da! We're fine!"

He backed down into the cabin. McKeon beamed, and raised his can. "A toast!"

Minogue slid in under the tabletop. The colors would be changed completely in another minute. He'd search for the first star out toward Wales.

"To our mad families, Matt! To the mad country that made us!"

Minogue studied the maudlin intensity in McKeon's face. Banish misfortune and all that? Everything counts and nothing matters, yes. What if this *lúdramán* was right. The Irish, he thought: for all our proprieties, our pragmatism, our loyalties here, we cheer the rebel hand.

"Come on now," McKeon said. "The world's gone mad — you have to admit. There's two highly educated girls, all right, women — out there — both of them the blackest, bloody pagans. One of them won't listen to anything except GOD — here, do you know them?"

"'Daddy's Girl'?"

McKeon cackled.

"My God, you do! Here we are, two gamógs up in dirty Dublin, doing our bit for some pagan ceremony or other! Madness . . . ! Come on now — put up your glass, your tin, there! Get rid of that long face there."

Minogue heard laughter outside, splashes. So there were mermaids after all. He'd look out from his perch at Tully Cross some evening searching for them in the water. He took a longer swig from the can.

"Mad," McKeon whispered. His eyes had gone moist in the dim light. Minogue didn't want to feel sorry for him. He pulled the curtain aside. "I want to see the water there," he said. "The colors."

McKeon's voice startled him.

> *"There was a wild Colonial Boy*
> *Jack Duggan was his name"*

Holy Jesus, Minogue thought. McKeon banged his can off Minogue's. "Come on there Matt, you know this one!"

It was Orla's laugh he heard.

> *"He was born and raised in I-er-land*
> *In a -h- a place called Ca-ha-s-el-maine*

"— arra, Jases, now, is the captain of the ship the only one singing? What? Sure we're home free now, Matt! It's the law of the sea, me bucko: sing!"

"I don't want either of the women to drown trying to get away from the sound of me singing 'The Wild Colonial Boy.'"

McKeon slapped him on the back.

"Ah God, you couldn't be that bad. Sure listen to me, man — I haven't a note in me head."

Minogue gave him the eye. McKeon laughed.

"Those two out there have us written off anyway," McKeon said with a yawn. "Well mine has, I mean. Orla thinks she has me codded. But she hasn't."

He popped another can and drank from it.

"About the singing, is it?"

"Christ, no! Orla hates me, man. I'm a pig. A bollocks. A male chauvinist pig bollocks. A *patriarchal* male chauvinist pig bollocks."

The boat yawed. Minogue cocked an ear.

"What are you thinking. Sharks is it?"

"They're in long enough."

"Ah, sit down. There's a ladder. They can climb out."

Minogue weighed his can.

"Aren't you a bit hard on yourself there?" he tried.

"Not a bit of it," said McKeon. "She hates me."

"Is she gay?"

"No, she fucking isn't. It's the times we're living in. Everybody hates fifty-one-year-old successful males. You listen to GOD, don't you? The one about families. 'Do You Believe'?"

"I think so. Maybe."

"Well okay. This is what it's all about. It's about me not being the modern sensitive chap, that's what I think. I love her, you know? She's me daughter like, but she drives me around the fucking twist. So I just ignore her. 'Da, bring me out in the boat. Today, half-seven.' 'Yes, love. Whatever you say, love.' That's how I've learned to operate."

Minogue drained the can. He could tell Kilmartin that he had a lost sibling in McKeon. A millionaire, Iseult had said.

"What would you suggest then?"

"I don't know," said Minogue.

"Well you're the bloody detective, aren't you? A Clareman too, aren't you?"

"Well, I was, I am I suppose."

McKeon tapped his temple.

"The second sight and all that, your crowd in Clare?"

"So they say."

"Come on. I should be the cop, shouldn't I?"

McKeon had a can out, opened and next to Minogue's hand before the inspector could say anything. He accepted it and nodded his thanks.

Minogue watched McKeon wipe a trickle of beer from the corner of his mouth.

"Did you ever wonder if yours hated you?"

"Well, when she wasn't so pleased with some of the edicts, when she was younger like."

"Really. I heard you were a pushover. The tough guy stops at the front door?"

"Was that in some review of the art thing as well?"

"No. Orla threw it at me in a row. 'Well Iseult's da doesn't be' . . . et cetera."

Minogue slid out from the bench. McKeon grabbed his arm. Minogue stared at him. He thought of Johnny Leyne.

"What's your hurry there, Matt? Here, would you like a smathán?"

"No, thanks. It's gone quiet out there."

"Ah, sit down, can't you."

"I'm going out and see about Iseult."

"They're in the nip now."

"I know."

"But you won't be looking?"

"I won't be looking, that's it."

"Hard to miss Iseult. Jases, she's the size of a, well . . ."

Minogue was suddenly sorry for him. McKeon had the bluster, but he was openhanded too. And he wasn't afraid to look at something straight on. Maybe his daughter did hate him. Minogue wanted to tell him that she'd get over it. He wanted to let McKeon ask him questions about gruesome murders and evil masterminds. He wanted to smile back at him and ask him tips for betting he didn't care about, about his boat and his adventures, about his tiled driveway or golf or whatever the hell people talked about these days. The damn beer must have some maudlin ingredient. He found himself winking back at the florid smiling face.

"A whale, Tom. It's whale watching I'm about."

The guffaws gave way to a song.

> "Are ye right there Michael are ye right,
> Do ye think that we'll get home before the night?"

Minogue waved him away when he tried to rise.

"I'm under instructions to keep you confined to quarters."

"Mutiny," said McKeon. "We can't have that."

"Until they're under wraps anyway."

The evening sky blinded Minogue for several moments. The water was lemon and gold to the shore side. He heard murmurs from the other side of the boat, a laugh.

"Iseult. It's Captain Cook here. Come in now, can't you."

"All right."

Teeth chattering, he heard.

"I'm coming over your side. Are you hanging on to some rope there?"

"Yes. Orla's just heading out a bit. I'm going to pull myself up the best I can."

"No! Don't be straining yourself there. I'll do the pulling."

Lines spread from Orla's drift through the water. Dimly he glimpsed her body as she turned and treaded water. Iseult was red.

"Great God," he said. "You look perished. Come on now."

He felt the boat give a little to his side. The rope ladder was off the back. He kneeled down and braced himself.

"That'll be a boll — that'll be difficult now to get on, love."

She grunted and pulled at the rope.

"I have me feet . . . but it keeps on going under the boat."

"Give me your hand there, yes. I'll take hold of your wrist now and you take hold of mine . . . use the other one to get ahold of that whatchemecallit."

He was reaching for her oxter with his free hand when he heard the cabin door open. He turned.

"Hi, Tom," he managed before Iseult lost her footing. For a moment he knew he could let go of her but also that he couldn't. His good knee hit the edge as he tumbled. Iseult let go. He brushed by her as the water closed over him.

He kicked but the coat was like cement. Keys, wallet, shoes, coat, change — all dragging him under: mustn't panic. His hand glanced off some part of Iseult. Bubbling, voices, a shout, bumping sounds. She grabbed his collar. Another hand grabbed his arm. His head was in the air. He opened his eyes. Orla had swum in. The water wasn't cold. He began to sink again. Should he try to get out of his shoes or this bloody jacket? Something slapped the water beside him. McKeon was shouting and laughing. He grabbed the tube. Styrofoam, more neon colors. He elbowed onto it and looked around.

"It's nice isn't it?" said Iseult.

The salt hurt his eyes. He reached down and felt for his wallet and keys. He tried to get further up the Styrofoam tube. It didn't surprise him that he didn't much care anymore.

"It is," he spluttered. "It's not bad at all."